Embracing the Change

EMBRACING THE CHANGE

THE RIVER RAIN SERIES
BOOK SIX

KRISTEN ASHLEY

Embracing the Change

A River Rain Novel

By Kristen Ashley

Copyright 2024 Kristen Ashley

ISBN: 978-1-957568-99-7

Published by Blue Box Press, an imprint of Evil Eye Concepts, Incorporated

BOOK DESCRIPTION

Embracing the Change
   A River Rain Novel, Book 6
   By Kristen Ashley

From *New York Times* bestselling author Kristen Ashley comes the
   new book in her River Rain Series, *Embracing the Change*.

That Kiss...

Gorgeous New York socialite, Nora Ellington has been waiting a
very long time for her happily ever after.

So long, she's given up on it and has decided, even though she's the
plus-one friend without benefits to a man she's head over heels in love
with, an HEA will forever be out of her reach.

Handsome billionaire Jamie Oakley thought he'd had two happily
ever afters in his life. However, neither lasted long, and both ended in
tragedy. He's not about to try it again or put his children through the
trauma Jamie has learned from experience undoubtedly will come
their way.

And he's made this decision even if the woman who's become his constant companion is a woman he loves straight to his soul....and wants with everything that is him.

But then, one night, Jamie loses control and kisses Nora.

He can't go there.

She can't go on without it.

They'll never be the same.

Or will they?

ABOUT KRISTEN ASHLEY

Kristen Ashley is the *New York Times* bestselling author of over eighty romance novels including the *Rock Chick, Colorado Mountain, Dream Man, Chaos, Unfinished Heroes, The 'Burg, Magdalene, Fantasyland, The Three, Ghost and Reincarnation, Moonlight and Motor Oil, Dream Team, River Rain* and *Honey* series along with several standalone novels. She's a hybrid author, publishing titles both independently and traditionally, her books have been translated in fourteen languages and she's sold over five million books.

Kristen's novel, *Law Man*, won the *RT Book Reviews* Reviewer's Choice Award for best Romantic Suspense. Her independently published title *Hold On* was nominated for *RT Book Reviews* best Independent Contemporary Romance and her traditionally published title *Breathe* was nominated for best Contemporary Romance. Kristen's titles *Motorcycle Man, The Will, Ride Steady* (which won the Reader's Choice award from *Romance Reviews*) and *The Hookup* all made the final rounds for Goodreads Choice Awards in the Romance category.

Kristen, born in Gary and raised in Brownsburg, Indiana, was a fourth-generation graduate of Purdue University. Since, she has lived in Denver, the West Country of England, and now she resides in Phoenix. She worked as a charity executive for eighteen years prior to beginning her independent publishing career. She currently writes full-time.

Although romance is her genre, the prevailing themes running through all of Kristen's novels are friendship, family and a strong sisterhood. To this end, and as a way to thank her readers for their support, Kristen has created the Rock Chick Nation, a series of programs that are designed to give back to her readers and promote a strong female community.

The mission of the Rock Chick Nation is to live your best life, be true to your true self, recognize your beauty and take your sister's back whether they're friends and family or if they're thousands of miles away and you don't know who they are. The programs of the RC Nation include: Rock Chick Rendezvous, weekends Kristen organizes full of parties and get-togethers to bring the sisterhood together; Rock Chick Recharges, evenings Kristen arranges for women who have been nominated to receive a special night; and Rock Chick Rewards, an ongoing program that raises funds for nonprofit women's organizations Kristen's readers nominate. Kristen's Rock Chick Rewards have donated over $180,000 to charity and this number continues to rise.

You can read more about Kristen, her titles and the Rock Chick Nation at KristenAshley.net.

ALSO BY KRISTEN ASHLEY

Rock Chick Series:

Rock Chick

Rock Chick Rescue

Rock Chick Redemption

Rock Chick Renegade

Rock Chick Revenge

Rock Chick Reckoning

Rock Chick Regret

Rock Chick Revolution

Rock Chick Reawakening

Rock Chick Reborn

Rock Chick Rematch

Avenging Angels Series

Avenging Angel

Avenging Angels: Back in the Saddle

The 'Burg Series:

For You

At Peace

Golden Trail

Games of the Heart

The Promise

Hold On

The Chaos Series:

Own the Wind

Fire Inside

Ride Steady

Walk Through Fire

A Christmas to Remember

Rough Ride

Wild Like the Wind

Free

Wild Fire

Wild Wind

The Colorado Mountain Series:

The Gamble

Sweet Dreams

Lady Luck

Breathe

Jagged

Kaleidoscope

Bounty

Dream Man Series:

Mystery Man

Wild Man

Law Man

Motorcycle Man

Quiet Man

Dream Team Series:

Dream Maker

Dream Chaser

Dream Bites Cookbook

Dream Spinner

The Fantasyland Series:

Wildest Dreams

The Golden Dynasty

Fantastical

Broken Dove

Midnight Soul

Gossamer in the Darkness

The Honey Series:

The Deep End

The Farthest Edge

The Greatest Risk

The Magdalene Series:

The Will

Soaring

The Time in Between

Moonlight and Motor Oil Series:

The Hookup

The Slow Burn

The River Rain Series:

After the Climb

Chasing Serenity

Taking the Leap

Making the Match

DEDICATION

To all of those out there who waited a while for their happily ever
after.
This one is for you.

PROLOGUE

VALENTINO

Nora

*J*amie pulled his lips from mine.

My first thought was to shout, *"No!"*

My second thought was that our kiss was so heated, so desperate, so deep, and it had lasted so...very...*long*, I needed oxygen.

I dragged in a breath.

In that space of time, Jamie took a step from me, meaning my arms were forcibly detached from where they'd been wound around his broad shoulders. Therefore, with nowhere to find purchase, they floated to my sides as I expended grave effort in solidifying my trembling legs beneath me.

I watched as he tore his hand through his dark hair, turned his head and looked at the floor.

My mind wasn't working properly, considering it was busy dealing with not only allowing me to remain upright, but also the array of pleasant sensations coursing through my body. Sensations I hadn't felt in so long, I forgot I could feel them.

But when my brain started to click in...

When what I was seeing in the haggard expression in Jamie's handsome profile started to penetrate...

I felt a tightness start to form in the small of my back.

I was not feeling haggard.

For the first time since I met him all those many years ago, I was feeling hopeful.

And for the first time in years—nay, *decades*—I was feeling truly and completely *alive*.

"Jamie?" I whispered, and I didn't like the tone of my voice. It was hesitant. Weak.

I was neither hesitant, nor weak.

Ever.

He looked to me, the drawn expression gone, there was a different tightness in his striking features now, and it corresponded with the steely light in his sky-blue eyes.

And his deep voice with that delightful touch of Texas twang he either couldn't or refused to filter out after all his years living in the city was firm when he stated, "That was a mistake."

If he'd slapped me across the face, I wouldn't have been more offended.

This was when I took a step back.

As my feet moved, those beautiful blue eyes framed with a fringe of thick black lashes dropped to my fabulous Valentino red Roserouche sandals, and when he looked at my face again, I was treated to yet another expression from the magnificent Jameson Morgan Oakley.

Chagrin and gentleness.

Though, not only that.

Worst of all (far worse)...understanding.

"Nora," he murmured, beginning to lift a hand my way.

"No," I said coldly.

His hand dropped and his lips thinned before he tried again. "Perhaps we should talk this through."

"I believe in the little you've said already that you've made yourself abundantly clear."

"I disagree," he replied.

"That's a problem for you," I returned.

"Damn it, Nora," he clipped. "Now, after what just happened between us, is not the time for you to get stubborn."

In that moment, I hated he knew me so very well. I *detested* that I'd let him in so thoroughly. I *abhorred* the fact, over the last few years, I'd given him everything he would allow me to give when I knew he had no intention of returning the favor.

Yes, our kiss had given me hope I'd been wrong about that last part.

And then he'd dashed that hope.

"I don't believe we have the kind of relationship where you're at liberty to tell me how I can behave." I paused, but not long enough for him to have the opportunity to speak. "No, wait. You're never at liberty to tell me how I can behave."

"What we have—"

I interrupted him. "We have nothing."

I felt the arrow I'd nocked in the bow myself pierce my heart at my words—words (in my defense) that were coming from place of deep hurt—because I knew I took things too far even before I watched him flinch so fiercely, his head jerked with the gesture.

"Nothing?" he asked softly.

Not nothing! my mind shouted.

We were friends. We were very good friends. The best.

That had grown recently.

But we'd been something to each other for decades.

Something important.

Something beautiful.

I fumbled to walk that back. "Jamie—"

"No, Nora." His voice was a sheet of ice forming between us. "Now I believe *you've* made yourself perfectly clear."

Damn it!

He turned to my door and didn't hesitate to walk to it.

I stood rooted to the spot, experiencing something the likes of which its occurrence in my life I could count on one hand.

A moment of indecision.

I had no earthly idea what to do, at the same time I knew I had to do *something*.

It was agony.

He opened the door but twisted back to me, his wide shoulder in his sublime bespoke suit jacket swinging with that mixture of strength and grace that was so inherently him, something about him (among many others) I found ludicrously attractive.

"Grow up, Ms. Ellington," he ground out after his eyes fixed on mine. "It was just a fucking kiss."

I blinked in shock, which was, apparently, what happened when you experienced a spasm of profound pain.

While I was still processing the strength of his blow, the door snicked shut behind him.

CHAPTER 1

CALVIN KLEIN

Nora

A *number of years ago...*

I SAT ALONE IN THE BALLROOM OF A NOTABLE HOTEL WITH A HALF-consumed martini resting on the table in front of me, watching my husband flirt with another woman.

This was not unusual. Roland was an inveterate flirt, and I wasn't too concerned about it.

Oh, make no mistake, it made me angry. It always made me angry.

So angry, the instant we arrived home, Roland and I would have a huge row, which would end in a sumptuously violent and all-consuming session of lovemaking.

Something to look forward to.

Nevertheless, people saw him doing it, and it never failed to be humiliating.

The only way to respond was to pretend I didn't care, a skill I performed so well, by the end of the evening, Roland would be infuriated, which harkened the volatility in his part of our lovemaking.

Even so, my eyes in a face that had assumed a deceptively entertained expression were resting on him, my fingers to the stem of my martini glass twisting it to and fro.

I was doing both wondering how I should approach Roland in a way he would actually listen to me and discontinue demeaning me in this manner (I could live without the makeup sex—our sex was all-consuming all the time, so, even if post-argument sex was fabulous, it wouldn't be a loss) when I felt someone sidle up to my side.

I turned my head to see a hotel employee bent toward me.

"Mrs. Castellini?" she asked.

"Yes," I answered.

"Your mother has sent me to get you. She says it's urgent."

I felt my brows draw together, but when Mother called, urgent or not, you came.

If it was urgent, you wasted no time doing it.

I abandoned my martini (alas) but grabbed my Judith Leiber and moved with the staff member out of the ballroom and through the hall crowded with the *crème de la crème* of New York glitterati. We were headed to where, in this hotel, which was used to host many a society function, was one of the more remote set of bathrooms.

The ladies being the facilities my mother always used when we were there.

When I saw two suited security guards standing outside, barring the door, my heart skipped a beat.

Was something wrong with Mother?

I hastened my step, and the staff member escorting me waved her hand to the guards at our approach. They each took a step to the side to clear my way to the door, but I didn't even glance at her or either of the guards as I pushed inside.

After I walked through the elegant lounge to where the basins and the stalls were, I stopped dead.

Mother was dumping what appeared to be vomit-covered towels into a basin.

And on her ass on the floor, propped against the back wall, her head with its extraordinary mane of strawberry-blonde hair lolling forward, her simple (but superlative) gold Calvin Klein slip dress askew and stained at the bodice, the skirt having ridden up to her shapely thighs, was the current belle of the hoi polloi.

Belinda Oakley.

I rushed forward, my heels clicking sharply on the tiles, asking, "What on earth?"

"Excellent," Mother said crisply. Having rid herself of the soiled towels, she turned to me. "You're here. Make certain she stays upright." She reached to a stack she'd clearly demanded of hotel staff and handed me a clean towel. "And see what you can do about her dress."

I made a face because contents expelled from a stomach were something I'd long since vowed I'd never deal with, and as such, with an iron will, I hadn't myself heaved in five years, and I'd certainly never been anywhere near someone else who'd done it. For my part, I'd not even done this when I had that horrible flu last winter, and Nanny dealt with my daughter Allegra's spit up.

"I'd say try to get some water in her, but I'm afraid it will come right back up," Mother carried on as I continued to grimace. "However, endeavor to do so. She needs hydration. And…Nora."

She said my name with such flinty inflection, as I'd been trained since cognition was even a glimmer of my existence, I focused entirely on her.

"No one comes into this room, except me and Oakley," she decreed.

With that, she swept out, I knew, to find Jamie Oakley.

Also, with that, I understood what was happening.

Mother liked Jamie Oakley.

Very much.

Further, Mother hated Jamie's father, AJ.

Even more.

I was well aware of the infamous incident that happened between my mother, the erudite, urbane Eleanor Ellington of the Manhattan Ellingtons, her pedigree so pure, there wasn't a big enough blue ribbon to stamp on it, and the rough and rowdy AJ Oakley of relatively new, and brash, and vulgar Texas oil money. Thrown into that inimical mix had been my father.

This incident was so well-known, even after all these years, everyone was aware of it. Including me, and it happened when I was a child.

Mother was...*Mother*.

She was also married at the time, and in their way, my parents were very much in love. Neither would ever stray, because, in Mother's words, "To do such, well..."—while delivering this pearl to me, at this juncture, she'd shivered with revulsion—"it's entirely crass, darling."

Upon reaching adulthood, I'd discovered not everyone, especially the men of our circle, but also quite a few of the women, held this same sentiment.

But as far as I knew, Mother and Dad did.

The story began when, at a party, AJ had slapped Mother's ass, which was inexcusable enough. However, he'd also done it with Dad right there.

He'd then declared loudly, for all to hear, "You get done with her, my man, I'll take that kind of sloppy seconds."

My father, Quincy Harrison Ellington, was a mild-mannered man. In the short years I'd been privileged to have him in them, I'd never so much as heard him raise his voice.

However, after his wife was assaulted in that manner, and then those words were uttered, he'd reportedly punched AJ Oakley with such force, the man was flat on his back on the floor.

My father stepped over his prone body and guided my mother away.

As you could see, quite the incident to make the rounds to the point it became lore.

It was my understanding AJ never set foot in New York City again, which, after such a mortifying debut, was understandable.

It was known widely that Jamie did not get along with his father. It was even hinted they hated each other.

Therefore, obviously, Mother thought Jamie had a good head on his shoulders, and he was one of the very few who, without jumping through hoops to get it, had her respect.

I knew she was off to find him, and doing it clandestinely, so no one would be the wiser about what was happening in that bathroom.

And I was stuck there with Jamie's gorgeous, and outrageously inebriated wife.

I knew another thing.

There was no way to get Belinda out of that bathroom without taking her through a hall crowded with people who would see her in this state, and that would travel like wildfire through the gossip channels of café society.

She'd be ruined.

And that would cling to Jamie.

This was why Mother had barred the door even to staff (because staff talked, and sometimes sold the tidbits that they'd witnessed).

I had to clean Belinda's gown as best I could (Lord help me).

I also had to try to get some water into her.

The first was imperative before it dried and got worse. Fortunately, Mother had tackled the worst of it. It was still unpleasant work.

Once I accomplished that, I went to the door and stuck my head out.

One of the security guards looked to me. "Can I have a carafe of ice water and a glass?" I then added, "Also a very strong cup of coffee."

He nodded.

"Please knock when it arrives," I continued. "I'll come fetch it."

Another nod, and I didn't wait for him to see to my request (I was an Ellington, and now a Castellini, I knew my request would be seen to *tout de suite*).

I headed back to Belinda.

I hadn't officially met her, or Jamie, though I'd seen them at several events since their triumphant arrival in the city.

She was flawless.

He was spectacular.

They were the It Couple: beauty, money, class, and for his part, it was known he was highly intelligent and lethally ambitious.

However, they (as was I, I had to remind myself, even if I didn't feel that way, as I never had) were young.

But this was an event to raise money for childhood leukemia. There were millions, maybe even billions of dollars in jewels and gowns and custom-tailored tuxedos and Italian shoes floating around that hotel.

This wasn't a frat party.

How on earth could she get in this state?

As I had this thought, she attempted to lift her head while slurring, "Jamie? Hun. I'm sho shorry. I promoish. Thish time, *I promish*, never again."

She then let her head fall.

It was the "this time" that got me, and when it did, a chill slid down my spine.

It was my understanding they had a child. An infant. He couldn't be more than one, or if so, not much older.

"Good Lord," I murmured.

The water came before Mother and Jamie did, and I was crouched, attempting to get the second half of the glass I'd poured for her down her throat when they arrived.

I turned my head and looked up at Jamie Oakley.

My husband Roland Castellini was the epitome of swarthy, masculine, sophisticated Italian/American good looks.

Jamie's features were not elegant or refined, but rugged and robust. He was more in line with the Marlboro Man than Armani. Which made all that was him, his tall, muscular frame encased in an impeccably tailored dinner jacket and trousers, incongruous in the most delightful ways.

I had this thought in a flash before the look on his face as he stared down at his wife washed it clean away.

Worry.

Anguish.

Heartbreak.

Oh yes, this wasn't the first time he'd seen his beautiful wife and the mother of his child in this state.

A knock came on the bathroom door, which prompted Jamie to continue his journey to his wife and brought me out of my crouch.

I looked to Mother. "I ordered a cup of coffee as well."

"Excellent idea," Mother replied. "Oakley, can you get her to the lounge?"

She didn't have to ask. As if she weighed as much as her slip dress, he'd already lifted Belinda in his arms, and with wide strides of his long legs, he was moving to the lounge.

I gave mother the glass of water and went to the door to fetch the coffee.

I took the tray from the waiter, which was full service, with a small pitcher of creamer, sugar bowl and a container of selections of sugar substitute, doing so with Mother hovering close so they couldn't see inside, even if I only allowed the door to be open wide enough so I could bring the tray in.

I set the tray down, stepped back, and saw that Jamie was on the couch with Belinda, her propped against his side, and Mother had given him the glass of water. He was doing much better—a practiced hand—at getting the liquid into her.

"I appreciate your time, and discretion, but you don't have to stay with us," Jamie murmured, not shifting his attention from what he was doing.

"I believe we do," Mother denied.

Jamie didn't argue, perhaps because he saw the benefits of having us there should they need anything further from the staff, perhaps because he knew of my mother, and as such, understood resistance was futile.

"How does she take her coffee?" I asked, feeling helpless, and oddly, a great deal more.

This centered around sadness...for him. Indeed, I felt such a depth of sadness for someone who was an absolute stranger, it was vaguely disturbing.

"With cream and three sugars," he said, then he lifted his astonishing blue eyes to me. They were so astonishing, even in the circumstances, having them aimed at me for the first time, I felt my breath hitch. "But now, after I get another glass of water in her, she'll take it black."

I nodded.

As time went by, and liquids went into Belinda, she grew more in control of her body as well as more coherent.

She didn't meet our eyes.

The pain had left Jamie's affect, and tightly reined anger had replaced it, so she didn't meet her husband's eyes either.

"Would you like me to order another cup of coffee?" I offered.

"No," he stated shortly. "Another fifteen, twenty minutes, she'll be fine to walk out of here."

Indeed, he had practice.

"I think now, we'll leave you," Mother announced.

Jamie looked up at us.

Belinda did not.

"Again, I appreciate all you've done." His arm around his wife tightened. "*We* appreciate it." He turned his head to Belinda. "Don't we?"

"Yes, of course," she murmured. "I'm sorry." She lifted her gaze to Jamie. "I knew I shouldn't have eaten those shrimp, hun."

I knew as one who, against my will, came into close contact with her vomit, that was such a lie, I had to stop myself from rolling my eyes.

I was aided in this endeavor by Jamie assuming a *You are so full of shit* expression as he held her gaze.

She wasn't so far gone she missed her husband's expression.

"You know my stomach isn't good with shellfish," she said defensively.

"We'll talk when we get home," he said resolutely.

Her gaze, still vague, drifted from him.

I knew by the way it did, they'd talk.

She just wasn't going to listen...or make an effort to change.

The sadness nearly overwhelmed me, making my legs weak.

It was definitely time to leave.

"If you need anything further, just ask the staff to find us," Mother ordered.

"We'll be fine," Jamie told her.

"Of course," she murmured, wrapped her fingers around my forearm and guided me to the door.

I couldn't control the urge to look over my shoulder at him as we made our way to the door.

Thank you, he mouthed when I caught his gaze.

I'm so sorry, I mouthed in return.

He shook his head in a defeated manner that made rage—actual *rage*—boil inside of me.

I feared I didn't hide it, and this fear came from the fact Jamie's eyes widened in surprise as I experienced it.

Thus, it was fortunate, with Mother's hand on my arm inexorably guiding my way out of the loo, the door closed between us.

SEVERAL DAYS LATER...

I ARRIVED HOME WITH MY BERGDORF SHOPPING BAGS, NANNY WITH ME, pushing Allegra in her stroller, only to be confronted by my husband in the foyer.

I stopped dead at witnessing the murderous look on his face.

I felt my cheeks flush with ire when he commanded Nanny, "Take our daughter to the nursery."

Nanny, not having missed his mood, quickly moved to heed his command.

But I said, "Allegra and I—"

"*You* are coming with me," Roland decreed.

He then turned on his Italian loafer and stormed out of the foyer.

I glared after him.

My husband and I had a...shall we say, *unusual* relationship.

However, I'd sought that purposefully.

Make no mistake, the quiet, genteel manner in which my mother and father regarded each other with respect, graciousness and only minor and rare gestures of affection was lovely, in its way.

But witnessing that until adulthood, then witnessing my mother losing it upon my father's passing and going on with her life as if my father had never been in it, hiding her grief, even from her children, I didn't want that.

I wanted adventure. I wanted passion. I wanted my lipstick smudging my husband's collar, telling anyone who would see it I couldn't keep my mouth off him. I wanted heated glances across the table that informed everyone around us they were gratuitous to our world, and we couldn't wait to be free of them so we could go at each other.

What I didn't want was every day to be the same. I didn't want the love I had with the man I decided to spend the rest of my life with only to be expressed behind closed doors.

And with the single-minded determination I began to show around the age of two (if the stories about myself I was told were true), I found that.

However, I was also finding there were downsides to getting what you wanted.

Taking in a steadying breath, I followed Roland to our living room.

I barely made it over the threshold before he hurled a large, exquisite crystal vase filled with glorious, long-stemmed yellow roses across the room. The vase hit the wall. The crystal shattered. The water splashed. The roses scattered.

"What the devil?" I demanded.

Roland whirled on me. "Explain to me...*precisely*...why Jamie Oakley is sending you roses?"

My stomach dropped, and it was far from an unpleasant sensation. Sadly, as a married woman—a married woman, I reminded myself, who was in love with her husband, no matter how exasperating he could be—the kind of sensation it was, was not one I should be experiencing.

"And thanking you," Roland continued. "Thanking you for what, Nora?" he asked. "Sucking his hillbilly Texas dick?"

Oh no.

Automatically, my chin lifted.

"You did not just speak those words to me," I declared, each syllable frosted with a layer of chill.

"*Why is that man sending my wife flowers?*" he bellowed.

"Calm yourself," I snapped.

"How would you feel if a woman sent me a gift?" he asked acidly.

"Exactly how I feel when you force me to watch you flirt with every blonde with fake breasts in your vicinity," I retorted.

"And what?" He threw out his hands. "This is some kind of revenge for my harmless flirting, you fucking Jamie Oakley?"

I'd argue the "harmless" part of that, but I decided to do that later.

"I do not know Jamie Oakley," I sniffed. "There was a situation with his wife having food poisoning at the leukemia gala that Mother and I dealt with, so I met him, of a sort. However, he was so busy seeing to his wife, he barely knew we were there."

Yes, I was lying to my husband, but you see, when Eleanor Ellington demanded you keep a secret, you did. Even from your husband.

Regardless that Mother demanded it, Roland had a big mouth and a competitive streak. If he held the knowledge that Belinda Oakley had a rather alarming drinking problem, he would find a way to use it.

So...yes.

To wit, I was protecting Jamie, not to mention Belinda, from my husband.

"He knew you were there enough to send you flowers," Roland pointed out.

"It was an unpleasant situation, and by the way, obviously Belinda also was there, and I'm assuming they speak to each other, so even if he was seeing to her, she could have told him we were the ones who helped her."

"Belinda Oakley's name isn't on the card," Roland noted.

Oh dear.

That was quite the oversight on Jamie's part.

And…

How lovely.

I fought my lips curling up.

"And you didn't tell me this because?" my husband prompted.

"Honestly, it slipped my mind."

"It slipped your mind," he repeated disbelievingly.

"I had a doctor's appointment on Monday, Roland," I reminded him.

"Yes, and now it's Tuesday, so it's been three days since the event when you could have shared with me you assisted Belinda Oakley in some dire food poisoning situation."

"It wasn't dire, she was fine. Eventually."

"You still could have told me."

Enough of this.

"Roland, I'm pregnant," I announced.

His body jerked. His eyes blinked.

Then his lips spread in a blinding white smile reminding me just how handsome he was, and the next second, I was in his arms, and he was kissing me, reminding me why I put up with his antics.

Mm.

Yes, this was the good part of getting what you always wanted.

When he finished with the kiss, he whispered, "You drive me crazy."

"That feeling is often mutual," I replied.

He grinned at me before he kissed me again.

Crisis averted.

And all was good again with my husband.

My family.

My *growing* family.

For now.

It would be several months before I saw Jamie Oakley again.

It was at lunchtime. I was in a restaurant, sitting alone at a table, for once early (rather than my usual late), waiting for a friend who would be joining me, when I noticed out of the side of my eye someone approaching.

I looked that way and up to see it was Jamie.

No, it wasn't the dinner jacket.

He was just… *transcendent.*

I smiled and moved to stand, but stilled when he lifted a hand, palm aimed my way, so I stayed seated while I waited for him to cross the last five feet to me.

When he arrived, he bent to kiss my cheek, and I scented the notes in his cologne were subtle hints of amber, pepper and tobacco.

Very him.

Very delicious.

When he lifted away, I murmured, "Jamie."

"Nora."

"Lovely to see you."

"And you."

"All's well?" I asked.

I knew I shouldn't have when the clouds overtook his eyes, but he smiled through them and lied, "Just fine."

"Good to hear," I lied in return. Then, to take us out of that unpleasantness, I went on to tease, "I must say, the flowers, I could tell, were magnificent. That is, from what I saw of them before my husband threw them against a wall in a jealous rage. You, or your assistant, mistakenly neglected to put Belinda's name on the card, I'm afraid."

"I don't make mistakes, Nora," he returned decisively. "Therefore, perhaps now, since he knows how it feels, he'll stop chasing skirt in front of his beautiful and kindhearted wife."

I couldn't contain my gasp.

And my gasp couldn't contain the warmth his words spread through the entirety of my body.

"I see you're expecting," he continued. "I wish *you* all the best."

You. With emphasis.

Not *you both.*

"Jamie," I whispered.

"I'm right here," he replied.

Yes, he very much was.

It took effort, but I finally found myself and grabbed hold.

As such, I informed him, "I'm not kindhearted. Ask anybody."

Jamie shook his head. "I think you've learned by now we all wear masks, Nora. I don't know what's behind yours, and unfortunately for the both of us, as things are, I'll never be in the place to find out."

After delivering those morsels, morsels that were at the same time poison and ambrosia, he took my hand from the table. He then proceeded to bend over it, lifting it to his lips, where he brushed them against my knuckles. He replaced my hand to the table, completing a debonair act of yesteryear that was highly effective, and "as things were" between us, entirely bittersweet.

He was still bent to me, his eyes holding mine captive, when he murmured, "I hope you're happy."

"I am," I replied quietly, and then to remind the both of us where we stood, I went on, "And Roland is over the moon."

"He should be," Jamie shot back, and the depth of meaning behind his statement was not lost on me.

Two could play that game.

"I hope you're happy," I repeated his words.

"My son is perfect."

After saying that, his lips tipped up, and there was a trace of forlorn in his small smile.

I returned it in kind.

And with that, Jamie Oakley straightened and walked away from me.

Sadly, I wouldn't reconnect with him in any meaningful way for years.

And when I did, we would both pine for the days when there was just a trace of forlorn to be felt.

CHAPTER 2

CAROLINA HERRERA

Nora

 *resent day...*

MY PHONE VIBRATED IN MY HAND WITH A TEXT.

I didn't look at it, at first.

I was in a state.

It had been two weeks since Jamie and my kiss.

Two weeks during which I hadn't seen him. Two weeks where I hadn't heard from him. Two very long, very alarming, very terrifying weeks.

Granted, I hadn't reached out to him.

I also hadn't walked out on him telling him to "grow up" and saying that kiss we shared—which was *not* "just a kiss"—was *just a kiss*.

We had not been apart for that long since three months ago, when he'd had to go on a multi-leg business trip.

And even then, shortly after week two began, he'd texted and asked if I wanted to fly to Florence to join him for the weekend before he had to head to South Korea for more meetings.

I'd flown to Florence.

The shopping was excellent there.

But that wasn't why I'd boarded a plane.

Before that, well…

It had been years.

Now, Chloe had gotten a wild hair that, before she and Judge had their first baby, and before Alex and Rix got married, which, according to Chloe, heralded the Baby Making Years where we wouldn't be able to do this kind of thing, we all needed to go on a family vacation.

She'd said, "Before you know it, Sasha, Sully, Gage…even Cadence will be hitched or shacked up, and it'll be *decades* before we can do something like this again."

This was entirely untrue. I'd taken many a vacation with my children when they were younger, including doing it with friends when they'd had children.

But Mika and I had discussed this with Genny, and we thought perhaps Chloe was feeling a little panicked about their new arrival, so against my better judgment, I'd agreed to go.

I loved Chloe (who happened to be Jamie's daughter-in-law, married to Jamie's son, Judge).

I loved Mika (naturally, as she was my best friend), her husband Tom (Chloe's father, Genny's ex-husband), and I loved Mika's darling daughter Cadence.

And with Tom came everyone else, all of whom I loved.

Including Jamie.

God, why had I agreed to this again?

I wasn't even a blood or by-marriage member of their family, for goodness sakes!

It was the wrong time to ask that question. I was in the car with three bags packed to the gills in the trunk (yes, we were to be gone only a week, no, I did not think for a second that I'd overpacked), and there was a yacht waiting to whisk us on a family Caribbean cruise.

To be able to escape thinking about the disaster that awaited me with Jamie being on that damned boat, I looked to my phone.

When I saw what was on the screen, I frowned.

Roland.

He'd been bothering me for *forever*.

What he thought we had to speak about, since our children were all grown and had moved on to lives of their own, *I did not know.*

(By the way, my children and their partners had been invited on this trip. But, in the time allowed, Allegra and Darryn couldn't make arrangements to adjust their schedules at the hospital, Nico and Felice were in Vermont teaching summer courses, and they couldn't make it, and Valentina and Archie were sadly in Allegra and Darryn's boat and hadn't had enough notice to arrange time off for a vacation.)

But I'd lost track in the last couple of years of how many times Roland had approached me at events, sent texts, made calls and left voicemails, practically begging me to meet him for dinner, which, when that came to naught, turned to drinks, which became requests for lunch, and I knew how desperate he was getting when he asked me out for coffee.

Yes, I drank coffee.

Yes, I'd meet friends for coffee (though, when I did that, mostly what we consumed was tea, and not the liquid kind).

But I didn't sit down for coffee with my ex-husband.

Roland, I'd painfully learned, had not been an inveterate flirt.

He'd been an incurable philanderer, and I knew there was no cure because I'd searched for one.

He, however, hadn't. Even if he promised on more than one occasion that he would.

As the docks came into view, I was in such a mood, I did what I rarely did anymore.

I read his text.

I know you're no longer seeing Oakley so CALL ME!

A chill spread across my skin because he knew.

Which meant everyone knew.

Only some of them suspected Jamie and I weren't actually *together* together.

But now everyone knew we weren't in any way together.

I cared very little about what people thought of me. I never had. Mother had taught me that from early on.

Oh, Mother was a stickler for the rules of society.

It was just that…she made them.

It was easy to follow the rules if you were the one who wrote them.

Why I cared that anyone knew I'd lost Jamie, I had no idea.

But I cared.

And Roland knowing?

I cared very, very much.

So much, my legendary iron control snapped, and I jabbed at my phone until I heard it ringing.

I put it to my ear.

"Good God, it's harder than fuck to get in touch with you," Roland snarled by way of greeting.

"Well, warmest regards to you as well, my not-so-dearest, but thankfully only ex," I drawled.

His tone changed to cajoling. "Nora—"

Oh no, we weren't doing this.

"Stop contacting me," I bit. "I cannot *begin* to imagine how you haven't received the signal I've been sending loud and clear but allow me to make it even clearer. I. Do. Not. Want. *Any.* Contact. With. You."

"I'm in love with you, desperately, I have been since the moment I saw you, and the biggest mistake I've ever made in my life wasn't losing you, it was hurting you."

I sat perfectly still in the back of a luxurious town car, seeing, without really seeing, the massive yacht Chloe had hired for our adventure (but of course it was massive, and openly opulent, so very Chloe—Lord, I loved that girl) looming larger and larger as we approached.

I did this while hearing my ex-husband's words rattling around in my brain.

The only reason I snapped out of it was noting Chloe, Cadence, and God save me, Jamie's daughter Dru hanging over the railing on the deck at the side of the yacht, waving excitedly at my approaching car (well, Chloe wasn't waving excitedly, that wasn't Chloe's way, but I could see she was watching my arrival).

"I can't do this now," I said in a small voice.

Roland, not one to miss an opportunity, or miss noting an opportunity was there to be exploited, and I'd regrettably given him both in my moment-of-silence response to his words and following it with a small voice, did not miss the opportunity.

He said quickly, "Listen to me, darling."

"I really can't do this now," I repeated.

"Dinner, tomorrow. Anywhere you like, but I'd prefer you came to mine so we can talk in private. I'll cook."

He was a fabulous cook. His Italian grandmother taught him. He didn't do it often, but I'd always loved every tidbit he'd presented to me.

"I'm leaving on a cruise in about thirty minutes."

That wasn't true. I was late, per my protocol (how else could I execute the perfect entrance?). The yacht was set to launch in about ten.

"Then let's make plans now for when you return."

"Roland—"

"Please, Nora, allow me the chance to explain."

My driver swung around to the red carpet that had been laid out to the gangway, and he got out of the car. But he didn't come to my door as I was on the phone. He went to the trunk to deal with my bags, handing them over to the white-uniformed crew that waited at the edge of the carpet for that purpose.

As this happened, fury roiled in that deep pit I'd buried the lost love and hope of a happily ever after with Roland (or ever having one at all), and for the first time in eons, I allowed it to froth over.

"As you're of that particular gender, and you're making this request, then you're in the position to explain to me, when a man breaks a woman's heart, how he feels it's within his right to request her time and attention in explaining *why* he did such a monstruous thing."

"Your heart wasn't the only one that was broken."

"Yes, but you did the breaking of yours."

"No, my darling, *you* did."

He wasn't serious.

"Pardon me?" I rapped out.

"As taught to you by your mother, you gave no fucks about me our entire marriage, or at least that's what you showed to the world, including me."

In total shock, I stared at the seat back in front of me.

Roland was not in shock, nor was he finished delivering it to me.

"And then, in the midst of us building a family, you fell in love with *him*. For fuck's sake, the tail of his acceptable mourning period had barely slipped by before you two were so all over each other, you practically crawled into each other's skin."

Unable to make it any louder, my voice was a whisper when I asked, "What are you talking about?"

"Those flowers, Nora, all those years ago. They *weren't* about you helping Belinda Oakley through some bout of food poisoning. They were Jamie Oakley staking his claim."

I continued to whisper when I stated, "You've gone mad."

"I have?" he asked snidely. "Then why, when you filed for divorce, and Oakley was then married to Rosalind, did he *still* come to my office with a smirk on his face and that odious drawl in his voice, congratulating me for my utter stupidity at letting the best thing that could ever happen to me slip through my fingers?"

My throat closed.

Jamie did that?

I had no idea Jamie did that.

Roland's tone again changed entirely when he went on, "Nora, please listen to me. I'm being very genuine when I tell you I've thought about it. I've had years to think about it, and I took that time.

Doing so, I understand now, my darling. I understand why you had to turn to him. I understand the part I played in that. And now that it's over between you two, we can both attempt to understand our behavior and find our way back to each other."

"Jamie is on the yacht I should be boarding as we speak."

This statement was greeted with Roland's silence.

"As I said earlier," I continued, "I can't talk about this now."

"Are you two reconciling?" he asked.

"That's really none of your business," I answered.

"Paloma said—"

A whooshing in my head drowned out whatever he said next, and he was still speaking when, with acid dripping from my words, I queried, "You're speaking to Paloma Friedrichsen about me?"

"No, the woman is a viper. We both learned that the hard way."

Oh, *we* certainly did.

"*She* approached me about *you*," he concluded.

I had a dawning understanding of what was going on with my ex-husband, precisely when it all started, and why, considering my arch-nemesis Paloma Friedrichsen was involved.

And, honestly, I couldn't fathom how my ex-husband could say her name in my ear when *she* was one of the women he'd cheated on me with.

But as I saw Cadence make her way down the footbridge, a confused and borderline concerned look on her face, my repeated words to Roland came inescapably true.

I couldn't do this now.

"I have to go," I declared.

"Can we speak when you return?" Roland pushed.

Cadence was getting closer.

"Perhaps," I muttered distractedly. "Goodbye, Roland."

"Until we—"

I heard no more, I disconnected.

The instant I reached for my bag to drop my phone inside, the driver opened my door.

I stepped out, pasting a brilliant smile on my face.

"My dearest!" I cried, throwing out my arms. "The fun can officially begin. Mother is here!"

The confusion and concern swept from my beloved girl's beautiful features, and she returned my smile.

"I love your dress," she said as she finished her trek to me.

"Of course you do," I replied as I wrapped my arms around her. "It's fabulous."

It was from Carolina Herrera's resort collection of several years ago. But it was Herrera, so it was timeless. A muted, flirty, feminine, off-the shoulder, chiffon floral print up top, juxtaposed with an above-the-knee, bold floral print at the bottom. I wore the wide, black with white polka dots belt it had been styled with on the runway. But the dress was a long way from matchy-matchy, so I paired it with strappy, gold, high-heeled sandals.

Cadence and I linked arms and followed the crew member carrying the last of my bags up the ramp.

"Is the gang all here?" I asked.

"Not yet, there are going to be some, um…late arrivals," Cadence said.

I wasn't surprised about this, considering it had been thrown together at the last minute, and the sheer number of people made it a scheduling nightmare. Considering who those people were, from Hollywood movie stars to busy billionaires, it was a miracle, the like Chloe Oakley crafted on not a rare occasion, that it had come about at all.

"Is everything all right?" I queried.

"No biggie," Cadence answered. Then she shot me another big smile. "It's all going to be *great*. I can't *wait*."

Her excitement was infectious, and although it didn't entirely clear away the unease I felt at my conversation with Roland, or the looming vacation that Jamie was to be a part of, it significantly alleviated it.

We made the starboard deck and Dru was there, giving me her usual tight hug, which told me that Jamie had not shared our rift with his daughter (truly, she was his stepdaughter, but that was semantics). Or perhaps he did, and Dru was being Dru. She was a sweet girl, along with smart, and as such, she made up her own mind.

When I turned to Chloe, she looked me top to toe and inquired, "Herrera 2019 resort collection?"

"How are you not of my loins?" I replied.

She smiled a cat's smile.

This further pressed my question, as did her tiered maxi-dress that both minimized and celebrated her pronounced baby bump.

We embraced.

When we broke, she stated, "Bon voyage champagne in the forward lounge."

I could use champagne.

"Excellent, are you coming?" My inquiry was aimed at all of them.

But it was Dru who answered, "We're the welcoming committee."

"Of course," I murmured, making my way toward the bow. "I'll see you when your duties are complete."

"You will!" Cadence cried, her exuberance still on show.

And since it was, I felt it somewhat odd.

I'd known her since she was a baby. I wasn't sure she'd ever taken a trip on a private yacht, but she hadn't lived a sheltered life. She'd traveled. Her mother was an explorer in every way that could be, considering Mika was a celebrated artist, and I'd learned, through Mika, that to be such, you had to thoroughly explore. They had money, quite a bit of it, so that hadn't narrowed their adventures.

Cadence had always greeted each day with the energy of youth and the enthusiasm of a voyager, so perhaps it wasn't that odd.

I made the panorama windows of the forward lounge, peeked inside, and I saw two things at once.

The lounge was a sublime mix of pearl-gray velvet, tufted-based, low, gold-marble-topped tables, sumptuous carpeting and a trio of dreamy cream curved couches adorned with gold, gray and cerulean toss pillows. A wide, circular, utterly divine crystal light installation adorned the ceiling above this conflagration of gorgeousness. There was a bar with cerulean velvet bucket seat stools at one side of the back of the space, and a table with four cerulean velvet chairs at the other side.

And Jamie was standing at the port windows, looking out at the city, holding, not a flute of champagne, but an old-fashioned glass filled with what I knew was his preferred bourbon and branch, rocks.

He was wearing a white button down, untucked, and gray-blue casual trousers, and even in such casual wear, he looked resplendent.

However, only Jamie was in there.

Were the others in their cabins?

My first inclination was to return to the girls and request directions to my own cabin in order to do some freshening up I did not need to do.

This changed when Jamie sensed me standing there, and he turned to look at me.

Upon seeing me, his mouth tightened.

So that was how it was going to be.

At witnessing his response, my mind made itself up, and I moved to the opened door to the lounge and sauntered through.

"Jamie," I greeted frostily.

"Nora," he returned stonily. His gaze moved over me. "Nice frock."

That blow was so low, I wanted to throw my charming, woven leather clutch at him.

This was because, when we were what we'd been, he'd tease me relentlessly about my extreme reverence of fashion, intermingling this with my devotion to shopping.

I didn't reply to his comment.

I noted, "I was told there's champagne?"

"I'll pour you a glass," he murmured, ever the gentleman (damn him), and beginning to turn toward the bar.

"As you know, Jamie, I'm perfectly capable of pouring my own champagne."

He stopped dead, scowled at me, but inclined his head.

I tossed my bag on one of the couches and moved to the bar, on which was an opened bottle of champagne, chilling in a bucket, curiously with only two flutes sitting beside it.

I was finishing my chore, wondering where in the hell everyone was, when Jamie made his approach.

"We should take this opportunity of being alone to come to some sort of truce for the sake of this holiday," he stated.

"Rest assured, I'll act in a civilized manner."

His face assumed a disbelieving expression before he returned, "Nora, I know you, so I can not rest in that assurance."

I felt my eyes widen. "I beg your pardon."

"You're all about drama."

He was correct, I was, when drama was appropriate, that being when it was fun or made a point.

He was very *in*correct when that drama might negatively affect people I loved.

And he damn well knew that.

I took a sip of champagne, regarding him around my flute, fashioning my retort.

When I'd swallowed, I rejoined, "It wasn't me sulking the last week after this trip was decided instead of extending an olive branch so we could navigate this holiday without issue."

"I'm sorry, did I miss a phone call? A text?" he asked.

I put my hand lightly to my chest in genuine affront. "You think *I* should have been the one to make the first overture?"

"I think *you* aren't in a position to throw that in my face when you didn't do what you accuse me of not doing."

"Because it wasn't my place," I shot back.

Blue fire lit in his eyes, but he pulled a sharp breath into his nose to gain control, and he said carefully, "I understand where your hurtful words came from."

Oh no.

We were not discussing that.

We were absolutely not discussing how I'd revealed how deep my feelings ran for him after that kiss, and he hadn't missed it.

I didn't get the chance to inform him of that fact.

He continued, "What I find upsetting is that you don't seem to understand where I was in that moment."

My God.

How had I missed he was this self-involved?

I was such a fool. He was a man. It should have been a given.

"Believe me, Jamie, I could not escape where you were at...*for decades*. Even if I had tried."

More blue fire before he struggled for control and unsurprisingly (this *was* Jamie Oakley) succeeded.

"So it's to be exchanging barbs and avoidance for the next week?" he inquired on a sigh.

With studied nonchalance, I took another sip of champagne before replying, "I'm game if you are."

He shook his head with disgust. "I can't even begin to comprehend how I managed to overlook how utterly immature you are, especially since it was right up in my face the entirety of our friendship."

"Well, we share something in common, considering I managed to overlook how self-absorbed, and I'll add, entirely clueless *you* are."

He got closer and his anger rose palpably nearer to the surface before he growled, "You're the first woman I kissed after my wife died."

You're the only man I truly loved in my entire life, and you managed to overlook that as well, even if it, too, was right up in your face the entirety of our friendship, I did not say.

"This is not news," I hissed.

"And you have no empathy for where my heart and head were in that moment?"

"There was another person there in that moment, Jamie, and I'll take this opportunity to remind you that other person was me."

"So it's all about you and what you were feeling, and you accuse me of being self-absorbed?" he fired back.

"No, it's all about the fact you want it to be *solely* about you when it's not. When we were both there, feeling deeply."

"You mean something to me, Nora, so when you lashed out when I was *feeling deeply*, sharing you thought what we had was nothing, you kicked a man I thought you cared about when he was down."

"And you're old enough to know you never tell a woman you just kissed, and kissed *thoroughly*, Jameson Oakley, that the kiss you shared was a mistake."

Yet again, his eyes flashed. "My words were lamentably unguarded, but also unintentional when I hurt you by saying that. Can you claim the same?"

"Absolutely," I spat.

He glowered at me.

I glared at him.

His head shot around to look out the windows.

It was then I heard the hushed rumble of the yacht's engines.

They weren't just starting up. In the intensity of our conversation, we'd missed their engagement.

They were working.

Thus, when I glanced to the side, I saw we were moving.

I felt my brows knit in confusion.

"What on earth?" I murmured.

Had everyone arrived?

And if they had, why had no one joined us in the lounge?

Jamie slammed his glass down on the bar and prowled to and out the open door to the deck.

Hurrying, I followed him.

He was at the starboard side where I stopped next to him and stared in total incredulity at Chloe, Cadence and Dru standing down on the dock, waving up at us (though, again, Chloe wasn't waving, she had one hand to her baby bump, and a smug look on her face).

There was a mild, panicked squeak to my words when I asked, "What's happening?"

Slowly, Jamie turned my way.

I looked up at him.

He stared down at me.

And then he spoke.

"It looks, sweetheart, like we've been parent trapped."

Oh. My.

Lord.

It hit me like a rocket.

Chloe.

That little *minx.*

This was…

It was…

Unconscionable.

When Jamie managed to talk the captain into turning us right back around, I was going to find her.

And then I was going to *throttle her.*

Metaphorically, of course.

But make no mistake, I was going to do it.

Meticulously.

CHAPTER 3

MICHAEL ARAM

Jamie

 *everal years ago...*

"We can't, it's not right. We can't do it like this."

Jamie stood at the front of the church with his daughter, who was in a mild panic.

There were reasons why, and they all centered around the hand-crafted, nickel-plated Michael Aram urn with its gold lid and base and the single white cast anemone fixed to the bottom that sat on a plinth at the front of the altar.

Or, more precisely, what lay in that urn.

However, Dru's words were not about the urn, or the occasion, but about the flowers adorning the church.

She had, he remembered distinctly, requested peach roses for her mother's funeral sprays.

They were her mother's favorites.

And Dru's.

Now, she was saying she'd ordered red, to match Rosalind's, and Dru's, hair.

"Darlin', people are arriving," Jamie said gently. "I've been told the vestibule is filling up. We can't keep the doors closed much longer."

As if his words rang to the back of the cathedral, they heard a door open, the low buzz of conversation coming from the lobby, and Jamie and Dru turned that way.

But, he suspected, only Jamie knew the woman who had closed the door on their guests and was walking swiftly down the aisle in their direction.

Her dress was prim with short, capped sleeves, an exaggerated, pointed collar buttoned up to the base of her throat, and a tie belt at the nipped waist, the latter two were black, trimmed in white. The skirt was wide. The style was reminiscent of the fifties, including the black gloves she wore on her hands that ended at her wrists.

He didn't understand, on seeing her making her way to them, why the weight of the day and his and his daughter's grief seemed less heavy, but it did.

When she made it to them, she stopped, tearing her sorrow-filled, warm brown eyes from Jamie to look at Dru.

"Hello, dear," she said tenderly.

"Uh, hi," Dru mumbled.

Nora Ellington looked back to Jamie. "Can I be of help?"

Of course.

Of course she was there to help.

How she sensed he needed it, he didn't know.

But she did, and she was there to offer it.

He had only spoken pleasantries and small talk with her since he'd seen her in a restaurant waiting for a friend years before, and now, when he needed her the most, she was there.

"We have an issue with the flowers," Jamie told her.

Nora's gaze swept through them, and when it came back to Jamie, she arched her brows in question.

"Dru wants red," he explained.

"Obviously," Nora stated, turning her attention to Dru. "Because of your mother's fabulous hair."

Jamie's throat tightened.

Tears shined in Dru's eyes, these coming from the sadness that she'd worn like a cloak since Lindy's diagnosis, and naturally more so the last week since she passed, but also in gratitude that Nora understood.

However, all his daughter had in her was to nod.

"Leave it with me," Nora decreed, dropping her head to the clutch she was opening to retrieve her phone.

"The service is to start in twenty minutes, Nora," Jamie reminded her.

"They can wait an extra ten minutes while I do my work," she decreed. "I'll spread word around your guests that there's a minor delay. And I'll see if the church can set up a coffee service in the meantime."

Jamie knew nothing about flower arranging, but he did know how much those sprays cost, and he could see with his own eyes how elaborate they were, so he could surmise there was no way a florist in New York City could switch all six of them out in thirty minutes.

He opened his mouth to say the words he needed to say to let his daughter down gently so this could be done for the both of them, but Nora spoke before he could get the first one out.

"Jamie, *leave it with me*," she stated softly, but nevertheless inflexibly.

What could he do?

He nodded.

She walked away, the phone already to her ear.

"Who is she?" Dru asked when Nora was out of earshot.

"A good friend," Jamie murmured.

Dru moved her attention from watching Nora walk away to her dad. She then leaned into him, though it was more like collapsing.

He took her weight and wrapped his arms around her to give her his warmth.

Dru offered the same in return.

They both stared at nothing, because everything had been torn away from them, and nothing, but what was standing there in each other's arms (except, for Jamie, he also had his son, who was currently greeting their guests in their stead), held meaning anymore.

———

THIRTY MINUTES LATER, ABOUT TWO MINUTES AFTER JAMIE APPROVED the opening of the doors to the sanctuary, was when the large team of florists scurried out of the cathedral.

And the six sprays adorning the altar sported bright red-orange roses.

Near-on the exact color of his beautiful wife's gorgeous hair.

They were perfect.

———

"SIR, I'M SO VERY SORRY, *SO VERY SORRY*, BUT WE HAVE AN ISSUE IN THE foyer."

Extreme irritation formed a hot ball in his chest, considering, during his dead wife's memorial reception, there should be no issue that required his attention in the foyer.

"What is it?" he clipped at the venue manager.

The man cleared his throat and further lowered the already low voice he'd been using. "There's a gentleman who's demanding entry who says he's Mrs. Oakley's husband."

Chet.

Dru's biological father.

Not Lindy's husband.

Christ, he hadn't seen that asshole in years.

Jamie's body stiff with rage, he moved toward the foyer, only to nearly run over Nora, who appeared for the sole purpose of blocking his path.

"Sweetheart," he murmured.

"I'll handle it," she declared.

His head ticked. "You'll handle what?"

"That man in the foyer," she stated. And before he could ask how she knew, she told him. "I was coming back from the powder room, and I overheard what he was saying." Her gaze drifted away, and she muttered to herself, "I should have stepped in right then."

"This isn't something you can handle," he shared.

She tipped her head to the side, and for the first time in so long, it seemed a millennium, Jamie felt the urge to laugh at the openly confused expression on her face that there might be something... *anything*...in this world she couldn't handle.

He didn't laugh because he had to say, "Dru's biological father is not a nice man."

"I already ascertained that," she huffed.

And with that, he knew Chet was causing a scene.

"I can do this," he told her.

"I have no doubt. That doesn't negate the fact you *aren't* doing this," she retorted.

He opened his mouth to refute her assertion, when several of his guests moved to his side.

Nora smiled benignly at them, coasted a glance through his eyes, and took the opportunity of Jamie being waylaid to hustle on her black pumps toward the foyer.

From where he stood, he couldn't see what was happening in the foyer.

All he saw was, five minutes later, Nora returning. When she caught his gaze, she swiped her hands together as if cleaning dust from them, sharing without words the mission was accomplished. After doing that, she looked away in order to take a glass of champagne from the tray of a passing waiter.

That was the last he saw of her that day.

He would never know how she handled Chet.

All he knew was that he, nor Dru, ever heard from the man again.

And that was all he needed to know.

Six weeks later...

DRU WAS, THANKFULLY, SPENDING THE NIGHT WITH SOME GIRLFRIENDS.

She needed that. To do normal things. To remember she was a teenager. To fiddle around with makeup and talk about boys and hopefully giggle and watch movies that Jamie (nor Lindy) would want her to watch because neither of them relished the fact she was growing up so fast.

He doubted she was giggling.

But he hoped for part of her time with her friends, she had some fun.

It was on this thought, Jamie's doorbell rang.

Jamie looked at his watch, then he set aside his book, got up and went to the door.

He peered through the peephole and saw Nora standing there.

He opened the door, and further saw she was carrying two handled paper bags.

He felt his mouth form a rusty smile. "This is a delightful surprise."

She lifted her right hand. "Crispy duck, glazed prawns with walnuts, and water dumplings."

On the side of the bag, it said MR. CHOW'S.

She held up her left hand. "Pistachio financiers and an assortment of macarons from Chanson." She dropped that hand, and finished, "More than enough for you and your daughter."

"Dru isn't here."

She appeared adorably stymied before she said, "Well, I hear Chinese leftovers are delicious."

All of a sudden, his smile felt less rusty. "You hear?"

She gave a delicate, one-shouldered shrug. "I give any leftovers to my housekeeper."

"Of course you do," he murmured.

She offered the bags. "But a nice dinner for you in the meantime."

He took the bags and asked, "Have you had dinner?"

Now she appeared surprised. "I don't want to intrude."

"You rang my doorbell."

"I did because they melt away."

"Who melts away?"

"All the people who have good intentions when something awful happens. Then the weeks pass, and they forget you're still living with it, you are because you can't escape it, but they get to carry on not thinking about it."

And his smile disappeared.

"I don't want to hurt you," she said quietly, watching him closely, the liquid brown of her pretty eyes filled with sympathy and concern. "I just don't want you to think everyone melted away."

Christ, she was something.

From the moment he met her, she'd been something.

He could still see her mouthing, *I'm so sorry* as she left him with the mess that was his first wife. He could see her crouched in her amazing gown beside a line of toilet stalls trying to get Belinda to drink water. He could also see her awkwardly taking a tray of coffee with the door mostly closed so no one could see inside.

Not a word, for days, weeks, months, now years, had been heard anywhere about what happened in that ladies room.

No, when Belinda imploded their lives and family, she'd done that on her own.

Nora, nor Eleanor, had breathed a word.

But Jamie had half fallen in love with Nora in that bathroom.

He'd had plenty of time to process this, considering, at the time, he'd been married to a woman he loved very much.

And he understood that part of it was all that was Nora Elizabeth Ellington Castellini (at the time, she'd since dropped the Castellini, fortunately for her, having that assclown out of her life) was all that Belinda Oakley was not.

But part of it was her generosity of time, and care, and discretion, which more than hinted at the significant levels of her compassion and integrity.

Not to mention, she was tall and voluptuous, had an aggressively lavish sense of style that was so unapologetically in your face about her obvious wealth, for a man like Jamie, who was unapologetically aggressive about acquiring wealth, it was arousing.

But she could be in a T-shirt and jeans, and she'd be beautiful to look at, because she was beautiful deep down to her soul.

He'd been right when he'd spoken to her in that restaurant, their time was not to come. She was still with Castellini when he was between Belinda and Rosalind, and he was very with Rosalind when she was done with Castellini.

And now, losing Lindy, he was just done.

Forever.

But she was still Nora, indicating with every move she made he'd been right about her generosity, compassion and integrity.

Like right now.

He stepped to the side. "Come inside and have dinner with me."

"Jamie—"

"This will be the first night I'm alone since she died."

That did it.

Nora stepped right in.

He closed the door and guided the way to the kitchen, not missing that Nora blatantly looked around and took everything in while he did.

He did not know her well, but he knew that was very her.

Nora didn't hide who she was or what interested her.

And now he was wondering if she'd ever worn a mask.

Nora was just...*Nora*.

He got out plates and napkins while she unearthed food.

"White? Red? A cocktail?" he offered.

"White," she ordered.

He went to his wine fridge.

It was in silence that wasn't entirely comfortable, but it wasn't uncomfortable, that they sorted their meals, and Jamie poured their wine, and they found themselves sitting at his island in his wife's kitchen.

"I'm not surprised Rosalind could best the Herculean task of creating a home that's both unequivocally homey, at the same time elegant and refined."

A dumpling he'd dipped in sauce that was trapped between his chopsticks and suspended halfway to his mouth froze in mid-air as he stared at her.

Nora noticed and said, "What I mean is, it's lovely."

"Thank you," Jamie replied.

"Well, no offense, but I suspect you had little to do with it," she teased.

"No," he said low, and her attention on him deepened. "For talking about her so openly. Talking about her, and talking about the fact she's gone, and we're dealing with that. Thank you. People skirt around her name, her existence, her loss, like she's some villain locked away in prison, and not the wife I loved who I miss, and I want to talk about, because I damned well fucking miss her."

Her lovely face softened before she asked, "Do you talk about her with Dru?"

He bit off a bite of his dumpling, chewed, swallowed and answered, "All the time."

Her expression became approving. "I'm glad."

"And you're correct." He circled his chopsticks in the air. "This is all Lindy. I had nothing to do with it."

Her eyes twinkled. Even so, that light didn't hide the sorrow she felt for him. "As suspected."

"She liked you," he told her.

"I liked her," she replied.

"I think she would have liked to know you better."

"She was a busy woman."

"As are you."

She lifted a shoulder and dropped a prawn in her mouth.

Once she swallowed, she murmured, "I should have made time to get to know her better."

"The 'should haves' will kill you if you let them."

She turned her head his way, and her tone was actually tender when she said, "You made a beautiful couple."

"I have a talent with that," he muttered cynically, snagging his own prawn.

"You've traveled a rough path, Jamie," she noted carefully.

"And I reaped the bounty, Nora. Belinda gave me my son. The time I had with Lindy. The fact she left me with Dru."

"Don't think for an instant you didn't give her bounty too," she admonished.

His laugh came, and it was so harsh, it wasn't a laugh at all.

"Do you doubt it?" she asked incredulously.

Jamie got a lock on his self-pity, reached out and touched her wrist, then went back to his food, saying, "Don't mind me."

"Please explain, if you would, why you laughed like that," she pressed.

He stopped building his duck pancake and looked to her.

"I hate my father. I think I've hated him since my first memory of him, which was watching him shout at my brother after he fell off a horse. I believe Andy was maybe ten years old. In my memory, the way my father spoke to him, I wouldn't speak like that to my worst enemy. I wouldn't even speak like that to my father, who I have no respect for, and this was his son."

"Lord," she whispered.

She had that right.

"Andy, my brother, had broken his collarbone in the fall. Mom couldn't take him to the hospital until Pop was done with him. I can't imagine the pain he was in, physically, standing there waiting to get the medical attention he needed. But I can imagine the emotional pain he was in, having his father shout at him like that, even if you factored out his ignoring his son was injured, but the fact remained, he was injured."

She stared at him.

"Yeah," he grunted, slathered some plum sauce on his duck, rolled the pancake and took a bite.

"You told me this because..." she prompted.

He swallowed his food, and shared, "I told you because I had a trust fund, on my mother's side. It wasn't enormous, but it was a foundation to start a life. But I didn't take a fucking dime from him, Nora. Not that he offered. He wrote me off when I left Texas and turned my back on the family business. But I wouldn't have taken it if he had. And I built this." He circled his chopsticks again, because she'd know New York real estate, considering her generational wealth, and all of it happening in New York City, so she'd know it better than most. "Neither of my children will ever want. Their children won't want. Dru will have the wedding of her dreams, even if I have to fly five hundred guests to a castle in Germany. I built that. All of it."

"And you couldn't save Rosalind," she said with soft understanding.

"And I had to watch my wife suffer and die," he agreed.

"I know I'm telling you something you know, but I still think it has to be said. It isn't your fault."

He nabbed his wine and took a sip before stating, "I do know that, but Dru needs her more than me. Lindy's gone. And I'm still here. I don't have a close relationship with Judge, my son. Circumstances with my ex-wife made it that way. He's built his own life, and I'm proud of him, but he doesn't need me."

"Survivor's guilt?" she asked, openly astonished.

"I would want Lindy to live on and continue her work, which, as a social worker, was actually important. I would want her to help Dru when she finds love, when she starts a family. I'd want her to enjoy what I worked hard to build for them—"

Nora put her chopsticks on her plate and sat back, snapping, "Stop it, Jamie. It didn't happen that way."

"I'm aware of that, Nora, but that doesn't stop those thoughts from coming."

"And girls need their fathers, make no mistake. I know, mine is gone. And I've met the one who donated his seed to make yours, and trust me, she needs you, Jamie. Don't ever doubt it."

"I'm sorry you lost your dad," he murmured. "And Eleanor. Your mother was a remarkable woman."

"I'm sorry you think you should have taken Rosalind's place. I mean, dear Lord, I didn't know her very well, but I knew her enough to know, if she was sitting here, listening to this, she'd be shockingly angry with you."

"And I know that as well, that still doesn't stop the thoughts from coming," he retorted.

She picked up her chopsticks and stabbed at a dumpling, grousing, "What I wouldn't give for a magic wand. You can't change the fates, but I could maybe do something about this alarming train of thought you have happening." She shoved the entire dumpling in her mouth, chewed angrily, then, still with food in her mouth, an indication of how angry she was, because Jamie reckoned, she never spoke with food in her mouth, she turned to him and said, "I have no idea if what happens is meant to be and it's simply our lot to deal with it. All I know is, the world would be a poorer place without you in it."

She swallowed, and it looked so rough, it hurt Jamie's throat.

But she kept talking.

"I mean, can you imagine if Rosalind hadn't met you, and she was still destined to leave this Earth the way she did, and Dru was stuck with *that man?*" She shivered dramatically.

It was cute.

But Jamie couldn't concentrate on that, considering he was reacting to her words, his chest swelling to the point it felt like it would burst, and his heart started beating faster.

Nora continued speaking, "Or having no one at all. *That* would be a tragedy." She shook her head and snatched up another prawn. "I have children, and so do you, so you know this as well. The last thing Rosalind wanted to do was to leave either of you, but I know for certain she felt content, even blessed, that she was leaving her daughter with you." She stabbed the air in his direction with the prawn caught between her chopsticks. "And you can take that to the bank, Jameson Oakley."

With that, she angrily bit down on her prawn, and still angrily, chewed it.

"Fuck, I'm so glad you showed tonight," he said.

She blinked rapidly several times. "What? Why? So I could rant at you?"

"Somebody needed to, so I'd get my head out of my ass."

For a moment, she seemed stunned, then she seemed pleased, after that, she looked so content, if she purred like a kitten, he wouldn't have been surprised. "Happy to be of service."

He chuckled.

It was rusty too, but it was authentic.

"Tell me about Dru, and your son," she demanded.

Jamie happily obliged.

And they decimated the Mr. Chow's, the bottle of wine, as well as the financiers, and several macarons besides, before he guided her back to the front door and down to her waiting car and driver.

Before helping her into the back seat, Jamie kissed her cheek, coming to the realization made even more poignant that night that they could never be.

And that had been so he could have Rosalind, and in the end, he could have Dru.

Jamie was both perfectly content with that, at the same time it chafed. Horrendously.

In the intervening time since their dinner together in his kitchen— this would be the time between Rosalind dying and Belinda eventually (or perhaps the more fitting word was "inevitably") overdosing, which brought Judge fully back into his life, they would meet for lunch a couple of times, and a few times more, they'd chat animatedly at events they both attended.

It wouldn't be until he realized he was unwittingly using Dru as his buffer to the world, and Dru was doing the same, and he had to let his daughter live her life, that Nora would come in and save the day yet again, becoming his plus one, with that growing to her becoming his near-constant companion.

She had her own apartment, and he had his brownstone. They both slept alone.

But they saw each other practically every evening and spent most weekends together as well.

He thought he had a handle on it. His affection for her. His feelings for her.

His growing yearning for her.

Then she'd worn those damnably sexy, red, high-heeled, fuck-me sandals.

And he'd been unable to control his rampant—and becoming with each second he spent with her more overpowering—urge to kiss her (not to mention, do other things to her).

He'd succumbed to that moment of weakness.

And blown it all to shit.

CHAPTER 4

PUCCI

Jamie

 *resent day...*

WITH NORA AT HIS HEELS, JAMIE STALKED TO THE COCKPIT AND knocked on the glass.

The captain was at the helm.

The chief officer came to the door.

"Uh...sir—" the man began.

Jamie was not the kind of man who asked for a manager. There was something abhorrent about that to him, the idea that anyone would feel so entitled they couldn't deal with the person they were dealing with and negotiate terms, and instead demand to speak to a superior.

If those negotiations didn't go your way, and the result was unacceptable, you simply didn't patronize that establishment again.

It took little effort to understand why he felt this way. His father probably asked for a manager everywhere he went. Though, Jamie had personally seen him do it repeatedly while he was growing up.

But in that moment, considering the circumstances, Jamie pushed through the officer, Nora at his back, and he addressed the captain directly.

"Respectfully, I request, at your earliest convenience, you turn us around."

"I'm sorry, sir, that isn't possible," the captain replied as Nora came to stand by his side.

And fuck him, the tangy, warm, orange blossom, jasmine and vanilla notes to her perfume always fucked with his head.

It did it in the lounge when he got close to her, regardless of how insanely pissed he was at her.

It was doing it to him now.

Jamie powered through her sexy-as-all-hell perfume.

"Can you explain why that isn't possible?" he requested.

"I have my orders," the captain announced.

Jamie fought grinding his teeth and asked, "And those orders would be?"

The captain stepped away from the helm, dipping his chin to the chief officer who took over, before turning fully to Jamie to address him.

And you had to hand it to the guy, he looked wildly uncomfortable.

"I was told you'd make this request, and I was told, under no circumstances was I to cut our tour short."

"My daughter-in-law gave you that direction," Jamie surmised.

"Well—"

"I can make it worth your while to violate her order," Jamie stated.

"I know who you are, sir, and I know that you can." He cleared his throat awkwardly. "However, I don't believe you can make it worth countermanding Hale Wheeler's standing counteroffer."

He heard Nora gasp.

And this time, he ground his teeth.

Because Hale was a member of the family.

And he was the richest man in the world.

Literally.

Jamie glanced at Nora, and both of them walked out of the bridge. They stood outside it as Jamie pulled out his phone and immediately called Hale.

Hale, who was supposed to be there with Elsa, and their new son Laird. Along with Mika and Tom. Genny and Duncan. Chloe and Judge. Alex and Rix. Ned and Blake. Sasha, Matt, Sully, Gage, Dru, Cadence…

And he and Nora.

Plenty of people around to run interference.

Not anymore.

Hale answered within two rings.

"Jamie—" he began.

Jamie cut him off. "Call the captain and have him turn this ship around."

"I can't."

"You can," Jamie asserted.

"Right, those mega-yachts are floating climate disasters, which wouldn't be my choice…ever, but with that said, *you* answer to Chloe if I do that shit," Hale returned.

"You cannot tell me you're going to strand Nora and I alone on a boat for a week for a vacation we didn't buy into because you're afraid Chloe is going to pitch a fit."

Hale had sounded guarded.

Now he sounded amused. "You clearly haven't witnessed Chloe pitching a fit."

"Nora, nor I, are finding anything funny," Jamie warned.

"I think maybe, and I say this with the utmost respect, you both should take this time we've given you to find out why you don't," Hale returned.

Could he have a new phone airlifted to him if he threw the one he had into the Hudson?

A uniformed woman approached and spoke to Nora, saying,

"Hello, I'm Amy, and I'm your chief steward. Would you both like to be shown to your cabins? We've settled you in. Dinner will be served at seven, which is a little under two hours from now, with cocktails before, and you might want to refresh and dress."

Trust Chloe to charter a yacht where they had to dress for dinner.

He had no doubt he was prepared, since Dru had commandeered his assistant and taken over his packing.

Christ, his own *daughter* was involved in this disaster.

"Sounds like you've got things to do," Hale said in his ear, and yes, he again sounded amused.

Nora was staring at Jamie helplessly.

Seeing that look on her face, a look she'd probably never assumed in her whole damned life, his fury escalated.

But he jutted his chin at her and said, "We'll have dinner. I'll take care of this. We'll be home later this evening."

"All right," she said shakily and followed the steward.

Jamie watched her go before he turned his full attention to Hale.

"You don't understand what you're doing with this, Hale."

"I think we know exactly what we're doing, Jamie."

"You'd be wrong."

But...

We?

"Exactly who's involved in this fiasco?" he demanded.

"Well, Chloe, me...I'm sure you know Cadence and Dru."

"Yes, I got those four," Jamie drawled.

"There's also Mika. And Genny," Hale went on.

Naturally.

"And Tom, Duncan. Alex wasn't a fan, but Rix thinks it's a scream," Hale continued.

"Fucking hell," Jamie muttered.

"And Judge," Hale finished.

It felt like he'd been sucker punched.

So he forced out his sardonic, "Excellent," and he hung up on Hale.

He then called his son.

"Dad—" Judge answered.

"Turn this fucking boat around, Judge."

"Dad, listen to me—"

"Turn it around."

"What's going on with you two?" Judge asked.

And there was one question answered, what had precipitated this drastic action.

They'd all definitely noticed he and Nora no longer spent time together.

"It's not your business."

"How do you figure that?" Judge returned, and his words were becoming aggravated.

"We're adults. I don't get involved in your relationship with your wife."

"Think about that," Judge clipped.

"About me not getting involved when you and Chloe fight?"

"Chloe and I don't fight. I tell Chloe something that's bothering me. She either decides it's important to factor into her life, or not. And then I realize, if it's not, it's not important, and if it is, all is copasetic."

"I've seen you fight, Judge."

"You've seen Chloe throw dramas. Everyone knows to ignore her when she does that. It eventually passes."

Jamie blew out an infuriated sigh.

"What I mean is, think about how you jumped right to that comparison," Judge carried on.

"Sorry?" Jamie queried.

"Whatever is happening with you and Nora being akin to my relationship with *my wife*."

Fucking *hell*.

Jamie grew silent.

"Yup," Judge said, ending that one-syllable word with a decisive pop.

"Bring us home. We'll have dinner together on the boat. We'll work things out. And when I get home, I'll find time to sit down with you and your sister and explain why this can't be what all of you think it is."

"You can talk to me until it's two thousand and ninety-nine, and I won't get that. Dru either."

"Judge—"

"You're allowed to be happy, Dad."

"Judge!" he bit, but he got nothing further out.

"Mom was whatever Mom was. That wasn't on you," Judge bit back. "Rosalind died. Her loss was hideous, but it happened. That wasn't on you either. Live your life, for shit's sake. And be happy."

"Don't talk to me like that," Jamie gritted.

"Don't do stupid shit to fuck up your life to make me talk to you like this."

Jamie shook his head. "I cannot believe you're buying into Chloe's matchmaking maneuvers."

"Oh yeah. You're right. When she's on one of those, we fight. But this one, Dad, *this one*, I'm with her *all the fucking way*." Before Jamie could say a word, Judge continued, "Love you to my soul. Now I'm saying goodbye so I won't hang up on my stubborn, stupid-ass Dad. Bye, Dad." But he didn't hang up, he ordered, "And don't call Dru. It'll be a waste of your time. She's in on this all the way too. Love you. Get your shit together. Have fun. Later."

And then his son was gone.

———

An hour and a half later, Jamie was behind the bar in the forward lounge wearing a suit and shirt, no tie, and he'd dismissed the steward because he could make his own damned drink, something he was just getting down to doing when Nora swanned in.

And swanning she did, wearing a long Pucci dress in the usual striking, but arbitrary pattern of that design house, this one in black, burgundy, red, cream, several blues, orange and green. The long sleeves were flared and hung down at least a foot at the back sides of her hands, and the V at the neck was deep and showed cleavage.

Oh, and the jersey material clung to her curves.

Right.

He was disinheriting both of his children.

Her long, thick, rich brown and caramel hair (those were her words to describe the color) was down and floating around her shoulders in waves. And the grace of her gait wasn't lost on him, nor were the different pair of gold, strappy, high-heeled sandals she'd donned for their evening *à deux*.

He might not understand the act of murder.

But he was beginning to understand the urge to commit it.

His first wife Belinda had an icy beauty every man, including Jamie, wanted to thaw.

His second wife Rosalind might have had fiery red hair, but she didn't have the countenance that went with it. She was warm and nurturing, from the moment he met her, to the last words she spoke to him.

Nora was a firebrand. She lived life no-holds-barred. She was rich, and she flaunted it. She had opinions, and she spoke them. She had attitude, and she didn't dilute it. And if she cared about you, she'd do anything for you if it was within her power, and if it wasn't, she'd find a way regardless.

As such, with hindsight, Jamie saw that sex with Belinda had been adequate. They were each other's firsts. They'd been learning. But in the beginning, Belinda was all about pleasing him, rather than being in the moment and letting it wash over them, or better, sweep them away. At the end, she was rarely ever sober, so he couldn't stomach touching her.

Intimacy with Rosalind was exactly like her personality. It was loving, giving, soft, sweet and on tap all the time. It was about whispers and touches that communicated adoration and complete connection. It had seemed impossible, and he'd often marveled at it, but it was true that nearly every time, their orgasms had been simultaneous.

Sinking inside his wife felt like coming home.

And now, after the kiss they'd shared, Jamie knew sex with Nora would be explosive. It'd be unpredictable. It'd be cat and mouse, or a fight for supremacy. It'd be combustible. It'd be consuming. It'd be heat and fire and the world would melt away. There would be no work. There would be no worries. There would only be Nora.

Jamie and Nora.

He wanted to experience that.

More, so much more it was like an ache, he wanted to give it to her.

But he couldn't.

After what Belinda put his son through, and what losing Lindy had put all of them through, he couldn't do it to his children.

Further, Jamie was an honest man, and extended that to himself, so he also knew he couldn't go through it again.

Love was pain.

His father taught him this important lesson with how he treated Jamie, and his siblings, but mostly with how he saw AJ treat Jamie's mother.

But he'd tried anyway, and found Belinda, then lost Rosalind.

Both had brought him to his knees.

Worse, the first had nearly destroyed his relationship with his son, and he'd had to watch his daughter lose the most important person in her life.

So...no.

He couldn't do it again.

"I'm manning the bar," he shared unnecessarily as she made her way to him. "And before you place your order, I need to tell you that I was unable to change Hale's or Judge's minds about our enforced weeklong cruise."

She stuttered to a halt and shot him a killing look he knew wasn't aimed at him, even if it physically was.

Unfortunately, he had to continue. "I also spoke with Tom, hoping I could appeal to his level head, and he'd intervene. This, too, was unsuccessful."

The conversation with Tom had been his second least favorite of the three, considering Jamie was certain Tom would step in, so hearing he wouldn't was far from fun.

Nora tossed an exasperated glance to the ceiling before she stalked behind the bar with him.

She put her miniscule bag that probably only fit her lip gloss on the bar, along with her phone, and lifted her arms with bent elbows, gold bangles jingling and flared sleeves fluttering as she waved her hands and waggled her fingers like a magician would do, all while she stated, "I called Mika, Genny, Chloe, no joy. I won't share what they said, because I sense you got the same from Hale, Judge and Tom. I then requested a rescue from Allegra and Valentina, which meant I faced further defeat. Both of them have been corralled into this farce by Cadence. Nico, however, said he'd find a speedboat and rescue us."

Valentina was her last born, a daughter.

Nico was her second born, her only son.

Jamie had met all her children, mostly in passing at the various charity events she organized. Though, on occasion, they'd dropped by her apartment when he and Nora were having dinner or watching a movie. He liked them all, even if they were nothing like their mother, who, until recently, he'd liked enormously (and he would again, after they got over this bump).

Her children were, to his surprise, a lot like Judge, Dru and Cadence, except they were married, or in Valentina's case, partnered up without the intention to ever marry, but with a life commitment.

And he was unsurprised that Nico would ride to her rescue.

The only person who hated Roland Castellini more than Jamie did was his son.

You didn't fuck over a son's mother.

He'd tried to teach his father that, and failed, only because AJ Oakley paid attention to no one but himself.

"Where's the muddler? I desperately need to muddle something," she mumbled irately, looking around the bar area.

And damn.

He had not forgotten that the woman was almost always uproariously funny.

Maybe especially when she was annoyed.

He just didn't need the reminder.

"Nora," he called.

She turned her head and tipped it to look up at him.

The perfect opportunity for a kiss, and worse, with her lips glossed with her usual perfection, he badly wanted to give her one.

Goddamn it.

"We're going to have to make the best of this."

"I haven't given up on Nico."

"I'm not sure a speedboat would catch up to us at this juncture or make it with the fuel limits."

"It feels like we're crawling."

"We are. We're probably going seven miles an hour."

Her eyes got big.

And occasionally, she could be cute.

He was in hell.

"But I hate to remind you of this, in the summers, your son lives in Vermont," he concluded.

Nico was an English teacher, his wife a history teacher, and during the summer, to make extra money, and enjoy what they both enjoyed, the outdoors, they moved to a cabin by a lake and both of them taught writing classes at a local college.

Nora made a feminine growly noise he'd never heard her make before (also cute, but all he could do was to wonder if she sounded something like that when she was naked, on her back and he did something to turn her on) as she located a muddler and started tossing mint and lime wedges from the bar caddy into two highball glasses.

Apparently, he was drinking a mojito before dinner.

"How are we going to make it to the Caribbean and back in a week going seven miles an hour?" she asked.

"It's doubtful that's our goal," he answered.

She stopped smashing mint, lime and sugar and stared up at him again.

"Be prepared not to leave this boat, sweetheart," he warned.

She turned back to the glasses and went to town with the muddler, saying between her teeth, "I…am going…*to kill many people.*"

"Nora," he called.

"What?" she snapped at her muddling.

He wrapped his fingers around her wrist.

She stilled but didn't look up at him.

So he called again, "Nora."

She gave him her eyes.

"Like I said, we're going to have to make the most of this."

"I don't feel like getting along with anybody right now."

"I understand."

She sighed dramatically, and got over it, he knew, when she inquired, "I should have asked, do you want a mojito?"

"Since you've started, sure."

"Oh, don't mistake me, Mr. Oakley. I'm perfectly fine to drink two."

He smiled at her.

Her eyes dropped to his mouth.

When he felt that in his cock, he let her wrist go.

That look she had on her face after he told her their kiss was a mistake came back, it wasn't as strong, but it still gutted him.

She wanted him.

And she was in love with him.

Yes, it gutted him.

Because he couldn't give that back.

That wasn't true, he was in love with her too.

Hopelessly.

He just couldn't follow through with it.

Because…not again.

Never again.

"After I finish these, I'll make your bourbon," she said while reaching for the rum.

And thank Christ she was strong, and kind, and smart, and could look out for herself, or what they had could be ruined.

They'd find their way back to it.

She just needed to save face.

And he needed to give her space.

It would be painful for them both, and that killed him.

But they were family now, thus it was unavoidable, and they were both the kind of people who, for the ones they loved, would suck it up.

"I'll have a mojito," he replied.

She nodded her head and didn't reply.

Her phone lit up, and the screen said Ex CALLING.

His neck got taut.

"Who's that?" he asked, even if he knew exactly who it was.

She glanced at her phone, then said, "Ignore it."

"Who's that, Nora?"

She looked at him again. "Ignore it, Jamie."

"Is it Roland?" he asked, and again he knew it was, because he knew the man had been sniffing around her all too frequently of late.

"It doesn't matter."

"It does."

"It doesn't."

"*It does*," he asserted. Then he stated, "Fuck it, I'll find out myself."

He grabbed her phone, took the call and put it to his ear as she cried, "Jamie! What are you—?"

"Castellini?" he demanded.

"Oakley?" Castellini queried.

Nora had gotten close and was pressing into his side, now with her fingers wrapped around his wrist, trying to pull the phone away.

Not gonna happen.

"What the fuck?" he clipped into the phone.

"Where's my wife? Why are you answering her phone?"

"First, she's not your fucking wife. Second, I'm answering her phone because she's busy making me a drink. Why are you calling?"

"Jamie, just—" Nora tried.

"That's none of your damned business," Castellini said in his ear.

"Seeing as I'm here, about to share a cocktail and then dinner with her while she's wearing a phenomenal fucking dress, and you're not, I beg to differ."

"Fuck you and put Nora on the phone."

"Don't call her again, Castellini," he ordered.

"*Put Nora on the phone!*" the man thundered.

"Don't call again," he said and then disconnected.

Nora was no longer pressed close, nor did she have her fingers wrapped around his wrist.

She was standing two feet away with her arms crossed on her chest and banked fury in her eyes.

He ignored the fury, even if he couldn't ignore what her pose did to her breasts and how that made his trousers fit too snugly in the crotch.

"I'll keep this for tonight, if you don't mind," he stated and slid her phone into his inside jacket pocket.

Her brows went up before she asked, "What if I do mind?"

"I'm still keeping it."

"Be my guest. Now, just to say, there are a few more corners around here you forgot to piss in," she informed him.

He disregarded that and asked, "Why is he calling you?"

She shook her head. "It doesn't matter."

"Nora, he cheated on you with every skirt he could con into bed."

"You don't have to remind me."

"So why is he calling. Are the kids okay?"

"They're fine."

He tipped his head sharply to the side in a *Talk* gesture.

She tipped her head to the side too, and queried, "Did you visit him at his office after I filed for divorce?"

He nodded. "Damn straight I did."

He was thankful when she put her hands on her hips. "Why did you do that? No,"—she shook her head—"why didn't you tell me you did that?"

"He obviously told you," Jamie pointed out.

"Yes, he did, right before I boarded this yacht."

That was surprising.

"Let's return to my earlier question," she suggested. "Why did you do that?"

"Because the man is a motherfucker, but he's not stupid, and he knew he'd made the biggest mistake in his life, and I wanted to rub that shit in. I did, and I enjoyed every fucking second of it."

She stared at him, her eyes moving all over his face, then down to his jacket, where her phone was hidden.

Some understanding dawned, she lifted her gaze to his and said, "These shoes look like they can perform miracles, but they aren't meant to be worn for a full bartending shift."

He felt his lips twitch. "Then finish up and let's sit down."

She made short work of completing the mojitos. The moment she was done, he claimed both of the glasses and jerked his head toward a couch.

He followed her there. She arranged herself on the seat. He handed her the drink and folded down beside her.

She was taking a sip, and he was trying not to notice how much he liked her perfectly shaped almond nails painted a shocking scarlet, when he ordered, "Now explain what just occurred to you."

She gave him an annoyed side eye he'd seen before, considering she often found it vexing he knew her so well, even when they weren't having problems.

She did this before she dropped her drink to the knee she'd crossed over her other long leg, and she said, "The fact you seem to hate Roland more than even I do is about AJ."

"Yes," he confirmed.

And it absolutely was about his loathing of cheaters because his father was an unapologetic womanizer.

It was also about Belinda fucking her dealer to get her fix after Jamie cut her off financially in a last-ditch effort to curtail her addiction.

But knowing much more about that illness now than he did when he was in the throes of dealing with hers, he understood it was a symptom of her illness. It was one of the more unpleasant ones, on a

list of symptoms that were all grossly unpleasant. Though he understood—even if it was difficult to live with—knowing where she was in
her disease, it was nearly impossible for her not to engage in that
behavior.

His father was another matter.

"Which brings me to the unfortunate pass that I can't be irritated
at you for your behavior," Nora finished.

He smiled over the rim of his glass and repeated, "Yes."

"Even if it's wholly outrageous you took a call on *my* phone against
my wishes, then confiscated it, again, against my wishes."

He repeated, "Yes."

She harrumphed and sipped her drink.

Christ, she was something.

He took a sip of his drink.

Yes, she was something.

A simple mojito she'd mixed in a snit, and it was the best he'd ever
tasted. Not that he was a mojito man, but he hadn't had just one prior
to the one in is hand. It was just that Nora had a particular talent
behind a bar.

Wordlessly, she raised a hand, palm up, scarlet-tipped fingers
slightly curled.

With a wry grin, he slid her phone out of his jacket pocket and
placed it in her hand.

She set it on the couch beside her.

"At this juncture, it might be good we make some ground rules," he
noted.

"If you're about to suggest we get along, don't waste your breath. I
believe the *Art of War* states the enemy of your enemy is your enemy."

Jamie chuckled. "Not exactly."

She took another sip and stated, "We'll have dinner, and it will be
pleasant, because we'll be discussing the varied acts of revenge we'll
engage in against our former loved ones the moment we return to the
city. Once those plans are set, in the morning, all bets are off."

"They think they're looking after us," he said quietly.

Her head tilted. "Are you no longer angry?"

He locked eyes with her. "Oh, sweetheart, I'm angry."

She studied him, and as she did, the tip of her pink tongue appeared in order to travel along her full lower lip.

He watched.

Avidly.

Oh, yes.

He was angry.

"However, when I referred to ground rules, I meant we should try to make the most of what could be a relaxing week and start by agreeing we're not going to dress for dinner," he clarified.

She gasped in horror, and since she was Nora Ellington, it was genuine.

She didn't hesitate to explain her reaction. "I packed an entire bag with evening wear."

Jamie sunk deeper into the couch and sighed.

Then he murmured into his drink, "Fine."

She aimed a smug smile into her glass before she took another sip, making him wonder what other ways he could coax her to feel that smugness.

Mm-hmm.

Definitely angry.

"And take this time that's been forced on us to come to an understanding," he continued.

Her bearing grew stiff. "I believe we already have that."

"Nora—"

She turned to him. "Jamie, no. It's been a trying day. I don't want to fight. I haven't had near enough time to wrap my head around what's befallen us. Let's enjoy our drinks, enjoy our dinner, get some sleep, and face whatever tomorrow brings...*tomorrow*."

He had a week to wear her down, therefore, he could give her that.

He lifted his glass her way.

She pulled in a visibly relieved breath and exhaled before she did the same with her glass.

However, Jamie wasn't going to leave it at that.

So he didn't.

Even if it was barely above a whisper when he said, "Just know, you mean the world to me."

"Jamie," she warned, her voice husky.

"All I'm going to say, darlin'," he muttered.

Nora took in another breath.

And exhaled.

CHAPTER 5

FERRAGAMO

Nora

$\mathcal{I}$ woke to darkness.

Per usual.

Thus, I pushed the satin eye mask to my forehead, and through the bright morning sunshine, stared at the circle of gold on the cream ceiling I'd discovered last night had soft illumination coming from behind it.

I didn't have to look at the rest of my cabin, which I knew had sweeping views, was decorated in soft grays, golds and navy blue, and was the likes only Hale Wheeler and the four men under him on the list of the world's most wealthy could afford.

I sighed, turned to the oblong nightstand beside the bed and picked up the phone to order coffee.

I then got out of bed and began my first-thing-in-the morning routine, being interrupted in exfoliating by accepting the arrival of my coffee service with a note communicated to me from the steward,

"Mr. Oakley is enjoying coffee on the aft deck, and we'll be setting out the breakfast buffet there soon."

Tremendous.

Another day alone with the man I loved, who did not love me.

I'd showered and was seated at the small vanity in the bathroom where, last evening, a member of the crew had arranged my cosmetics. I was sipping coffee and preparing for the day when my phone lit up.

I glared at it.

Because it was Mika.

I took the call, put it on speaker, and continued shading my eyelids, stating, "I'm not speaking to you."

I heard her laugh even as she replied, "You answered."

"Only because I have a reason to do so."

"We can talk about that in a second, after I share my chagrin that you're answering at all."

"If you don't wish to speak to me, why did you call?" I queried.

"I was testing the waters, because if you didn't answer, that would mean you're getting busy...*finally*...with Jamie."

I huffed.

"Nora—"

"We are not that."

She spoke gently when she asked, "What's been going on with you two? Why haven't you been spending time together?"

A morsel of news: the scene of the kiss with Jamie, particularly after it, was so painful, I'd told no one. Not even my dearest friend.

But now was the time to do that.

"He kissed me."

There was sheer joy in her voice as she asked, "Last night?"

I put my makeup brush down and moved on to foundation. "Two weeks ago."

"Wait. What?"

"Two weeks ago, he kissed me. It was the best kiss of my life. Then, seconds after he tore his mouth from mine, he told me the kiss was a mistake."

"Oh God," she groaned.

Not that I needed confirmation, but if I did, there it was.

Jamie saying that was a wound no woman needed inflicted.

"Indeed," I clipped.

"He's not—"

I finished for her. Sarcastically. "Over Rosalind? You think?"

"What I was going to say is, he's not allowing himself to move forward."

"I'm sensing that's not something he has in his power."

"He's stronger than he thinks, he just needs to be reminded of that."

And I knew who she thought should remind him.

I simply disagreed. Vehemently.

"This is not why I answered the phone," I informed her.

"We should talk this through, Nora. Especially now that I know about the kiss."

Hell no, we were not doing that.

"If you utter a word about that to a *single soul*, Mika, I swear to *God*, I truly won't speak to you again. You can't even tell Tom."

There was a beat of silence before she said, "I have to tell my husband. You can't ask me to keep anything from him."

"Fine," I spat, only because I knew Tom would be circumspect. "But none of those other traitors can know."

"You're on a luxury yacht with the man you love, we've hardly locked you in an iron maiden."

I put my beauty blender down so I could more fully focus on delivering a very pertinent message.

"Allow me to paint you the picture, my dearest," I began. "Say Tom Pierce was hung up on his first love, the inestimable Imogen Swan. Yes, he had deep feelings for you, he was attracted to you, he liked spending time with you, he admitted you meant the world to him, but he would not allow himself to go there with you. Now, tell me how you'd feel being stuck on a ship with him for a week."

"Belatedly, I'm seeing your point," she mumbled.

"I'm sure you are," I stated coldly.

"Maybe we can talk about this later."

Oh, we'd talk about it later.

But only when I was ready.

"*Much* later," I stressed.

"So why did you answer my call?" she inquired.

"I have a task for you to perform, and considering you owe me, you're going to see to it before we return."

"That task would be?"

"I want you to find out where Paloma Friedrichsen is the minute we make land after our excruciatingly slow tour of the Atlantic seaboard."

Her tone was guarded when she asked, "Why would you want to know where Paloma is?"

"Because Roland called yesterday to impart his desire to discuss reconciliation."

"Oh my God," she whispered in a mixture of horror and wrath.

Obviously, she knew all about Roland, and she hated him slightly less than I did, and definitely less than Jamie did.

I went on like she didn't speak, "And he shared with me, Paloma had told him that Jamie and I were through."

"What is that woman up to?" Mika groused.

I went back to blending. "Why, fucking with me, of course."

"Why?"

"Because she can't get to you, and you stole her last chance at the delicious lifetime meal ticket that was Tom Pierce."

"I knew she was bad, but I cannot wrap my head around any woman who did what she did to you having the sheer audacity to cloud your life again."

"Your taste is far too good when it comes to the people you spend time with, case in point, me being your best friend," I drawled.

"What a cow," she muttered.

I had a different c-word I would use to refer to that woman, but I sadly had too much class to utter it.

"I'll get Teddy on it," Mika declared.

Perfect.

Indeed, with this reminder of her assistant, who I *adored*, I also realized I could enlist Teddy in devising and executing a flawless plan of vengeance against that silly...*cow*.

Once Teddy knew, he would live for that.

"I'll let you go," Mika finished.

"Farewell."

"Wait. Nora?"

I picked up my tube of concealer. "I'm still here."

"I didn't know about the kiss."

I sighed. "Allow me at least forty-eight hours after your traumatic betrayal before I'm forced to begin to entertain thoughts of forgiving you."

I heard the humor in her, "Okay, I'll allow that."

And she would find it humorous, considering we both knew I'd forgive her.

Eventually.

"Goodbye, Mika."

"Try to make the most of it, Nora."

Impossible.

We rang off and I finished with my subtle, on-a-yacht makeup. With a curling iron, I then refreshed some of the waves in my hair that needed it, and did a half-up, half-down style. I spritzed on my perfume and donned my Ferragamo dress that was stark white with a pattern of a spread of oranges on the branch with leaves. It had cape sleeves, a plunging neckline and was completely backless (thank you, Dr. Fierstein, for my still perky breasts), with the added feature that the sleeves could come up to wrap around the neck to make the dress a halter and expose the arms.

I did not do this last.

I paired the dress with bronze, kitten-heeled slides, minimal gold jewelry, massive, black-framed sunglasses, and steeling myself for whatever was to come, I headed to the aft deck.

I found Jamie sitting at a table adorned with an extraordinary bouquet of fresh flowers. He was wearing khaki trousers and a blue button down I knew on sight would cause hot flashes with what it did to the color of his eyes.

Fortunately, he was wearing a handsome pair of Tom Ford sunglasses, something I saw when he heard me coming and turned my way. Unfortunately, those sunglasses swept me from top to toe to top again, and his beautiful lips formed a sexy smirk that instantly affected three very private places on my body.

"Good morning," he rumbled.

The three affected areas were more affected at his rumble.

"It is?" I replied.

The sexy smirk turned into an even sexier bright white smile.

I stopped by the table and took in the silver coffee service, his half-full cup and opened laptop with papers strewn around, his attractive attaché that had files stuffed in it resting on one of the other chairs.

"You haven't eaten?" I inquired.

"I was waiting for you."

"That was unnecessary," I remarked.

He pushed back his chair to get up. "Do you know me?"

I very much did.

He was a morning person, so he'd probably been up for hours, and further, was likely quite hungry.

But beating that, he was a down-to-his-bones gentleman.

Therefore, I didn't reply.

I went to the buffet and made myself a plate that included lots of fruit, a spoonful of scrambled eggs, two rashers of bacon, and an almond croissant.

I liked food, and I partook of it at will.

Mother had instilled in me that you should always have whatever you wanted when you wanted it, "The key, dear, is careful moderation."

My careful moderation differed from hers, which was why she had been a size six, and I was a size twelve, and would happily go up a size, if most of the designers I wore made clothes in it.

Since they did not, I reined my version of moderation in a notch.

I began to seat myself at the table across from the space Jamie had claimed but froze when his voice came from the buffet.

"If you sit there, I'll pick you up and put you in the chair beside mine that has a damned view."

I looked to him and noted, "Every seat has a view."

"Not that one."

He was right.

That one had a direct view into the aft lounge, which was smaller, more intimate, but no less well-appointed than the forward lounge.

Even so, it wasn't the peaceful vision of sun glinting off the sea with land in the distance lazily floating by.

I shifted so I would be seated right next to Jamie (damn him).

I poured my coffee, and due to habit, therefore, without thinking, refreshed his (he liked his coffee) as he filled his plate and folded down beside me.

"Thanks, sweetheart," he murmured.

It hit me why he was expressing gratitude, and I could have kicked myself for personally delivering the hit that we shared many intimacies, even if we weren't ever actually going to be *intimate*.

I forked into a sliver of cantaloupe and remarked, "You do know what 'vacation' means?"

"I'll shut it down now that you're up," he replied.

I put the melon in my mouth and said no more on the subject of his work, something he enjoyed, so, frankly, I wasn't surprised he'd brought some on vacation.

"Sleep well?" he asked.

I did.

Sumptuous fare, good wine and Jamie being charming as he always was, and last night was no exception, did that to me.

"I'm refreshed," I said by way of answer.

"Good," he murmured. Then he shared, "I spoke with the captain, and I was correct. There are no stops scheduled for this tour."

I looked to him. "Don't they have to refuel?"

Jamie speared some scrambled eggs. "Apparently, they're stocked up. Though, my guess is, if they have to stop to do anything, they've planned to do it when we're asleep, on order of my devious, and annoyingly brilliant, daughter-in-law."

"Marvelous," I drawled.

The tines of his fork pierced a strawberry as he stated, "I took a tour of the ship. There's a small screening room, and they have a great library of films and Internet access, so we can watch anything we want."

At least there was that.

Jamie carried on. "The captain also said, whenever we wish, he can drop anchor, and we can swim in the ocean."

It was mid-July. But considering, at the pace we were going, the shoreline sliding by us was probably still New Jersey (slight exaggeration, but maybe not), I was Nora Ellington. And as such, I was not about to entertain swimming along the Jersey shore.

Or any shore for that matter.

Swimming was to be done in swimming pools.

Oceans were about beaches where you could sit atop a lounger under a cabana, sip a fruity cocktail and read a book. Not *swim*.

Fighting a delicate shiver at the very thought, I glanced into the beyond, where there were some plush couches under the overhang where we were seated, and beyond that, there was a small, zero-edge pool that looked more like a jacuzzi.

"When we're not in the jacuzzi, which is heated, that is." Jamie read the direction of my gaze. "The captain told me that in case we wanted to get into the sea."

"Ah," I said, my eyes still trained to the waters even as I placed a bite of eggs in my mouth, not about to share my thoughts on getting into the sea. Because I knew if I did, Jamie would tease me, and I loved it when he teased me, so I wasn't ready to suffer that so early in our enforced holiday.

"Also talked to the steward."

I turned to my busy-morning companion.

"Probably not a surprise," he started, "but they feature daily house-keeping service of the cabins, nightly turn downs, and they can launder or press clothes if needed."

"Of course they can."

His lips tipped up before he went on, "They also have anything we might have forgotten, toothpaste, shampoo, sunscreen, charging cables."

"I think I'm covered."

"Just in case."

I tipped my head to the side to confirm I heard him.

He kept going. "I further confirmed that breakfast is whenever you swan onto the deck."

I put my fork down in affront. "I do not *swan*."

He chuckled even as he said, "Nora, you totally swan."

Okay.

I swanned.

And we were getting into Jamie Teasing Territory.

Moving on.

"We'll let them know when we're ready for lunch," he continued. "She told me they ask for an hour's notice, if we can give them that heads up. Also, if we want snacks, just let them know, though the screening room is equipped with a full-service snack bar."

Again, I was unsurprised.

Jamie kept going. "And I shared we're fine with dinner being at seven. She gave me a menu of what they have planned, and it seems they've been informed I don't like bell peppers and you don't like scallops."

"Chloe is thorough," I stated with peeved admiration.

"She is that," Jamie said before he took a bite of toast.

I quickly moved my attention from his lovely white teeth biting into the bread and returned it to my plate.

"They have boardgames, a game console, playing cards and a small library that has a number of books," Jamie said.

"It seems we're all set," I murmured irritably.

"I thought we could watch a movie after breakfast, then after lunch, sit in the hot tub until we need to get out to prepare for dinner."

I had never seen Jamie's bare chest.

I desperately wanted to see if his body was what was promised through his clothes.

An aside: the promise was *promising*.

What I equally desperately *didn't* want was for him to know—since it would forever be look, but don't touch—I needed to avoid any view of him bare *anywhere*. Therefore, I'd have to sit with him in that dratted jacuzzi, so he didn't guess why I refused to do so.

"Sounds like a plan."

"But now, over breakfast, we're going to finish our conversation from last night."

My head whipped his way at the surprise attack.

He waved his fork side to side at the same time he shook his head. "Not that. Roland."

My eyes narrowed behind my shades. "What about Roland?"

"Why were you speaking to him before you boarded?"

"Because I was in a bad mood, considering I knew I'd be imminently dealing with you. So, after he texted me, I called him because he seemed like an excellent candidate to use to expend my bad mood."

"I would normally not disagree," Jamie noted.

"And why do you disagree now?"

"Because he called again only two hours later."

I shrugged, picked up a rasher of bacon and said, "I essentially hung up on him after our brief chat."

"Did he know you were about to board a yacht?"

I swallowed my bite of bacon and replied, "I did share that information."

"Did he know I would be on said yacht?"

I turned fully to him. "Would you grace me with the knowledge of why you're interrogating me about this?"

Even with his sunglasses, I could read his expression was dumbfounded.

His next word was dripping with it. "Why?"

"Yes, why?"

"The man has no reason to contact you, so he should not be contacting you."

"I can't argue that fact."

"And yet, he's contacting you."

"Jamie—"

Jamie returned his attention to his breakfast, stating, "He needs to be informed in no uncertain terms that his communication is unwelcome, and it must cease immediately." His chin tilted my way slightly, but I knew he was pinning me with his eyes through his shades when he finished, "And if it's me who has to drive that point home, I'll gladly accept that task."

Visions of Jamie pressing Roland against a wall using a hand full of his shirt and tie, "driving that point home" assailed me, and I cared very little what it said about me, I found it titillating.

Even so, I said, "You need to stop worrying about Roland."

His fork clattered on his plate, the sudden sound surprising me so much, I gave a slight jump as Jamie turned fully to me.

"Right, we're here."

Oh dear.

I wasn't sure what "here" meant.

But I was sure I didn't want to be there.

He carried on. "I know you don't want to talk about it, and I'll give you more time, but I *do* want to talk about it. However, for now I'll just say, I can have you as I'll allow myself to have you."

As he'll allow himself to have me?

What on earth did that mean?

"And in so doing, *I have you*," Jamie continued. "You mean something to me. You're mine. You're a part of my life. You're a member of my family. And I think you know I take care of those I love, Nora. That being the man I am, I cannot countenance this jackass annoying you or taking your time or infiltrating your life in any way that does not involve the children you share. Am I being clear?"

You're mine.

I take care of those I love.

You're...

Mine.

Those...

I...

Love.

"Nora," he called. "Am I being clear?"

"Jamie," I said quietly, "I can handle Roland."

"Then handle him, or I will," he threatened.

I noted he was agitated. Significantly.

And someone shoot me, I couldn't abide that.

"You need to calm down, honey," I whispered.

"I will, when your ex is handled."

I reached out and curled my fingers around his forearm.

"I'm not your mother, darling," I reminded him carefully.

"I know you're not," he retorted tersely.

"Maybe we should talk about your depth of reaction to this," I suggested. "Roland did not treat me right, but he's not your father."

"It isn't about my father."

My brows shot up so far, he had to see them over my marvelous, and large, sunglass frames.

"Right, it's not entirely about my father," he allowed.

"Then perhaps whatever the rest of it is, is what we should discuss."

"The first time I met you, you were pouring water down the throat of my drunk and very stoned wife."

I took my hand from his arm and withdrew into my chair.

"You wanna talk?" he asked, his Texas twang becoming more pronounced, "We're talkin'."

"You don't have to go through that again."

Evidently, he did, because he kept talking about it.

"In order to deal with her confidence issues in that kind of environment, oh...and the fact she was already well on her way to becoming a junkie, she snorted a good deal of coke, got so high, it freaked her, so she'd already downed a bottle of wine before we even left for the event."

"Jamie—"

"The next morning, it took a fight the decibel level of which meant our neighbors called the police for her to admit that to me."

Good God.

My poor Jamie.

I put my hand in my lap and decided just to listen to him.

It was a mistake.

"You don't want to discuss this now?" he taunted.

"I'm giving you the chance to say what you need to say."

"No, Nora. I'm saying what *you* need to hear. You were stunning that night."

I sucked in an unladylike breath in an effort to cool the warmth that created in me.

"Belinda was covered in vomit, and you looked like Vogue styled the candid shot they took that evening that made it to the society pages."

"All right," I said hesitantly when he didn't go on.

"And he cheated on you?" Jamie demanded. *"Repeatedly?"*

"I'm not going to defend Roland, but there's more to a woman than being photogenic and having stylish taste in evening gowns."

"I know, and I met that 'more' that night in all you did for Belinda and me."

Lord.

"And again, when you got Dru her roses when she was forced to say goodbye to her mother."

This had to end.

I was going to start weeping.

"And again, when you came to my house and got my head straight about the gifts my dead wife left me and how I needed to stop thinking like an ass and get on with it."

I had to put a stop to this.

"I don't—"

That was as far as I got.

"So no. Fuck no, baby," he growled. "He doesn't get to shit all over you and then take a goddamned second more of your time *unless it has to do with your children.*"

I pressed my lips together.

"Now, am I clear?" he asked.

"You're clear, darling," I whispered.

"Good," he bit off. "So what movie are we watching?"

I had the insane desire to burst out laughing.

Mercifully, I did not.

"You pick today. I'll pick tomorrow," I proposed.

He turned back to his plate and muttered, "*Barbie.* I've been meaning to see it, but I haven't had the opportunity yet. And I know you want to see it too."

I'd been waiting for him, so, no. I hadn't seen it yet either.

"Dru loves it," he kept muttering before he put more eggs in his mouth.

I knew she did. She'd rhapsodized about it for half an hour the first time I saw her after she'd gone to a showing.

I knew from what I'd heard, I'd love it too.

And the killer of it all, one of the many things that destroyed me when it came to Jamie, was that I knew Jamie was the kind of man who was going to love it too.

CHAPTER 6

BADGLEY MISCHKA

Nora

I was fully dressed for the evening meal, it was time to leave my cabin to join Jamie for cocktails…

And I was pacing the floor, phone in hand, panicking.

It was our third night on board.

Jamie and I had breakfasted together the last two mornings.

Jamie and I had watched *Barbie* after our first breakfast (we'd both liked it, and after talking about it for some time, I could say that Jamie liked it even more than I did), and we'd returned to the screening room to watch *Rear Window* after dinner that evening.

Jamie and I had sat in the hot tub that first afternoon (yes, his chest was all it promised it would be in clothes…and then some—also yes, it was *torture* sitting in a hot tub with that man and his amazing body). And we lazed in the aft lounge the second afternoon, Jamie alternately reading and working, me catching up on the editions of *Vanity Fair* I'd brought along with me.

Jamie had teasingly accused me of being a witch after I made him a

French martini during cocktail hour last night, something he'd liked so much, he requested I make him another one before we headed in to view *Rear Window*.

We did not talk about the kiss.

We did not talk about the limits of our relationship.

We did not talk about the words we'd hurled at each other.

We did not talk further about Roland.

We absolutely did not talk about his assertions during breakfast that first morning.

We relaxed. We chatted about my children. We made a bet on the gender of Judge and Chloe's baby (they didn't want to know, so no one knew—and by the way, I said boy, Jamie said girl). We shared our mutual frustration that Dru wanted to "go it alone" and therefore was refusing Jamie's financial assistance, and as such, she had two roommates, and they were living in a small apartment in Queens. We discussed how we both knew the tea that Ned had a woman, but he hadn't shared this information with either of his daughters. We then discussed the reasons we thought Ned had not disclosed this information. We got on Jamie's laptop and ordered Alex and Rix's wedding present together.

I made Jamie laugh. He made me smile.

And through all this, I woke up to what was happening and started panicking because…

I was his damned *girlfriend*.

No, I was more.

We were more.

We just were that without sex.

I was his (he said so his damned self!).

He was mine.

I loved him.

He loved me (he said that too!).

So what in *the hell* was going on?

On that thought, I engaged my phone in order to call in assistance.

Mika answered on the third ring with the quip, "I see my forty-eight hours of Nora purgatory is up."

"I think I'm Jamie's girlfriend," I blurted.

"*What?*" she shrieked in delight.

Yes, Mika Stowe, coolest woman on the planet (and that wasn't my title for her, it was many others, though I agreed with it) *shrieked with delight.*

"Don't get excited," I cautioned.

"How could I not be excited? *I knew it!* Hey!" she cried suddenly. I heard what seemed to be skin slapping against skin. And then, "Stop that! Te—"

There were jostling noises and then I had Teddy's voice. "Nora, darling, we must speak."

"Give that back!" I heard Mika shout.

"What's going on?" I asked Teddy.

"Do you know that Paloma is seeing AJ Oakley?"

My stomach took a dive.

"*Seeing?*" I asked.

"*Seeing,*" he confirmed.

"I saw them at an event together some time ago, but—"

"Well, he's—"

Teddy didn't finish because Mika was back. "Talk to me about this being-Jamie's-girlfriend business."

"We already know she's his girlfriend," Teddy stated in the background, then demanded, "Hand me the phone."

"No, this is more important," Mika refused Teddy.

"You don't deal with catty bitches enough," Teddy's voice retorted. "When they're making moves, that takes priority over *everything.*"

I was in the unfortunate position I couldn't agree or disagree.

Everything seemed to be a priority.

"Mika," I said commandingly. "Tell Teddy I'll talk to him in a second."

"Nora says she'll talk to you after she talks to me," Mika said to Teddy. Then to me, she said, "He's pouting, but I'm back."

"All right, I should be up top, mixing Jamie a cocktail right now, so I don't have a lot of time," I began.

Then I ran it down as quickly as I could.

All of it.

Jamie answering my phone, then seizing it when Roland called. His "You're mine/I take care of those I love" speech at breakfast the morning before. His confusing comment of "as I'll allow myself to have you." His extreme agitation that Roland was pestering me. The whole spiel about Belinda and my Vogue-style society page shot and the rest of it. And last, there was the entirety of that mind mess, yet no kissing, touching or making love, but there was a lot of our usual getting on swimmingly with each other.

So…yes.

I told her *all of it*.

I finished with, "And now, I'm in that short Badgely Mischka mini-shift-dress I have. You know, the one with the tropical print, three-D sequined flowers and the same print sheer balloon sleeves."

"I know it," Mika confirmed.

"It's too short."

"You have great legs."

"It's too young."

"You're as young as you feel, and you look fantastic in that dress. Please tell me you're wearing the silver sandals with the four-inch stiletto heel."

"I'm wearing the silver stilettos," I whispered. "It's a fuck-me outfit, Mika."

"It's a fuck-me outfit, sister," Mika crowed.

"He's not ready to go there," I reminded her.

"That dress is gonna make him ready."

"He said 'as I'll allow myself to have you,' which means *he won't allow himself to have me*," I stressed.

"I think after he gets a look at you in that dress, he's going to allow himself to have a lot more of you," she returned.

"Oh God," I moaned, then executed a graceful fall to seated at the end of the bed I wished someone (though, not Jamie, he'd tease me relentlessly about it) was there to witness, because it was *perfection*.

"Just…ride it out," Mika advised.

"How?" I snapped. "Like I said, my dearest, *he's not going there*."

"Okay, allow me to let you in on something," she began.

"Do it fast, because I don't have a lot of time. Jamie is waiting, and I still need to talk to Teddy."

"Right, then. This whole yacht thing was not about you. We know you're there. It's about Jamie getting his shit sharp."

Oh.

That made sense.

"If I were ever to diet, which I'd never," she kept on.

"Never," I agreed on a faint shiver at the very thought.

"But if I were, put me in a room with a brownie, I'm good. For a while. But not for very long. Then that brownie is *in my belly*."

Completely made sense.

Chloe was *genius*.

And…

Oh dear God.

I was a brownie, and Jamie had been on a very long diet.

"Therefore, ride it out," Mika finished.

Oh *God*.

"Can I talk to her now?" Teddy asked petulantly.

"Are you done with me?" Mika asked me.

"I think so." My voice was trembling.

"You got this, Nora. Stay the course."

God!

"Here's Teddy," she said.

"*Thank you*," he stressed snottily. "Nora, darling?"

"I'm here," I replied.

"I don't have much more…yet."

Then why did he want so badly to talk to me?

"But I think we both can agree this is sinister news," he went on.

We could definitely agree on that.

"Indeed," I said.

"So dire, I'm activating the G-Force."

This was such news, I forgot about being Jamie's brownie and gasped.

The G-Force was Teddy's group of friends. They were all gay

(hence, the "G") and they were all connected. They could find out anything, and they did. In fact, after Elsa was folded into the family, several of them acknowledged they were informants of hers when she was still in the gossip game.

They could also ruin you if they so desired.

One could just say, Truman Capote's lesson to the swans, which should have been passed down generation to generation with alacrity, was not learned by every female in Manhattan. Swans all over the place were making the same mistakes with the G-Force. And if they didn't stay on the Force's good side, as the saying went, shit got real.

Usually (as in, *always*), their maneuvers were only made on behalf of members who felt they'd been wronged.

It was a huge honor they might consider my plight for one of their skilled and precise strikes.

"Do you think they'll take it on?" I asked.

"I already know they will," Teddy purred.

"Oh my God," I breathed with sheer, unadulterated glee.

"They love you. You're a gay icon. You're our Babe Paley."

I just knew they were all over going Capote. Though (in my opinion), Babe hadn't deserved the Capote treatment.

Fortunately, the G-Force was on the side of good.

Not to mention…

How sweet.

"With better hair and less of a stick up your ass," Teddy continued.

"I knew I *adored* you," I stated.

"Obviously," Teddy returned.

"Though, we can agree, Babe was eventually hindered by bad sixties helmet hairstyles."

"We can certainly agree *that*," Teddy replied. "Although we love you, it's important to note, part of this is about the fact Paloma hasn't exactly stayed in the good graces of the G-Force."

I was completely unsurprised.

"Color me stunned," I drawled.

"Get off the phone, Teddy," Mika ordered in the background. "She should be having cocktails with Jamie right now."

"Fine," he snapped at Mika, then to me, "I'll let you go, beloved. We're on it on this end."

"For the G-Force, cocktails and closet privileges at my place." I declared. "For you, pick your boutique."

"Even if it's Chopard?" Teddy tested.

"Dearest," I cooed. "Who are you talking to?"

There was a pause, before, "I adore you too, Nora. And that classless piece of trash is not going to mess with you."

My eyes started stinging.

"I have false eyelashes on, Teddy," I warned.

"Of course, ta-ta," Teddy said.

Then Mika was back on the phone. "Knock him dead, babe. Speak soon. Love you."

"Love you too."

We rang off.

I couldn't say my panic was gone.

I could say I had hope for the first time in decades I'd get the happily ever after of my dreams.

So, absolutely.

The panic was not gone.

I went to the full-length mirror on the inside door of the closet, checked my dress (Mika was right, I had amazing legs), my lipstick and my lashes, and then I headed out.

There was a small bar in the aft lounge, so Jamie and I had decided to meet there that evening for a change of pace, and because the space was smaller, and thus less formal, but more relaxed.

I entered with a smile on my face that had a lot to do with the exceptionally cut blue suit and crisp, pristine white shirt Jamie was wearing.

My smile faltered when I noted he was prowling the floor like a caged tiger.

It died when he caught sight of me, stopped dead and pinned me to the spot with a lethal expression on his handsome face.

Oh dear, it appeared he seriously liked my cocktails and was not one with having to wait.

His gaze swept the length of me, settling on my legs, before he growled, "Are you fucking shitting me?"

"I beg your pardon?" I demanded.

His eyes raced to mine. "Did you miss something in your report about your chat with Castellini, sweetheart?"

I was confused, and communicated that by inquiring, "What?"

"Maybe the fact that he," Jamie bent toward me ominously, which gave notice of what was to come, before he roared, "*asked for a reconciliation!*"

I actually felt my face lose all color. "How do you know that?"

Jamie straightened, tipped his head back and thundered to the ceiling, "*Jesus Christ!*"

I dashed toward him and snapped, "For heaven's sake, keep your voice down."

His chin slanted into his throat, and he speared me with a venomous look as he snarled, "Fuck that. Fuck him. Why the fuck didn't you tell me?"

"I'm obviously not going to entertain his notion," I sniffed.

"Why didn't you tell me?" he repeated his question.

"How did you know?" I shot back.

"Tom phoned."

Tom?

Tom betrayed me?

Counting this whole yacht situation…

He did it *again*?

I lifted my phone in front of me and spat, "I need to make a call."

Whoosh! My phone was gone and flying through the air to plop on a sofa, seeing as Jamie swiped it and tossed it there.

"Jamie!" I yelled.

"Do not be angry at Tom," he ordered. "Mika shared with Tom, as spouses do. Then Tom did some math. Which brings me to my next topic of conversation, the fact that Paloma Friedrichsen, who fucked your husband when he was still your husband, and who tried to fuck *me* when my wife was dying of cancer, is the one attempting to fuck"

—he flapped a hand irately through the minimal space between us— "*us* up."

Damn, I'd forgotten that little tidbit about Paloma's sheer nastiness, making a play for Jamie when Rosalind was ill.

How could I forget that?

I couldn't linger on it. Jamie was still glowering at me.

"I put that together too, and I'm handling it," I assured.

I also needed to tell him that Paloma was definitely *with* his father, which did not bode well, but I didn't think now was an advantageous time to convey this information.

I heard his phone vibrate in his jacket pocket.

He ignored it in order to ask caustically, "You're handling it?"

"Yes," I hissed.

"Like you're handling Castellini?"

"I'm handling him too."

It was then, I heard my phone vibrating on the sofa cushion.

I ignored it because Jamie announced, "From where I'm standing, you're not handling either of those pieces of shit at all, darlin'."

"*I* didn't maroon me on a floating palace with you," I reminded him. "My hands are rather tied as we become intimately acquainted from afar with the coastline of Delaware."

He dropped his head, tore his hand through his thick, dark, hardly-silvering-at-all hair, leaving his fingers curled around the back of his strong neck, before he grumbled to his shoes, "Fucking hell."

"Jamie, rest assured, the G-Force is on Paloma, and I'll make it very clear to Roland upon our return that his attention is unwanted."

His phone had stopped vibrating, as had mine.

But his started up again right away, and after his head shot up, he dropped his hand and spoke his next, so did mine.

I couldn't make note of either to him, not only because he was speaking, but also due to what he was saying, and the low, deep, threatening voice he used in saying it.

"No, baby, *I* will make things clear to Castellini, and *I* will be certain that *cunt* steers *very* clear of you."

That was the c-word I would have used in regard to the P-word, and oddly, I didn't find it vulgar at all when Jamie used it.

"What the fuck is a G-Force?" he asked before I could dispute his assertion he was going to butt into my operation.

I flipped a hand out. "It's a kind of special operations unit, society style, made up of gay men."

He stared at me like I'd lost my mind for a beat before he returned his gaze to the ceiling once again, this time to mutter, "Fuck me."

"Jamie, your language is appalling."

He looked back at me. "Darlin', you've set a pack of gay guys on a bitch on a mission. I suspect in most cases, gay guys can get the job done. But we're talking Paloma Friedrichsen here. She's made a living off sucking cock to keep her in heels and jewels, but she is not of an age she can turn that kind of man's head anymore. Which means she's desperate. Evidence of that, the last time I saw her, she was with my father, and no woman who is not alarmingly desperate would touch his shriveled ass and depleted bank account with a ten-foot pole. She's dangerous, and she has *you* in her sights."

So he knew about AJ.

Maybe?

"I think she's actually seeing your father," I felt it safe (ish?) to disclose.

"I know she is."

Well, it was good I didn't have to confirm that for him.

"And I've got him on his back foot, Nora. You know that."

I did.

Jamie had been working for years to destroy his father in the way that would hurt him the most, that being decimating his finances and his pride.

He was close to succeeding in the first, the second would be harder, considering the false pride a man like AJ Oakley had was coated in steel.

But he'd get there, mostly by annihilating the first.

He wouldn't get there, though, without backing AJ in a corner.

And a cornered predator was unpredictable.

Not to mention vicious.

This was something that had been worrying me for quite some time. It did the same to Dru (we'd talked about it once). But we'd both agreed Jamie was smart, savvy, and his reputation and money made him untouchable.

At least, we hoped so.

"Therefore," Jamie continued, "Paloma making moves, and Pop being Pop, after he took hit after hit for his part in the Core Point debacle, I do not see good things."

I didn't either. And I worried at this juncture in our conversation that he might not find solace in me reiterating how effective the G-Force was.

The Core Point debacle had been devastating for AJ Oakley. His part in that athletic company's coverups of sexual assaults, which had led to the outing of AJ being involved in the same in his other business dealings, had been crushing.

He'd been removed from boards, even the one of his own company. He'd had deals die. He was a pariah in any polite society. Not that he'd ever cared about that, but then again, he'd never been a pariah. Even the media, who used to feed on his extreme political incorrectness, had lost interest in a loud-mouthed old man who seemed to behave as he did in a frantic attempt to remain relevant.

After that, AJ had vowed "dirty" revenge against Jamie (consequently, Dru's and my growing concern).

I didn't know how we didn't cotton on to the unholy alliance of Paloma and AJ.

Well, at least I hadn't.

Jamie seemed to have his finger on that pulse.

I was taken out of my gloomy thoughts when Jamie said, "Now we need to talk about that dress."

I felt heat in my face, and it hit other parts of me when I focused on him and caught the look in his eyes.

I noted immediately AJ and Jamie had one thing in common.

If they had a reason to be, they were both predators.

But, I was seeing, they were very different kinds.

For the life of me, I didn't know why, since the look in his eyes was what I'd been wanting from him for a very long time, but I took a step back.

He took one forward.

Oh my.

"Jamie," I whispered.

He didn't reply.

He was again staring at my legs, which had suddenly started trembling.

"Sir. Ma'am."

Both our heads turned sharply to see the captain standing just in from the interior doorway to the lounge, beyond him, a magnificent view of the formal dining room.

He cleared his throat. "I'm sorry to interrupt, but we've received an urgent call from Mr. Tom Pierce."

The look on the captain's face, those words coming from his mouth, my hand darted out, colliding with Jamie's as his did the same my way, and he curled his fingers tightly around mine.

"We'll be increasing our speed and changing course toward shore," the captain continued, and his eyes locked on Jamie. "I'm sorry to be the one to inform you, sir. Your daughter-in-law has gone into early labor. Mother and child are in distress. They're sending a helicopter to collect you and Ms. Ellington from the ship. Mr. Wheeler's plane will be meeting you at a local airstrip. I suggest you both change clothes."

Jamie's voice was so guttural, it felt like it flayed at my flesh, and his grip on my hand was vise-like when he said, "Thank you."

The captain dipped his chin and left.

I turned instantly to Jamie, got close, put my hand on his chest and pressed deep.

When I looked up at him, I saw his face was ravaged with worry.

My heart squeezed.

"It's going to be fine," I whispered.

He nodded mutely.

"Let's change, darling, so we'll be ready and won't lose a second."

He nodded again but didn't move.

"Let's go," I stated firmly.

He still didn't move.

So I took charge.

I pulled him to the stairs and took him to his cabin, which was at the opposite end of the yacht from mine.

I left him there.

And learned I could run in four-inch heels.

Because, once I saw Jamie yank off his suit jacket, I turned toward my own cabin.

And that was exactly what I did.

CHAPTER 7

RALPH LAUREN

Jamie

They received the news somewhere over New Mexico.

Considering Hale, Elsa and Laird were on the plane when he and Nora met it, so they needed the additional seating capacity for transport to the hospital, Rix and Harvey, Duncan's best friend, had both driven to the local airport to pick them up.

Harvey, a rabidly genial man, was unusually quiet.

Rix looked wrecked.

It felt like Jamie hadn't had any oxygen from the minute the captain gave them the news until they hit the maternity waiting room, and he saw Duncan surge out of his chair and jog to them, a massive smile on his face.

He took Jamie's hand, and with his other, clamped the muscle where Jamie's shoulder met his neck and squeezed.

Duncan didn't delay in speaking.

"Chloe and baby are fine," he shared the information they got on the plane, but Jamie, knowing thoroughly how painful love could be, refused to believe it until he saw it. "She lost a lot of blood, so they're going to keep her here for a day or two. Their baby boy is adorable as fuck, and so tiny. But he's breathing on his own, sucking and can keep himself warm. They're gonna keep him here with Coco, but when she's good to go, he's good to go."

He.

Judge and Chloe had a boy.

Nora had been right.

Duncan looked over his shoulder, grinned largely, clapped Jamie's neck and stepped aside.

Through all this, Nora was at his side, clutching his biceps with both hands, but they dropped away when Dru fell into his arms.

He wrapped them tight around his daughter and rested his cheek against her brilliant hair, pulling in her scent, feeling her health and relief and joy seep into him.

She tipped her head back, and he lifted his.

"Let's go see Judge," she whispered.

He nodded, needing that like he needed air to breathe, but he let her go and turned to Nora.

She looked like a Ralph Lauren ad. Medium-wash, western-inspired denim shirt, tailored white slacks, tan belt.

Her eyes were soft with relief and bright with tears as she lifted her hand to cup his cheek.

At her tender touch, the beauty in her expression, the memory of her the last few hours, not to mention how she'd been in his life the last few decades, it happened.

What he thought would never happen again.

But he was done.

It was over.

The fight. The denial.

The pain.

All of it.

Though, the instant he heard Castellini was making plays to get her back, and then Jamie saw her in that fucking dress, it had already been over.

She'd been at his side in a plane for the last five hours, holding his hand.

Before that, she'd been at his side in a damned helicopter, also holding his hand.

In fact, she'd been at his side the last nearly two years, and long before, looking after him, taking away his crushing loneliness and going so far as to make him laugh. A lot.

So Jamie took her face in both of his hands, angled his head, and captured her mouth.

She made a soft sound of surprise, but she was Nora. His Nora.

She didn't pull away.

No, she wrapped her fingers around one of his wrists.

The kiss was hard and long, but closed mouthed, and he hoped it communicated all he felt for her, all she was to him, and all they were going to be in the future.

Jamie only ended it when he felt the wet of her tears on his lips.

He raised his head and looked down at her beautiful face.

The tears were not for what he just gave her, because Nora didn't think like that. She didn't think about herself first.

The tears were about what he was about to receive from Chloe and Judge.

"Go," she whispered.

Yes. He was right.

Those tears were about the gift he was about to receive.

He nodded, pressed his forehead against hers, then let her go and moved to take his daughter's hand.

Dru was staring up at him, lips parted, even more joy and relief in her eyes, but he couldn't process that now.

"Show me the way, darlin'," he prompted.

She squeezed his hand, and he traded chin dips and nods with Harvey's wife Beth, Mika and Cadence, who, with Tom, had chartered their own plane and beat them there (they'd brought Dru), as well as Sasha, Matt, Gage, Alex, and Mi, Chloe's best friend, along with Mi's husband, Jacob. All of whom were in the waiting room.

And now, all of them had eyes to him, there were some smirks, some happy smiles, some expressions of delighted surprise, this because of what they'd witnessed between Jamie and Nora.

He ignored all of that as Dru led him down the hall and to a room. She stuck her head in, turned back to him and graced him with a radiant smile before she pushed through and guided him in.

Tom was standing, looking out the window.

Genny was perched on a chair in a manner she could pop out of it at a second's notice.

Both of their gazes came to him as Dru backed out and closed the door.

But he only had eyes for what was in the bed.

Chloe lay there on her back, her head having fallen to the side, and incidentally, into the throat of her husband, because Judge was stretched out beside her, turned to his wife, his arm tight around her, his head bent, face in her lustrous dark hair.

They were both fast asleep.

Jamie moved to the bed and couldn't stop himself from reaching out and smoothing back a lock of hair that had fallen on his son's forehead.

He'd felt this feeling, once, the day Judge was born.

And Christ, it was the most beautiful feeling in the world.

His gaze darted to Chloe when he heard her sleepy-tired-soft, "He'll tell you it was his idea, but he lies. It was mine."

Jamie had no idea what she was talking about, he was just thrilled he'd have the opportunity to find out, but that time wasn't now.

"Okay," he whispered, moving his hand to cup the top of her head. He bent and kissed her forehead then lifted up and ordered, "You done good, honey. Now go back to sleep."

Her eyes drifted closed, her lips curled up, and she turned her own head to fit it back into her husband's throat before she did as told.

Jamie looked at Judge, who had not woken through this.

He felt a hand on his back.

He turned to see Tom standing close.

"Come with me," Tom said quietly.

Jamie followed Tom out of the room and further down the hall.

To the nursery.

The nurse there hurried to get them gowns and masks, they washed their hands, and then Tom led him to a clear-sided hospital bassinet that was on rollers.

Resting in it, wrapped in a plush blue blanket with a deep satin border, his eyes closed, his cheeks chubby (regardless of his size), was the new most precious being on the planet.

Tom put his tanned hand on the baby's blanket, bringing into stark relief how tiny he was.

"Five pounds, twelve ounces, allow me the privilege of introducing you to Jameson Thomas Oakley," Tom announced.

Jamie felt his body buck as the bolt of happiness seared through him, and his gaze shot to Tom.

"I know," Tom said on a smile. "Hale and Elsa already gave me the honor, but this one feels just as fucking amazing as the last one."

Jamie was not one of those men so desperate to deny the fact his existence in the grand scheme of things would one day melt clean away, so in an attempt to lengthen the stamp he put on history, he named his offspring after himself.

Hence, his son's name was Judge.

But *fuck*, it felt good that Judge and Chloe honored him this way.

"They say they're going to call him JT," Tom continued. Jamie's friend's eyes warmed and he took his hand from JT's belly. "You can touch him."

Jamie immediately moved in, bent over the bassinet, and touched a gentle finger, sliding it from between his grandson's closed eyes along his little forehead, and he whispered, "Hey there, JT."

JT's diminutive, pink, bow mouth made sucking motions, and then he settled.

It was the sweetest greeting Jamie had experienced in his life.

JAMIE OPENED HIS EYES TO DARK CUT THROUGH WITH LIGHT THAT WAS not the muted glow of the city, or the stark moonlight hitting the sea, but moonlight sifting through trees.

He felt silk on his hands, because tucked tight to his front was a warm body.

And in his nostrils was Nora's tangy, flowery scent.

He felt her round ass snug in his groin, but that pleasant sensation wasn't what made him curl his arms stronger around her to pull her even closer.

No, he did it because his mind was filled with recent memories.

Of the crew on the yacht racing around to get them packed, Nora doing it with them.

Of Nora screeching over the whirring helicopter blades *"Just leave them!"* when they were using the ten seconds it added before their takeoff for the crew to shove her bags into the bird. She did this even though they already knew they'd be waiting at the airstrip for twenty minutes before Hale and Elsa arrived in their jet.

Of Nora's wide eyes, open surprise, and expressive hope after they left the hospital and went to Duncan and Genny's sprawling mountain house to have a glass of champagne to celebrate before they crashed, and Genny said, "I'll run and make up a couple of rooms for you two."

Whereupon Jamie replied, "We only need one."

Nora had not said a word. Nor had she made it a thing.

After gifting him with a wondrous expression, she'd simply followed Genny to help her, and Mika went along with them. And when Jamie finally made it to the room, she was in the bathroom, unpacking his dop kit so he didn't have to go rummaging for his toothpaste.

She'd then futzed around with her own things, her indication she wanted him to get ready for bed first.

The only hesitation she'd shown was when she walked out of the bathroom wearing a stunning nightgown of shimmering, pale pink silk edged in exquisite cream lace that fell to her calves.

"Which side is yours?" she asked.

He was standing in his pajama bottoms at one side of the bed, staring at how gorgeous she was, though he thought his position shared the answer to her question.

Since it hadn't, his answer was to move to her, herd her to that very side, then hook her at the waist and pull them both into bed.

He'd turned out both lights then situated them as they were now.

With her scent, and her feel, and her nearness, and his son whole, and his son's wife healthy, and his grandson breathing, Jamie had passed out within seconds.

Now, Jamie was awake.

And he had to make a decision.

That wasn't quite true. It was mostly made.

But when they woke the next morning, he'd have to make it official, because after the morning, he couldn't walk it back.

But first, he had to make an admission.

He was scared shitless.

An outsider looking in would think he was born with it all.

He was not.

He'd convinced himself he'd had it all when he'd won Belinda's heart.

He did not.

He'd earned it when Rosalind entered his life and brought Dru with her, and she'd entrusted both of them to him.

Then he lost half of that.

Now, he had a shot at it again.

On this thought, he felt an odd, soft bump hit the bed, this being explained when he felt a cat walk up his leg.

One of Genny and Duncan's pets.

The cat stopped at his hip, and he felt it staring down at him through the dark.

He figured it'd jump away, but instead, it started to move toward Nora.

He was about to intervene, but was too late. The cat touched her, and she moved.

She swept the feline into her arms and cuddled it, cooing drowsily, "Your Chloe did fine, Puck. Did you ever doubt?"

Jamie heard a loud cat purr.

He kept hearing it even as Nora's body melted into his as she fell back to sleep.

She liked animals.

That did it.

Decision made.

The cat was still purring when Jamie settled into Nora and drifted asleep.

———

JAMIE WOKE AGAIN, BUT THIS TIME, THE SUN WAS SHINING THROUGH THE pines.

And he was now on his back, Nora pressed down his side, her arm resting along his stomach, her head on his shoulder.

Having her there after how long he'd waited to have just that, what he didn't want was to move, but he had to use the bathroom.

He was also keen to get back to the hospital.

He carefully extricated himself from her hold so he wouldn't wake her and went to the bathroom.

When he finished and walked out, he froze at the sight of her makeup-less face, her bed-tousled mane of hair, and her pretty sleepy eyes, a sight he'd never seen.

And finally, he got to see behind the mask, and what she'd been hiding was even more beautiful than what she gave the world.

She was sitting up on her ass in the bed, her knees to her chest, her arms wrapped around her shins.

She let them go, and moving both legs at once, gracefully swung them over the side, found her feet and walked his way.

She stopped at him and got up on her toes to press a kiss to the underside of his jaw, and then he heard the bathroom door close.

He sat on the end of the bed to wait for her to come out and glanced around.

He'd been to Genny and Duncan's large mountain house before. It was rustic, cozy, but still impressive, imposing and refined in a way all the logs, wood, stone, western and Native American motifs could not hide.

Taking it in now, he decided he was buying a house in Prescott, Arizona. And if he couldn't find one he liked, he'd build one.

On this thought, Nora came out of the bathroom and headed to one of her open suitcases, stating, "I'm assuming you wish to whisk away to the hospital *tout de suite*."

He was relatively certain he'd never "whisked" anywhere.

But her words made him smile.

And knowing his decision had been made caused warmth to rush his chest.

"Come here," he ordered gruffly.

She stopped, turned, and regarded him.

"Jamie, I think we should—"

He cut her off by indicating the bed they'd slept in together with a flick of his hand. "I'm pretty sure you've caught my drift, but let's make certain of that, shall we?"

She stood there, staring at him, and it was cute how he could tell she was barely breathing.

But since she needed to do that, and he needed to end the hell he'd been putting her through, he didn't hesitate to carry on.

"You were right. That kiss wasn't a mistake. I've been wanting to do that for fucking decades. I fell in love with you in that ladies room, Nora, and it might not be right I did when we were both married, but it happened. I've loved you ever since. I'm terrified of having you, and life making it go to shit. But I can't fight it anymore, and more importantly, I can no longer put you through me trying to do it. I want you in my bed and in my life. In my children's lives. I want to be in your children's lives. And when we figure out where we're going to land, and just saying, your apartment is fantastic, but I'd prefer my brownstone, and I'm okay with you redecorating it. Even though Lindy's touch is all over it, it'll be your home. So you'll need to make it yours. But once that's done, we're getting a dog and a cat, or maybe two. Of both."

"I should have come to you," she whispered.

Jamie smiled again. "Yes, you should have. But why did you say that?"

"Because…it's so very strange, darling, but I find I can't move."

If she couldn't, Jamie sure fucking could.

He got up, went to her, and pulled her into his arms.

She put her hands on his chest just below his shoulders and looked deep into his eyes.

"I want to kiss you so badly, it's a goddamned ache," he announced. "But I can't kiss you, because I did that, so I know how it'll go. That being, it'll make me want to fuck you. And we don't have time for me to do that properly, since I need to see my son, my daughter-in-law and hold my grandchild."

Her smile was soft and sweet as she rested her weight against him, "Then let's get to the hospital."

Jamie chanced allowing himself to touch his mouth to hers.

It was a mistake, seeing as, when he came away, her gaze was languid and loving and happy.

Fuck.

He'd nearly messed this up.

Thank Christ he'd pulled his shit together.

Finally.

He gave her a squeeze. "You'll take longer, so you go first. I'll get us some coffee."

"Your wish is my command."

It would be.

He told her that with a wolfish grin, and her eyes grew large.

Before that affected his groin any further, he let her go and gave her a gentle shove toward the bathroom.

He then found a T-shirt to pull on before he walked down to the kitchen to get their coffee.

IT WAS SUPREMELY SATISFYING TO BE THE MAN WALKING BEHIND NORA Ellington when she swanned into a room.

He'd done it before, but he'd never been hers. Not officially.

Now he was.

And it felt tremendous.

Thus, his lips were twitching smugly when he did so.

Nora was speaking.

To Chloe.

"Oh, glorious! You got the peignoir set I sent you!"

The room was crowded, but Jamie's eyes went right to the bed.

Chloe was wearing a baby pink nightgown with a deep, wide vee neck that had little red roses with green leaves embroidered on it. Decorating the end of the bed was a filmy robe with those same roses, what appeared to be trailing down the sides of the sleeves.

Chloe was pale, still looked tired, with bruising created from effort and fatigue shadowing under her eyes sharing how bad it had been.

But mostly, she looked like Chloe.

"Of course I did. It's the first thing I packed in my baby bag. Didn't you get my thank you note?" Chloe replied before Nora bent over her and moved her head so they could kiss both cheeks.

Judge stood by Chloe's bedside, and Jamie was concerned to see his son's wife was bathed, refreshed, her hair gleaming, and she was in a lovely nightdress. But his son was disheveled, wearing the crumpled clothes he'd been in the night before, and he clearly hadn't gone home to shower and change or taken the time to freshen up in Chloe's hospital bathroom.

He also appeared to be standing sentry beside her bed.

Jamie's gaze moved to Tom, who caught it, jutting up his chin in understanding and shared concern. Then Jamie looked to Duncan, who gave a slight shake of his head in the same.

After that, Jamie noticed Alex, who had moon eyes and a love-struck look on her face.

He followed her gaze and saw Rix standing and holding a tiny bundle to his massive chest, his entire focus on the baby in his arms.

"Rix, stop hogging Jimmy," Chloe ordered. "Give Jamie a chance to meet his grandson."

Jimmy?

He thought his grandson was to be called JT.

"Not gonna," Rix denied, even if he looked at Jamie and grinned as he started his way.

"He's going to kidnap him like he keeps trying to kidnap our dogs," Chloe complained to Judge.

"No he's not," Judge stated flatly.

His son's tone snagged Jamie's attention, but Rix was now there.

With utmost care, Rix and Jamie did the exchange.

And the minute Jamie had him, he understood and accepted the fact, for the rest of his lifetime, he'd be falling in love again and again and again.

Nora got close to inspect him, and within a nanosecond, turned and decreed, "Obviously, sheer *perfection*. You are so clever, my darling girl."

Chloe preened. Judge scowled.

Jamie looked to Rix.

His attention was on Judge, and his mouth was tight with worry.

Jamie turned his attention to Chloe.

She felt his regard, then mouthed, *Do something. Please.*

Fuck.

As he suspected, Judge had it bad.

Carefully, he bent at the same time he pulled JT up his chest to give his little sleepyhead a soft kiss, before he asked Nora, "Want to hold him?"

"You took an *age* to ask," she replied, even if he'd had hold of JT maybe a minute.

She went in, doing it deftly, but delicately.

Once she had his grandchild held snug against her, Jamie turned his attention to his son.

"How about we take a walk, Judge?" he suggested. "Maybe I can drive you home so you can get a shower."

"I'm good here," Judge replied.

"Hup," Rix grunted quietly, and the room started to clear, this being Duncan, Genny, Tom, Mika, Alex and Rix.

All but Nora, and obviously, Chloe.

Nora moved to the window, swaying the baby gently side to side, removing herself from the conversation that was to come as best she could with JT in her arms.

Judge tracked her with his eyes like she was a threat.

Oh yes.

He had it bad.

"Judge," Jamie called.

"Yup," Judge answered, not taking his gaze from Nora, or more to the point, his boy.

"Judge," Jamie repeated inflexibly.

His son looked to him and bit, "What, Dad?"

Jamie continued to repeat himself. "Let's take a walk."

"Like I said, I'm good here."

"I think you need—" Jamie began.

"Judge, *mon beau,*" Chloe interrupted him, raising her hand Judge's way, and he caught it immediately, like she was weak, and she couldn't hold it up on her own.

Shit.

"Please, go home," she continued. "Have a quick shower. Then come back to me. And bring me a donut from Bosa."

"I can send Gage to Bosa,"

"I don't want Gage to get me Bosa. I want *you* to get me Bosa."

"Chloe—"

"Judge, honey, I want you to go with your dad, now, so you can be back fast."

Jamie watched helplessly as his son put up an epic struggle to beat back every instinct seizing his body, a feeling Jamie knew all too well.

He won when Chloe whispered, *"Please."*

Judge nodded, bent and pressed a hard kiss on Chloe's mouth.

He straightened directly, looked to Jamie and grunted, "Let's go."

Judge then moved. Fast.

Jamie glanced at Chloe, who nodded to him, to Nora, who gave him an across-the-room air kiss, and he hustled after his boy.

Judge didn't speak all the way to his and Chloe's townhouse, but he drove like they had a trunk full of loot and the police were in hot pursuit.

Jamie didn't speak because he needed his son to concentrate on driving and not killing them.

But when they got upstairs to the kitchen from the garage, and Judge was jogging to the next flight of stairs, completely ignoring their two dogs, Zeke and Montana, who were jumping around him, Jamie followed into the living room and stopped him by calling his name.

Judge turned on him. "Not now, Dad."

"Now, Judge. You need to get this shit out before you go back to your family."

"I don't have any shit," Judge lied. "I need to shower, get Chloe her donut, and get back to her."

"Judge—"

"*Not now!*" Judge roared.

Jamie didn't flinch.

But he did ask, "What happened?"

For a second, Judge just stood there.

Then he bellowed, "*Fuck!*"

Jamie could tell he needed to let the dogs out, but he didn't move. He just kept his focus on his boy.

"God, I get it. *Christ*, I get it," Judge said as he started pacing.

Both dogs followed him.

He stopped abruptly and swung to Jamie. "I should never have gone along with pulling that shit with you and Nora on that boat."

"We're fine. Better than fine," Jamie assured. "We can talk about that later. Now, tell me what happened yesterday."

"Everything's been perfect. Minimal morning sickness at the beginning. She's had great energy. Fucking *glowing* since the fucking *beginning.*"

Jamie nodded. "I know, son."

Judge threw both of his hands up in agitation. "So how the fuck did that happen?"

"I don't know."

His voice was tortured when Judge shared, "They pushed me out of the delivery room."

Goddamn fuck.

"Come here," Jamie urged.

Judge shook his head. "No. I can't. I need to shower. I need to get back to them."

"Chloe is fine. JT is fine. You need to ground yourself in that fact."

"How?" Judge clipped. "You didn't see...you didn't hear...fuck. *Shit!*"

Jamie watched his boy as he dropped his ass to the arm of a couch, bent double and wrapped his arms over the back of his head, both dogs worried and snuffling him.

Jamie got close as Judge said to his thighs. "I get it. I didn't even lose her, and I get how everything can turn to nothing in a flash, and you can't *handle it.*"

Jamie crouched by his son and reached to put his hand on his back.

"You're going to handle this, Judge," he said quietly.

Judge's torso shot up, dislodging Jamie's hand, and he clipped sarcastically. "Doing a bang-up job of that, aren't I?"

Jamie stayed low and stated, "You're having an honest reaction to a traumatic situation, and you're entitled to that."

"I have a wife and kid to look after."

"You're still human."

"I can't be human, I've gotta be—" he cut himself off.

"Everything?" Jamie filled in for him.

Judge's eyes were haunted when he looked at Jamie. "God, I get all of it now. Everything you went through."

"This isn't about me, it's about you, but I'll tell you about me to move this along. When the captain of that ship told us Chloe and JT were in distress, I froze. I was immobile. I might still be standing there if Nora didn't kickstart me. And I'm not embarrassed about that. I love you. I love Chloe. The fact I was so far away and powerless to help when I heard that news wrecked me. There is nothing wrong with feeling love. It can make us weak, like that, but even if it does, it never ceases to make us strong."

"If that's the case, then what the fuck with you wasting time claiming Nora?" Judge asked.

"I stopped wasting time. We're together. Get ready to have another stepmom."

His son's eyes rounded. "Shit. Really?"

Jamie stood while grinning and confirmed, "Really."

"Stepmom? That was fast," Judge muttered.

It wasn't fast.

It took decades.

"Obviously, we have to work up to that part," Jamie told him. "That's important, but it's not what's important now. What's important now is you stop being so damned hard on yourself. Yesterday was terrifying. That was yesterday. Today you have a healthy wife and a beautiful son. Trust me, buddy, life is too damned short to get stuck somewhere you don't need to be. I've learned that twice, the second time very recently, and I learned it the hard way. Don't turn away from feelings. Feel them. Then get on with it. Yesterday scared you, because it was fucking scary. Admit it. Feel it. I'm here to talk to about it. But in the end, today is today. And you need to get on with it."

In an agonized voice, Judge shared, "I love her with everything that's me, and I overheard them talking about the possibility that they'd have to save one or the other."

Fuck.

Jamie pulled his son to his feet and into his arms, and he held tight.

Judge's arms went around him, and he grabbed fistfuls of his dad's shirt.

"I would have picked her," he said quietly into Jamie's ear.

"I know," Jamie murmured.

"She'd never forgive me."

"I know."

"And I would have had to live with that decision, but even knowing it was the right one, it would have destroyed me."

Jamie let out a deep sigh and repeated, "I know."

Judge pushed his forehead in Jamie's neck, and Jamie gave him a moment.

"It didn't happen that way," his son said.

There it was.

"No. It didn't," Jamie confirmed.

He felt Judge nod against his skin.

Then he pushed away, stepped away and finally gave some attention to his dogs.

"Can you take them out while I shower?" he asked.

"Absolutely," Jamie answered.

"I need you to drive back," Judge admitted.

"I can do that," Jamie agreed.

A shaky smile hit his son's mouth. "Stepmom?"

Jamie's return smile wasn't shaky. "Eventually."

"I guess, once you get your head out of your ass, you don't mess around."

"Nope. And stop talking to your father that way," Jamie mock scolded.

Warmth hit his boy's brown eyes. "I love you, Dad."

Damn, he'd been so caught in all he'd lost, he hadn't taken time to recognize his many blessings.

He was learning.

"Love you too, buddy. Now go shower."

Judge nodded and headed to the stairs.

Jamie grabbed the leads hanging beside the front door and took the dogs out.

When they got back, he fed them and the cat, Venus.

And when his son came downstairs, they went to get his daughter-in-law a donut.

It was that afternoon.

Duncan and Genny, Tom and Mika, and Jamie and Nora were drinking cocktails in Duncan and Genny's great room.

Dru, Sasha and Mi were hanging at the hospital in case Chloe needed anything.

Gage had gone to let Chloe and Judge's dogs out again.

Matt, who was a practicing vet, had been called away on some horse emergency, and Cadence had asked if she could tag along, he'd said yes, so she went with him.

Hale and Elsa were upstairs, taking a nap with Laird, since Laird, in a new place and not feeling it, had made their night last night not very restful.

Alex and Rix had gone home due to the fact that Rix was like Judge's twin from another mother, and as such, he acutely felt Judge's pain. Not to mention, Rix loved Chloe like a sister. He was as demolished as Judge had been about what had happened, he was just better at hiding it. But Alex hadn't missed it, so she was seeing to her man.

Heddy, Genny's friend, had swung by the hospital to check on Chloe and meet JT.

And now, they were discussing Duncan heading into town to grab copious tapas from some place called *El Gato Azul* for dinner when Duncan's first son, Sully, prowled in.

"What the fuck are you all doing here?" he demanded in lieu of greeting.

Sully had a job in Texas and hadn't been able to get on a flight until late that morning. He'd told them not to bother coming to get him, he was renting a car in Phoenix.

"What are *you* doing here?" Duncan asked his boy.

"I went by the hospital first," Sully answered. "Coco was sleeping. Judge was *out*. JT was adorable, but he was also out. I called Gage, and he said he was meeting Sasha, Dru, Mi and Jake at COLT Grill for some barbeque, like serious shit didn't just go down. And you all are sitting around with cocktails. So again, the fuck?"

Good.

They were all sleeping, with Judge being *out*.

"That family needed some time without everyone hovering over them," Duncan explained.

At that, Sully got over his pique and moved further into the room. "What are you drinking?"

Genny lifted her glass. "Nora whipped up some watermelon sangria. It's delicious. Have some. There's plenty."

Sully turned to his dad. "Please tell me we have beer."

"Who are you talking to?" Duncan asked as reply.

Sully came in and kissed the cheeks of the women, shook the hands of the men, but gave his dad a hug before he went to the kitchen.

Jamie sipped his bourbon. Nora could mix a mean cocktail, but he drew the line at watermelon sangria.

On this thought, he turned to her sitting beside him on a couch (Puck, incidentally, was tucked to her side, and since he'd already noticed Puck was partial to Chloe, Jamie made note the cat had a type, one it shared with Jamie). She was swiping all over her phone.

"What are you doing?" he asked.

"I'm looking up baby stores in Phoenix," she murmured, then she turned her attention to Genny. "The results I'm finding are dire, my dear."

"I have some things on reserve at some stores in LA. I finalized purchase on all the boy stuff when we got the news," Genny replied, and concluded, "They deliver."

Being the true New Yorker she was, Nora made a hilarious face when Genny said the words "in LA."

Which meant Jamie was smiling.

He was also counting his blessings.

Because...yes.

Finally.

He was learning.

———

THE CALL WAS EXPECTED, AND IT CAME EARLY THAT EVENING.

Jamie took it while stepping out on the back deck.

"How are you doing?" he asked his son.

"Well, it happened." Judge blew out the words on a sigh.

"How'd it go?"

"We were all asleep. I woke up first and saw it. He'd slipped in and out like a ghost. I waited until Chloe woke up. She opened it. She says it's a Bird Baby sterling silver cup. I got the Tiffany's part from the box."

The ghost in that scenario was a man named Rhys Vaughan.

So far, Chloe was the only one to have met him, and she did this only briefly.

Jamie had had him investigated, but according to every record on two continents (he'd been told by Chloe, Rhys was Welsh, something she derived from his accent), he didn't exist.

So, yes, very much a ghost.

"And?"

"And, on the bottom, it's engraved, *To, Jameson Thomas Oakley. Love, Uncle Corey.*"

Jamie nodded even if his son couldn't see him doing it.

The story was tragic, convoluted, and bizarre, but tech billionaire, Corey Szabo, now deceased, father to Hale, best friend to Genny, and mastermind who was so good at that shit, he was able to perpetrate his maneuvers from beyond the grave, had set everything in motion.

Including, in a definite but roundabout way, Jamie and Nora being able to finally be what they were meant to be to each other.

Unquestionably convoluted and bizarre, but the results were far from tragic.

When Laird came into the world, his grandfather, even being dead, had sent him a like present.

So they knew it would happen.

And it happened.

"Is Chloe okay?" Jamie asked.

Chloe had been particularly close to Corey.

"She cried. But they were happy tears, kind of," Judge said.

"How about you?"

"I'm lucky I have a great Dad who's been through it, so he gets it."

Jamie drew in breath through his nose, so much, it expanded his chest, and then he let it go.

"Fortunately, considering Operation Parent Trap, we have the time off, so Nora and I are going to stay for a while," he shared.

"They're releasing Chloe tomorrow," Judge shared in return, and Jamie was relieved to hear humor in his tone.

That was much more like his son.

"Excellent."

"Will you and Nora move to the guest room in the townhouse?" Judge asked. "I want you close."

"We'll do that first thing tomorrow."

"Of course you will," Judge muttered.

Yes.

Of course he would.

"It's feeding time, so I gotta go," Judge said.

"Right. Love you, buddy. And proud of you."

"Love you too. Tell everyone we're doing okay."

"I will."

"See you tomorrow, Dad."

"You will, Judge."

"Later."

"Later, son."

They hung up.

He went inside.

Everyone was watching him.

"So?" Genny prompted huskily.

She'd loved Corey most of all.

"An engraved Bird Baby Tiffany's cup," he told her.

She bit her lip and tears hit her eyes. Duncan slid an arm around her and drew her close.

Mika dropped her head to Tom's shoulder.

Jamie moved to Nora to grab her wineglass, which was almost empty, so she needed it filled.

Death.

Life.

Blessings.

And they were moving on.

CHAPTER 8

VERONICA BEARD

Jamie

The next morning, Jamie woke in another fun new position. With Nora playing the big spoon.

He allowed himself long moments to enjoy it before he looked to the clock on the nightstand and saw it was early.

Nora wasn't an early riser.

And although he'd very much like to start both their days in a way it'd be starting the day right, Jamie didn't want the first time they made love to be in Duncan and Genny's guest room.

Or Judge and Chloe's.

It had been too long of a wait, and that was all his fault.

But they were going to have to wait a little longer.

He sighed, caught her hand on the arm that was draped around his waist and pulled it carefully to his lips so as not to wake her. He touched his mouth to her knuckles.

With equal caution, he set it behind him and slid out from in front of her.

When he got back from the bathroom, she was up on an arm, blinking crossly at the window.

Those annoyed eyes came to him.

"What time is it?" she asked.

"It's six," he answered.

"Is there an actual six o'clock in a day where I don't have a cocktail in my hand?"

Damn, she was funny.

He chuckled, walked to her and sat on the bed in the crook of her lap. "Yes, that would be the one referred to as six *in the morning.*"

"I don't recognize this in Nora Time."

"Then go back to sleep, baby," he murmured.

"No." She shook her head. "I can't. We need to pack. And our rental car is being delivered this morning. I also need to go over Hale's grocery list. He might miss something."

Chloe and JT arriving home that day, they all had their assignments.

And it was Nora doing the assigning.

Her and Elsa.

"And, of course, I have to go through the motions of looking fabulous before all that happens," she concluded.

"You look fabulous now," he told her.

And she did. Cute and soft and entirely too fuckable for their day's schedule.

"Stop looking at me like that, Jameson," she snapped. "We haven't discussed it, but I believe we both understand we cannot consummate this delightful change to our relationship in Genny and Duncan's guest room with your daughter ensconced right across the hall."

He lifted his eyes from where they'd gotten caught on her mouth.

"Or Judge and Chloe's," he added.

"One question," she demanded.

"What is it?" he asked.

"Were you going to ravish me in the aft lounge before we got our dire news?"

He burst out laughing at the word "ravish."

But, fuck him, he was about to do just that before they got their news.

So he was forced to answer, "Yes."

She looked away and huffed out an exasperated sigh.

He caught her chin and brought her back to him.

"We can make out in Genny and Duncan's guest room," he suggested in a low voice.

"Have you seen your chest?" she queried haughtily, glancing down at it like it caused offense and he needed to apologize for it.

He was chuckling again when he answered, "Yes."

"Well, allow me to inform you, as a heterosexual female, that it would be nigh on impossible to simply *make out*, as you so eloquently put it, with you and your bare chest, and not have that get out of hand."

Good to know.

"I could put on a T-shirt," he offered.

"I've seen it already this morning. It's taunting me now. You'd have to put on a snowsuit to take my mind off it."

Jamie again burst out laughing.

Nora waited until he was done before she spoke again, but she wasn't fooling him. Her face was soft, her expression content. She loved to make him laugh.

And Jamie loved that she did, and more, that she brought so much laughter back into his life.

Yes.

He loved that quite a bit.

"If we must be up and mobile at this godforsaken hour, I need coffee," she ordered imperiously.

"I'll get right on that."

"You do that."

"Kiss first."

She lost all snootiness and whispered, "Jamie."

"Quick one."

"I have morning breath."

"No tongue."

She rolled her eyes.

Jamie stole a kiss.

When he pulled away, she was pouting, and that didn't fool him either.

Her expression was no longer content.

It was happy.

So…good.

Jamie had managed to start their day off right, nonetheless.

DRU AND HALE WERE IN CHLOE AND JUDGE'S KITCHEN, COOKING enough food to refrigerate and freeze, it would keep that couple fed for a month.

Sully and Gage were outside, exercising the dogs.

Elsa was in the study, doing some work.

Laird was in Tom's arms, and Tom was out on the back deck.

Genny was in an armchair, JT cradled in her lap.

Duncan was at work, and so were Matt, Rix, and Alex, and Mi and Sasha had had to go back down to Phoenix to do the same thing.

Mika and Cadence were on a run to the grocery store to get something Hale had forgotten.

And Chloe and Judge had arrived home with JT half an hour ago.

Jamie's son had his wife cuddled to his chest where they both lounged on a couch, Chloe covered with a blanket, so Judge was as well. Venus was curled at their feet.

Jamie was in the other armchair, legs stretched in front of him, crossed at the ankles, waiting for his turn with JT.

All this was as it was when Nora floated down the stairs.

She stopped at the foot of the couch and stared severely at Chloe.

"Your postpartum wardrobe is unacceptable, darling," she announced.

Judge's gaze raced to his dad.

Jamie simply fought smiling and shook his head to communicate that, yes, Nora had undoubtedly snooped in Chloe's closet, but no, he didn't need to be concerned, because that was all she'd done, and she had a purpose in doing it.

Which she would handle, Jamie knew, right now, because when it came to clothes—or anything she deemed important, like a woman who took pride in her appearance, as Chloe did, needing not to lose hold on the woman she was when motherhood became a part of her life—Nora didn't fuck around.

"I know, I didn't have time to—"

Before Chloe could finish reminding everyone she'd given birth five weeks early, Nora spoke.

"No matter. Jamie has a laptop and that's what express shipping is for."

"There are some things I've been meaning to get from my shop in Phoenix," Chloe said.

"I'll bring you a pad and paper, darling. You make a list. I'll call Mi. She can package them up and I'll arrange for them to be couriered immediately," Nora said. She looked to Judge and raised her brows. "Pad and paper?"

"Study, also kitchen," Judge answered.

Nora glided to the kitchen.

"I love her so much," Chloe said dreamily, watching Nora go.

"Me too," Judge replied to her, but his eyes were on Jamie.

Jamie didn't fight that smile.

"Are you unpacked?" Judge asked him.

"Yes," Jamie answered.

"Is there anything you need?" Chloe asked.

"No, honey," Jamie said gently. "We've got all we'll ever need."

She tipped her head so she could see Judge. "They always fight, but I'm always right."

"I think maybe we should skirt that subject for a couple more days, baby," Judge advised.

"Skirt what subject?" Nora asked, returning with a pad and paper, which she handed to Chloe.

"Nothing," Judge said.

"My brilliant matchmaking skills," Chloe said over him.

Judge sighed.

Jamie heard Genny swallow a giggle.

Nora crossed her arms over her stomach, but she put out one hip so she could better tap her toe.

Christ, she was something.

And he was an imbecile.

Why had he fought it for so long?

How had he managed to do that?

He had to settle in the fact it was done now.

Or it would be, officially (or, more officially), when they got their asses home.

"We do need to discuss how infernally outrageous that was," Nora declared.

"Sweetheart," Jamie tried to intervene.

"You can't be complaining," Chloe stated.

"I'm not complaining." Nora waved a hand blithely. "But that does not negate the fact you stranded your father-in-law and I on a boat for a week. This, my darling, in the game of life and love, is known as foul play."

"It wasn't *a boat*," Chloe returned. "It was a mega-yacht."

"I also won't argue the amenities, dear," Nora shot back. "No one could accuse you of not having good taste. But again, you *stranded* your father-in-law and I on a *mega-yacht* for a *week*. This isn't a Disney movie."

Chloe snuggled back into her husband and smugly retorted, "It seemed to have worked out like one."

"Well, obviously, that can't be argued either," Nora drawled.

Jamie chuckled.

Genny let her giggle loose this time.

Judge pulled his wife closer.

"However, I must elicit a promise from you at this juncture," Nora went on.

"And that would be?" Chloe prompted.

"You never engage in that behavior again without involving me, and when I say that, I mean from the very beginning. I don't want to miss a thing."

"Well, Gage is here, working with Judge now, so that will be difficult for you, since you live in New York. Matt, the same. Sully is in Texas, also difficult for you. Sasha down in Phoenix, ditto. But when I get down to Ned and Blake, you can be in on it."

At Chloe's declaration she intended to continue meddling, Judge cast a beleaguered glance at the ceiling.

Nora, however, swept a hand to indicate the floor at her feet. "I've made this sacrifice several times, braving the wilds of Arizona for this family. So that's no excuse not to involve me. I'm uncertain I can handle Texas, because of a certain someone who lives there. But I'll do my best."

"Then you're in," Chloe decreed. "Now, are those cargo pants Veronica Beard?"

"Yes," Nora answered.

"This season?"

"Yes."

"Can you get me a postpartum pair?"

"I'll get my phone and do that now, darling," Nora vowed, then she was off to find her phone.

"Judge," Jamie called.

Both his son and his son's wife looked at him.

"Once things settle, I'll be looking into buying a property here," Jamie told him.

Chloe's face lit up.

"Wonderful," Genny murmured.

But Judge.

Fuck.

His boy looked happy, relieved, excited and humbled, all at once.

"That would be awesome," Judge said low.

"Not to live, but I'll definitely be out here more often," Jamie explained.

"We'll take anything we can get," Judge replied.

"Absolutely," Chloe added.

At this point, he had to shift because Genny was there, handing over JT.

"Not a surprise," she said after Jamie had curled the light bundle to his chest. He looked up into her blue eyes. "They're hard to resist."

She was very right.

She smiled at him, he returned it, then he moved it to the bundle in his arms.

JT was awake, his unseeing eyes staring, his little baby fists moving randomly, and Nora had been correct.

Sheer perfection.

He shifted his gaze to see Judge whispering in Chloe's ear, and Chloe listening with rapt attention.

Yes.

Sheer perfection.

THAT EVENING, EVERYONE HAD RETURNED TO DUNCAN AND GENNY'S, except Dru, whose flight to go home left the next day.

Sully was going to drive her down to Phoenix to catch it before he got on his own.

She'd asked if she could sleep on Chloe and Judge's couch so she could have more time with them and JT before she had to leave.

Judge wouldn't hear of it, since the couch in the study was a pull-out, so she was sleeping there.

But now, Jamie was standing at the back doors which were made of glass, and looking out at his daughter, who was sitting on a step on the flight that led down off the side of the deck to the open space shared by the complex.

He smelled her first, and felt her second, when Nora pressed against his arm.

Jamie wanted all the time he could get with Chloe, Judge and JT as well.

But he also really wanted to get home to see to some pressing business.

"You need to get out there," she said quietly.

He turned his head and looked down at her. "Dru can be an alone-time person."

"Dru, right now, needs her father to remind her, even though he's not her biological father, he's still her father, and even though she does not share blood with her big brother, he's still her brother. Last, the pairing she wanted for her dad came about, but that does not now mean she'll be cast out, emotionally or otherwise."

It felt like his insides had frozen because he hadn't thought of that.

"Jesus," he whispered.

"There's alone, darling," she whispered back. "And feeling alone because you can get it in your head you don't belong. So, my dearest, you need to assure her she does so that doesn't take root."

It was good she was so damned smart.

He bent his head to kiss her, she met him halfway, then she stepped away, and he moved out.

He sat down on the step beside his daughter and playfully bumped her with his shoulder.

He thought perhaps Nora was wrong when Dru did what she would always do. That being resting against his side and putting her head on his shoulder.

"You good?" he asked.

"That was scary," she answered.

She meant the way JT had come into the world.

He reached out and took her hand, holding it tight and bringing it to his knee as he agreed, "Yes, it was."

"But everything's okay now, and I'm glad," she went on.

"Yes, darlin', everything is okay."

She moved her hand from his hold, but only so she could play with his fingers.

Jamie felt that tighten his chest.

She did that as a little girl. She'd been fascinated by his hands when she was little. But she hadn't done it in years.

He also knew why she'd been preoccupied with his hands.

Chet had used his in fists on Rosalind before she'd left him, and Dru had witnessed it. And even when Chet wasn't doing that, he'd not been a man prone to acts of affection, physical or otherwise.

When Jamie had asked after Dru's fascination, Lindy had told him her daughter hadn't seen a man's hands be gentle and used to communicate love.

After that, Jamie had loved and hated Dru's captivation with his hands, so he was relieved when it faded away, at the same time he missed it.

Therefore, now, he was delighted to have it back.

He cleared his throat and remarked, "I think you get your mission was accomplished with Nora and me."

"Yeah," she mumbled.

"You okay with that?"

She lifted her head and tipped it to look at him. "Why wouldn't I be?"

"I'm just checking."

"I like her."

"I hope so."

"I like her, Dad."

He used his free hand to touch her nose as he smiled at her. "You'll always be my girl."

She looked away.

Damn.

"Dru?" he called.

"I know." She sighed and put her head back on his shoulder. "I'll always be your girl."

He caught her hand in his hold and bounced it once on his knee. "I mean it, Dru."

"I know you do."

She sounded despondent, and Jamie didn't like it.

He hadn't had a lot of time for her the last two days, considering everything that was happening.

He should have found it.

"You're worrying me a little bit, honey," he said.

She moved her head to look at him again and whispered, "She got Mom's roses."

And his chest tightened again.

"You remember that?" he pushed out.

"I'll never forget it."

"You've known Nora awhile, and you haven't mentioned it. I thought, since it was an emotional time, it slipped your mind. And since it was an emotional time, I didn't want to remind you."

"I wasn't…" She trailed off and looked to the trees. "Wanna hear something stupid?"

"I want to hear anything you have to say, but I doubt it's stupid."

She looked back to him. "You're right. This isn't stupid. But it's… weird."

"I'm sure it's not."

"Okay, then maybe a little creepy," she mumbled.

"Dru, out with it."

Her eyes had fallen to his shoulder, but they came up to his, and she blurted, "After Mom died, after we met her, at the church, I used to make up dreams, before I fell asleep, that Nora would come back and make you happy again."

Jamie grunted, the invisible blow she landed was so solid.

"I know, creepy," she said quickly. "It isn't like I didn't miss Mom."

"Of course not, darlin'," he forced out.

"I don't want you to think—"

"I don't think anything but that you care about me. I used to wrack my brain to figure out what would make you happy too, after we lost your mom."

"Did you come up with any ideas?"

He smiled through the sadness he'd never lose that he hadn't bested that impossible feat. "No."

She dropped her head to his shoulder again.

He rested his against it.

They sat together for a while and didn't talk.

Dru broke their silence.

"How did she get the flowers there so fast?"

"I've no idea," Jamie murmured.

"It was like magic." She lifted her head again, so he did as well, and she looked to him. "I think that was why I fixated on her. It was all so...we were so..."

"Sad," he supplied when she faltered. "Devastated. It was all so inconceivable."

Her smile was small. "Yeah. All those. And then this woman in a pretty dress shows up and makes flowers appear out of thin air. So it seemed she had magic, and I guess, well..." She shrugged. "I guess we needed magic."

Jamie could definitely see that, because at that time, they did need Nora's magic.

"And now, she's with you," she whispered. "And it makes me happy. But it also makes me sad."

And he could definitely see that too.

"I will never not love your mom and I will never stop missing her, even if Nora makes me happy."

"She gets that. Nora, I mean."

"Yes," he confirmed.

"It wasn't a question, Dad. She gets it. I like that about her."

"She liked your mom, and we haven't had time to talk things through, but Nora is not the kind of woman to replace another woman. She's the kind of woman to embrace another woman. We'll never lose your mom that way, darlin', and you don't have to try to make things easier on Nora by hiding that part of you. Nora wouldn't have that, and I won't either."

She pulled her lips in and rubbed them together.

"Did you worry you had to do that?" he asked.

She let her lips go and said, "You loved Mom a lot, Dad."

"I loved your mom with everything I had that I didn't give to Judge and you."

Her face scrunched, and she hid her emotion by dropping her forehead to his shoulder.

"She knows that, right?" Dru inquired of his shoulder.

Oh, Nora knew that, for certain.

"Yes."

"How does a woman come after something like that?" Dru asked.

And there was more of Nora's magic.

"She understands that life keeps going, and love has no limits, and the man I am that she can love, Lindy helped create, so she's grateful I had what I had with your mom. She's grateful for me, and because she liked Lindy, she's grateful your mom had it too."

Dru nodded her head against his shoulder, before she mumbled, "I heard you laughing."

"Sorry?"

She still didn't raise her head when she said, "This morning. I heard you laughing."

"As you know, Nora is funny."

"Mom made you smile a lot. But she didn't make you laugh. Not like that."

Right.

"Darlin', what I have is different with Nora because they're two different women. One is not better than the other. It's just different."

"Okay," she said softly, still not lifting her head. "And don't get me wrong, I like she makes you laugh. Even before you guys sorted it out, I liked how happy she made you."

And *damn*.

He'd been a total fucking imbecile.

"Things will be changing," he warned.

She looked at him then, and the smile she gave his comment wasn't small. "I guessed."

"But you will always be a part of it, Dru. I might not have been able to adopt you, but you're mine. You're my little girl. You're my daughter. I raised you. I claim you. And Lindy left me the most precious gift she had to give when she left you to me. I'll always think that. Always, honey."

Tears filled her eyes, and she said, "I know that, Dad."

"Never forget it."

She shook her head. "I won't."

"So, why are you out here by yourself?"

"Because I was feeling funny because I'm not really…you know."

Yes.

Nora had been right.

"Tell me."

"I'm not feeling it anymore."

"Tell me anyway."

She knew him, and when he was like this, she knew she wouldn't get away with hiding anything from him.

So she rolled her eyes and said, "I just felt like a third wheel." She glanced back at the house and her lips quirked. "Or in this case, a sixth."

"You're not, you know."

"Ugh!"

And there was his Dru.

Jamie grinned.

"I already told you I don't feel like that anymore, *Dad*," she finished.

"Just making sure," he muttered, his lips still tipped up.

They heard footsteps on the deck and looked up the stairs to see Judge coming down.

He sat behind Dru and mussed her hair while she batted irritably at his hands.

Judge did this saying, "No fair you two squeezing out the older child and giving him a complex by whispering secrets to each other on the deck steps."

"We were talking about Dad and Nora," Dru didn't quite lie.

"I think JT really cramped Dad's style," Judge announced.

He definitely did.

"Eww! Gross, Judge!" Dru cried.

"He's just a man," Judge kept at her.

Dru made a mock-gagging face.

Jamie started chuckling.

"So, I'm asking for an island to get over my possible-new-stepmom woes," Judge stated. "You should ask for a car," he advised Dru.

"Why do you get an island, and I only get a car?" Dru asked in return.

"Because I'm the eldest so I get special treatment," Judge razzed.

Dru blew a raspberry at him.

"Neither of you are getting gifts because I found someone special," Jamie stated.

"You ruined it." Judge immediately fake-blamed Dru.

"Like Dad was ever gonna buy you an island," she retorted.

"I think he was close," Judge muttered, shooting a smile Jamie's way.

"You understand now," Jamie said to him. He turned to Dru. "And if it's your choice, you'll someday get it. But trust me, right now, sitting here with you two, I feel like the luckiest man alive."

"Dad!" Dru cried and threw herself in his arms.

He held her close and looked over her shoulder to Judge.

"I'd say you suck, because you ended all the fun, but you don't, which also sucks," Judge said.

Jamie started chuckling again.

Dru pulled away, wiped under her eyes and then smacked Judge's arm. "Don't be a jerk!"

"Ow!" Judge yelled, rubbing his arm dramatically. "Dad! Dru's picking on me!"

Jamie had no clue if Nora sent Judge out to drive the point home. Maybe. Maybe it was Chloe.

And maybe it was that his son was just as determined to make sure Dru didn't get lost in all that was happening because the only person she biologically belonged to was gone.

It didn't matter.

Judge had driven the point home.

Biology didn't matter.

Family did.

And Jamie had the greatest kids on Earth.

CHAPTER 9

BOTTEGA VENETA

Nora

*J*amie and I were sitting in the back of his car. His driver had picked us up from the airport.

Our luggage was wedged in the trunk, and we were headed to my apartment.

I was hoping this wouldn't be just his first stop, but his only one.

I was also gearing myself up to make certain it was, by inviting him up for the evening if I found it wasn't.

I had no idea why I was hesitant about that. I'd never had an issue with sharing my desires.

It was just now that the time was nigh (very, *very* nigh), I felt timid about it.

One of the vagaries of being a woman, or perhaps being human, that I wasn't fond of.

It was mid-evening New York time, early for us in the time zone our bodies were accustomed to.

So truly, there were no longer any reasons why we couldn't fully embrace the change to our relationship at my apartment.

The last several days with Chloe, Judge and JT had been fabulous, but Jamie and I had lives to get back to, and that family had to get used to being a family without a whole host of loved ones trooping through all day.

This meant our parting was bittersweet, at the same time necessary.

Jamie was currently on his phone, scrolling through his email.

I was on mine, scrolling through my schedule.

My eyes caught on something, and I turned fully to him.

"Darling, can I assume we'll be back to regularly scheduled programming now that the parent trap was successful?"

Jamie turned fully to me, a handsome smile on his lips, his hand reaching out to capture mine.

One thing I noticed of late that was delightful and tortuous (both for obvious reasons) was that Jamie was an exceptionally affectionate man. He held hands. He snuggled. He cuddled. There was close contact when sleeping. Hell, I couldn't even walk past him and be in reaching distance without him touching me, even if it was only to trace his finger along the back of my hand as I passed.

In other words, for the last couple of days, the tortuous had beaten out the delightful.

He'd been gentlemanly before, guiding me by a touch at the small of my back, standing beside me with his arm curled around my waist.

But this was very different.

And very gorgeous.

And very much—too much—to handle when I was cut off from all the rest.

"Are you talking about the store opening we agreed to go to this Saturday?" he asked.

Hale and Elsa had some friends who had a store where they sold furniture they refinished. They'd been able to grab the lease on the space next door to expand their business to include selling vintage stoneware, china, glassware and home décor. And Saturday was their grand opening.

Jamie and I had agreed to go together before we had our little— shall we say—hiccup.

I sensed I knew his answer, but I also needed him to confirm.

"Yes," Jamie stated (indeed, that was the answer I'd sensed). "We're back to regularly scheduled programming. We're dining with Mika and Tom, Hale and Elsa before we go, correct?"

I nodded, not quite able to process the relief that we had that back, along with all the rest.

Jamie lifted my hand, kissed my knuckles, then rested our hands on his thigh before he went back to his phone.

I looked out my window.

The sun was setting. There were sirens in the distance. People were strolling the streets, one of them was a man who had what appeared to be a very fluffy, and not at all small, husky dog bouncing in a pack on his back. He was emerging from the stairs to a subway terminal.

A driver in a car close by suddenly hit his horn and didn't feel like taking his hand away, the shrill sound splitting the air then continuing to rend it.

Ah, New York.

It was lovely to be home.

Not long later, we slid to a halt outside my building, and neither of us moved until the driver opened my door.

I alighted, and when Jamie did as well, I felt great hope.

And then he murmured, "Thanks, Vincent," before he looked between Vincent and Arnold, my doorman, and ordered, "All the bags."

All the bags.

Including his.

As the hope burst into reality, a thrill raced up my spine (and in another secret place as well).

Jamie put a hand to the small of my back and guided me into the lobby.

As Jamie led us to the elevators, I smiled at Charlene behind the concierge desk, and I knew how bright it was by the way she blinked in surprise at me.

I'd always been friendly to the staff. Mother had taught me so.

"They are, in a sense, family, my dear," she'd said. "They share our homes and lives. Of course, they're paid to do so. But a home is a home, and no matter why you're in it, if you are on a regular basis, you should always understand you're welcome there."

In other words, it wasn't like I'd never smiled at Charlene.

I'd just never smiled that brightly at her.

We made the bays, and Jamie tagged the button.

I dug my keys out of my Bottega Veneta clutch and handed them to him.

Therefore, when we entered the elevator, he touched my fob to the reader and hit the button for my floor.

"Your bag?" I murmured.

"I'll need to leave some things here," he said. "Might as well leave the things already packed."

I felt my lips curl up.

I knew how fiendishly smug my smile was, and I could not care less.

We were let out on my floor to see the usual table across us that held two vases of bright, fresh flowers, this sitting below a striking abstract painting, and, hand returning to my back, Jamie directed me to one of the two sets of double doors situated on either side of the table.

The set on the left.

Charlene had called my housekeeper, Alyona, I knew, because we were still a few feet from my door when she opened it.

"Welcome back," she greeted through a smile.

"Lovely to be back," I replied, going to her and touching cheeks before I swept in.

"Congratulations, Mister Jamie," I heard her say behind me.

"Thank you, Alyona."

"Miss Nora texted pictures, he's adorable," Alyona told Jamie.

"He's a lot more than that," he replied proudly.

I moved into the living room and tossed my clutch on one of the sofas.

Jamie moved directly to the bar cart.

Alyona followed us but stopped just inside the entryway to the room.

She was a live-in. And salaried. And I'd been away for nine days, most of which (not including that day, obviously) I'd given her off to have her own holiday.

Even so, I didn't like to take advantage of her hours, and seeing as it was on the wrong side of 7:30, she needed to be off duty.

She knew my penchants with that, so she followed us and said, "I've prepared some sandwiches, there are chips, and I got that chocolate cream torte you like, Mister Jamie."

Hmm.

Seemed Alyona might be prone to matchmaking too.

"You spoil me," he said to her, and after she smiled at him, he asked me, "Martini, sweetheart?"

"Please," I replied.

He went back to Alyona. "I'll have a bag coming up too."

Alyona's eyes widened and grew happy, and she looked at me.

My smug smile returned.

"For tonight, you can unpack just the essentials, dear," I told her. "Then you're off. Thank you for waiting for us to return."

"Always," she said, directed a large, happy grin to me, then she left to go to the service elevator in order to direct the arrival of our luggage.

I sat down next to my purse, flicked off my pumps and curled my legs under me.

Jamie made my martini, his bourbon, and he walked my drink to me.

I took it and murmured, "Thank you, darling."

He stayed standing and sipped his drink before he said, "I'm going to call Judge and Dru, let them know we got back all right, and make sure everything is good with both of them."

He'd been making a concerted effort not to be overpowering, but definitely to make certain his daughter remained well aware of her place, at the same time keeping his finger on his son's pulse, not only because he was a new dad, but how that came about.

Thus, I understood his need to do this, and nodded.

Jamie bent and kissed my cheek before he walked away, taking out his phone.

I grabbed my clutch to get my own.

I then sent a group text to my children.

I'm home. Talk among yourselves to find a time, and one of you handle setting up that computer thing so we can all catch up. Kisses, Mother

I immediately got from Allegra, *For the last time, Mom, you don't have to sign off texts.*

My lips were again curled when I fired off, *The death of manners is the death of civilization as we know it.*

As I was hitting send on that, I got from Nico, *It's called Zoom, Ma. Or Skype.*

Out of habit, I shivered in revulsion.

I loved to hate my son calling me *Ma.* It was hideous. He just simply refused to be broken of the habit.

Though, if I was truly honest with myself (which, heavens, about this, I was *not*), I really hated that I loved it.

I prefer Skype, Allegra replied.

Valentina entered the conversation. *We don't need a Skype for you to tell us you've FINALLY made it official with Jamie.*

Oh dear.

That, I knew, could be blamed on Cadence. My last and Mika's only were thick as thieves and just as diabolical.

Wait. WHAT!?!?! That was from Allegra.

About fucking time. That was from Nico.

Right? And that was from Valentina.

Language, Nico. That was me.

So I guess that boat thing wasn't as bad as you thought it would be. Yeah, Ma? Again Nico.

It was the new baby. Babies make everyone feel lovey. And that was

Allegra, which gave me pause, considering she'd been married for several years now, and it was all fine and lovely that Jamie was a grandfather. He was tall and straight and built and virile (I hoped), and his hair had miraculously only silvered just a little.

But I was *not* ready.

I'll tell you about it in the Skype. I cut in. And then I sent, *Follow directions. Decide among yourselves when, tell me, and I'll be there.*

Love you, Mom, and so happy for you and Jamie. Allegra.

What she said. Valentina.

Later, Ma. Nico.

I sipped my martini and sent more texts, one to Mika, telling her Jamie and I were safely back in the city, and one to Teddy, informing him of my return, and I was ready when he was to begin to make plans.

Jamie returned shortly after I received Teddy's response of, *More soon, my dearest.*

But instead of coming to me, he went to the window and looked out at the city.

"Everything okay?" I asked.

He turned to me, and every molecule in my body stopped moving when I saw the look on his face.

It appeared he was very much still on Arizona time and thus, not at all tired.

On no, he was not.

Not at all.

His gaze moved over me curled in my couch before it came back to my face.

"Everything's perfect," he said, his deep voice thick.

Through a mouth that was suddenly dry, I inquired, "Why are you all the way over there, darling?"

"Because Alyona hasn't retired to her rooms yet."

I pressed my lips together.

"And I'm struggling with the urge to ravish you on the couch, something that would not only be rude to Alyona, but the first time I sink into you is not going to be on your couch," he concluded.

Oh my.

I swallowed, and my nipples tingled.

"Goodnight, Miss Nora and Mister Jamie," Alyona, with excellent timing, called from the back hall.

"Goodnight," I returned, my voice sounding choked.

"Are you hungry?" Jamie queried.

I was. The food on the plane wasn't appealing, so I'd only eaten the roll and the salad.

"Peckish," I answered.

"Can you wait?" he asked.

"Yes," I whispered.

"Right then, sweetheart, I suggest you make your way to the bedroom, because if you don't, in about three seconds, I'm going to carry you there."

I needed no further coaxing.

I stood.

But I didn't go to the bedroom.

I went to Jamie.

His eyes flared.

I took his hand.

At that, his eyes warmed.

And I guided him to my bedroom.

Alyona had left the lights on at the nightstands.

I led Jamie to one, put my martini glass on it, took his drink and set it beside mine.

My heart hammering, my legs feeling like jelly, I took him in, wearing his dandelion yellow, polo necked, long-sleeved, lightweight sweater and off-white trousers. Drinking it all in all at once. His careless but sophisticated style. His height. The breadth of his shoulders. His elegant clothing woefully inadequate at disguising his rugged masculinity. All of that, for the first glorious time, invading the ultrafeminine whites, creams, golds and powder blues of my bedroom.

All of it making my belly flutter and areas south grow wet.

I felt like a sixteen-year-old girl who'd caught the attention of her greatest crush.

And it was a beautiful feeling.

"I love you," I whispered.

In an instant, his eyes dilated fully.

Then he was kissing me.

Straightaway, I discovered our first wasn't a fluke. It wasn't two adults who had been starved for touch finally getting what they'd been craving and taking advantage of that fact.

Oh no.

It wasn't.

It was about two people deeply in love who'd denied themselves and each other the intimacy they needed to seal the silken steel bonds they'd been creating.

Jamie's arms closed tight around me, his tongue swept into my mouth, and he fed, not like a man famished, but like a king claiming a feast as his due.

It was *so* Jamie.

It was also *delicious*.

I clutched him to me, sliding my fingers into his soft hair, and he leaned into me until we were falling back to the bed.

His weight hit mine, and taking it, I caught fire.

Quite simply, from that point on, my actions were no longer my own.

They were a craven need to have him, *all of him*.

A need I couldn't, and didn't, deny.

I touched him, stroked him, pulled desperately at his clothes.

He arched away to yank off the polo.

Confronted by his wide, furred chest that was now mine to do with as I wished, I went right in to taste his corded throat, trail my lips along his bulging pectoral.

As I did, Jamie worked at my blouse. He then rolled to his back, taking me on top, and sat us both up, me straddling him. It was then the heady sensations of want and triumph assailed me at feeling his hardness strain against me through his trousers.

He pulled the blouse down my shoulders and tossed it away, right before he went in, his lips closing over silk around the tight nub of my nipple…

And drawing deep.

So…very…*deep*.

I whimpered and arched into the sensations, into Jamie.

Jamie.

In my bed.

In my life.

Soon to be in me.

At what I was thinking, feeling, I fisted my hands in his hair, and he growled animalistically, and as such delightfully, when I pulled his head back and claimed his beautiful mouth.

I was so lost in my feelings for him, in what he was doing to my body, what I could finally do to his, all we were sharing, I wasn't close to cognizant of any of our fierce, blistering, uncontrollable acts. The strokes. The nips. The scratches. The draws. The violently desperate disposal of clothing.

The ruthless kisses (Jamie's).

The intoxicating licks (mine).

The ravenous bites (both of ours).

Though I did come to when Jamie positioned me on my back, pushed my thighs apart, then sunk between them, and his mouth clamped on me.

Good *Lord*.

I cupped a hand on his head as he laved, moaning, "Honey."

"Precisely," he grunted into my flesh, a wave of heat scorching over me at his word, the feel of it, even if I didn't know if he was claiming that endearment for himself, or describing what he was tasting.

I had no more thoughts as he suckled and licked and eventually slid a finger inside, after a few strokes, making it two. He managed to make the act of going down on me voracious and gentle, loving and selfish, arrogant and generous, commanding and sweet.

It was *heaven*.

I was writhing under his ministrations, the fire building, blazing, consuming me beyond control.

"*Jamie*," I gasped my warning.

He didn't heed it. He sucked hard at my clit and thrust deep with his fingers, my entire body tensed, and then, I couldn't stop it, I couldn't wait for him, I exploded, flew apart...

Combusted.

I was still climaxing, so I vaguely felt his mouth and fingers retreat, but it wasn't vague in the slightest when I felt his cock invade.

The first stroke was sure, swift, commanding.

The king, indeed, was claiming his due.

I moaned at the feel, the stretch, the need to accommodate his size and circled him with both arms and legs.

He then did what he'd been doing from the start.

He made love to me at the same time he was fucking me.

I opened my eyes and saw only him, his rugged features having turned savage in the sex act.

He was just...

Extraordinary.

"Harder," I whispered.

Jamie obliged.

"Faster," I breathed.

Jamie drilled into me.

God, I'd feel fucked for the next week with how brutal he was taking me.

I *adored it.*

To communicate that, I raked my nails up his back until I could fist my hand in his hair while I clamped the other to the tight curve of his clenching and releasing ass.

"Again," he growled his order.

He wanted me to climax *again*?

"I—"

He cut off what I was going to say by dipping in and nipping my lower lip sharply.

I tasted him and me in the enchanting, vicious bite, so I tightened around him *everywhere*.

He grunted at the feel and released my lip.

"Again, Nora," he demanded.

"Baby," I rasped.

Even though I wouldn't have imagined it was humanly possible, he drove in harder, faster, *deeper*, grunting, "*Again.*"

The orgasm rising and cresting in a second, clamping onto him with all four limbs (and other places as well), I did as told and came again.

"Yes," he bit out then shoved his face in my neck, and I heard his deep groan while he hammered inside me, filling me with his seed.

Languidly, his thrusts slowed until he slid in to the root, and I felt his lips trail up my neck to below my ear, where he teased, "You don't sound like an uptight society maven when you come."

I rolled my eyes to the ceiling and fought smiling.

But my lips huffed, "I'm far from *uptight.*"

He lifted his head, looked down at me, and honest to God, it took everything in my power not to burst into tears at what I saw.

It wasn't simply his usual handsomeness made more so (much, much more) from sex and satisfaction.

It wasn't the natural magnetism and constant hum of energy that always exuded from him either.

It was the happiness he showed without hiding it in the slightest, which overlaid a deeper contentment that seemed so settled, anyone who didn't know him would think it had always been there.

When it absolutely had not.

I'd given him that.

Me.

So yes, it took everything I had not to cry.

Instead, I rested my hand on his cheek.

He turned his head and kissed my palm.

I really, very much, and very deeply, and very delightfully *loved this man.*

He looked back at me.

He then kept teasing, "You sound like a wanton hussy."

I gasped in (false) affront.

"It's exquisitely hot," he went on. "When you climaxed in my mouth, I thought I was going to come all over your satin comforter."

"Don't be vulgar, Jameson," I admonished. I then educated, "And the comforter is the fluffy one, folded at the end. Under us is a *coverlet*."

He grinned, white and wide, and muttered, "Right."

"You're not going to remember that, are you?"

"No, and not only because I don't care what it's called, but because you'll be there to remind me."

Oh dear.

I had to stop myself from crying again.

He slid out but immediately glided his hand over my hip and in between us to cup me tenderly.

Oh, *wow*.

What a lovely thing to do.

"Jamie," I whispered.

"You okay here?" he whispered back.

"Yes," I told him.

"I went hard."

"I know, I was there. And if you'll remember, I asked for that."

His lips curved. "Totally a wanton hussy."

I turned my head away to pretend he was annoying me.

"Nora," he called.

I turned my head back.

"I love you too, sweetheart."

Oh no!

The tears came before I could even begin to try to stop them.

Jamie rolled us to our sides and held me close as I wept into his throat.

Abruptly, his arms tightened, and he ground out, "Fuck, I'm such a goddamned idiot for putting you through what I did."

My tears stuttered to a halt as I pulled my face out of his throat to look up at him.

"You are not," I retorted.

"Baby, look at the state of you."

"These are happy tears."

"Tears you wouldn't have cried if I'd fucked you after that first thing we went to together, which was when I wanted to do it, but I wouldn't admit to myself how much I wanted it."

I loved to know that was when he wanted it, because that was when I wanted it too.

But we couldn't dwell on that.

"Well, you didn't do it then," I stated emphatically. "You did it just now. And I don't remember complaining."

"You burst into tears," he pointed out. "That's pretty much the definition of a complaint."

"I did so because, like I said, *I'm happy*. You make me *happy* Jameson Oakley. So stop ruining it."

His lips twitched. "All right, sweetheart."

"Don't ever refer to yourself as an idiot again," I commanded.

"Order received."

"Now, while I clean up and put on an entrancing nightgown that will make you want to attack me again, as penance, you have to go get the sandwiches. Oh, and refresh my martini."

He rolled me to my back, with him rolling his weight onto me, before he put his face close to mine and warned in an utterly *scrumptious* rough, deep tone, "I'm going to let you be bossy in this bed this once, darlin'. I suggest you don't get used to it."

I trembled beneath him.

He rewarded me with that roguish grin he'd given me the morning after we'd gone to Arizona, but this time it was better.

Because this time it disappeared because he was kissing me.

Oh yes.

Much better.

CHAPTER 10

SAINT LAURENT

Nora

$\mathcal{I}$ woke with Jamie's hands moving over me.

"Darling," I whispered.

Those hands became fingers fisted in the silk of my nightgown, jerking it up.

I shivered in anticipation and pressed back into him.

He shifted so his mouth was at my neck, and one of his hands dipped into the bodice of my nightdress, cupping a breast and rubbing a thumb over my nipple. His other hand dove between my legs, his middle finger working miracles, making me very happy I had not re-donned my panties the night before.

When both our breathing was labored, and I couldn't stop rubbing my backside against his hard cock, I whimpered in protest when he removed his hand from between my legs, but only so he could caress my hip, before he trailed it down, gripped my thigh and hiked it forward.

I felt his long frame shift down, then I felt him glide inside.

My head fell back to his shoulder.

His middle finger returned to my clit, and his cock thrust in and out of me.

When he made me come, I noticed distractedly that I *did* sound like a harlot.

No, an absolute *trollop*.

I *adored* it.

It was *perfect*.

A few minutes later, I found I loved the rough, rich rumble of his much more.

After his orgasm left him, Jamie slid inside and wrapped his arms around me before he murmured in my ear, "Clean you up and then you can go back to sleep."

"What time is it?"

"You don't want to know."

I suspected I didn't.

He kissed below my ear, my shoulder, then he slid out of me, climbed over me, and did what he said he was going to do.

He came back after returning the washcloth to the bathroom, and in the early morning light, I saw the stark beauty of his naked body, including his very handsome, and endowed even soft, cock.

Mm.

He sat on the bed and pulled the hair away from my face. "I'm going to shower and then get on with my day. Even though I'd like to take you out on an official date to celebrate our change, I think here tonight again. I've been sharing you too long."

"I love that idea," I said softly. "Do you want me to ask Alyona for something specific?"

"Her salmon *en croute*."

I could have answered my own question.

It was his favorite.

"Consider it done."

He bent and touched his mouth to mine, moved away minimally, and ordered, "Now, back to sleep."

I smiled at him, thinking that would be impossible, him in my home, my room, my shower.

My life.

Fully.

Completely.

But considering the orgasm he gave me, after I enjoyed watching the backside of him walk away, and heard the shower start, I fell right back to sleep.

I WAS AT MY VANITY, FINISHING MY MAKEUP, WHEN MY PHONE LIT UP.

Mika.

Delightedly, I took the call and put it on speaker.

"Hello, darling," I purred.

"*You guys did it!*" she gloated.

I was unsurprised she read that in the tone of my two words.

I'd been correct the evening before, and it wasn't (only) that I received more that morning.

I was going to feel headily and splendidly fucked for at least a week.

Nevertheless, I refused to dignify Mika's shout verbally, but I did allow myself to smile.

"How was it?" she asked.

"A lady never tells," I replied.

"Oh my God, don't even with that nonsense," Mika returned.

I brushed on blush, sharing, "Jamie is uniquely skilled at making love and fucking at the same time."

"*Really?*" Mika breathed.

"I can't explain it, dear. I didn't even know such a thing existed. But I can assure you, *it does.*"

"That sounds amazing."

"That would be putting it mildly."

"I'm so happy for you, honey," Mika gushed.

She wasn't the only one. "He is too."

"I could tell," she said. "It was like he was a different Jamie, at the same time, he wasn't. There was just something…*peaceful* about him the whole time you two were out here. And that's saying something, considering why our family reunion came about."

Blush brush frozen in mid-air, I stared unseeing at myself in the mirror as something altogether marvelous curled contentedly deep inside of me.

"Nora?" Mika called.

I went back to brushing. "He doesn't hide I make him happy."

"I love that about him."

I stopped brushing.

"He does seem peaceful, doesn't he?" I asked softly.

"So do you," she said, just as softly.

"I'd…given up on thinking I'd have this," I admitted.

"I know, honey. I can't even begin to tell you how thrilled I am for you. For you and Jamie. How thrilled we *all* are for you."

That snapped me out of it.

"Well, darling, rein it in. Chloe is already far too proud of herself for this happenstance, when Jamie and I did most of the work. It's like she burnt the sugar on top but is claiming the creation of the entire crème brûlée."

I heard her happy laugh. "No one steals Nora Ellington's thunder. Not even Chloe Oakley."

I dusted some highlighter along my upper cheekbones. "Precisely."

"I'll warn Chloe."

"Thank you."

"Tom and I are coming back in a couple of days. I'll let you know when we decide, and we'll get together after we're back."

"All right, dear. I'll see you then."

"So happy for you, Nora."

There was a grave depth of feeling in my, "I am too, Mika."

"Love you," she whispered.

"And I you," I returned.

We rang off.

I finished my makeup, rose, and went into my massive closet.

Alyona was in there, moving things around.

At this affront to my meticulous closet organization, I arched my brows in query.

"I'm doing Mister Jamie's laundry, but when it's done, he'll need space."

I fought grinning like an idiot.

But I had a feeling, when I saw the light hit her eyes, I didn't quite hide that urge.

Alyona left, and I dressed, then reached for my Saint Laurent, black patent, slimline, small sac shoulder bag.

I switched out what was needed, found Alyona to confirm dinner plans and times, and then I headed out to peruse *proper* baby stores, upon which I arranged the shipment of a few things for JT.

JAMIE SAT BACK IN HIS CHAIR AND ROARED WITH LAUGHTER.

Regardless of how handsome he looked doing it, and how attractive it sounded, I frowned at him.

He continued to laugh.

I forked off a small wedge of puff pastry, salmon and cream sauce and put it in my mouth.

Jamie eventually got control of himself and returned to his own food.

But he did it muttering, "I cannot believe you sent seven thousand dollars-worth of baby things to Judge and Chloe."

"Darling, I hate to inform you of this, but...*we're rich*," I returned. "Being so means we can do things like that."

Humor was still infusing his striking face as he speared one of Alyona's delectable, buttery, herbed new potatoes, and he said, "Yes, sweetheart, but that doesn't mean we should."

"Your son is very concerned about waste, or the environment, or," —I flicked my fork out nonchalantly—"whatever young people worry about nowadays. They'll use it all, then they'll find someone else who can do so. I mean, we *are* going to the grand opening of a store this weekend where everything in it will have been *previously owned*." I gave a subtle shiver. "That whole generation does that kind of thing. *Someone* has to keep the economy flourishing."

"Fuck, you're something," Jamie said warmly, his amusement still on the surface, as well as in his words.

I loved his words, affect, *and* tone.

I carried on eating, that contented feeling in my belly purring, and did it sharing, "Alyona made space for you in my closet."

"Do I need to order a medal to be engraved, give her a bonus, or both?" Jamie teased.

I rolled my eyes.

Jamie ate more potatoes, his own eyes twinkling.

"I have reservations for us at Le Bernardin for tomorrow," he announced after he swallowed.

Shocking.

And beautiful, considering he'd selected the best restaurant in the city for our first outing being official.

I addressed the shocking part.

"How did you manage reservations on such short notice?" I asked.

"It wasn't short notice. I had Monica phone them last week."

My Jamie, planning ahead.

And if I wasn't careful, that smug smile would be permanently affixed to my face.

Monica, by the by, was his assistant.

"That still had to be a squeeze," I noted.

"Monica has connections," he replied.

She did. She was quite the whiz. I was glad he had her. And this wasn't the first time I had that thought.

"I've considered, maybe I could ask all the girls, and by 'all,' I mean both of mine and the one of yours, to lunch here on Sunday," I told him.

"Am I invited?" he asked.

"Of course. I'll ask Nico too. He might be able to come down for the day."

"Works for me," he murmured.

We continued eating comfortably and silently until Jamie remarked, "I noticed you don't wash your hair every day."

I looked to him. "I don't. Every third day. Why?"

"When is the next wash day?"

"Tomorrow morning. And again, why?"

He sliced into his salmon, declaring, "Because you have a fantastic shower, so I'm fucking you in it tonight."

Oh my.

I bit my lip and crossed my legs under the table.

"Exactly," he rumbled, his eyes locked to me. "Stop looking at me like that," he ordered. "I love Alyona's salmon, but I don't think it'll taste the same cold."

I returned my attention to my plate and took a steadying breath.

We ate in uncomfortable silence then, and for my part, I tried not to wolf down my food.

"Nora?"

I lifted my gaze to him.

He reached his hand along the table my way, so I took it.

"Thank you for waiting for me," he finished.

I squeezed his hand, but said, "I love you gave me that, Jamie. But that's the last we'll speak of it. I didn't suffer."

"Nora," he warned.

"Unduly," I allowed. "But why go back when we're here?"

He nodded his head, only once. "I agree, but that doesn't negate the fact you need to know I understand where I was then, and more importantly, where I am now."

"I understand," I confirmed.

"I'm glad, but the reason it's important to me you do is so you won't think I'll slide back."

Oh, my lovely Jamie.

"I don't think that, Jamie," I said quietly.

"Then we're set."

"We very much are."

He squeezed my hand, rubbed his thumb along the inside of my wrist, and let me go.

We finished dinner and then enjoyed Alyona's raspberry mousse with chocolate shavings.

After that, Jamie fucked me very thoroughly in my shower.

I just *knew* his chest was *everything*.

But it was nice to know it was that and multi-purpose to boot.

———

THE NEXT EVENING, WEARING MY SHOULDER-BARING, BLACK, BOW NECK, chiffon, drape back Saint Laurent blouse with the dark gold, satin Saint Laurent maxi-skirt, I swanned…

And believe me…I *swanned*…

Into Le Bernadin.

I did this at Jamie's side.

I saw a couple of people I knew.

I noted Jamie did the same.

But it seemed like everyone was watching us make our way to our table.

This didn't come as a surprise to me.

We were, obviously, fabulous.

Jamie had been right all those years ago. He had a talent at making a beautiful couple.

I was just filled with glee I was part of it now.

Being Jamie, he stood while I seated myself in the booth seat, and only when I had, did he angle into the chair opposite me.

We both shook out our napkins before the waiter could do it and put them on our laps.

Jamie ordered his bourbon. It was a cosmopolitan night for me.

When the waiter left, Jamie opened his menu, looked down to it and casually declared, "Half the men in this room want to fuck you."

I tsked and opened my own menu, saying, "Please, darling. I appreciate your attempt to stroke my ego, but I don't mind I don't turn heads like I used to."

It took a moment before I realized I had his focus.

"What?" I asked when I'd caught his gaze, but he didn't speak.

"Do you really think that?"

"I hesitate to remind you of this, considering you know it very well due to your father, but it's very rare that men of our set have the intelligence and confidence to spend time with age-appropriate women."

"I do know that. I also know half the men in this room want to fuck you because half of that half have told me."

I blinked.

He looked back to his menu, stating, "It's a trait that should be weeded out of our gender, but it perseveres for reasons I can't comprehend that, no matter their age, some men relapse to the locker room, and often. Especially when another man of their acquaintance starts seeing a woman they want." Just his eyes lifted from his menu when he again looked at me. "And you are an object of fascination and desire for a good number of them."

"Are you…quite serious?" I asked.

He shrugged his shoulders in his lovely black velvet blazer (by the by, our clothing also matched splendidly). "That kind of man collects trophies, and you can't be unaware you're a lioness in this animal kingdom. In fact, you're the alpha. As such, they've been rabid for you for years."

It was wonderful he thought that way, but that wasn't what I'd been referring to.

"What I mean is, when they thought we were together, they said those things to you?"

He slapped his menu shut decisively and set it aside. "I advise you never go to a locker room."

I couldn't believe this.

"How crass," I snapped.

"I'm not immune, sweetheart. It was with singular gratification, having had you…repeatedly…that I walked in here with you tonight, knowing what they do not, and having what they'll never have, but want very badly. And I felt that before I had you." He shot me that roguish grin I loved so much. "Though, doing it feels much better now."

I returned to my menu, shaking my head. "It never fails to baffle me how you lot rule the world."

"This is part of why Castellini wants you back."

I raised my gaze to him again.

"That and you're you, and he knew what a huge fuckup he perpetrated all those years ago," he concluded.

"Shall we not speak of Roland, let's say…ever again?" I suggested.

"I'll agree to that only after you know, his mistake was forgetting he fell in love with you and making you a trophy the first time, and it's the same now. It's the way men like him need to think so they can take what they want and move on to the next with zero scruples. And they do this completely unaware it actually emasculates them because it shares they don't have the balls to commit to the hard work a relationship can be, so they can pretend not to care that they'll never earn the vast rewards that hard work will get you."

I snapped my menu shut, set it aside and shared, "I hope you don't feel threatened, because that's just ludicrous. There's no competition, Jamie."

"I know that, Nora," he replied. "But have you made it clear, now that we're back, that he's not to infiltrate your life anymore?"

I waved a hand. "He hasn't factored in the last two days of happiness I've enjoyed since I've been home."

At my words, Jamie awarded me a contented look before he shifted slightly in his seat as the waiter put our drinks on the table.

Jamie did this last, murmuring to himself, "So it'll be me making it clear. And I'm fine with that."

"Anything to start?" the waiter inquired.

"Order for me, darling. I can never make up my mind when I'm here," I said, reaching for my drink.

"Ms. Ellington will have the tuna to start, I'll have the oysters," Jamie said. "We'll order seconds and mains later."

"Excellent." The waiter took our menus and slipped away.

And it was. Jamie was very good at ordering.

I took a sip of my drink and put it back to the table, saying, "I think I should deal with Roland."

"As you wish, so do it," Jamie returned.

I felt my eyes narrow. "Again, he is not so important that he requires priority placement on my to-do list."

As I said this, Jamie watched me over the rim of his glass while he took a sip.

It was inordinately sexy.

He returned the drink to the table and leaned toward me. "You have, my beautiful Nora, become quite well acquainted with my cock these last two days."

I had.

That first night. The next morning. The shower. After the shower. That morning. Before we came out tonight.

I was very correct about his virility, thankfully.

And one could say, he was quite enamored with the blouse I was wearing that night, and it was unlikely I'd ever forget the charming way he shared that with me.

Further, it was clear Jamie felt like making up for lost time, just as I was making it clear I had no issue with that.

Even with all of this, I glared at him.

He sat back. "So, being a man, and knowing how men think, you need to trust me on this and not let it play out any longer. He knew you were on a cruise...with me. So he left you alone. We're out tonight. People we both know are here. And people talk. He'll learn you're back, and he won't delay in pressing his suit. So you can't delay in telling him to go fuck himself."

"I don't think he's the problem you think he is," I remarked.

He raised his brows. "Do I have to talk about my cock again?"

I couldn't help it, I chuckled.

Then I said, "No."

"Thus, we're agreed."

Ugh.

I huffed out a peeved breath. "Fine."

Jamie smiled, again reached for his drink and took a sip.

And I watched the alpha lion in this particular jungle lazily and indifferently enjoying his rule of his domain.

Never in my life would I begin to comprehend just how magnificent a happily ever after could be.

But I was beside myself to find I was in the midst of learning just that.

———————

THAT NIGHT, IN BED, IN THE DARK, AFTER MAKING LOVE, I LAY WITH MY head on Jamie's shoulder, smoothing my palm through his rough chest hair.

"I like JT better," Jamie said apropos of nothing.

I tipped my head back to look at his shadowed face. "Pardon?"

I watched his chin dip down. "Chloe calls him Jimmy. I like JT better."

"Hmm," I hummed, and put my cheek back to his shoulder.

"What?" he asked.

Drat.

Would that I'd been smart enough to keep some of me back so he couldn't read me so completely.

This was never a pleasant subject for Jamie, and with my concerns about his plans of annihilation, it wasn't for me either.

His arm around me gave me a slight shake when I didn't answer.

"Nora, *what?*"

I put my chin to his shoulder to look at him again, only to see he'd angled his head to do the same to me.

"Chloe refuses to call him JT, which Judge prefers, because he likes that it honors both you and Tom."

"She told you that?"

I shrugged a shoulder. "I asked."

"She doesn't like the name JT?"

"She doesn't like the name AJ, and as such, refuses to shorten her son's name to initials in the same manner."

He righted his head and said to the ceiling, "That's very Chloe."

It was.

And this brought us to something we hadn't discussed in some time, but, as much as I didn't like it, we were there, and it needed discussing.

"Maybe you should share," I suggested quietly.

"I'll share when it's all done," Jamie replied.

"I think they should know. It's not like they're going to phone AJ or some gossip magazine," I pointed out.

"I know, sweetheart. But when I share that my father isn't actually my biological father to anybody, *I* have to be ready."

This was true.

I pushed up so I could look down at him. "Do you think he knows?"

"AJ?"

"We know he doesn't. Your actual father."

He shook his head as an answer to me that he didn't think his biological father knew.

"Are you going to tell him?" I asked.

"When I officially take it from Pop, I'm going to give my birth father the ranch."

I gasped at this astonishing news. "You are?"

"He's been a ranch foreman for over forty years, working a ranch all his life. He's got his own now, and two sons who work it with him. His father was a ranching cowboy. It's in his blood. He'll run Oakbilly Gulch, definitely better than Jeff, even better than Pop, and his sons will run it better than both of them after he's gone."

Jeff was Jamie's older brother. Jeff was also a wastrel, a sneak, and a pissant, and I felt qualified to make those judgments, even if I'd never met him, from all Jamie had told me about the degenerate man.

"Do you care that he runs it well?" I asked. "You don't have many happy memories from there."

"I care that my mom loved him. I care that he loved my mom. I care, if she was still alive, me doing that would make her happy. That's what I care about."

Jamie so very loved his mother, the beautiful Cordelia Oakley (I could also say she was beautiful, considering I'd seen pictures).

He told me the story, and I still felt the depth of the honor I'd experienced when he'd bestowed it on me.

The story was, after her passing, Jamie had found his mother's journals. As such, he'd read about the love affair she'd carried on with the foreman of the ranch her husband owned. She'd also written about him asking her to run away with him.

She'd had three children by that time, and she was well-acquainted with AJ's nastiness, not to mention the way he wielded his wealth as a weapon to perpetuate it, which she feared would mean she'd lose her children, so she didn't feel she could.

Jamie's real father couldn't stick around and watch her husband treat her like a chattel.

He'd unknowingly left her pregnant with his son, found himself a wife and started his own family.

So, when AJ had finally set her free, she didn't go to the man she loved to tell him what they shared. She didn't want to negatively affect his life, because, by then, he had what he'd always wanted. A wife. A family. And his own ranch.

It was a tragic story, one Cordelia bore the brunt of, but through her journals, she'd unwittingly left some of it to Jamie.

I moved a hand to stroke his jaw and said carefully, "This plan of yours is keeping you from him, and your two brothers, and, darling, none of you are getting any younger."

"I know," he murmured.

"It's also keeping all that from Judge and Dru."

He said nothing to that, except emitting a soft grunt.

All right.

We were done talking about this.

For now.

I settled back beside him.

He curled his hand on my hip, the pads of his fingers digging in. "I want you to know, you're heard, Nora. Let me think about it."

"Okay, honey," I whispered.

"Have a good night?" he asked.

"The best. Dinner was remarkable. The chefs there are very talented. And my company was second to none."

He rolled into me so we were side by side, and then he tangled us up together, but he made no reply.

Then again, the physical reply he made worked very well.

"We're spending a lot of time at my apartment after you proclaimed we'd eventually be living at your brownstone," I remarked.

"And we'll continue to do so until the bed I ordered is delivered. I can't have you in the bed I shared with Lindy, and I can't ask you to share that bed with me."

God, I loved him *so much*.

Even so, I was me.

So I asked, "What if the bed you selected doesn't fit with my decoration plans?"

"Then we'll get rid of it."

"Who's wasting now?" I teased.

I could hear the smile in his voice when he said, "Shut up and let me sleep. You never do the work. If I'm going to make us both come in the morning, I need rest."

"It isn't *me* who refuses to let me on top."

"I'm not a woman-on-the-top kind of man."

"Because, if you were, you wouldn't be able to control the rhythm."

"Precisely."

"And force."

"Correct again."

I sighed dramatically before saying, "If you were anybody else, I might find this vexing."

There was outright humor in his, "It's good I'm me then."

It was indeed.

I snuggled closer.

Jamie held me tighter.

And not long later, we both fell asleep.

CHAPTER 11

DIOR

Nora

$\mathcal{L}$ate the next morning, my phone rang in the elevator as it rose to my floor, bringing me home after I'd attended the most desperately annoying committee meeting of women who were planning to raise funds to pay for an exhibition to be brought from a museum in France and displayed at The Frick.

I looked at the screen, felt my face get soft, and took Jamie's call.

"Hello, darling," I greeted.

"Hello, baby," he replied. "I know you have your Skype with your kids soon, but I wanted to run something by you quickly."

The elevator doors opened, and I stepped out, saying, "I have twenty minutes, and I can text them to share I might be a few minutes late if you need more time."

"I sense I won't, but I don't want to make assumptions."

Again, Charlene had warned Alyona of my arrival because my front door was open before I got there.

I smiled at her, pointed to the phone, and mouthed, *Jamie*.

She nodded, her gaze brightening with joy for me (I truly adored my Alyona) before I walked inside.

I went to the living room and sat down to get my weight off my high-heeled sandals while saying to Jamie, "I just got home, I'm no longer teetering on four inches, please share."

"I asked Monica to pack a few more things to send to your place."

"If the assumption you were referring to was that I wouldn't have a problem with that, you assumed correctly."

"No," he said. "In making that request, I thought I'd ask her to pack all my clothes to send to yours, so we could live there while you get started on any changes you wish to make to the brownstone."

I stared at the beautiful round coffee table situated between the sofa and two armchairs across from me.

"Nora?" Jamie called.

"You wish to move in?" I asked.

"Temporarily, until we both move to the brownstone. Is it too soon for you?"

I couldn't begin to describe how not soon enough it was.

"No, it is *not.*"

"Sweetheart," he murmured warmly.

"Please instruct Monica to see to transferring anything you need. And in the meantime, Alyona and I will tackle the Everest of finding space for your things in my closet."

He was chuckling through his, "I'll amend my request to Monica."

"I've had an idea about the brownstone," I announced.

"Of course you have," he said with continued humor.

"I'd like to ask Dru to share the task of redecoration with me so we can retain some of her mother's stamp on the home you all shared in ways that are meaningful for you both, but only Dru can share with me. This would also serve the purpose of Dru feeling she had a part in putting her stamp on the place, so it'll aways feel like her home."

The silence coming over the line was so complete, I wondered if a black hole had taken over the satellite we were bouncing off of.

Thus, it was my turn to call, "Jamie?"

His voice was hoarse in a way that hurt to hear, even if it was still lovely, when he said, "You don't need to do that, baby."

"You're very wrong about that, darling," I replied.

"I don't want, and I'll be clear, Lindy wouldn't want to be a shadow over our lives together."

"I think we can both agree that Rosalind was never a shadow, Jamie," I assured. "I not only cannot erase your history to make you all mine, I wouldn't want to. You are what your history made you, and *that*, I'm proud to claim as all mine."

"Fuck, I love you," he grunted.

"And I love you. Now, would you like to talk to Dru, or would you like me to?"

"I think that should come from me."

"All right, darling," I murmured. "Now, is that all? I don't wish to let you go, but I have a busy day. First, as you know, the call with the kids. Then, as you also know, Mika is coming over for a late lunch. And news to you, after that, the G-Force will be descending."

"The G-Force?"

"Yes. Remember, I told you about them on the boat?"

"I remember, but I thought I was dealing with Paloma."

Oh, my Jamie.

He had so much to learn.

"You don't *decline* an offer from the G-Force to get involved, my dearest. Good God. That would be akin to learning you're to be awarded the Presidential Medal of Honor, and saying, 'Yeah, thanks, but I'm good.'"

I heard his laughter, which, after our emotionally charged discussion, soothed me, and then he said, "Keep me informed of their schemes so I can be sure they don't negate mine."

Curiosity piqued. "What are yours?"

"Calling her and informing her that my father is keeping her due to using credit that's running out. Further, the bank that holds the note on his over-leveraged ranch is going to call it, considering I own controlling shares in that bank. And last, I don't think she'll like squeezing into the two-bedroom apartment she'll be sharing with Pop and Jeff if she doesn't cut her losses right now."

This sounded like a good plan, though not a comprehensive one.

However, Jamie wasn't done.

"I'll then tell her, if she ever fucks with you, or anyone I love, I'll make it so she longs for a two-bedroom apartment, because, if I can reduce AJ Oakley to that, which I can, and am, I can ruin her, which I can, and will do, if she doesn't stand down."

"Although this seems thorough, I still think whatever the G-Force would do would be more entertaining," I murmured.

He chuckled.

Then he said, "Now, if you're good with that, I'll let you go."

"I'm good with it, more than good. Text when you're on your way home?"

"I will. Much love, sweetheart."

What a divine way to end a call.

"Much love to you too."

We rang off and I rose from the couch to go to the kitchen to make myself a Perrier with lemon and lime before I went to the study to take the call from the children.

Glass in one hand, phone in the other, I hit the study.

I'd redecorated it post-Roland to rid it of the cloying, dark masculinity he preferred, so now it was bright, elegant and feminine, decorated in creams, salmons and peaches.

But before I moved to the desk where the PC was, I walked to the inlaid bookshelves, which were covered in pictures.

The one that had pride of place (for now, I often rearranged them) was a photo of all the gang at Mika and Tom's wedding last year.

I smiled at it and then looked next to it, where a formal portrait of Allegra and her husband Darryn sat.

My daughter had elected to wear her grandmother's vintage tulle extravaganza of a Dior wedding gown. Darryn had elected to wear a white jacket for his tuxedo, which worked beautifully with Allegra's dress and his midnight skin.

I hadn't been certain about Darryn for Allegra because doctors, on the whole, could be arrogant, surgeons often thought they were gods, but neurosurgeons thought they were *the* god. And Darryn was a neurosurgeon. And frankly, no one wanted to be married to a man who thought he was god.

But he'd won me over because he loved my girl unreservedly, showed it openly, he had an acerbic sense of humor I *adored*, and he was, indeed, delightfully arrogant because he also happened to be frighteningly intelligent, he knew it, and he didn't suffer fools.

My Allegra was a nurse practitioner. They worked at the same hospital and had a stunning, newly built apartment in Battery Park.

I moved along to the wedding photo of Nico and his Felice. My daughter-in-law had gotten married barefoot and with flowers in her hair. She also made her own jam and maintained an herb garden on the fire escape off their apartment in the East Village. Being the good mother I was, regardless of all of this, I loved her anyway.

(Not true, I tried to love her, however, she wasn't very lovable, but I could pat myself on the back because I hadn't given up—on the other hand, she also wasn't my biggest fan, but sadly, she wasn't as good at hiding it.)

Then there came the picture of Valentina and her Archie. He was a cameraman at sporting events, she was the assistant to a line producer of a network evening news program. He resembled a bear. She had my grandmother's delicate, petite frame. He was rough and rowdy. She could make a party out of a funeral.

They'd had their own commitment ceremony in the Bahamas that no one was invited to, so in my Valentina's "wedding" photo, she was wearing a bikini.

I still had not forgiven her for that, any of it.

I didn't care they didn't want to be married.

However.

A *bikini*?

And...

I wasn't invited?

With a good deal of practice, I mentally set that aside, moved down the line and stopped at a black and white photo of Mother and Dad.

Mom was wearing Dior (again, Christian Dior had been her favorite). Dad had a precisely folded pocket square in his dinner jacket. Clamped between my mother's two darkly enameled, perfectly manicured fingers was a long, elegant cigarette holder bearing a lit cigarette (ah, a tragic indication that ignorance was *not* bliss). Dad had his arm around her and was smiling down at her like she hung the moon. She was smiling haughtily at the camera like her husband had just given her the stars.

It was one of the only photos that depicted how much they did indeed love each other.

Of course, they were much younger. The photo had been taken before their children came along (I had a younger sister who moved to Florida after her divorce five years ago, and we both had a younger brother who was a law professor at Yale—we were all close, emotionally, but sadly not close locationally).

So, for Mother and Dad, in that picture, love was in first bloom, and they hadn't yet settled into their personalities, their responsibilities, their places in society or the people they would become.

But I knew their first-bloom love had never died, I just wished they both felt freer to express it, share it with their children, and mostly, each other.

I wondered if Mother would have been different if Dad couldn't allow her to pass within reaching distance without gliding a finger along the back of her hand.

Perhaps not. Perhaps it would be her beautiful little secret.

But perhaps she would.

I was just glad I knew before I lost her (and yes, it was to lung cancer), that Jamie had her approval.

I wouldn't have cared if he hadn't (case in point, she wasn't Roland's biggest fan, lesson learned: always listen to Mother).

But I was glad to know Jamie did.

My phone vibrated in my hand, and I looked to it.

It was a text from Mika, and I hoped she didn't need to cancel our lunch. She would be great help with the overhaul of the closet.

I sat behind the desk, started the computer up, and looked at the text.

It was a photo, the sight of which, I gasped in delight.

It was a picture of a slender, white, long-haired cat with some nuanced gray shading around her eyes and ears. She had blue eyes and an expression on her face that stated plainly *I cannot be dealing with you now.*

In our conversation yesterday to set up lunch today, I'd told Mika that Jamie had said he wanted to adopt some pets, and since I'd been considering the same since the children had left (I just never got around to it), I decided to stop faffing about and see to that…for Jamie and for me.

I'd told Mika about this by asking her if she knew of any reputable shelters I should patronize.

Another text came in as my rhapsodizing gaze moved over the picture of the cat, and Mika told me, *Her name is…get this…Heiress!*

At this news, my thumbs flew over the screen, demanding, *I have the call with my children now. Please contact whoever has custody of this animal at once to share I'm interested and wish to meet her as soon as schedules allow.*

On it, Mika texted back.

I saved the photo and sent it to Jamie, with the message, *We shall be meeting this darling soon. Warn Monica your schedule will need to be fit around it.*

I was clicking into Skype when my phone vibrated on the desk.

I turned it over to read Jamie's reply of, *Trust you to find the most condescending cat in New York in only three days.*

I didn't share that I hadn't found her, Mika had.

I said, *I can't be anyone other than me.*

Thank God, he replied just as that annoying loop-de-loop sound of a Skype call coming in sounded.

I put my phone down and hit the camera to start the video.

Nico came up on screen.

He looked like his father, except far more handsome.

"Gotcha, Ma. I'm bringing in Allegra and Val now," he said.

Shortly after, Allegra, who looked quite a bit like me, and Valentina, who, as mentioned, looked very much like her maternal grandmother, were in squares on my screen.

"She's glowing," Allegra said, grinning hugely.

"Mom's totally getting herself some," Valentina replied.

"Fuck. Stop talking about that," Nico demanded.

"I love this *so much*," Allegra enthused.

"I'm delighted you do," I entered the conversation. "Now, I'd like all three of you, Nico, you as well, if you feel like a day trip, to come to lunch with Jamie and Dru on Sunday."

"I'm in," Valentina said.

"I am too," Allegra said.

"I'll talk to Felice," Nico put in. "Are spouses invited?"

"Always," I drawled, though, if given a choice, I'd invite Darryn and Archie without reservation, Felice, with some reservations, and I would pretend to be very sad she couldn't make it (since she often opted out of family gatherings), but in reality, I wouldn't be sad at all.

"Yay! Darryn *loves* Jamie," Allegra announced.

"Not as much as Archie does," Valentina returned. "Since he gave us those courtside tickets to the Knicks, Jamie has been Archie's favorite person."

"It isn't a competition, Val," Allegra retorted.

I cut in before my two daughters could start bickering. Something, regardless of how much they loved each other, they were prone to do.

"I want no argument about this, you all knew it was going to happen, but when I move in with Jamie at his brownstone, I'll be transferring the apartment to Allegra and Darryn."

All my children's stunned faces just stared from the screen.

"This apartment has been in the family now for three generations," I reminded them. "And it always goes to the firstborn. So I don't want any squabbling. Nico and Valentina, you know I'll find a way to balance it out for you."

"You two are moving in together?" Nico asked.

"Yes," I answered.

"You're leaving Grandmother's apartment?" Allegra asked.

"Jamie's brownstone is far from uncomfortable," I noted.

"What's going to happen to Alyona?" Valentina queried.

Oh dear.

I hadn't thought of that.

Jamie had Monica, of course, but she didn't cook, or clean, (though she did handle Jamie's groceries and dry cleaning and the like). Jamie had a cleaning service that came in once a week, one that Monica managed.

He also didn't have a small apartment where Alyona could have her own space.

"We…haven't discussed that yet," I admitted.

"Well, you need to," Nico asserted. "Alyona has been with us for twelve years."

She had indeed.

"If you're leaving the apartment, just rent one for her, close to Jamie's, so she can come to work every day from her home like normal people do. It's utterly *archaic* to have a live-in these days, Mom," Valentina declared.

"That's actually a good idea," Allegra said.

"I have good ideas all the time," Valentina retorted.

Again, I cut in, "I'll discuss it with Jamie, then discuss it with Alyona. They get along. I'm sure it won't be a problem."

"Good," Nico grunted.

As you could see, I'd also instilled the philosophy that staff was family with my own children.

"How's JT doing?" Allegra asked.

"He's so *adorbs*. I *love him*, and I haven't even met him yet," Valentina decreed (obviously, I'd texted them all pictures). "We should all plan a family thing in Arizona sometime later this summer."

"I don't have time off to go to Arizona," Nico said. "Maybe we could do something around Thanskgiving."

"Darryn's mom would murder me if I wasn't at her table at Thanksgiving," Allegra noted.

Darryn's mother, Jaclyn, had maneuvered that tradition, with no fight from me. I was no cook. And I unwaveringly gave Alyona time off at Thanksgiving and Christmas. But Jaclyn cooked beautifully. I was always at Mika's.

And since Nico, Felice, Valentina, Archie and I were invited to Jaclyn's for every Christmas dinner, that worked splendidly too.

Would Jamie wish to go to Jaclyn's for Christmas dinner?

Would Jaclyn, who was already cooking for fifteen people, want to add Jamie and Dru?

She would, but Jamie...no.

Because he and Dru went to Arizona to have Christmas with Judge, and I couldn't imagine him wishing to make a change from that.

My.

It seemed Jamie and I needed to get our heads out of the clouds and have some important conversations.

"Ma, you okay?" Nico called.

I tuned into the conversation. "I'm fine. You two don't seem to have an issue with the apartment going to Allegra."

"Since you've been drilling that's going to happen into us since we were babies, it's not news, Ma," Nico drawled. "And anyway, Felice would have a conniption if I tried to move us into that humungous space."

She would. And then she'd realize she could house refugees here, and she'd be pleased as punch.

Darryn would redecorate, of course, but since he had superb taste, I didn't mind.

"I don't have long to talk," Nico said. "I have to snarf down a sandwich and get to my next class."

I truly wished my son didn't use words like "snarf."

Per usual, I said nothing.

I also understood why this was a lunchtime call, which wasn't exactly convenient for any of them. It was so he could sneak it in, and Felice wouldn't be the wiser or around to hear my voice over a computer.

Per usual, I buried that.

"What time for lunch on Sunday, Mom?" Allegra asked.

"Anytime after noon. We'll eat at one thirty," I told her.

"I think Felice and I can manage that," Nico said.

This made me happy.

All of it.

All right, maybe the Felice part didn't make me ecstatic, but I couldn't wait to see my son.

We caught up a bit more, then Nico had to sign off. I continued to chat with my daughters, until they both had to get back to work from their lunch breaks.

And after I shut down the computer, I picked up my phone again.

Because I couldn't delay any longer.

It would be awkward, considering I hadn't heard from him, so there was no springboard from which to deny his suit, but I'd promised Jamie.

So I called Roland.

He didn't answer.

But his voicemail did.

Thus, with no other choice, I left a message.

"Roland, although it's not yours to know, but considering your recent behavior, and our last chat, I feel it's fitting to share that Jamie and I are moving in together. As I believe you're aware, my partner is not fond of your attentions toward me, and I'll reiterate, I don't welcome them either. Therefore, unless it has to do with the children, I require that you don't contact me. This can't come as a surprise. The house we built, you burned down. There is no phoenix that will rise from those ashes. So allow us both to move on."

With that, I hung up.

Then I took my phone, my drink, and I went to my closet to form a preliminary plan to find Jamie no small amount of space.

Because the space I gave him in my closet was a metaphor for the space he occupied in my heart and in my life.

And that was not small at all.

CHAPTER 12

HERMÈS

Nora

"This is classic Hermès," Ryan intoned, staring at the scarf draped over his hands with awe. "I've been obsessively checking The RealReal for this exact scarf for *two years*. Not a single listing."

"Take it," I said.

Four sets of eyes whipped to me.

Teddy and Mika, however, both lounged on my closet chaise, didn't blink.

Teddy, because he knew I was generous.

Mika, because she knew, me giving that scarf away meant it'd be an excuse to buy another.

That said, the loss of that scarf meant Jamie could fit at least three of his lovely ties somewhere in that closet, so I wouldn't be replacing it.

"Are you sure?" Ryan asked.

"I don't speak words unless I'm sure," I replied.

Ryan gleamed.

The other three looked on with jealousy (yes, the G-Force was in the house).

"We *are* here making space," I reminded them (and yes, within ten minutes of their arrival, I'd recruited them into my closet reorganization efforts). "I can't send everything to storage."

The men in my closet redoubled their efforts at rummaging.

A masculine throat was cleared.

I turned to the doorway and saw Jamie standing there.

Oh yes indeed.

I needed to make a great deal of space.

He was wearing a dark gray suit with a darker gray vest that had thin lines in it that formed a check pattern. White shirt. Light gray tie. And then there was the razor-sharp line of a white pocket square.

He didn't go out and buy his clothes.

Monica employed several stylists, and with their guidance, all of his suits were tailored for him.

Including this one.

"Oh. My. God," I heard breathed behind me.

"I can't believe it. It's impossible. He's even better in person," came another reverent whisper.

"I feel faint," was a third.

My brows drew together as I moved toward Jamie. "Darling? Did you text?"

"Yes, I texted," he said, dipping his chin when I made it to him, an invitation I accepted, getting up on my toes to brush my lips against his.

When we broke, I murmured, "I don't know how I missed it."

His gaze moved to the room as his lips twitched. "I do."

"Of course," I said, and turned to his side, whereupon he took one hand out of his pockets where both had been resting (yes, even through our kiss, very sexy) and wrapped his arm around my waist.

"Jamie, allow me to introduce you to Ryan, Bryan, Byron and Wallace." I indicated each in turn. "Gentleman, this is Jamie Oakley."

They rushed forward as one.

"Of course."

"Yes, lovely."

"Good to meet you."

"Charmed."

Jamie shook hands with each of them, before he remarked, "I take it you're the G-Force."

There were smiles, nods, and Byron did a little preening.

"Pleased to meet you," Jamie said, then moved from me to give Mika a kiss on her cheek and shake Teddy's hand and clap him on the arm.

"Sadly, I'm afraid we need to cut this short," I announced to the boys.

"Please don't do that on my part," Jamie said. "I have some calls I need to make and a few emails I can return."

He came back to me and cupped my jaw.

When he did, I was sure it was Byron who I heard sigh.

"Take all the time you need, sweetheart. I can entertain myself," he said.

"All right."

He dropped to give me another swift kiss before he smiled to our audience, and walked out, shrugging off his jacket.

When he did this last, I heard another sigh (Byron) and a muted moan (I didn't know who that was, I was just glad I had enough control that it wasn't me).

Jamie tossed his jacket on the bed, aimed another smile our way as he walked to the bedroom door, loosening his tie, and there were two more muted moans.

The instant he was out of eyesight, Bryan declared, "We must take that bitch down *immediately*, so Nora and that fine man have no obstacles in their path."

"They're moving in together," Mika pointed out. "They already don't have any."

"Don't spoil the fun," Teddy mumbled to her.

"We're taking her down anyway," Byron decreed. Then he turned to Bryan. "Did you hear that she visited Ned Sharp's lover's table at

DANIEL and not so subtly hinted that Ned was *her* castoff. Like *she* scraped off the great Ned Sharp."

Bryan rolled his eyes and made a face.

"It's simply *bad form* to walk up to your ex-lover's new lover's table *at all*," Wallace griped.

I felt Mika's gaze but ignored it to watch and listen.

It must be said, there was one spill I was very adept at wiping up, and that was spilled tea.

"I'm so happy Ned found somebody," Ryan oozed. "That horrible Helena is *such* a bitch. Do you remember that time she told Mamie that Gucci was common? *Gucci!* Princess Diana carried Gucci!"

There were infuriated nods all around.

Ryan carried on. "It's about time Ned moved on. I hope he claims her officially soon, like Nora and Jamie have done."

"And *I* hope Blake's grown up enough to let her daddy find some happy," Wallace declared.

Blake was Ned's daughter, Alex's older sister.

She'd not exactly behaved with decorum her whole life. It was only recently, after a humiliating experience at the altar of her own disas-trous (and incomplete) wedding, that she'd started to get her act together.

And I, too, hoped she'd grown up enough to allow Ned to find his happiness.

Byron pouted. "Sadly, the bitch is in Texas now. I mean Paloma, not Helena. I haven't seen Helena in *ages* and have no idea where she is. I'm just glad she's not here."

"I'm pretty sure she returned to hell for her annual visit with her brother Satan," Wallace remarked.

Byron and Ryan snickered.

But Bryan beamed. "Yes, but let us not forget, Paloma is in... *Texas*...having to bang...*AJ Oakley* only to earn *Coach* bags."

They all started cackling.

And you could see why I adored them.

In the ensuing thirty minutes, I gave away another scarf (Prada), a costume bracelet (Chanel), and a brooch (also Chanel). It wasn't much of a dent, but the boys seemed happy.

Mika and I then walked them to the door with their promises they were "all over it" the instant Paloma returned to the city or pulled any shenanigans.

We did cheek touches, but I gave Teddy a hug, before I closed the door to them and turned to Mika.

"Would you like to call Tom over to have dinner with us? Alyona's made a roast. I'm sure it'll stretch."

"I'm supposed to be heading to Hale and Elsa's. Hale's cooking his bolognaise tonight."

Hale could have his own restaurant, he was that good of a cook.

"I didn't leave with the guys because you know what they were talking about when it comes to Ned, and I don't. So obviously, I have to throw a fit that you didn't tell me, and then demand you tell me," she finished.

Oh dear.

"It was just rumors," I hedged, because I told her everything.

Except this.

And it actually wasn't just rumors.

Ned was getting bold. He'd even been seen out with his latest lover, something he used to keep strictly behind closed doors. Partly so his girls wouldn't be upset about it, mostly so it wouldn't give his ex-wife, Helena, a reason to make his life a living hell, something she excelled at.

However, considering Jamie and my situation, and how we'd dragged everyone through it along with us, I felt the unaccustomed need to allow Ned his privacy.

Jamie and I had talked about it, of course. But only because we'd been stuck on a ship together, so we were doing a lot of talking (actually, that wasn't true—I'd been dying to gab to someone about it, and Jamie would be the most circumspect, so I picked him, only to find he already knew).

"Liar," Mika returned.

I blew out a sigh. "Right. Ned is seeing a woman. Actually seeing her, out in public. As far as I know, it's gone on for some months."

"Do you know her?"

I nodded. "I've met her, and I like her. She's the Executive Fashion Editor at *Millicent*."

Millicent was a fashion magazine on par with *Vogue*. It had been named after one of my grandmother's friends, the New York fashion icon of the 40s and 50s, Millicent DeBonnay. In fact, there were rumors (untrue ones, according to my mother, and she would know) that Walt Disney himself had fashioned a certain very famous witch with much the same name after her, at her request.

Mother had never had a single issue of that magazine in her house, nor had my grandmother, and this was because Grandmother had never forgiven them for not naming the magazine after her. It'd caused a huge rift between Millicent and Grandmother too. In fact, the first time I met Millicent was at Grandmother's funeral.

She'd been genuinely distraught. However, that was what happened when you allowed something trivial to get between true friendship, and Millicent wasn't innocent in their rift. She'd rubbed it in Grandmother's face even knowing it was upsetting to her.

Indeed, Millicent had lost a number of friends due to that honor being bestowed on her.

Sometimes, humility paid. Or you did.

Mika's eyes widened. "You mean Marlo Winslet?"

"You know her?"

"She approached me about doing a spread, Cadence and I, with me wearing clothes in my wardrobe I'd found over the years, and Cadence working with one of her editors to select and model new fashion. We had lunch to discuss it the day before we had to fly to Arizona."

What an exciting idea!

"Oh my goodness, are you going do to it?" I asked.

"Yes, because Cadence wants to. Now, seriously, she's seeing Ned?"

I nodded.

"I love that for him," Mika murmured.

"She's a mite young," I noted.

"No she isn't," Mika returned. "Yes, she's, what, ten, fifteen years younger than Ned?"

"I don't know her exact age, but I'd put it around there."

"But she isn't twenty-two," Mika pointed out.

"I don't carry judgment about this, my dear. That's not why I mentioned it. I want him to be happy and have someone to share his life with. I don't think Alex would mind either. But..." I tipped my head to the side. "Blake."

Understanding dawned on my friend's face.

Even so, Mika declared, "Marlo might not be old enough to be Blake's mother, but she isn't old enough to be her sister either."

"Again, this is not my issue," I asserted. "Though, as you know, even if he's going out in public with her, he's not introduced her to our group. If we're at an event together, he'll ask Blake to be his plus one, like Jamie did with Dru before me."

"Tom says Ned is dedicated to the effort of building the family he neglected when they were growing up," Mika mused.

"Well, that's an honorable pursuit. But they're both grown women now, who should be pleased their father has someone he enjoys spending time with. So perhaps I should talk to Chloe."

Mika burst out laughing, before saying, "Please God, no. At least give us a few weeks to get over what we all had to do to you and Jamie before we're dragged into another one."

I could give her a few weeks.

Short ones.

So I promised I would, and she went with me to the hearth room, where Jamie was on the sofa with his laptop.

They said their farewells, we all shared how we couldn't wait to meet for dinner before the store opening in a few days, and Mika assured us she could find her way out, before she left us.

I fell to the couch and lifted a knee so I could get to the side of my ankle to take off my sandals.

"Allow me," Jamie said, holding out a cupped hand.

Watching him with loving (and grateful) eyes, I put my foot in his hand.

He tugged at straps and pulled off the shoe, we switched, away went the other shoe, and I could curl up comfortably at his side when he lounged beside me.

This, I did.

"You don't have a drink," he noted.

"I'll run and make one in a second," I said. "But first, the G-Force outed Marlo and Ned to Mika."

He winced.

Oh yes, he'd been a part of dragging our loved ones along in our prolonged finally-getting-it-together love story.

"Perhaps you should talk to Ned," I suggested.

"I will," he agreed.

"We have other things to talk about," I noted.

He leaned forward to nab his bourbon and tipped it in offering to me.

I scrunched my nose since bourbon wasn't a favorite.

He sat back with his drink and asked, "Those things would be?"

"You know I talked to the children today," I began.

He studied me acutely. "Yes. That didn't go well?"

"It went splendidly. But they reminded me of our now established traditions…and Alyona."

"Ah," he murmured.

"Jamie, I don't cook, and not only because I never learned how, but because I have absolutely no interest in doing so."

He took a sip and rested his forearm on the arm of the sofa.

"I do cook, sweetheart," he replied. "I have to admit, I wouldn't feel comfortable with Alyona living with us, because I don't have a private, contained space for her like you do. But if you wish for her to carry on with you, I don't think it'll be difficult to find an apartment for her close by that she likes and is convenient to her, and she can continue to do all she does for you. That is, finding an apartment won't be difficult, as long as we retain a broker to start looking for that apartment right now."

I was pleased he had the same idea as Valentina. I just hoped Alyona was amenable to it.

"Let me talk to Alyona," I murmured.

"This won't be a hardship. I'm sure Alyona won't mind not having to cook when I have a mind to. Not to mention, Monica is rushed off her feet as it is, and it's coming time to promote her. She's far too clever to be a PA for very long. I can get a new one who doesn't have to see to the things Alyona does. It'll be fine."

"I'm glad you think so."

He raised his brows. "Now, these established traditions?"

This might be more difficult, but even so, we had to sort through it.

"Thanksgiving really isn't a thing for us," I shared to start. "Allegra goes to Darryn's family. Since she does, and I don't cook, Nico and Valentina take that opportunity to dine with Felice and Archie's people."

He nodded.

"But Christmas is another matter," I went on. "The morning and afternoon are changeable with them coming to me, or me going to them, or however it fits in everyone's schedule. But without fail, for dinner, we all go to Darryn's mother and father's house."

"But Dru and I have been going to Judge," he finished for me.

I nodded.

"Through his life, I have not had a lot of time with my son, Nora," he said low, watching me closely.

Wretchedly, Belinda and AJ had made that so.

Jamie kept speaking. "I don't want to declare that takes precedence over your family's traditions, but we're going to have to find a way to balance this, because I love you very much, and I like your kids, and I don't want to tear you away from them. But I also want to be with my boy during the holidays, and now, more than ever, it's easier for me and Dru to go to him."

I looked to his laptop on the coffee table and sighed.

"Is this going to be a big issue?" he asked, bringing my attention back to him.

"It's just annoying to have the reminder that even perfection isn't perfect."

Jamie gave me a small smile, leaned in and touched his lips to mine, then leaned back.

"We'll figure it out."

I was sure we would.

"I know you don't want this reminder," Jamie continued. "But eventually, like mine, your kids are going to have kids, which means they'll make their own traditions and won't want to be rambling all over the city or boarding planes. In the meantime, we'll settle into a pattern of spending time with them. But my son grew up mostly without a father. And now my son *is* a father. I have to have a mind to that, which means asking you to have one too."

"I don't want to tear you away from your children either, Jamie."

"So we'll figure it out," he repeated, more firmly this time.

Yes, we would.

With my lips tipped up, I reached out and touched his strong chin.

Then I said, "I'm going to dash and make a drink."

"Stay still," he ordered as he pushed out of the sofa. When he was on his feet, he looked down at me. "What do you want?"

"I'm feeling a gin gimlet tonight, darling."

"Coming up," he murmured, and sauntered from the room.

After the glory of the vision of him was out of sight, it struck me that change was good, but it wasn't always easy.

In the end, though, I knew Jamie was right.

We'd figure it out.

And then it would be just fine.

I had this thought not taking it further and realizing, change wasn't good for everybody.

For some, they'd strike out at those who were affecting it.

Some would do that spitefully.

And others would do it viciously.

CHAPTER 13

CHLOE

Nora

"This is mildly disturbing," my son mumbled.

"Shut up! She hasn't even allowed me to touch her yet, but still. I *love* Heiress," my youngest snapped.

"Not the cat, the cat *bed*," Nico corrected.

I sat on the sofa in my living room with my legs crossed, a Perrier with lemon and lime in hand, my eyes on my newest dearest darling, my beloved Heiress the cat, lounging on her cream silk, ruched-back, circular cat bed that had jeweled nailhead trim (it even had its own tiny toss pillows!).

She was licking a paw, pretending she wasn't basking in the attention.

She was *life*.

Evidence of this: the instant the delivery men set that bed down on Friday, she'd daintily stepped into it, and then rightfully claimed it as her throne.

I was considering buying one for every room.

I didn't share that.

No, I shared something else.

"I'm trying to find one of those small-animal carriers so she can go on the town with me," I declared. "Sadly, they all seem to be designed for dogs, which I find offensive. I had no idea the prejudice against felines in the fashion world. It's disgraceful. And Lagerfeld even had Choupette!"

My son and daughter (*and* daughter-in-law, though, Archie was grinning) both stood there staring at me.

"Fortunately," I waxed on, "she and I did some exploration in my closet, and we found she fits in my Chloe Woody bag, and she can stick her head out of the top. I just need to get a little pillow sewn to put in the bottom so she's comfortable in there."

Dru, sitting across from me, laughed softly.

Jamie, seated across the space on the bench of the grand piano, legs spread, elbows on his knees, looking delectable, chuckled.

Both my children (and daughter-in-law) kept staring me.

Archie was still grinning.

Yes, it was Sunday.

Yes, it was time for family lunch.

Yes, I loved Dru's laughter, my children's usual horror at my very existence and everything I did with it, and Jamie looking so handsome in his lightweight gray sweater and medium-wash jeans, an outfit he took from *our* closet where his wardrobe was now situated.

I loved all of this so much, I decided to have a family Sunday luncheon at least once a month.

Jaclyn could have Thanksgiving and Christmas.

I would have this.

"You can't take a cat on the town like you can carry around a dog, Mom," Valentina proclaimed, going to plop down in the armchair next to Dru.

"I can do anything I like," I retorted.

"It's not good for the cat," Felice shared dourly as she moved to sit across from me on the sofa.

I looked to her. "Dearest, she was in a cage three days ago." I swept a hand toward Heiress—who, on Thursday afternoon, had taken precisely five seconds to recognize she'd finally found her true home —currently had her little nose in the air and was pre-nap blinking. "Now she's lying on a bejeweled cat bed. She's not dim. She knows precisely how good she has it, including picking the Chloe, which goes with her coloring, over the Fendi, which did not."

Felice aimed a long-suffering gaze at her husband in response to my pitifully bourgeoisie ways.

Per the protocol I'd created after I'd come to understand my son was serious about her, I ignored her.

Felice's attention wandered, and she noted, "That's a new piece," toward the glass sculpture on the plinth across the room.

"Dad and Nora found that at a vintage store last night," Dru announced.

I watched Felice's eyes widen at the news I'd entered a vintage store, then her face blanked, not only as if she couldn't process this knowledge and make sense of it, but she had no desire to try.

"It's a Seguso," Dru continued. "Gemma and Jadyn were thrilled Nora bought it. They were worried they wouldn't be able to move it. It's not exactly at a price point they're used to stocking."

If the smirk that was now on her face was any indication, Felice appeared to be able to process that without any problems.

Dru also went to the opening last night. She'd come with some friends. And she'd talked me into buying the Seguso.

Because Drusilla Lynch had very good taste.

Alyona strolled in at that moment and put a tray of mini crabcakes and quiches down on the coffee table, announcing, "Some munchies."

Only Alyona, who had labored over complicated hors d'oeuvres, like crabcakes and quiches (at least I thought they seemed complicated, I would have no way of truly knowing), would describe them as "munchies."

"You're working on Sunday, Alyona?" Felice asked in horror.

Hmm.

No.

I shot a warning look to my son.

We'd had this discussion more than once.

Felice could look down on my bourgeoisie ways. But in her rabid progressivism, she was *not* allowed to make Alyona feel uncomfortable about how she chose to earn a living.

Alyona shot an exasperated look at Felice.

"People work on Sundays, Felice, and I'm one of them," Alyona said.

"Felice—" Nico began.

"Well, I can bring food in, and I can wash up too," Felice stated stubbornly.

Alyona straightened from the tray. "Yes, but you won't, because it's my job, and that's *my* kitchen, and unless I approve the caterers, no one does anything in it but me."

With that, she huffed off.

Felice blushed.

I sipped my Perrier.

Nico came to sit on the arm of the sofa by his wife, murmuring, "I keep telling you—"

"Whatever," Felice snapped quietly.

When she felt my regard, Dru tore her surprised gaze from Felice, and I sent her a rueful smile.

She sent a reassuring one in return.

Jamie had such a lovely daughter.

Through our nonverbal exchange, Archie fell on the crabcakes.

The front door opened.

We all looked in that direction to see tall, dashing Darryn striding in.

But I tensed when I saw the homicidal expression on his face.

"It wasn't my fucking idea," he said instead of greeting any of us. "In fact, I was against it."

Allegra hustled in after him, looking harassed.

"Mom—" she began.

"What's going on?" I asked, sliding to the edge of the sofa.

"My son in town, and he doesn't even tell me," Roland said from the door to the living room.

I froze.

What on earth was *he* doing here?

"Dad! You promised to wait in the hall," Allegra cried.

Out of the corner of my eye, I saw Jamie stand, so I did too.

"He was loitering outside the building," Darryn shared.

"I wasn't loitering," Roland snapped.

Darryn went on like Roland didn't speak. "He talked Allegra into letting him come up with us."

In homing in on Jamie, I'd missed that Nico had stood too.

Oh dear.

And presently, my son demanded of his father, "Why are you here?"

"To talk to your mother, of course," Roland returned.

"Does she want to talk to you?" Nico asked.

"No, she does not," Jamie answered for me.

"All right, everyone—" I tried.

Roland interrupted me. "It's actually fortuitous you're all here, including you, Oakley, because I am officially done with being the bad guy, and you should know what you're getting into."

He directed that last to Jamie.

My heart squeezed.

"So you're a magician now?" Valentina sneered.

God.

I hadn't forgotten how wounded she'd been at her father's betrayal (oh no, a mother never forgets something like that). They'd been particularly close. She'd been daddy's little girl.

Of course, I had not shared *why* we'd split up, but children found their way to learn things.

And they'd learned them.

"Darling—" I tried again, my eyes on my youngest.

I failed again.

Valetina was laser focused on her father. "Drop the satin curtain and *voila*! You're not a cheating bastard anymore?"

With that, my heart bled.

"Valentina, my lovely, maybe you should go to the study while I deal with your father," I suggested.

"Fuck that, Mom," Valentina retorted. "He's hooked me. I'm interested. How is he no longer the bad guy?"

"I cannot believe you're speaking to me like this," Roland ground out.

"I cannot believe you're crashing a family lunch where we're bonding with our new sister and probably soon-to-be stepdad," Valentina returned, then her eyes pierced her own sister and she finished, "Thanks, *Allegra*."

And Allegra, also wounded by the failure of her parents' marriage, had always had a soft spot for Roland.

Her face flushed.

Darryn put an arm around her shoulders, but he murmured, "Sorry, but you bought that, baby."

"Your mother didn't care," Roland stated, getting everyone's attention again, as I felt Jamie come to stand at my side.

"She didn't care about what? You fucking everything that moved?" Nico asked.

"Nico," Felice whispered, reaching out from the seat she still occupied on the couch to wrap her fingers around his forearm.

He shook her off.

Instead of showing chagrin for her husband or finding another way to support him during this emotional scene, her face got hard.

Oh my.

Was there trouble between those two?

"It doesn't matter if I did, because she didn't care," Roland said to my son. "You knew your grandmother. And you're a grown man now. Imagine having that woman as *your wife*."

"Dude," Archie entered the conversation, "are you seriously blaming your ex for you cheating on her?"

"You didn't know Eleanor," Roland retorted.

"I didn't need to, man. That's whacked," Archie shot back.

"It is, totally whacked. Grandmother was awesome," Valentina asserted.

"She was cold as an icicle," Roland stated.

Before anyone could say or do anything, Nico exploded, and that was when all the men, plus Valentina, moved.

Toward Nico.

"*Fuck you!*" he roared, bumping chests with his father.

Darryn got there first, wrapped an arm around his chest, and pulled him back, but even though Darryn was six four, and quite built, and my son was no slouch, but he was not, Nico fought it. He didn't win, but he fought it.

Dru sidled up next to me and took my hand.

Dear Lord, she was witnessing this debacle.

My chest threatened to cave in.

Nico stopped fighting Darryn and jabbed a finger at his father. "Tell yourself that, you asshole. Convince yourself that Mom did shit to deserve you *shitting all over her.* All over your marriage. All over *your family.* Tell yourself that, you motherfucker."

Roland looked struck.

"Nico," he whispered.

"You didn't take us to school, *Mom* did," Nico bit out. "And she was standing outside *every fucking day* to walk us home. She might not have made us after-school snacks, but she sat with us while we did our homework, so if we had a question, she could help. We had family dinners every night, and you weren't around for most of them, because you were working or off fucking one your whores. She was *a Mom.*" He threw his arm out to indicate the room. "*We* were a family. I'm sorry you weren't a part of it, but that was *your choice*, not hers, and not *ours.*"

Jamie turned to me during Nico's speech, and the warmth coming at me from his beautiful blue eyes set in his stony-angry face was probably the only reason I kept my feet.

"You went to the best private school in the city because of the work I had to do," Roland returned.

"*Had to do*," Nico scoffed. "Bullshit," he fired back. "You came from money. So does Mom. And newsflash, Dad, I'd give it all up if I could erase just *one time* hearing her crying at night in your room when it was late, and you still weren't fucking *home.*"

At that, the warmth in Jamie's eyes turned to fire, and he aimed it at Roland.

As for me, the threatening ended, and my chest caved in.

I had no idea my son had heard me.

Quick glances at my daughters and their forlorn expressions directed my way told me they'd heard it too.

But I couldn't focus on his new knowledge.

At Nico's words, Jamie was done, I knew, because he stepped in and asked Nico, "Have you finished?"

Belatedly realizing we had a large audience, and I was a part of it, Nico glanced sheepishly at me and said, "Christ, Ma. I'm so sorry."

"That's all right, dearest," I whispered.

Jamie took that as Nico's assent, because he moved between Nico and Roland, with Darryn and Archie coming in at his sides, and he said, "You can leave right now, or we can remove you. Choose."

Roland scowled at Jamie, then he looked between Darryn and Archie and declared, "I never liked either of you for my daughters."

I also had not forgotten my ex could be petty.

I just wished he hadn't said that to his sons-in-law, because it would far from ingratiate him to his daughters, and he had one who still cared, but if he crossed Darryn, she would not.

"That's okay, seein' as we don't give two shits," Archie replied.

Roland's scowl intensified before he turned stiffly on his foot and marched out the door.

Archie followed him, and I heard the front door slam.

"You were kind of harsh, Nico," Felice said quietly.

Oh no.

Nico whirled on his wife. "I was? You know how it was for us with him out fucking around?"

She lifted a feeble hand. "I was just saying—"

"What?" he demanded. "What were you *just saying*? Or, I should ask, what would I give a shit about you saying, since you seem to have an awful lot to say about fuckin' *everything.*"

"Nico," I warned.

Nico visibly pulled it together, and said to his wife, "You have more to say, we can move it somewhere else. If you don't, then for fuck's sake, don't say anything."

She screwed her lips up angrily.

Yes, my son's marriage was in trouble.

I didn't want to admit it, but if forced to do so, I would have said I'd seen it coming.

It wasn't that they were from two different worlds (she hailed from upstate, both her parents were teachers, and they'd gone barefoot to my son's wedding too). It was just that...

Well...

He'd married his mother.

Opinionated and outspoken.

The problem was, Nico didn't agree with her opinions, considering quite a number of them were judgments about the life he was born into, something which was out of his control.

He'd turned his back on it because he was Nico. He made his own way. He'd always wanted to be a teacher. He was a teacher. He'd never been into owning things. Now he didn't have a lot of things. He'd always liked to earn his own money, so at sixteen, he'd gotten a weekend job in a bakery. Getting up at five in the morning to make bread and pastries, going home to his apartment on the Upper West Side, and having cash he earned to take a date to the movies.

But he'd also turned his back on it for her, living in a cramped, one-bedroom in the East Village, growing herbs on the fire escape, when he had a trust fund he'd never touched that could purchase them a property four times the size for when their family expanded.

She could make her jam and grow her herbs, but their children's schooling would be paid for, and they'd all have closets where they could put their clothes.

"I'd like to discuss why Allegra let him come up here," Valentina groused.

Darryn again got close to his wife, but it was me who spoke.

"She loves her father. She's allowed, Valentina. So I'll hear not another word about it."

But Allegra looked distraught. "I had no idea he was going to say any of those things, Mom. And he promised, he *swore* he wouldn't come inside unless you invited him. He said he just needed a word with you."

Darryn gave the fullness of it. "He told her you two were talking reconciliation. That you'd ended things with Jamie. And, once Jamie learned you were getting back together, Jamie interfered."

Fucking *Roland*.

"That isn't true, Allegra," I asserted, my voice trembling with unhappy emotion.

"I know that *now*," Allegra mumbled.

"He's a fucking piece of work," Nico clipped.

I hated women going out in leggings. Occasionally, yes. The constancy with which I saw it, absolutely not.

I hated the seating in some of the theaters on Broadway. It was too close, the seats too small. I couldn't enjoy a musical when I was eating my knees and practically sitting in my neighbor's lap.

I hated the communal tables some of the new cafés and restaurants had. I didn't want to eat or sip my coffee with strangers.

But the thing I hated most of all was how much my son hated his father, how hurt all my children were, and that for some reason, the man had listened to the message I left on his voicemail, and he'd still shown up at my building and ruined an important lunch.

I knew why that was too, and Allegra would admit it to me in private.

She'd told her father this was happening today. And he knew why, since I told him Jamie and I were moving in together. And in an act of sheer jealousy and spite, Roland had acted on it.

Oh, and I hated that Jamie had been right.

I had a feeling, if he'd dealt with this, Roland wouldn't have caused that scene.

I walked to Nico, lifted my hands and smoothed the skin on his face, leaving my hands on either side of his head.

"Thank you for defending me, my champion," I said softly.

"Ma—"

"And I don't know what your father is going through right now, but he's still your father. So feel these feelings, my handsome boy, then I hope you find your way to reaching out to him. Because he wasn't a good husband, and perhaps not around as much as he should have been, but he loves you all very much."

"I wouldn't hold my breath for that, Ma," Nico warned.

"Yeah, totally, Mom," Valentina added.

I drew in a deep breath, and let it go, along with my hold on my son.

I stepped away and said, "So be it." I looked to Jamie. "Darling, can you make me a martini?"

Jamie was studying me intently even as he said, "Of course."

"I'll take one too, please, Jamie," Allegra requested.

"I'm just gonna do shots of vodka," Valentina announced, following Jamie to the drinks cart.

"That's my girl," Archie encouraged on a smile.

I felt attention, so turned to Felice just in time to watch her quickly rearrange her features from distaste to benign.

"Would you like a drink, Felice?" I asked.

"No. I'm good, thanks," she said shortly.

"You must be Dru," Darryn said to Dru.

Damn, it'd slipped my mind they hadn't met yet. At a function several months ago that Darryn couldn't attend, she'd met Allegra. She'd met the rest earlier when they'd arrived for lunch. Darryn, no.

"Yes, and you're Darryn." Dru offered her hand, and Darryn took it.

"I'd say welcome to the family, but that isn't usually the way we play. Normally, it's Nora being hilarious, her kids pretending they don't think she is, when they do, and me stuffing myself so full of Alyona's food, I have to wear untucked shirts every time I come here so I can unbutton my pants."

Dru burst out laughing.

Thank God for Darryn.

"You'll be pleased to know I made your favorite chicken salad, Darryn," Alyona shouted from the kitchen.

"Allegra needs a sister wife," Darryn shouted back.

Allegra turned her eyes to the ceiling.

I felt an arm slide along my waist, and I looked up at my boy.

"You okay, Ma?" he asked.

"I'm fine," I assured.

"I lost it. It was uncool. I'm sorry."

"You're home, Nico. This will always be your home, even, in a way, it will be when it's Darryn and Allegra's. You're free to behave however you like at home."

"Oh, yeah," Darryn called to me. "Thanks for the future new digs, Momma."

I chuckled.

"Darryn!" Allegra snapped.

I looked to Dru to see her reaction to this, considering I knew Jamie had spoken to her about my redecoration plans, and she'd agreed to help, but I had not had the opportunity to discuss it with her and get a sense as to how she really felt about it.

But she was smiling at Darryn.

"Losers!" Valentina yelled from the bar cart. "Jamie and me just made up a cocktail and *everyone* has to drink it."

"Is it a riff on a Long Island?" Archie called.

"You know me so well, loverboy," Valentina cooed.

"I'm in," Archie declared.

Dear Lord.

Valentina at the helm, we'd all be sloshed in an hour.

But maybe that wasn't a bad thing.

I sought Jamie's gaze, and he didn't make me work for it. His was on me.

All right? he mouthed.

I nodded.

He sent me a gentle smile.

I hadn't been all right.

But receiving his smile, I was on my way to getting there.

And witnessing this byplay between Jamie and me, our children hadn't been all right.

But they were definitely on their way to getting there.

I SAT IN BED BESIDE JAMIE, SMOOTHING LOTION INTO MY HANDS.

"I'm concerned about Nico and Felice," I announced.

Jamie, with Heiress lounging on his ankles (she knew who her daddy was, my precious darling furry girl), wearing attractive glasses because he was reading a book (I'd just joined him after an epic rundown of the day's events over the phone with Mika), turned his gaze and peered at me over the frames.

"You should be," he stated.

"What's your take?" I asked.

"He loves her, so it's going to destroy him, but he's not going to be able to put up with her acting like she's better than his mother every time he spends time with the both of you. Or, I'm sorry if you haven't already put this together, but it's something you should be cognizant of, sweetheart, every time she talks shit about you. Which I would guess is often."

"I would guess that too," I mumbled.

Jamie nodded. "And that isn't about him being a momma's boy. That's about his wife's rampant disrespect. Her treatment of Alyona was unconscionable. She's so up her own ass about how the world is supposed to work according to her, she doesn't see that Alyona takes pride in what she does. She belongs in this house even more than Felice does, and her efforts to humiliate you by using Alyona only serve to make Alyona think Felice looks down on the decision she's made as to what she does with her life."

I made a face, because this was very true, and it was the reason I broke my vow never to get involved in my children's relationships and spoke to my son about his wife's behavior toward my employee.

Jamie carried on. "Nico won't be able to ignore it if they have children, and he won't be able to stop Felice from talking shit about you to his kids, which will do his fucking head in. So before it gets to that, he's going to let her go."

This hurt me so much, I was unable to move or speak.

"It happens, darlin'," Jamie, reading my response, said quietly. "Life has a way of burning off the rosy glow of first love and making things come into sharp focus. There's nothing wrong with the lives we live, just as long as we don't fuck anybody over to live them, and we're conscious that others aren't as fortunate. He didn't turn his back on his life, he pivoted to embrace his future. She thought he'd turned his back on his life. She thought he agreed with her. She was mistaken. And she doesn't like that very much."

"I can see her being mistaken. My children tease me about the way I am," I explained.

"I noticed, but it's teasing, and it's rooted in love. She's not dumb, Nora. She saw what she wanted to see. When it became clear it was what it actually is, that's what caused the problem."

Unhappily, because I was keenly aware that I played a part in my son's marriage issues, I shifted to pull the covers out from under me and settle them over me.

When I was in, Jamie asked, "What are you thinking?"

"That it isn't all that fun to be the cause of Nico's troubles in his marriage," I answered.

Jamie shook his head.

"Stop thinking that, Nora. It has nothing to do with you. Please know, I will be cordial to her for as long as she lasts, but I'm going to say it like I see it, she's a judgmental bitch. I'm all for social justice. What I don't like are these self-proclaimed social justice warriors who are so grounded in their beliefs, they think they speak for everyone, when they don't. She tuned out after that big scene, because if she tuned in, she'd have to confront the reality that you're a human with feelings, regardless you live in a palatial apartment. You can be hurt. Your life isn't always roses. And you *were* hurt. Gravely. But you kept your family together. It was *you* who earned the respect you received today, not only from your children, but from Darryn and Archie. This tells me she's not a listener, but she fancies herself a preacher. She doesn't understand there isn't a single decent preacher on this planet who isn't, first, a damn good listener. If they don't have that skill, any word that comes out of their mouth loses meaning, because they've lost touch. She has no idea how this world should be because she's lost touch."

My Jamie was so very wise, and I felt better.

Not great.

But better.

So I nodded.

Jamie remarked, "I always liked your son. I respect him a good deal more now."

"Well, at least something positive came from the day," I mumbled.

Jamie set his book aside so he could turn to me and pull me up and into his arms (Heiress didn't like this much, but she'd be back, I'd noticed she didn't tend to stray too far from her new daddy).

"Before you say it, yes. I should have let you deal with Roland," I proclaimed.

"That wasn't what I was going to say. You told me you'd contacted him, today was all on him. Even I couldn't guess he'd pull that move."

"Your cock didn't warn you?" I asked, trying to inject humor in our dreary discussion.

The corners of his eyes wrinkled, and he said, "That wasn't man shit, that was spoiled-boy-tantrum shit. So no, my cock doesn't know anything about that."

I laughed and tucked my head in the crook of his shoulder.

Jamie stroked my back. "Another positive, your kids love you very much. Felice looked like she was sucking lemons when Nico was describing how you were a great mom. It isn't something she understands, but she can't deny you love your kids, show them in a number of ways, and were always there for them. It explains why they rally around you, something she probably won't allow herself to understand either. But she doesn't like it."

"How long do you think they have?" I asked.

"I'd put money down on them fighting all the way to Vermont, if she didn't give him the silent treatment. And I think he'll think that's fucked up, because he went through some serious shit today, so she should be all about him. As such, I wouldn't worry about buying her a present at Christmas."

"Well, that's a relief," I quipped to hide my dismay my son's wife was more than likely not supporting him after that awful scene. "She's immensely difficult to buy a gift for."

"I have no doubt," he murmured with humor.

I looked at him. "Are we going to make love?"

He tipped his head to the side. "If you want to. But I thought maybe just cuddling and reading might be a nice change of pace."

Ah.

My Jamie.

He wanted to make love. He had an active libido. It was a miracle he'd gone without for so long between Rosalind and me (truth told, I didn't know if he actually had, I didn't ask, and wouldn't, but I would listen if he cared to share).

No, he was offering me a different kind of intimacy, and showing me a window into our future that wasn't always about performing and grand gestures, but sometimes having quiet times and togetherness.

And I loved when Jamie made love to me, but frankly, tonight, I needed cuddling.

"I've been neglecting my book," I noted.

He looked to my nightstand, then to me. "Get it, darlin'."

I turned and grabbed my novel, and my reading glasses.

Then I turned back to Jamie and cuddled in.

We each found a comfortable position to be able to hold our books and turn pages.

I fell asleep before Jamie.

But I woke when I felt my book slide from my fingers, the lights going off, and he tangled himself in me. Not long later, Heiress returned and draped herself over both our ankles, because she loved her daddy, but she also loved Mother.

Witnessing even one of your children's pain was impossible to take, so doing that with three was excruciating.

Even so, I fell asleep in Jamie's arms, and he in mine, because we had tomorrow, our children had tomorrow.

So it was all right for now.

CHAPTER 14

OSCAR DE LA RENTA

Nora

The next morning, I stood sipping coffee, my hip resting against the green marble countertop of my very long, wide, fastidiously organized galley kitchen.

My eyes were on Alyona.

"This week's menu is on the counter. If you have any changes, let me know. I'm going to go pick up that Prada blouse you needed mended, and I'll be stopping by the market on the way home," she said this while drying my breakfast dishes.

"Alyona," I called quietly.

"Don't," she whispered harshly.

I lifted my cup from the saucer and took a sip, not removing my eyes from her.

Alyona, a second-generation Russian immigrant, and as such, she had instilled in her an impeccable work ethic and a passionate countenance, couldn't hold it in for long.

She slapped a towel down on the marble and turned to me.

"I shouldn't complain," she stated.

"I'm not sure that's true," I replied.

"It isn't my place."

I gave her a look.

"Okay," she snapped. "She makes me feel...*irrelevant.*"

My lips tightened.

"I know my picking up your dry cleaning and dusting your shelves isn't going to change the world," she continued. "But I take pride in taking care of you, in taking care of them." She swung an arm out randomly to indicate my children. "Maybe my work isn't important, but still, I checked, and I make more money than she does, *and* I don't have to pay rent or live somewhere where I have to commute three hours a day to get to work. So I don't know why she looks down on me. I know my place. But she doesn't have to *put* me in my place."

With her speech and learning she'd gone so far as to actually compare her salary to Felice's, it was a wonder my mouth didn't crack, my lips got so stiff at her words.

I forced them to move when I declared, "What you do is very important to me."

She snatched up the towel and started polishing the marble with it, mumbling, "I know."

"And it's just important, Alyona," I stressed. "Don't let Felice make you think any differently. You don't have to work to find a cure for cancer to be doing something important. This world is able to go around because of all the things everyone does to make it do so. Heavens, the only contribution I've made is my three children. I'm very proud of that, and I don't mind I'm now doing nothing but enjoying my retirement."

"You raise a lot of money, Miss Nora," she returned.

I shrugged that off. "The fact remains, if you have pride in what you do, and you do it well, which you very much do, no one should steal that from you."

Still polishing the sparkling counters, it was Alyona's turn to shrug.

"Nico adores and respects you," I carried on. "It breaks my heart, but it seems clear that you'll be in this family far longer than Felice, if that make you feel better."

"It doesn't," she was still mumbling. "He was so happy on their wedding day, even if…" She turned from the counter to me. "Who wants dirty feet at their wedding? That was weird."

I smiled, because it *was* weird.

After I took another sip of coffee, I asked, "Are you okay with all of that?"

"I'm sorry, Miss Nora, but she's just annoying."

Felice was that.

No need to dwell, time to move along.

"Right. Now we have to discuss Jamie and the future," I said.

Alyona's irritable face turned panicked.

I raised my brows. "Didn't you just hear me say you'd be with us longer than Felice?"

"Mister Jamie doesn't have a housekeeper."

"No, and so you know, I'll be redecorating his brownstone, and when that's done, we'll be moving there. Allegra and Darryn will take over the apartment."

She seemed concerned at the same time perplexed. "Will I work with Allegra and Darryn?"

"If you want to, however, that would be for the three of you to decide," I answered. "Though, I'd prefer you go with me. There's no apartment for you in Jamie's space, so he's hiring a broker for you to work with to find one close to the brownstone so your commute isn't unpleasant. Obviously, as it is here, I'll be paying for your accommodation. The only change is that you won't be living with me, or, that is to say, us. Oh, and you'll get a raise, since you'll be taking care of both of us, and not just me."

For a second, she did nothing.

Then she started my way, so I had to set my cup and saucer aside and accept her hug, which I returned.

It didn't last long before she stepped out of my arms.

"I want to come with you," she confirmed verbally what her hug had already communicated.

"I'm glad." And I very much was.

She looked down to my coffee cup. "Are you done with that?"

I nodded.

She whisked it away.

And we were back to normal.

I went to the menu and approved it, before I reminded her, "I'm in committee meetings all day."

"I remember."

"I'll be home around four."

"Okay."

"Have a good day, Alyona."

"You too, Miss Nora."

I walked out and found Heiress eschewing her cat bed to sleep on Jamie's pillow (I understood her decision).

I gave her a scratch. She gave me some purrs.

Then I grabbed my bag and went out to face the day.

WEDNESDAY AFTERNOON, DRU AND I STOOD IN THE FOYER OF JAMIE'S brownstone.

As mentioned, she was a sweet young woman who I liked very much, but I could tell, right then, she was uncomfortable, and I was concerned she didn't want to be there, but she was doing it for her dad.

The only way I could help her with that was to get on with it.

"To start, let's do a bottom to top, dear," I suggested.

She licked her lips and nodded.

Yes, uncomfortable, and maybe nervous.

We then toured every inch of Jamie's home, the one Rosalind Oakley created for her family, and left with them.

When we were finished, we ended up in the library, which was full of books and leather furniture and a fireplace with a large television over it.

And I was studying yet another wedding portrait.

This depicted a glowing, flame-haired Rosalind wearing a cream Oscar de la Renta, full-skirted, to the calf wedding dress, Jamie, handsome in a tuxedo, with a much younger Judge at Rosalind's side, and a little girl Dru wearing a pretty cream bridesmaid dress at Jamie's side.

Judge looked a mite awkward. Perhaps it was his age. Perhaps it was that he didn't know his place in that new family.

Rosalind, Jamie and Dru were all beaming.

"Uh…well? Do you have any ideas?" Dru called.

I turned to her. "Your mother decorated in, well…" I smiled at her as I swept my arm in front of me. "*Jamie.*"

Dru glanced around, then she burst out laughing.

"Oh my God," she pushed out. "She totally did."

"I can't say I hadn't noticed it before, I had. It just came very to the fore in inspecting the entirety of it. It's not as if it's overwhelmingly masculine, but she definitely balanced the scale more to that side so her husband would not only be comfortable but able to wallow in his many successes."

The humor left her expression.

"Mom was super proud of Dad," she said softly.

"It shows," I replied.

"He really needs you to, um…change things."

It was me talking softly when I said, "I know."

"I think he, um…uh…needs you to make it very *you.*"

"I know that too."

"I know he doesn't want to erase her," she said swiftly.

"Dru, darling," I replied, going to her and taking one of her hands in both of mine. "I think we both know he needs that because he wants it for me. Our mission here is to give him what he needs so he can assure himself that I'm fully aware of his feelings for me, at the same time make it his space, your space, Judge's space, and retain Rosalind's space."

Gratitude shone in her eyes even as she noted, "That's a hefty order."

"I believe we're up for the challenge."

Dru added her other hand to both of mine and gave them a

squeeze. "I love how much he loved her, and even though it might seem bizarre, I love how much he grieved for her, because it showed how much he loved her, and it felt good, having someone share that with me, even if what we were feeling felt awful."

"Of course, dearest," I whispered.

"But I'm sorry he didn't see what was right in front of him for so long so he could be happy again."

"Oh, Dru," I said, pulling her hands to my chest. "That's very lovely. Thank you."

"I should be thanking you for making him happy. He's, I don't know how to say it except, he's *back*."

I *adored* she felt this from Jamie.

"Outside my children, this is my greatest triumph," I declared.

She smiled before she let my hands go, and she pulled me into a hug.

When we stepped away from one another, I said, "I think this room, we don't change. It's so very Jamie, it *oozes* him."

"I agree."

"The front room, darling, let's go there to feel the space and brainstorm."

She grinned at me. "Awesome."

We came up with some ideas, decided to share those while we interviewed a few interior designers, and we headed out.

Dru was a flautist, a talented one, and as such, she was quite busy with session work, and she was booked to be at a studio soon.

An aside, to augment her income, on days she wasn't booked, she was a substitute teacher. She had, I noticed, not shared this with Nico and Felice the Sunday before, and since she didn't, I didn't either. However, she'd seen Felice's behavior with Alyona, and I didn't need to crawl into Dru's head to know she worried that Felice, a full-time educator, might look down on Dru doing it for extra cash.

We headed down the steps to the car I'd hired for the day, but Dru paused before getting in the back, her attention aimed across the street.

"What is it?" I queried.

She turned her head my way. "I just...got a strange feeling that man was watching us."

I looked across the street. "What man?"

"He's gone. He took off when I looked at him."

Considering Hale was a billionaire, Genny was a famous actress, Tom was a retired tennis star, and Elsa was an up-and-coming celebrity interviewer, and frankly, all of us were very photogenic, our group had no small amount of attention from gossips and the media, so I asked, "Was it a paparazzo?"

"He didn't have a camera." She shook her head. "Maybe I was wrong. It's not a big deal."

She ducked into the car.

I watched her do it, standing on the sidewalk, unmoving.

Something was off with her, I just didn't know her enough to know what it was.

But I didn't like it.

"Ma'am, is something wrong?" my driver of the day (today, the agency sent David) inquired.

"No, nothing," I murmured, and folded in beside Dru.

David closed my door and got behind the wheel.

He took Dru to her session.

He then took me to Mika's so we could have a drink and a gab before I headed home to have dinner with my Jamie.

As we were wont to do, Mika and I lost track of the time.

So I was late arriving home that evening.

Alyona opened the door for me, and I wasn't sure I understood the look on her face.

"He's in the bedroom," she murmured.

I felt my brows draw down in confusion, but she took my bag and jerked her chin to the hall.

Swiftly, I walked down the hall.

When I entered our bedroom, I saw Jamie in a position I'd seen him in before, but it was much different this time.

He was sitting on the French Provincial bench at the end of the bed, leaned forward into his elbows at his knees.

Heiress was sitting beside him, her tail twitching, her face saying to me *Do something!*

I moved to him, calling, "Jamie?"

His head came up, as did his torso.

I moved to stand in front of him, and the instant I did, he reached for me, grasping my hips and pulling me closer, between his legs.

He then held my hips and stared at my belly.

I rested a hand on the top of his head, gliding it down to the side, as I whispered, "Jamie, what's the matter?"

He slid his hands up to span my ribs and tipped his head back to look at me.

"Dru is very excited about the plans you're making for the brownstone."

Oh, my Jamie.

I moved my hand again, to cup his jaw. "I could tell."

"She says you're not changing the library."

I shook my head. "No. Rosalind gave that to you, so it will remain."

He fell forward and buried his face in my stomach.

I wrapped both hands around his head. "Jamie."

"I hate this," he said into my stomach.

"You hate what?"

He tipped his head back to look up at me and put his chin to my stomach.

For Jamie, it was oddly boyish, and terribly sweet, but even so, it made me no less concerned, so I smoothed my hands over his hair as he answered, "I hate that I have to tell you this."

My hands stopped moving. "Tell me what?"

"That sometimes, I miss her."

I cupped his face in both hands, moaning, "Oh, my darling. Of course you do."

"I wouldn't change us, Nora."

"I know, honey," I whispered.

"The fact remains."

"I know."

"It's excruciating to experience that loss, at the same time think, if it hadn't happened, you would be alone. We would not have what we have. We wouldn't have a future."

Unfortunately, these horribly conflicting thoughts he was sure to have hadn't occurred to me.

I brushed his hands aside so I could sit in his lap.

He wrapped his arms around me.

"And the fuck of it is, I can't stand the thought of you being alone," Jamie went on. "That's the worst of it. You have so much love to give. It causes physical pain to think of you not having a man to give it to. It just gets worse, thinking that man would not be me."

"This has to be very confusing," I noted.

"As fuck," he agreed.

There was nothing I could say but, "I'm sorry."

His arms gave me a squeeze. "I hope you know, even with what I'm saying, that I've moved on. I understand she's gone. I'm not pining. I'm not only prepared, but happy to look forward to a future with you."

"I know."

"Don't forget that," he demanded.

"Don't stop talking to me about these things, even if you think you shouldn't. I want all of you, Jameson Oakley. I would not be best pleased if you buried any of you away from me."

"Fuck," he grunted.

"What?" I asked.

"Alyona has dinner ready, but now I have to fuck you."

"Can you hurry?"

We'd never hurried, even in the mornings. Jamie was a lazy lover, in all the varied delicious ways lazy could be.

His brows rose. "Is that a challenge?"

I fiddled with his collar. "If you wish to take it that way."

He surged up, and since I was in his lap, so did I, but he did it to his feet, and I did it in his arms.

Heiress leapt away with obvious outrage.

Jamie tossed me on the bed.

Oh my.

He went right to work on my sandals.

Once they were gone, I sat up, grabbed his tie and used it to pull him to me.

Before he kissed me, I asked, "Can you manage this feat without messing up my hair so Alyona won't know what we've been up to?"

"No."

I pouted.

He grinned. "Baby, when we're done, you won't give a shit about your hair."

"Jameson, there has never been a day in my life I didn't give a shit about my hair."

His lips came to mine, his eyes holding mine, and he proclaimed, "Get ready, today's that day."

And that was when he kissed me.

Twenty minutes later, both of us dressed, and both of us with sex hair, we walked to the living room with Jamie going on to the kitchen to tell Alyona we were ready for dinner.

And he'd been right.

I didn't give a shit about my hair.

CHAPTER 15

PRADA

Jamie

That Friday, Jamie negotiated walking through the busy lunchtime tables to where he saw Ned seated, his menu set aside, a bottle of San Pelligrino already on the table.

Ned got up when he saw Jamie, and their greetings included handshakes and claps on the arm.

They took their seats, putting their napkins on their laps, with Ned starting it.

"I was pleased when your assistant asked mine for this lunch."

"It's been a while," Jamie agreed.

Ned's eyes warmed. "Congratulations on JT."

Jamie smiled at him.

"And on Nora," Ned continued.

Jamie smiled again.

The warmth faded from Ned's eyes.

"So it fucks with me that I have to share all I have to share with you," he concluded.

Jamie's smile died.

This lunch was about them being friends, and extended family, and not seeing each other for a while.

It was also for Jamie to broach the difficult subject of asking after Ned's love life, which would also hold a warning, because Nora knew, and Chloe would find out, and Jamie had learned that when Chloe, or Nora, set their sights on something, things could get dicey.

Before he could ask, the waiter was there.

"Drink, sir?"

"The sparkling water is fine," Jamie replied.

The waiter poured the water. Jamie quickly picked up his menu to make his decision, they both shared their preferences, and the waiter took off.

Jamie didn't fuck around. "What news do you have to share?"

"Were you aware that Paloma was feeding Roland information about your relationship with Nora?"

Ah.

This was about that.

Jamie took a sip of his water, put it down, sat back, and replied, "Yes."

"Were you equally aware she was doing this to have her path cleared to make a play for you?"

Jamie went still.

Ned read his response and nodded. "She was. And just in case you doubt my sources, this comes from Blake. She hears things through some female grapevine we're not privy to, and she says the person who told her knows she's close with you, so she told her so Blake would warn you."

"How could she ever imagine...?" Jamie trailed off and shook his head. "Paloma knows I detest her."

"I'm not sure you made that clear."

"No, Ned. I made it very clear when she made a pass at me while my wife was dying."

Ned flinched before he murmured, "Good Christ."

"Yes. She's a vulture. When she's not being a viper."

"Perhaps desperate times," Ned suggested.

"I don't give a fuck what it is," Jamie clipped.

He'd not had time to find a way to get in touch with Paloma and share some truths.

The priority level of that had changed with this lunch.

"I hesitate to share that isn't all the bad news I have," Ned said.

"Terrific," Jamie muttered.

Ned didn't make him wait. "Roland, and I can only assume this is through Paloma, is making a number of meetings."

"To do what?" Jamie asked.

"To gather the capital to buy the note on your family's ranch."

Jamie could do nothing but stare at his friend.

"Roland isn't in ranching, he's in shipping," Ned stated. "But even with that, I can't imagine what he's trying to do, outside of fuck with you."

Oh, he was doing that.

"The note isn't for sale," Jamie stated.

"It doesn't have to be. AJ can pay it off if he remortgages with Roland's group."

"Goddammit," Jamie bit.

He needed to stop delaying. With Chloe pregnant, then JT coming, and Nora and he what they were, then becoming who they are, not to mention, Jamie had to be emotionally ready to do all he needed to do, he hadn't leaned into his father in order to decimate his resources so he could call the note.

By Texas law, his father was not as yet in default, but in Jamie's estimations (which were never wrong), AJ had three months of assets before that would happen.

Once it happened, they'd send a 30-day breach trust letter, which would include the twenty days AJ would be given to cure the default, something he wouldn't be able to do.

Unless someone bankrolled it.

"This is bigger than Paloma making a play for a meal ticket," Jamie said to his glass, his mind turning through the possibilities. He looked to Ned. "Roland is definitely angry Nora and I are together, but this is even bigger than that. I don't recall Roland ever playing nasty. Inside his sandbox, yes. Outside it, no."

"The both of them do seem to have a healthy interest in messing with the two of you," Ned agreed.

"And AJ is determined to stop me doing what he knows I'm doing," Jamie added.

"An unholy trinity," Ned murmured sympathetically.

"Why doesn't Paloma just make a play for Roland?" Jamie groused.

"He's already had her, and she's far too old for him, Jamie," Ned said. "He wants Nora back because he doesn't want anyone else to have her, particularly you. You're worth more than he is. You have more respect than he does. Her finding someone else after all these years, and it being you, is a one-two punch for a man like Roland. If she's alone, he can convince himself he broke her and she's pining for him, something that strokes a man like Roland's ego. If she's moved on, especially trading up, he's unable to do that. And he wouldn't hesitate to use an ex-lover if she proved useful to him. Apparently, Paloma is making herself very useful."

"His relationship with his children is hanging in the balance on this, Ned. There's enmity there. Nora has good kids, they're loyal to her, but she's not averse to them having a relationship with their father. If they got wind of this, I don't think that will be in the cards for him in future."

"It's the bed he's making, Jamie," Ned replied, reaching for his water. "He may learn he can't act like a petulant child until the day he dies. He might not. Obviously, my family knew his family. His mother spoiled him." Ned took a sip and put the water back before he shrugged. "He's always been a brat. Eleanor bemoaned Nora's choice before their marriage, and after. And Eleanor was very rarely wrong."

"And Nora is learning that the hard way, which is not something I can allow to go on, I just have no fucking clue at the moment what to do about it."

"You'll think of something," Ned assured.

Jamie blew out a frustrated breath.

"I hate I had to share all of this," Ned said.

"I'm sorry you hate it, but I'm glad you shared," Jamie replied.

Ned inclined his head.

"Now, since our conversation hasn't been comfortable, we might as well get it all out of the way with me telling you not only Nora, but Mika, know about Marlo."

Ned's lips thinned.

"And I can assume you understand, if those two know, then Chloe isn't going to be far behind," Jamie finished.

"Blake and Alex don't know," Ned said.

"I'm aware." He watched his friend closely. "Is there a reason why?"

"They've had to compete with my work, and me fighting with their mother, for my attention all their lives, and they lost. Those things aren't in the way anymore. But not much time has passed since I removed them. I don't want them to think they suddenly have another obstacle to my love."

"It doesn't work that way, Ned," Jamie said quietly.

Ned shook his head. "Blake is blossoming. Alex is happy and getting married very soon. It isn't the time."

"And Marlo feels about this…?"

Ned looked away.

Mm-hmm.

"Do you care about her?" Jamie asked.

"She's an extraordinary woman," Ned said to the napkin in his lap he was adjusting.

"You've waited longer to find someone to share your life with than I have, Ned, but take my advice. Don't fuck this up. The girls will understand, and perhaps it might be rocky with Blake at the start, but she'll come around."

Ned finally looked at him. "I just need more time."

"Don't take too much," Jamie cautioned.

Ned held his gaze a beat before he nodded.

And their lunch was served.

THAT EVENING, WHEN HE ARRIVED HOME, ALYONA OPENED THE DOOR for him, and he smiled at her.

"Hello, Mister Jamie," she greeted.

"Alyona. Good day?"

She nodded. "Miss Nora is in the study."

"Thanks, darlin'."

He moved in and saw his little girl prancing his way, so he bent and picked her up in his arms.

As was becoming her habit, Heiress moved to rest her paws on his shoulder and sniff his neck while he carried her to the study.

He found Nora on the sofa, the coffee table in front of her covered in papers.

She glanced up at him. "Darling, remind me never to accept the assignment of creating seating charts *ever again*. I must have had a moment of insanity when I agreed to this torture."

"The Frick thing?" he asked, moving to her and bending to brush his lips against hers.

When he straightened, she shook her head. "No, the ballet thing."

"Ah," he murmured.

Her eyes narrowed on him, reading him, he knew, when she asked, "How did lunch with Ned go?"

Jamie lifted a leg high to step over both of hers in the space between sofa and table, and then he (and Heiress) sat down beside her.

"I wouldn't count on him calling a family meeting with his daughters anytime soon."

She huffed.

He smiled, but said, "It has to be on his time when he's comfortable with it."

"Marlo Winslet doesn't strike me as someone who will wait very long for a man to extricate his head from his ass," she remarked.

"You waited for me."

"I was hopelessly in love with you."

He grinned at her and said, "Maybe Marlo is in love with Ned."

She looked to the charts. "We can hope so...for Ned."

"Ned had some things to share with me too."

She refocused on him. Acutely. "Why does your tone warn me to brace?"

"Because it's some fucked-up shit."

Her eyes widened, then she lifted a hand to roll it at him to prompt him to divulge.

Jamie did so.

He told her about Paloma, which made Nora appear annoyed. He then cautiously told her about Roland, which made her look shocked. And he made sure she knew AJ had to be involved in this, which made her openly contemplative.

"What?" he asked.

"I don't know," she hedged.

He knew her too well, so he noted, "I think you do."

She shifted in her seat as if preparing, for what, he had to prepare for, before she said, "You may consider me crazy, but I think in that mess, Paloma is the mastermind."

"I love you, sweetheart, but you're giving her too much credit. If Roland isn't, AJ is."

"Roland can be petty, but this is beyond the pale."

"You haven't lost you, *twice*. And I'll add, in losing you, for all intents and purposes, he lost his children. I don't agree with it, but I can see how that would take things beyond the pale."

"There's something I haven't shared...about Paloma."

Jamie felt the skin at the back of his neck stretch taut.

"What?" he pushed when she didn't go on.

"Well, as you know, she was with Tom for a time."

"I know this."

"And Tom broke things off when he started seeing Mika."

"I know this too."

"And Paloma wasn't happy about it."

"I could guess at that."

"Well, she intended to do something about it. And not long after Mika and Tom realized their undying love for each other, I got a call from Hale."

Now, he was confused. "Hale?"

"Hale, who told me that Elsa had told him that Paloma had been doing some pretty intense digging, and she was close to finding out the name of the woman Tom had an affair with."

The air Jamie sucked in at that hissed between his teeth.

And then it hit him.

"So you intervened," he guessed.

"Not exactly," she dissembled.

"How *not exactly?*" he pressed.

"I believe it was Hale who made certain the woman wasn't found."

"And you?"

She fluttered out a hand. "Well, it was light work, darling. She'd already burned a great many bridges."

"But you burned the rest of them so there were no more invitations, which meant cutting her off from her means of existence, as she wouldn't easily be able to meet men of a certain standing, married or not."

She bit her lip to communicate he was correct.

She then continued, "And she might, well…be banned from the Prada boutique on 5th Avenue."

Jamie sighed.

"And the one on Madison," she continued.

Jamie rested his head on the back of the sofa.

Heiress took this opportunity to climb out of his arms and settle between them on the sofa.

"And the one on Broadway," Nora mumbled.

Jamie returned his gaze to her.

"Prada is her preferred house. Almost to the point she'd made it her signature," she explained.

"And you cut her off."

"Hardly," she drawled. "They have boutiques all over the world, and you can buy online, darling."

"Do you think maybe, in the several times we discussed her, I might need to know this?"

"Would you believe me if I said it slipped my mind?" she tried.

"No."

She smiled. "It's good for our relationship to know I can't lie to you."

"Nora, this is about you," he pointed out. "She's pissed as shit at you. This isn't about you having things she doesn't. This isn't a society catfight. She's coming at you."

"Tom's business is not mine to tell, Jamie," she said softly.

"I know all about his business, Nora. We're close. He's confided in me. And you know why."

Her face scrunched.

She knew why. Then again, everyone did. Belinda made sure of that.

When he'd sought connection and intimacy in another woman's arms, that woman not his wife, he'd been separated from Belinda and had already filed for divorce.

When Belinda leaked the "affair" to the press, she didn't mention that part.

"We were no longer together," he told her.

"You don't need to explain this to me."

Was she insane?

"Of course I do."

"I know the man you are, Jameson. Even if you didn't say that to me, I could have guessed," she snapped.

Jamie sat solid.

"I also knew her issues. And that a custody battle and quite a bit of money were at stake. She was a woman playing her options, and you paid," she continued.

"Judge paid," he forced out.

"Both of you paid," she declared. "I honestly don't care what people think of it, but before the ink was dry on my divorce to Roland, I went on the prowl. I slept with a number of men. I did this before I realized it wasn't my choice to do it, he'd driven me to do it as a form of revenge. It drove him up the wall I was taking lovers, and to all appearances, something Roland didn't miss, I enjoyed doing it. I came to my senses. But although our stories are very different, I do know how it feels to have a spouse betray you as they fill their driving need to have something else. I also understand having the desire to feel attractive and rebuild your confidence so the way they treated you, like you were worthless, as was your love, doesn't dig in, fester and ruin you forever."

Christ, he loved it that she got that.

Got him.

Always.

With what had happened with Belinda.

How much he'd lost of Judge.

How much he'd gained, then lost, with Rosalind.

"Fuck, are you real?" he asked.

"I'm sitting right here."

He was pleased to note at that juncture she was wearing a dress.

"I need to go down on you," he stated.

Her eyes flared and she retorted, "This is a problem for you, since I suddenly have the overwhelming urge to have you in my mouth."

"Nora—"

She smiled a sultry smile as she leaned toward him. "You know you're going to let me have what I want, Jamie."

Her hand went to his crotch.

"Fuck," he bit out.

"I'm sorry, darling," she murmured as she shooed Heiress from between them.

She then made to move as if she was getting on her knees on the floor.

"Not on your knees," he grunted.

Her eyes went from his lap to his face. "If I don't—"

"I'll let you blow me, baby, but Nora Ellington does not get down on her knees."

A different flare lit her eyes before she nodded, then she unzipped him.

Remaining beside him on the sofa, she bent to him when she released his hard, throbbing cock from his trousers.

He'd learned she didn't fuck around when she did this. She wasn't about teasing, and she wasn't hesitant.

She was about results.

This wasn't about hurrying through an unpleasant task.

No, Nora used skill, precision, dedication and urgency to provide the ultimate explosive experience.

As such, Nora worked his cock with mouth and hand until she gave Jamie that experience, and their sexy little secret, Nora Ellington swallowed.

Jamie had barely come down before he ordered, "Straddle."

"Jamie—"

"Get astride me," he demanded.

She hitched a leg over him.

He dipped a hand under her skirt and into her panties, feeling she was drenched.

Her head fell back.

He worked her, and he watched his work in her face, getting mildly hard again while listening to it as it heightened, crested and crashed over her.

He slid his hand from between her legs to cup her ass inside her panties when she collapsed against him, her forehead in the side of his neck.

And she brought them back to their earlier discussion.

"She's the mastermind," she murmured into his skin.

"I hate to admit it, but I think she is."

"I don't think a call to her is going to change her mind."

"I hate to admit this too, but I believe you're correct, and further, this is not my forte, dealing with women like that."

"Leave it to me."

Oh no.

"Not gonna happen," he replied.

She lifted her head. "Jamie—"

"No, Nora."

"Jamie!" she snapped, post-orgasm mellowness vanishing.

"You're not in the line of this fire," he clipped.

"You're not either."

"Acquiring the ranch is a waiting game at this juncture. If Pop doesn't find an ally, and at this point, he has only two, Roland and Paloma, he's fucked. The only recourse we have is me uncovering who Roland is conning into getting involved in this mess and convincing them not to get involved in this mess. The ranch is leveraged for more than it's worth. I can't imagine anyone with a lick of business sense getting involved in the first place, so we might be worried about nothing."

"I *can* imagine, if they don't like AJ, and they want to fuck him nearly as much as you do."

Christ, he was off his game.

He hadn't thought of that.

And his father had a lot of enemies.

"Damn," he muttered.

"This is a good course of action," Nora approved. "Find them. Stop them. Obviously, Paloma is not going to win you. And Roland isn't going to win me. If you can put a stop to your plans being stymied to take the ranch, eventually, none of them are going to have any ammunition to hurt either of us."

Roland was a pest.

Paloma was a vulture.

And AJ was a snake.

Thus, Jamie wasn't certain Nora was right.

But there was nothing else he could do.

Beyond the ranch, he'd taken everything AJ had. Roland was his woman's ex, and the father of her children, so Roland might think his hands weren't tied, but Jamie understood, in some ways, his were. And he wasn't comfortable fucking with a woman. Paloma wasn't his favorite person, but she had nothing but fading looks. He couldn't live with himself if he found a way to leach blood from that stone.

"Fuck," he muttered again, dropping his head back to the sofa.

Nora curved a hand around the side of his neck and pushed up so he could see her. "We'll be just fine, darling."

Jamie was pleased to hear the strength behind her assertion.

She believed that.

But Jamie had a bad feeling that something was coming.

And Jamie had not made the life he'd made by ignoring his intuition.

It wouldn't take long at all for him to discover, as usual, he was very right.

CHAPTER 16

VAN CLEEF & ARPELS

Nora

It was early the next week, and Dru and I had just finished meeting with the first of the three interior designers we were interviewing regarding the brownstone.

Not unusual for New York traffic, four blocks from my building, we encountered gridlock.

I took this opportunity to think back on the time I just spent with Dru, because gridlock was annoying (no matter how usual it was, you never got used to it), and the time I spent with Dru was absolutely not.

It was Dru who started it, asking if I wanted to pop somewhere for a coffee after the meeting.

Obviously, I said yes. Though, I was somewhat concerned about what this may be regarding, considering we'd just discussed new design schemes for the brownstone. I was worried, now that the project was becoming more real, she'd started to have issues with it.

I would find she had issues, but they were other issues, and just as heart wrenching.

I learned this once we were seated in the bustling café with our lattes, and she appeared uncomfortable.

That was when I started it.

"You know, you can talk to me about anything," I told her carefully.

She ticked her head, her fabulous flame hair shifting across her shoulders, before she announced, "This is going to sound silly, or, I don't know, disrespectful."

Oh dear.

"Nothing is silly if it concerns you," I replied. "And disrespectful to whom?"

I braced when I saw actual pain in her eyes before she admitted, "Mom."

Oh dear wasn't the half of it.

"What about your mom, darling?" I prompted gently.

Like she was confessing a dirty secret, she shared, "She wasn't into clothes. I mean, she was. She liked getting all dolled up to go out on the town with Dad. But that wasn't like...*every night.*"

"All right," I murmured when she stopped speaking.

"And well, so...um, we didn't really have any of those mother-daughter bonding experiences while shopping. Because she wasn't like...into that. I mean, not really. She had her own style, but it was pretty laid back." She smiled a soft smile. "She was more about Dad, me, and her practice. You know?"

Oh, I knew.

I knew that was something Dru wanted, but she didn't get it, simply because it wasn't Rosalind's thing, but it would turn out it was Dru's. She'd just not had the chance to grow old enough with her mother in her life so they could possibly explore it.

My heart bleeding, I replied, "I know."

"And it's just that...I guess, uh..."

When she seemed to be having difficulty, I repeated, "Again, you can tell me anything."

"Well, you're into fashion," she said on a rush. "Designers. I mean, you knew the name of the Chloe bag that Heiress picked, not just the designer, but the *name of the bag.* And you always look more than put together. You're always on the best-dressed lists. It seems to come so easy to you and, the thing is…" she trailed off.

"You're into fashion too," I stated.

Something animated came over her, so much of it, she bopped in her seat. "Yes, but more. I'm like into…the *art* of fashion. The beauty that designers create. Or how they push the envelope. How they style things. How they build a runway."

"Would you like to go to a runway, or several, with me during Fashion Week?" I asked.

Her eyes turned into sea-green flames of excitement. "Seriously?"

"Of course," I replied. "I'd love it, dear. Neither of my girls are particularly interested. Mika will go at a push, if she's not busy with a project. You'll be granting one of my greatest wishes." I leaned toward her. "I've *always* wanted to share my love of fashion with someone."

"I would really, really, *really* love that," she whispered.

Yes, I could see she would.

She would also really, really, *really* love to share something with the woman in her father's life. Something that was ours. Something that we'd have forever. Something she could have with a woman in her life who was older than her, who could mentor her, who could be there for her when a woman like that was needed.

It took everything (and I mean *everything*) not to burst into tears that she was giving me this honor.

Once I locked that down, I declared, "Then, it's done. Fashion Week is in September. I'll start getting the invitations very soon. When I do, we'll go over them and decide which ones we want to attend."

"Oh my God, that would be awesome," she breathed.

It would be.

It would be *everything*.

For both of us.

"And you also must come over and go through my closet with me. I'll show you my favorite pieces and share why they're that," I invited.

"Oh man, I *need* to do that," she stated. "I just…I don't know. I can't seem to get a lock on what's *me*."

"Darling, that takes years," I reassured her. "I'll show you pictures when I was in my early twenties." I shivered, largely and genuinely. "I wouldn't admit this to just anyone, but I owned several"—I leaned in again and went on in a dire voice—"*tracksuits*."

Jamie's beautiful girl burst out laughing.

Watching her, my work, in that moment, I knew was done.

But I also knew our conversation meant I had a job with Dru for the rest of my life.

And I couldn't wait to dive in.

Once I went over this loveliness in my head two or three times, and after sitting in the gridlock without moving for twenty minutes, considering I was done for the day, it was sunny and lovely outside, I told my driver to head home, and I'd walk from there.

I'd gotten out, made my way to the sidewalk, and barely traversed a full block before I heard my phone vibrate in my bag.

I pulled it out, looked at the screen and took the call from my Allegra.

"Hello, dearest," I greeted.

"Hey, Mom," she replied.

"You're well?"

"Um…kind of."

My step slowed. "Kind of?"

"Okay, I know I shouldn't tell you this, but I am because I think you should know, but I can't unless you promise not to tell Val."

"I can't make promises about something I don't know."

"Mom—"

"Allegra, you know I'll be appropriate, especially when it comes to you children. Out with it."

"Damn," she mumbled.

She knew I'd be appropriate.

I headed out of the thoroughfare to stand next to a building in order to focus on my girl.

"Allegra," I prompted.

"Right, you know Darryn's cousin who recently got divorced?"

Oh no.

I sensed I knew where this was going.

"Yes," I said reluctantly.

"Well, um...Nico called Darryn and asked for her contact info so he could get a referral for her attorney."

Yes, I knew where it was going.

"Damn," I whispered.

"Yeah. And no. Felice is a pain in the ass, Mom."

My ears perked up, because neither of my girls had ever given any indication about how they felt about Felice. They tended to support everything their brother did, love him unreservedly and act like he walked on water.

Of course, I encouraged that.

"Her holier than thou act gets on my nerves," Allegra said. "I swear, a couple of months ago, you know, when Darryn gave me that Alhambra Van Cleef & Arpels watch, we went out to dinner with them, and I showed it off. She actually got her phone out, looked up the price of the watch, engaged the calculator and told me how many school lunches we could have paid for with that watch."

I grimaced.

"I thought Darryn was going to throw her over the table," Allegra carried on. "We're lucky his parents have money, as do mine, so we don't have student debt. But it isn't like he sits around playing video games and mysterious forces stop by to give him money. He worked hard to buy that watch for me. And just to say, the hard work he does is stressful and saves lives."

"It's a beautiful watch, darling. I hope Felice saying that didn't make it any less meaningful to you."

"It didn't, Mom," she said on a sigh. "I'm just saying, she's a pill, and it sucks, but I'm kinda glad Nico is thinking of scraping her off."

I was "kinda" glad too, even if it broke my heart.

"Well, I won't share this with Valentina," I promised.

"That's good, because even though I'm kind of glad Nico is seeing the light about her, if Valentina knows he is, she'll wiggle in there and make it happen. And if she does that, it's not gonna be pretty."

"Valentina isn't fond of Felice either?" I queried.

"She hates her, Mom. Do you know how she is with Archie?"

Oh no!

How could Felice be anything with Archie? He was as amiable as they come.

"How is she with Archie?" I asked with dread.

"Well, first, that whole 'no one is invited to our commitment cere-mony' thing was all about Felice. Archie didn't want her there, ruining it for them. So, the only way they thought they could do it, without Felice showing or making a big thing about not inviting Felice, was to do it on their own."

At learning this news, I experienced a buzzing in my head so strong, I thought it might explode.

Although I understood why they made that decision, I was furious they felt forced to make it, and in so doing, they did not have the ones they loved close at hand to celebrate something so beautiful and important in their lives.

Allegra wasn't done.

"This came about because she can pretty much rattle off the name of any NFL, NBA or MLB player who's been accused of raping a woman, can go on about how cities pay for arenas when team owners are billionaires, and I could continue. Val told me she practically went stalker with how many articles she sent him about those hockey guys who got busted for what they did to that poor woman. In the end, he had to block her. All this, like Archie having a job taping a game means he's directly responsible for everything wrong with profes-sional sports. Archie is so freaking over it, it isn't funny. He almost didn't come to lunch that Sunday when he found out she was going to be there."

Oh dear.

I understood it was bad, I was learning it was very bad, but with that, I realized it was far worse than I thought.

"Just to say, I'm not a big sports person, and a lot of it has to do with all those things," Allegra kept on. "But Darryn is really into foot-ball and basketball, and her yammering on about all that stuff ticks him off too. I mean, it's like she doesn't know, you know, *of course*

Darryn isn't down with sexual assault. But they're just *games*, they're *entertainment*, and how the players and the owners behave, and all that shit isn't a reflection of fans of the game, but the individual owners or players. You know?"

"I know," I murmured conciliatorily.

"And I don't want to get into telling you how she lectured Darryn about how he should turn his back on the NFL because of that taking a knee thing. It's none of her damned business how he feels about that, though, obviously, he felt a man should be free to express himself by taking a knee or any way he wishes. Bottom line, though, frankly, she's in no place to lecture a Black man about how he feels about anything. Or, really, lecturing *anybody*."

"No, she isn't," I stated flatly.

"You have to talk to Nico, Mom."

I blinked at the pavement. "For goodness sakes, why?"

"Because, even if he doesn't scrape her off, she has to stop this crap with, I don't know, *everything*."

"Allegra, you and your sister are grown women, and I'll add, your men are grown men. You can speak up for yourselves."

"You get in his shit about how she is with Alyona," she pointed out.

"Yes, because that's mine to 'get in his shit' about, as you put it. Now consider how you'd feel if I came to you with complaints from Nico and Valentina, Felice and Archie about Darryn's behavior."

First, she made a scoffing sound before she declared, "Darryn is a god."

He might not expect anyone to treat him as such, but my daughter did it all the same.

It was adorable.

"Yes, Darryn is perfect." He wasn't, but it was close. "I said that as a for instance," I explained.

I heard her heavy sigh.

"Though, I don't think now is the time for either of you to confront Nico about his wife," I advised.

"If he's thinking of ending things with her, maybe now is the perfect time," she replied.

"I can't tell you what to do, I can only advise. Now, you can phone him, and he can get defensive, and dig in, which could delay him making an important choice about his future, which will shorten the time he has to find happiness after she's gone. Or you and Darryn and Valentina and Archie can support him through this tough time. Perhaps, if he confides in you, *gracefully* share how her behavior upsets you. But otherwise, let your grown-ass brother make his own way through this morass."

"Did you just say 'grown-ass?'" she teased.

"Is he not that?" I asked archly.

"He is. But I'm loving how Jamie is wearing off on you."

That wasn't Jamie.

I wasn't sure, but I thought it was Mika.

Or Cadence.

"To end, my dearest, we need to rally around your brother."

"Yeah," she muttered. Then she asked, "You okay about what Dad pulled?"

After that Sunday, she and I had a short conversation about it, during which, as I suspected, she'd admitted she let slip to her father we were having a blend-the-families lunch. After that day, I'd spoken to all my children to take their pulse and allow them to take mine.

I moved away from the building and continued walking while I assured, "As I've said. I'm fine."

I wasn't, knowing Roland was up to no good with Paloma and AJ, but if I could help it, none of my children would know about that.

"Dad's been calling. I'm not answering. Darryn intervened, phoned him, and told him he needed to back off and give me time."

Yes, Darryn was nearly perfect.

"Has he stopped calling?"

"Yeah," she said.

She sounded sad.

She loved her father.

I just hated being able to fully feel that was difficult for her.

"Take your time to find the way you wish to share with him how that made you feel, then reach out when you're ready," I advised. "He'll listen to you."

"It sucked you guys got divorced, and why," Allegra began. "But it was cool how neither of you ever badmouthed the other to us kids. So I honestly don't get what his thing is with this. Why he suddenly changed."

I did.

Paloma.

"Maybe, when you're ready to talk to him again, ask him," I suggested.

"Yeah," she muttered.

"I'd like that Sunday lunch to be a monthly thing. Would you like that?" I asked.

Her voice perked up. "That'd be awesome. Maybe we could do a 'round the houses. Every month at a different person's place."

"An excellent idea, dearest."

I turned the corner, and halfway down the block, saw Arnold standing outside my building in his sharp gray uniform, and I was glad of it. I'd overestimated how far I could walk in my Louboutin heels.

"My house next. I'll talk to Darryn," Allegra said.

"That would be lovely."

"Speak soon. Love you, Mom."

"Love you too, darling. Goodbye."

"Bye."

We hung up and I was about to drop my phone in my bag, smiling at Arnold, who had stepped toward the door in preparation for opening for me, when suddenly, I was slammed against the side of my building.

I opened my mouth to shout, but it died in my throat when I saw Chester "Chet" Lynch, Dru's biological father, standing in front of me, shoving me against the stonework with a forearm against my chest.

"You think you can be her mom?" he snarled.

I stared in his enraged eyes.

Arnold's whistle was going off frantically.

"He thought he could be her dad," Lynch continued.

"Move away from me," I demanded, shoving at his middle to push him off.

And Arnold was there, pulling violently at his shoulder. "Get away from her. Now!"

"You're gonna learn, you fuckin' *bitch*."

His spittle landed on my face on the last word, and I feared he was loading his mouth to deliver more, but Arnold shoved him off and kept shoving him down the street.

Now Charlene was there, asking, "Mz. Ellington, are you okay?"

Lynch spat at Arnold's feet, turned and jogged away.

"Mz. Ellington!" Charlene called urgently.

I looked to her. "Yes. I'm fine. I'm all right."

"Do you want me to phone the police?" she asked.

On Drusilla's biological father accosting and threatening me?

Not on my life.

Or…not until I talked with Jamie.

"No. I…not now. I think I just need to get upstairs," I said.

Arnold returned. "She okay?"

"She wants to go upstairs," Charlene told him.

"I'll escort you Mz. Ellington," he offered.

I nodded.

We all returned to the building with Arnold taking me all the way to my floor.

I knew Charlene shared because Alyona wasn't at an opened door, she was standing in the vestibule.

I knew what I must look like when she rushed forward and took my arm. "Oh, my goodness."

"You got her?" Arnold asked.

"Yes," she answered.

"Get her to call the cops."

At his words, Alyona's face paled.

"Thank you, Arnold," I said over my shoulder as Alyona led me inside.

"My job," he replied.

"And you excel at it."

He tipped his cap to me.

Alyona took me to the sofa in the living room and pushed me down.

"Charlene said you were attacked," she accused, like I did it to myself.

I waved my hand in front of me. "It wasn't an attack. More a confrontation that got a little physical."

"Miss Nora!" she cried in distress. "We need to phone the police immediately."

"It was Dru's biological father, Alyona."

Her eyes went huge.

"So first, I need to talk to Jamie," I decreed. "He'll be home in less than two hours. I can talk to him then."

She looked dubious. "I think maybe you should call Mister Jamie now."

"I think now I need to get my shoes off and my head together so I can help Jamie decide what to do about this."

And whatever "this" was, was something we did not need when Jamie was trying to figure out what to do about the Roland/Paloma/AJ situation.

Fortunately, he had an ace investigator named Kateri True Arrow who had already uncovered Roland's possible partners in the scheme to refinance the Oakley Texas ranch, and Jamie was hard at work scheduling meetings with them.

But we didn't need another headache.

I was beginning to think I should call Chloe to ask after the company she hired that yacht from and whisk Jamie away myself.

Alyona shook her head like I was making a big mistake then she asked, "Do you want me to help with your shoes?"

"No. I can manage. I'm going to go change. Jamie and I are in for the night. I can get comfortable."

Alyona continued to look reproving as I got up and went to my closet.

I switched my slacks, blouse and heels with a Brunello Cucinelli cotton-silk, zip-up felpa and matching pull-on pants (not *exactly* a tracksuit, I told myself as I donned it). Even if I normally would put on slippers, I left my feet bare.

After that, I went to the bathroom, cleaned my face of Lynch's spittle and moisturized.

While seated at the vanity, applying powder and mascara to get me through the evening, abruptly, I felt an uncontrollable rage boil inside me. A delayed reaction to being manhandled by a wife beater and deadbeat father.

Unable (unwilling?) to get a lock on it, I went to my purse, pulled out my phone, and did the only thing I had the power to do in that moment.

I called my children's father.

"I think we've said all we intend to say to each other," Roland said by way of greeting.

"I do believe you've lost Nico forever," I retorted. "But I don't know. He's a good man. And men need their fathers. And because life is life, eventually he will need you. Now, in those times, he can turn to Jamie, or you can get your *fucking shit* together and behave like a decent human being in an effort at making it easier in future to mend this rift with your son."

I was a little miffed at myself I'd lost it a bit in the midst of delivering that, but only a little.

"Nora—"

"Valentina wasn't a lost cause, and please make note of the past tense, Roland. She *wasn't*. Until your antics that Sunday. You're holding on to her by a thread. And by the way, the one you thought you'd never lose, the hold you have on her is unraveling too. In short, whatever nonsense you're up to, *stop it*. Before it's too late."

"I was your first love," he spat.

"You still are," I pointed out. "It's just that I don't love you anymore."

"What we had...the passion, the fire—"

Oh my God!

Men!

"Roland, *get over it.* You poured a cold bucket of water over that fire then kicked dirt on it to make certain it was snuffed out. It's *done.* How you can know who you were to me, what you gave me, what we had together, what you *destroyed,* and think you still have some right to do harm to me, I will never understand. *Stop hurting me.* For the love of God, *please.* Let me *be happy.*"

"Nora, *bellisima,*" he said softly.

"Goodbye, Roland," I said resolutely.

Then I hung up.

After that, I went to the bar cart and made myself a very stiff drink.

———

HEIRESS AND I WERE ON MARTINI NUMBER TWO (WELL, HEIRESS WASN'T partaking, she was just keeping me company).

This one, like the first, I'd just waved the vermouth over it in an act of faith to the art of martini making. There was a silver toothpick shoved full of bleu-cheese-stuffed olives rolling around in it.

And this was as I was when the front door opened, then crashed shut.

I jumped.

Heiress leapt off the couch to investigate.

Jamie stalked in, murder in his eyes.

"Darling—" I didn't really begin.

"First, are you okay?" he demanded.

Uh-oh.

"You know?"

Of course he knew. It was a stupid question. It was written all over his face.

It could be any culprit, Arnold, Charlene, but I was betting Alyona.

"Arnold told me," Jamie bit out.

Oh.

I was wrong.

"The question is, why didn't you?" he asked.

"I was waiting until you got home."

"You were…? Nora—" He cut himself off, looked away, tore his hand through his hair, then leaned toward me and bellowed, "*Have you lost your mind? You were attacked!*"

"You say it like it is, Mister Jamie," Alyona encouraged from where she now stood in the doorway that led to the dining room, her arms crossed on her chest, her glare settled on me.

Jamie glanced at her then scowled at me.

"I don't need to be attacked by you too," I snapped at Jamie. Then looked to Alyona. "Either of you."

Alyona stuck her nose up in the air.

"I'm not attacking you." Jamie brought my attention back to him. "I'm pissed as fuck, and not all of it is at you. Though, Nora, my beloved, part of it *is* at you. I can't believe you fucking waited until I got home."

Hmm.

"I'm also calling the police," Jamie continued. "Which is a useless endeavor at the moment, since the motherfucker has had hours to get away."

"I know who he was, which is another reason why I waited for you to get home."

Jamie's head ticked.

"It was Chester Lynch," I announced.

Jamie's entire body went still as a statue.

So his "The fuck?" was tight.

"He said something about me thinking I can be Drusilla's mom, you thinking you're her dad, then he made a threat. That's all he got out before Arnold pulled him away."

"What threat did he make?"

I shook my head. "Something like, 'you'll learn.'"

"You'll learn what?"

I shook my head again. "I don't know. He said very little. Arnold was there in a flash. And I was surprised to even see him, so much so, I was paying scant attention to what he was saying."

"Are we phoning the police?" Alyona asked.

Jamie looked to her. "Yes. Can you take care of that?"

"Right away," Alyona said, and dashed off.

"Jamie," I snapped.

He looked down at me. "What?"

"It was Dru's biological father."

"And...he attacked you. Arnold said he threw you up against a building, which, sweetheart,"—he came to sit next to me and took my hand—"you didn't answer my question. Are you okay?"

"I was just shocked. He didn't hurt me."

"Fucking fucker," he bit off, but lifted my hand and kissed the back of it.

He then put his arm around my shoulders and pulled me to his side as he settled us both back into the couch.

"I'll handle Dru," he declared. "But we have to make a complaint. It needs to be on file in case he intends any more of his bullshit."

That possibility didn't thrill me, not making the complaint, not Lynch having more antics up his sleeve.

But I couldn't dwell on it when there were other priorities.

"How are you going to handle Dru?"

He looked down at me. "Tell her what happened."

I stared up at him. "Won't that upset her?"

"She hasn't seen him since she was five," he shared. "She calls me Dad because I'm her dad."

"But—"

"Nora, honey,"—he pulled me closer—"she knows what kind of man he is, and if she was here, she'd be right with me, telling you to report it to the police."

"It will still upset her."

"He's skilled at upsetting people, as you've personally experienced, but welcome to my world where you're powerless against anything but damage control when it comes to that guy." He took my martini glass out of my hand, threw back a sip, then handed it to me while murmuring, "Now I need to sic Kateri on that clown's ass, see if she can find out what he's up to."

"I think we need to talk about Dru some more," I suggested.

"I think I'm going to have a chat with Arnold. I want him to escort you to and from your cars. I'll also chat with your hire company. I want your drivers escorting you in and out of wherever you're going."

"Although he didn't approach to invite me to breakfast at the Plaza, maybe we can brainstorm why he might suddenly have returned."

"The police are coming," Alyona announced.

Jamie peered over my head at her. "Thank you, Alyona."

"Would you like a drink?" she asked Jamie.

"I can get it," he told her.

I felt her leave us, and Jamie turned back to me.

"That's what Kateri is going to find out," he said.

"Jamie, he seemed very angry."

Jamie studied me.

"If we're going through with reporting this, I think you might want to call Dru now, to warn her, in case he goes to her," I suggested.

"Fuck," Jamie clipped, then he pulled out his phone.

He got up and went to the bar cart, putting his cell to his ear.

I then listened to his side of the conversation, which was fraught, mostly around Dru's concern for me.

I took in a deep breath, and let it go.

He ended it by assuring her that Kateri would be on it by morning, I would be looked after, and she needed to be vigilant, and if she was concerned, he'd get her security. It was clear she declined this, which didn't make me happy.

He then completed the call and brought his bourbon back to sit next to me.

When he was settled, Heiress had come up to get a belated greeting from her daddy, and he was scratching her ears, I remarked, "I'm not sure Dru should make the call about security."

"I'm sure. She shouldn't. Once I stop saying hello to Heiress, I'm contacting my team. She'll never know she's being followed."

That made me feel better.

"Do you know what's become of him? Lynch?" I asked.

In hindsight, I realized, Chet looked rough. Not downtrodden and, say, homeless or anything. Just like he'd done quite a bit of hard living in his years on Earth, and it showed on his face.

Jamie stopped scratching Heiress, which earned him a nasty look and her walking over Jamie's lap to get to me, so I took over as he alternately sipped, texted, and answered me.

"He's rattled around. Pennsylvania. Connecticut. New Hampshire. New Jersey." Sip. Type. "He tried to be a rambling man with Lindy. Once she had a baby, she wanted roots." More sipping. More typing. "It was one of the things they argued about." Still more typing, but no sipping. "He remarried. Twice. Divorced. Twice. No other children." I heard the whoosh and he looked to me. "How did you get him to leave Lindy's memorial reception?"

"I asked him to leave, and when he refused, I called security, and they made him leave."

"That's it?"

I nodded.

He seemed bemused. "We haven't heard from him since then."

"Well, the reason why had nothing to do with me. I'm sure his ego took a hit at being escorted out, but it wasn't that dramatic. Eventually, they were less escorting and more simply following since he just left." I tipped my head to the side. "Did you hear from him frequently before?"

"He came to me on a regular basis, demanding money."

"Oh Jamie," I whispered. "Did you give it to him?"

"In the beginning,"— he took another sip—"yes. It would buy him leaving us alone, particularly Lindy. Eventually, when he tried to extort five million dollars from me so I could adopt Dru, no. After that, the number of demands decreased, but they continued until Lindy got sick. And surprise, he never sued for custody, even if he threatened it repeatedly."

I could add Chester Lynch to my hate list, and I did, at a position very close to the top, sandwiched between AJ Oakley and Paloma Friedrichsen.

Jamie kept speaking. "Dru was seventeen when her mom died. Less than a year away from reaching her majority, which meant he had nothing to hold over us anymore. With Lindy gone, this is maybe why he fucked off for the last five years."

He was staring into his bourbon, and he'd been speaking, but I sensed I lost him.

"Jamie?"

He turned to me. "I don't believe in coincidences."

"What?"

"Ned learns Roland is making moves. You find out Paloma is attempting to interfere with us. Pop's over a barrel. And suddenly, Chet shows up?"

"Oh my God," I breathed as what he was saying struck me.

"Pop said he'd play dirty, and this is as dirty as you can get, unleashing that asshole on you, maybe on Dru, thus on me."

"He wouldn't," I whispered. "Dru is for all intents and purposes his grandchild."

He swirled his bourbon. "So was Judge, and he fucked him over his entire life in an effort to steal him from me, and in the meantime, keep him from me."

"That's...it's...it's...*diabolical*," I stammered.

He lifted his glass to me. "Say hello to AJ Oakley."

My eyes narrowed on him. "That was a long text."

"It was."

"Am I going to have security?"

He looked steadily into my eyes. "Yes."

I blew out a sigh and buried my fingers in Heiress's ruff. "This is outrageous."

"What it is, is all they've got. If I can shut Chet down, and I can shut Roland down, then I can shut Pop down. And in a few months, it'll be over."

"Until you hand the ranch to your real father. Which will make AJ lose his mind, and it'll be an emotional juggernaut for you."

"Until that," he muttered into his drink, before taking another sip.

I was definitely looking into hiring that yacht.

I wasn't sure I could afford it.

But I was looking into it.

"Before the police get here, you should know, Allegra called."

At my declaration, Jamie's attention returned to me.

"She told me that Nico contacted Darryn to get the number of his cousin's divorce attorney."

"Surprised at how fast this is, but not that it's happening," he murmured.

"Yes. And Allegra also shared that none of them, my girls or their men, like Felice."

"Hmm."

"Did you read that?" I asked.

He shook his head. "No. But I'm not surprised. She isn't very likeable."

Indeed.

"Oh, and I called and told off Roland."

His focus narrowed on me. "You did what?"

"I called and told Roland, if he didn't desist in harming me, he'd lose them forever. I have no idea if it sunk in." At Jamie's look of concern, I brought my shoulders forward and released them. "It was an out-of-control moment after the situation with Chester Lynch. Delayed reaction. I got angry, and he was the one I wanted to take it out on."

Carefully, Jamie said, "You do know, sweetheart, that if this is AJ, Roland might know about unleashing Chet."

I scoffed. "That is not Roland's style. He's acting like an ass, but he'd lose his mind if he knew someone put their hands on me. And there's no way he'd make Dru collateral damage."

"You know him better than me," he muttered.

I hoped I did, because, if Roland had anything to do with bringing Chester Lynch back in Jamie and Dru's life...

All bets were *off*.

CHAPTER 17

PATEK PHILLIPE

Jamie

Six years ago, it was just Jamie, Lindy, Dru and Jamie's longing to have his son more a part of their lives and deeper in their family.

Now, late morning after Nora had been attacked, Jamie's phone was overheating with all of the texts he'd been receiving from his massive, extended family.

Dru, he'd learned, had shared with Chloe.

And then it swept through the Oakley/Swan/Holloway/Pierce/Sharp crew like wildfire.

He wasn't complaining. It was good for him, for Nora, for Judge and Dru.

However, imminently, Jamie needed to leave to meet a colleague for lunch, this colleague also one of Roland's who Kateri had uncovered was considering investing in Oakbilly Gulch, when his phone didn't buzz with a text.

It lit up with a call.

From Elsa.

He loved Elsa, but he didn't want to answer because he didn't have the time.

She was family, so he took the call.

"Hey there, darlin'," he greeted.

"Hi, Jamie," she replied.

He got down to it. "I'm sure you've heard, and Nora's okay. Shaken up, but fine."

"I know. I spoke with her earlier this morning. But, well, I just talked with a friend, and what they told me I couldn't delay in telling you."

Marvelous.

This didn't sound like good news.

Jamie sat back in his office chair. "What's that?"

"My friend works for a nighttime news magazine, and she told me they're in talks with Chester Lynch to do some kind of exposé on you. Something about how you used your money and influence to keep Dru from him."

Jamie let out a controlled breath.

At least they knew why Chet was in town, even if they didn't know why he was accosting and threatening Nora.

Jamie should have thought of this. It was an AJ Oakley play right down to its DNA.

And Elsa being involved in that industry was another indication it was good to have a big family.

"It's a reputable news magazine," Elsa continued. "If they took it on, they'd get in touch with you for your side of the story."

"I have seventeen audio files of Chet Lynch using threats to sue for custody of his daughter and offers to end his harassment of his ex-wife, who he called, texted, repeatedly showed at her place of work and often times turned up where she got her coffee or when she was out with her friends. He did this in order to verbally abuse her. It goes without saying, I also have witnesses who will attest to all of this and will do so gladly. In these audio files, you'll hear that he did all of that in order to extort over three quarters of a million dollars from me, which he received, before I cut him off."

"Whoa," Elsa replied.

"Two of those audio files record his attempts to extort five million dollars to allow me the privilege of adopting Dru, who, at that time, he hadn't laid eyes on in six years."

"Damn," Elsa murmured.

"Further, I'm still in possession of all Lindy's account statements and day planners, and they will show that Chet never paid child support and never showed for his visitations with Dru. Even if he said he would, and we had Dru ready to go with him, regardless we didn't want her to. The media doesn't need to know that Dru also didn't want to go with him. But a little girl waiting for her father to give some sign he gives a shit about her, bag packed and ready to go, and he never shows will not play well for Chet."

Elsa sounded gleeful when she agreed, "No, it won't."

"I'll drop a few of those files in a shared folder and send the address to you. I have no issue with you passing them on to your friend. If they require more to kill that fucking story, I'll see they get that too. But the stipulation is that there will be *no story*. They do not have my permission to use what I gave them. They will not have my cooperation if they go ahead and air whatever Chet is claiming. If they do, I'll give the rest to someone else, and I'll sit in front of a fucking camera myself and share that I asked for this to remain private, but your friend's magazine dragged my daughter and my deceased wife into a spotlight they did not ask to have shined on them. And Elsa, I won't mince words."

"Not a lot of productions want to be used as some asshole's personal tool to continue abusing his daughter, Jamie," Elsa replied. "At least none of that caliber. If you can send those files, my guess, when they hear them, they'll retreat from Lynch. But I'll tell them you're not super thrilled this guy is pulling this shit after he did all the rest."

"That would be appreciated, Elsa."

"There are other, less ethical news outlets that won't blink at sharing what he has to say, though," she warned.

He knew that. "Then I hope their libel insurance is up to scratch."

"Sorry you have to deal with this guy," she said.

"I had Lindy in my life for seventeen years, and Dru will be in it for the rest of it. He's a piece of shit, but with what I got, dealing with him is worth it."

"Yes," she agreed quietly.

His phone told him he had another call, and when he checked, he saw it was Nico.

He didn't want to take that one either, but if Nico had heard about what happened to Nora, Jamie had to.

"I have another call coming in," he told Elsa. "You have my thanks for the heads up, but sorry, I have to let you go."

"Of course, Jamie. Speak soon."

"We will. And thanks again."

They rang off, and he took Nico's call.

"Hello, Nico."

"Sorry to disturb you at work, Jamie."

"That's all right. Everything good?"

"If you're fishing about whether or not I know what happened to Ma, I do. Cadence called Val, Val called Allegra and me."

"I see."

"I just spoke to her, and she says it's all good, but Mom always says that shit. So I'm calling you, and I know I'm putting you on the spot, but that was some fucked-up shit, so I really need to know if she's okay."

"Nora's strong, Nico. You know that," Jamie replied. "She was shaken up last night. But Alyona and I were with her, he didn't hurt her physically, and she was herself this morning. I can promise you I'll keep an eye though."

"Right," Nico mumbled.

"I'm sure she won't mind if you came down this weekend to see for yourself," Jamie invited.

"I'm already planning on it. Is it cool if I show on Saturday and stay the night with you two?"

"It's your home, so definitely."

More mumbling with his, "Cool." And then he cleared his throat and said, "Uh…Felice won't be with me."

"That's too bad," Jamie lied. "Maybe next time."

And more mumbling with, "Maybe."

He felt Nico's pain. Coming to the realization you needed to end a marriage was not fun and games.

But Jamie looked at his Patek Phillipe watch, and saw he had to leave in no less than five minutes, or, if New York traffic delayed him, as it tended to do, he'd be late for his lunch.

Even so, Jamie inquired, "Is there something else you needed to speak to me about?"

"I…yes, um…no. No, not really. Just worried about Ma."

"We don't know each other very well," Jamie said carefully. "But I hope you know I love your mother, what we have is serious, it has a long future, but not only because of that, also because I like all of you, I want to build strong relationships with you and your sisters. So I also hope you know if you need anything from me, I'm here."

"Boy, you get to the point, don't you?" Nico remarked.

"Life is too short to fuck around when shit is important," Jamie returned.

"Yeah, it is," Nico muttered.

"So, is there anything you need from me?" Jamie offered.

"I…maybe this weekend, you and me, you know, just the guys, can have a chat?" Nico requested.

"I'd like that."

"Okay, we'll do it."

Did Jamie detect relief in his tone?

Christ, Roland was such an asshole.

"I'm sorry, but I have to let you go now," Jamie said. "I need to be off to a meeting."

"Oh, right. Yeah. Anyway, thanks for assuring me Ma's okay."

"She's good. See you on Saturday. Look forward to it."

"Yeah. You're busy, so I'll call Ma and tell her I'm coming."

"Right. Take care, Nico."

"You too," Jamie replied.

They ended the call, and Jamie had just enough time to text Kateri about the latest developments with Chet and make a note for himself to deal with the audio files for Elsa when he returned, then he was up and on his way to the door to his office.

It opened and Dru peeked her head around.

He came to a halt.

He should have known this would happen. She was very bad at hiding how distressed she was last night. He didn't buy her consistent reiterations she was fine, she'd stop by that evening to check up on them, and he should let her go so he could see to Nora.

But woefully he was a father who had a now-adult daughter he couldn't coddle and protect, and if she expressed her wishes, he had to abide by them rather than sending a car for her and all of her clothes and moving her in with him and Nora.

"Hey, darlin', this is a surprise," Jamie greeted.

She smiled at him and slipped in.

"Is this a good time?" she asked, walking his way. "You look like you're off somewhere."

It wasn't, and he was.

But for Dru, he always had time.

She made it to him, they kissed cheeks, and she stepped away.

"I have a lunch," he told her. "But I can text and say I'll be a bit late."

"This won't take long, promise," she said.

"You okay?" he asked, watching her closely.

"I just...well it hit me, last night, with my bio-dad rearing his stupid head again, that I'm twenty-three now."

He smiled at her. "You are."

"So, I don't need his permission for you to adopt me."

Jamie's stomach dropped and his throat closed, but oddly, neither were unpleasant sensations.

"He can kiss off," she went on. "I'll officially be an Oakley, and he'll just be the pathetic loser he always was."

"Darlin'," Jamie whispered, his voice choked.

Her eyes were bright with tears of happiness because she knew his answer to her suggestion.

And setting him up, she clobbered him with the rest of it.

"Now I can tell you, I saw him. My bio-dad. Last week, he was lurking across the street from the brownstone. He was there, then gone, and he's aged a whole lot. I wasn't sure it was him. Until what he did to Nora, that is."

Christ.

"Why didn't you tell me?" Jamie asked.

She tossed up her hands. "Because I wasn't sure it was him, Dad. You and Nora were finally together. We have JT. All is good. It's happy. It's as it should be. We don't need that jerk messing it up."

He didn't like this. It smacked of stalking. Not only of Nora, but of Dru.

However, if she hadn't put that together, he wasn't going to do it for her.

And she had security on her, so they'd inform him if this was the case.

Jamie let out a sigh. "You can always tell me anything, especially if it's important."

"I know, but that doesn't mean I *want* to tell you, especially if it's going to be upsetting. I didn't know he'd go psycho and assault Nora."

There was a sliver of pain and embarrassment in her eyes, as if Chet's bullshit had something to do with her, when it didn't, so Jamie took her in his arms. As usual, they both held on tight.

"You've told me now," he said to the top of her head. "And I'll get my attorneys on drawing up adoption papers."

She tipped her head back to look at him. "Maybe we can have a big dinner to celebrate or something? I mean, JT can't fly, so we'll have to wait for when that's groovy for him to do, but that won't be bad. Only a month or two. It'll give everyone the chance to fit it in their schedules."

"That's an excellent idea. Would you mind if Nora planned it?"

She melted into him. "I'd love that."

And he loved she did.

"So would she," he murmured.

"Her shower for Elsa was the bomb."

"I have a sense she'll pull out all of the stops for this."

"I might have to bust into my trust fund to find a dress," she teased.

"It's yours, you can bust into it whenever you want."

He watched his daughter's eyes sparkle before she queried, "Can I walk you down?"

Best offer he'd had all day.

"Yes," he agreed, turned her to his side and slid an arm around her shoulders, guiding her to the door. "Can we drop you somewhere?"

"I can take the subway, Dad."

"That wasn't my question."

"Okay, yeah, I have an audition and interview down in Soho," she told him as they moved through the outer office, and he lifted his chin to Monica so she'd call down to Vincent to have him pull around.

Monica picked up her phone.

"Is this interview for something you're excited about?" he asked.

"It's not gonna happen, so I'm trying not to be."

Jamie hit the elevator then gave his girl a *Spill* expression.

She spilled. "It's to be in the band for Ashe's new tour."

That artist was not of his era, but even Jamie had heard of the hyper-popular female singer, Ashe.

The elevator doors opened just as Jamie's face split into a grin. "That's fabulous, darlin'."

They moved into the elevator as Dru warned, "Don't get excited. Everyone wants to be on this tour. It's going to be huge, and they'll have dates all over the world."

This didn't thrill him. Some of those tours lasted a year, or even longer.

But it'd be a huge coup for his daughter. It'd be tough work. But Dru loved to travel, so she'd not only see more of the world, she'd do it being able to network extensively in her chosen field.

"It's good you don't go in cocky so you'll make an effort," he said after hitting the button for the lobby. "That means you'll go for it. But I can know you'll get it even before you show up."

She rolled her eyes.

Jamie kept grinning.

They hit the lobby, got in the car, and Vincent dropped Jamie first, so he didn't have the opportunity to call Nora and share all the news before he had to meet his lunch partner.

And luckily, New York traffic cooperated, so he was only a few minutes late.

JAMIE WAS WALKING ACROSS THE LOBBY OF NORA'S BUILDING WHEN HIS phone vibrated with a text.

He hit the button for the elevator, then pulled out his cell.

Elsa.

The Lynch thing is dead. I'll keep my ear to the ground if he's shopping it around. My friend's pissed they were duped, so she said she would too. I'll be in touch if I hear anything.

He considered asking her to ask her friend if AJ, Roland or Paloma was involved in any of that mess, but decided to let Kateri do her work and ferret it out.

Thus, he returned, *Means a lot. Owe you one.*

He was in the elevator, and it was going up, when she returned, *No markers in family.*

So Jamie was smiling when he got off the elevator.

Alyona had the door open, and he aimed his smile at her.

She returned it and said, "Good evening, Mister Jamie."

He walked into the apartment and turned to watch her close the door.

When he caught her eyes, he said, "Nora told me you're coming with us to the brownstone."

She nodded.

"Then we're going to know each other for a long time, Alyona, and as such, I'd like to invite you to just call me Jamie."

That earned him another smile before she replied, "Okay...Jamie."

He winked at her and asked, "Where's Nora?"

"Study, and warning, she's in a bad mood."

This was concerning, but he didn't ask Alyona about it.

He went to find his woman so he could ask her, then do something about it.

He found Nora seated behind the desk, and he thought he discovered why she was in a bad mood, because, strewn over it were large diagrams which were obviously seating charts.

She turned her head to look up at him when he arrived, her foul mood undisguised even as she greeted, "Welcome home, darling."

Jamie moved to her and put a hand to her charts to brace himself as he bent low to kiss her.

He didn't move far away when he broke the kiss.

"Haven't found the key to the perfect placements?" he asked.

She shook her head.

"No. I have. I'm like a savant with seating charts. That's why they always ask me to do them," she said airily. "If you're asking after my scowl, it's because I love our people very much, but having Mika fawn all over me for two hours, Tom demand to prod the back of my head where it didn't even hit the wall of the building, my daughter racing here on her lunch hour to take my blood pressure, my other daughter texting every five minutes, not to mention fielding texts from Dru, Cadence, Chloe, Genny, Elsa, and even Blake all day, I've definitely decided to kidnap you to a yacht, but we won't be gone a week. We'll be gone a year."

Jamie carefully nudged her charts aside before he rested against the edge of her desk, and said, "We'll definitely do the yacht thing. I didn't get to fuck you there."

She tsked and gave him a side eye, but neither hid the rose in her cheeks and the fire in her gaze at hearing his words.

"But we have to wait to go for a few months so you can plan and then we can throw a celebration dinner when the adoption papers are filed making Dru officially mine."

She stared at him, lips parted in wonder.

Then she surged out of her chair and threw herself in his arms.

She even gave a little hop of excitement.

Yes, his elegant, sophisticated and droll Nora did something as cute as that in her happiness for him and his daughter.

Therefore, Jamie was chuckling when she leaned back, but not out of his arms, and he saw her face beaming.

"How did this come about?" she asked.

"She stopped by the office and informed her unusually slow father that she was no longer a minor, so we didn't need Chet's approval."

Nora fiddled with his tie. "You are not slow. You're already her father, so obviously, adoption became superfluous, therefore, you stopped thinking about it." She lifted her gaze to his. "Though, it's absolutely, positively lovely it's going to happen anyway."

"Dru wants you to plan the party."

More beaming. "Consider it done."

"Now, I have more good news, and some bad news."

She frowned dramatically.

Jamie chuckled again, and asked, "Which do you want first?"

"Definitely good."

"I spoke with Charles, and you were correct. Pop fucked him over on some deal about three decades ago, and Charles never forgot it. Thus, when Roland started fishing around, Charles jumped on board for the sole purpose of being in line to hammer a nail in Pop's coffin."

Charles VanderMeer was who he'd had lunch with that day.

"Oh my," she whispered with verbal delight.

"And Charles shared that, even though Roland doesn't know it, the other four investors he tapped who were willing to buy into this scheme were doing it for the same reasons."

"And this means?" she prompted.

"It means, I'm struggling with letting them have it, just to spread the joy of fucking Pop over."

"Jamie," she said softly.

Damn.

"I know. I can't. I need that ranch in my possession so I can give it to my birth father."

"Did you share with Charles that you had uses for the ranch?"

"I did, and he was amenable. That said, he's asked if he and the others could play with AJ for another few weeks. Give him hope he has a lifeline, then yank it around the time AJ runs out of funds, is facing default, and then I can move in."

"Obviously, you said yes to this," she purred.

His lips tipped up. "Obviously." He tilted his head to the side, "Though, one thing I wasn't certain about during our lunch was that he said Roland had contacted him just that morning, making some murmurings about how he may no longer wish to be involved in that deal."

Her expression turned thoughtful as she murmured, "That's interesting."

"What did you say to him last night?"

Nora tipped her head to the side. "Nothing I've not said before."

"Could it have gotten through?"

At that question, she lifted a shoulder. "No idea. Possibly. But if I had to guess, how honest his son was with him was probably what started to make him think."

Jamie could see that.

"Now, dearest, hit me with it. What's the bad news?" she asked.

Reluctantly, he told her why Chet was in town, and that Dru had seen him outside the brownstone.

"I worked with Elsa to kill the story," he finished. "But that doesn't mean he won't shop it around."

"So that was who Dru was looking at," she said.

"You saw him too?"

"No. But she mentioned someone watching us, and she seemed... not quite right about it. I put it down to the media attention our group gets. She never seems comfortable with that."

"Well, she recognized him."

He hated to see it, but there was no beam from her eyes now.

"This is unsettling, Jamie."

She was very right.

"She has a man on her at all times, as do you," Jamie reminded her. "They've been informed of this latest. Elsa is going to keep her ear to the ground in case Chet, Pop or Paloma looks for some other place who will air his lies. I can't imagine she'd be able to catch the story anywhere he shopped it so we could kill it. But Kateri also knows this is a possibility, she has even more connections, so maybe, between the two of them, we can cut him off at the knees."

"So, hopefully, we've sorted the two major issues. Charles and his cronies can have some fun with AJ. And in a few months, this will all be over."

"Hopefully."

"And then, Jamie,"—she pressed deeper into him, her gaze serious —"it'll be time to deal with your real father."

Yes.

It would.

As she always did when this came up, she made her point, then sensed his emotion around it, so she changed the subject immediately.

"In the meantime, Nico is spending the weekend with us, I have a *fabulous* adoption party to plan, and Allegra tells me my blood pressure is *perfect*."

"Excellent news, baby," he murmured.

"Oh, and I'll need a new dress for the party, so will Dru, and this means *shopping*."

She was beaming again, and he knew she loved shopping, but she'd also told him about her conversation with his daughter about designers and style, so he knew that beam was about a lot more than just shopping. Thus, Jamie decided talking was done, making out was in order, so with her between his legs, his ass on her desk, that was what they did.

He let her go to change out of his suit so they could relax and have dinner. Then read for a while, make love and go to sleep.

It wouldn't be until the next afternoon, when Charles called him, that Jamie would learn that Roland had completely stepped away from the Oakbilly Gulch deal.

So either Nora or Nico got to him.

That was good to know.

One down.

Two to go.

CHAPTER 18

TOM FORD

Jamie

Saturday afternoon, Jamie was in the hearth room, while Mika, Cadence, Tom, Dru, Allegra, Valentina and Nico (Archie was shooting a game, Darryn was on call) were sitting around the dining table, still chatting, and giving it time before they had dessert after consuming Alyona's gut-busting lunch.

He left them after he got a call from Judge, everyone yelled out hello (and demanded more baby pictures), and he moved to the hearth room for more privacy.

Nora had exquisite taste, every inch of her apartment was stunning, which made him look forward to what she and his daughter were going to do to the brownstone, but this was his favorite room in the house. It was the only one that had any masculinity to it, if you counted black velvet couches with crystal and gold lighting features as masculine.

But he liked the one dark feature wall, and the couches in there were insanely comfortable.

He settled in one and asked his son, "Everything going well?"

"JT is growing like a weed, mostly out," Judge told him. "He's getting a buddha belly. It's cute as fuck."

Jamie chuckled even as he reminded himself to look for real estate in Prescott. The lives they lived and where they lived them, at that juncture, it was out of his control how much he'd miss of his grandson in this time.

But Jamie was determined not to let that go on too long.

"Chloe's good," Judge continued. "She's getting her energy back, even though we've found that good-night's-sleep-is-a-memory thing for parents is very real, and it's tougher for her because she's breast-feeding."

"You're with her on that, though. Right?" Jamie prompted.

He heard the smile in his son's voice, a reaction to Jamie's quiet order, when Judge replied, "Yeah, Dad. She tells me I don't have to get up and hang with them. I tell her, if she'd just pump so I could feed him and she could sleep, *she* wouldn't have to get up. But she feels like hogging all that action, and when Chloe is really into something, I've learned the best thing to do is just let her do it."

Jamie chuckled again.

Judge kept speaking. "Though, she says she's going to give me a shot…eventually."

"That's good, buddy. Feeding your child is a bonding experience."

"I totally get that. In fact, sharing that is how I got her to give in and let me feed my boy…*eventually*."

Jamie shared more auditory amusement.

"She goes down to her shop in town a few hours a day while Genny watches JT," Judge told him. "Or she drops him at my office, and then I have to fight everyone off because they want a piece of him. Alex has fallen in love. Rix has fallen in love with her falling in love. He told me he's gonna knock her up on their honeymoon."

"I hope he does," Jamie said, looking forward to the trip to go out for their wedding, one that was happening that coming autumn, and he was looking forward to it for a bevy of reasons.

On that thought, Jamie picked up his earlier thought and made a mental note to set up some house viewings while they were out there.

"I do too," Judge said into Jamie's thoughts. "He also shared, when he lost his legs, he gave up on the idea of having kids. Didn't think he could protect them if something really bad happened. It's fucking awesome he doesn't feel that way anymore."

It absolutely was.

Predictably, it had been a rough road Rix had to travel after he lost both legs in an accident when he was a firefighter, first the physical journey, then the emotional one.

But Rix was a tough nut, and he fought to the other side. Now, it was all about getting on with life, love, and making babies.

"You hear from Chet again?" Judge asked.

"Not a word. No whisper out there he's causing any trouble. Doesn't mean we won't be blindsided by it."

"Do you have any idea what his deal is now?" Judge asked. "I mean, Dru's of age. Why doesn't he just piss off?"

At his son's question, Jamie made a decision.

And it was a big decision.

He then set about initiating that decision by explaining all that had been happening.

Everything.

Roland. Paloma. Chet.

AJ.

And finally, he said, "I haven't spoken to your sister about this, but I need..." he trailed off.

Was he going to do this?

"What, Dad? You need what?" Judge prompted when Jamie left it too long. Then he suggested, "A posse to go to Texas and kick Granddad's ass?"

Jamie wanted to smile at that.

He just couldn't.

"No, because, Judge." *Fuck*. "Because AJ Oakley is not your granddad."

Judge was silent.

Jamie was in it now, so he had to give it all.

"I found your grandmother's journals. She had an affair. I'm the product of that."

"Holy fuck," Judge pushed out.

"I know it's a lot to lay on you over the phone—"

"It'd be a lot to lay on me in person," Judge said. "You've known about this for a while?"

"It took some time for me to get over losing your grandma before I could read her journals. It then took more to convince myself I had a right to her privacy. I missed her and wanted to be closer to her. So I read them, and I'm glad I did, for more than this reason. But yes. I've known it for years. I didn't tell you because, well, frankly, son, I wasn't ready."

"It's yours to share when you want to, Dad. I'm just…is it bad that I'm really freaking happy Grandma cheated on Granddad?"

Miraculously, considering their subject, Jamie felt his lips twitch. "No. But it wasn't like that. It was a love affair, buddy. They loved each other. Deeply. He wanted to take her away from him. Give her a good life. But she had three kids, and they both knew how AJ could be, particularly Mom. If she humiliated him like that, he'd bury her, and my birth father."

"Christ, the tentacles of his bullshit stretch forever," Judge groused.

They were about to come to an end.

"What he did to you, how he used Belinda," Jamie began, "and learning what was in those journals was what prompted me to deal with him in a final way, Judge. Mom felt trapped. Well before the final years of her marriage, she felt trapped, and he purposefully made her feel that way. It was a relief to her when he replaced her. So, part of why I made that decision has always been the fact that I plan, once that ranch is in my hands, to give it to my real father…and your two uncles."

"Holy shit, I have uncles too?"

"Yes."

"Please tell me these ones aren't fuckwads," Judge begged.

Jamie felt a lightness in his chest at Judge's reaction to all of this.

He'd been avoiding it for a long time, not wanting to besmirch his mother's memory, not wanting any drama, but definitely wanting AJ firmly over the barrel before he pulled the final plug.

But fuck, it was good to finally have it out there.

"I've looked into all of them, and they're good, decent, hard-working men. They own a ranch they all work not far from Oakbilly. The sons are both married, one to his high school sweetheart. The younger one to a woman he met twenty years ago, and they've been together since. You also have cousins. Three boys and a girl. They're younger even than Dru, but they seem like good kids."

"Jesus, this is a lot," Judge muttered.

Jamie's stomach twisted. "Too much?" he asked.

"No, Dad. I think it's awesome. I should have known you weren't of his blood. You don't look like him. And you don't act like any of them. Have you reached out to these folks?"

"I'm going to do it after I get the ranch."

"Can I ask why you're waiting?"

Good question.

"Dad?" Judge pushed.

"I keep trying to think how I would feel if the product of a relationship with a woman from my past, even a woman I cared about deeply, approached me decades later."

"I know how you'd feel," Judge stated instantly. "You'd be shocked, but, as long as they didn't show up to milk you for money, you'd love it."

His son was correct.

However...

"Not every man would, Judge," he cautioned. "And he's been with his wife for forty-five years. She might not like it that much either."

"I hear you," Judge said quietly. "But if he loved Grandma...and Dad, you're no slouch. You've made an amazing life for yourself, and you're a great guy. I think this man will be super freaking happy to know you're his. And if his wife loves him, she'll only dig that he has more family to add to their own."

Fuck, he hoped so.

Jamie moved them on. "So…first step. Telling you. I'll tell Dru soon. Once we know Chet isn't going to bother her. And then I'll figure out when I'll reach out to this man."

"What's his name?"

"Morgan Rawlins."

"Holy *fuck*," Judge whispered.

That made Jamie smile, because he knew why Judge said that.

"Mom told Pop that she gave me my middle name after her side of the family, the Morgans," Jamie told his son something he already knew. "Her journal refutes that. She named me after my father. Which means, I inadvertently gave you your middle name after my father."

He could hear the smile in Judge's, "Shit, AJ is gonna lose his mind."

AJ was going to lose his mind.

There was a knock on the door, then Nico stuck his head in.

"Damn, sorry, I thought you might be done," he said.

"No, don't go," Jamie called. "We're finishing up." He went back to Judge. "Sit with this. Process it. I'll let you know when I talk to Dru. And then we'll get together and figure out what's next."

"Okay, Dad. Thanks for telling me."

"Thanks for handling it so well."

"Not a problem, since I think it's the shit. I can't wait to tell Chloe. If you hear her shriek of glee all the way to New York, you know I've done the deed."

And his son made him laugh.

Through it, he said, "Much love to you, Judge. Give Chloe and JT a kiss for me."

"You got that back, and I will. Later, Dad."

They hung up, and Jamie focused on Nico.

"You sure you were done talking to Judge?" Nico asked. "Honestly, I can come back."

"We were done, Nico."

And he'd been in the thick of it with Judge, but he knew the minute Nico showed late that morning that he needed to make sure there was time for this chat.

He knew this when Nico came through the front door wearing a brown Tom Ford button down and jeans, nice boots, and a brown military-style Tom Ford jacket.

Jamie sensed this was not an outfit approved by Felice.

It wasn't like Nico had been in flipflops and a T-shirt that last time he came home. But the short-sleeved button down and faded jeans he'd worn that time were both probably purchased at the Gap.

Nico was reclaiming himself, and undoubtedly, Felice wasn't a fan.

He watched Nico move to the sofa across from him and sit down.

"I'm going to make this easy on you and let you know that Darryn is a great guy, but he tells his wife everything," Jamie said quietly.

Nico looked to the fireplace. "Right."

"I've been divorced," Jamie reminded him, getting his attention back. "And lost a wife to cancer." He let his lips tip up ruefully. "I've got all the shitty experiences under my belt."

"I love her," Nico blurted.

Jamie nodded.

There was pain in Nico's face, and his voice, when he asked, "Is sometimes love not enough?"

Jamie thought of Belinda.

"I hate to tell you this, but yes. Sometimes love isn't enough."

Nico's face flushed with emotion, but he asked, "Are you cool with talking about this?"

"I'm very cool with it," Jamie assured.

"This is a lot, we don't know each other very well, but I don't want you to think I've got some kind of screw loose."

Jamie might speak plain and do it as a habit, but he wasn't going to remind Nico that he'd witnessed how he was with his father, so he knew, when Nico needed someone to turn to of maturity who'd been there, his father was not going to be that.

Instead, he said, "I can't say I haven't fallen into this trap in my life-time, more than once. Too many times to feel comfortable. And that's because I should have been smart enough to figure it out long before it became uncomfortable. That's to say, I understand that somewhere in our evolutionary history, men decided that talking and expressing their emotions is a weakness. And they made that decision because women do it, so they segregated it into feminine and masculine, with anything they erroneously deemed as weak being feminine. Women can feel and share. But even though men feel just as much, they cannot. And frankly, that's just, plain, fucking stupid. Like women, we feel hurt, joy, sorrow, elation, betrayal. Burying emotion and becoming an asshole no one wants to deal with doesn't seem like a wise answer to life's many issues. Getting shit out with someone you can trust, working your way through it, and hopefully finding some answers is a better way to go about it. Don't you agree?"

Nico was staring at him, but he used his mouth to say, "You really don't hold back."

"Like I said, not when shit is important. And you're important, Nico."

If Castellini had been anywhere near him in that moment, Jamie might have been moved to cut him gut to gullet at the look on Nico's face when Jamie said that. Because it was clear Castellini had not made a point of being absolutely certain his son knew he was important.

Fortunately, that moron was nowhere near.

And Jamie had to pay attention, because Nico was talking.

"Okay then, straight up, it's like she thinks she married a different guy. The longer I'm with her, it's like she hates everything about me."

Jamie nodded again.

"She has a real problem about class," Nico informed him.

"I'm sorry to say, that wasn't lost on me."

Nico flinched. "Did she say something to you to make you uncomfortable?"

"Not personally. But I wasn't a fan of the digs and looks she gave Nora."

He watched Nico's jaw bulge, sharing he wasn't big on that either, before he pointed out, "I mean, I can *not* be rich. It's doable, obviously. I can give away my trust fund. I can ask Mom and Dad to disinherit me. But that's fucking lunacy."

"It is," Jamie agreed.

"She cares about everything. At first, I thought that was incredibly cool. She reads *The Times* religiously. She knows how senators and congresspeople vote. But she spends a lot of time up in her phone, watching these TikToks that serve no purpose but to piss her off. I've told her she's feeding into the algorithms, and seeing stuff that only sounds in her personalized echo chamber, without getting any alternate perspectives, but she doesn't listen. I've asked her to stop, or at least cut back her screen time, and, I don't know, maybe spend some time with me. She says she will, then she doesn't, and our lives are permeated by what she consumes. One day, we can't eat at Chick-fil-A. She reads something, the next day, we can. And that's with everything, Jamie. *Everything.*"

Jamie could imagine that would be very frustrating.

Nico continued, "And, a month ago, she said she wanted to leave the city. Move to Vermont. Use my trust fund to buy some cabin or something. Plant a big garden. Slaughter our own pigs and chickens. I mean, slaughter our own meat, for chrissakes."

Jamie grew up on a ranch. The circle of life was not lost on him.

That said, he liked his steak, but he'd never slaughtered an animal and he had no desire to do so.

"This Vermont full-time idea is out the blue," Nico told him. "She never hinted at wanting to leave the city. She told me she loves it here. She can go to protests. She can go to poetry readings. All that shit. Now, she wants to raise pigs and figure out how to make our own Oreos organically and go off the grid. It's freaky."

Jamie leaned forward and put his elbows on his knees. "No one stays the same. We all grow. Mature. Change. And sometimes, if you're in a couple, when you do that, you grow apart."

Nico nodded, right before he shook his head.

"I think she's always been like this. I think I was like...one of her causes. This poor little rich boy she can show the way. But, serious to Christ, there's only so many times a man can listen to a woman shouting at him because he forgot to clean out a Ziploc when he's just done."

Jamie sat back, saying, "I can imagine."

"I feel like a fucking failure," Nico mumbled.

"You aren't. It happens. It would be a fail if you knew it was over, if you ignored the red flags, and you gave more of your life to it."

"I kinda married Mom, except the not-funny, totally not-self-aware, naggy, judgy flipside of Mom."

At that, Jamie smiled a soft smile.

Because he'd married his mother too.

In Rosalind.

Loving, generous, kind.

His last woman was all his pick.

Hilarious. Loyal. Devoted. Outspoken. Stylish. Gorgeous.

And a fantastic lay.

"Why are you smiling?" Nico asked.

"Because I had a great mom, like you do," Jamie explained. "My second wife was a lot like her. She made me very happy. But your mom is all my choice. I came from means, but I made my own way in this world, and your mom is the woman I've been working to earn all my life. And I finally won her."

Jamie leaned forward again and gave him the wisdom.

"Nico, what I'm saying is, we all make mistakes, but the only good ones are the ones we make when we fall in love. I fell in love with a woman that was going to die young, and in doing so, cause me immeasurable pain. But while I had her, I was enormously happy. You fell in love, and you were happy, and you got married. The key is, once you realize it's a mistake, don't make it a failure by not recognizing it for what it is. If you're feeling there's no common ground between you and Felice, then it isn't only to save yourself, it's to save her, that you cut her loose so you *both* can find what you need. If you love her," —he sat back again—"then, I know it sounds like bullshit, but it can be an act of love to let go."

Nico's voice was thick with emotion when he said, "This is gonna suck. We haven't even been married for two years."

"Do you have a prenup?"

Nico nodded. "Totally. Dad flipped his shit when I proposed to her without discussing that." A fond, sad smile hit his lips. "She didn't even read it when she signed it. She's totally not about money."

"That can change when hearts are broken," Jamie warned.

Nico shook his head. "When I go home tomorrow, if she asks me for a divorce before I'm through the door, I won't be surprised. We both know it." His voice dropped to a whisper when he repeated, "We both know it."

"I hate that you—" Jamie began, but there was a sharp rap on the door.

He looked that way to see Tom come in, and he was leading a charge.

Everyone was coming in.

But Jamie homed in on Nora.

She looked distraught.

"What's going on?" he asked.

Nora came right to him and sat beside him as Tom asked, "Where's the remote for this TV?"

"I'll get it," Nico said, reaching to a pearl-velvet box on one of the coffee tables and opening it.

When he grabbed the remote, he tossed it to Tom and Tom aimed it at the television over the fireplace.

Jamie looked to Nora.

"Again, what's going on?" he demanded.

"Elsa called. I'm so sorry, darling," was all she said before she jutted her chin toward the television.

Jamie looked that way.

Tom had found a news channel.

And on the screen, he could see his childhood home engulfed in flames.

Not telling his body to do so, Jamie took his feet.

Nora came up beside him.

Tom turned up the volume.

"...at the stables, where there are known to be thoroughbred horses. The fire then jumped to the main house, along with several other outbuildings, something that's confusing at this time, considering the distance between them and it hasn't been a windy day. More fire crews are coming in, but as you can see,"—the reporter on screen turned and moved to the edge of the frame to give the viewer the full scene of the entirety of Oakbilly Gulch consumed by flames, the reporter then turned back to the camera—"it doesn't seem like they've been successful at containing what, no other way to describe it, is an inferno, Evan."

The screen went to someone sitting in the studio. "Paula, any word on AJ Oakley?"

Back to the reporter, who shook her head. "We've been told Mr. Oakley's son, Jeff, and the senior Oakley's girlfriend, former supermodel Paloma Friedrichsen, were at the house when the fire started, but we haven't seen either of them. And no word on AJ Oakley."

Evan the newscaster came back on screen. "I'm sure you'll stay on top of it, Paula," he said. "We'll circle back to you when..."

Tom turned down the volume and looked to Jamie.

"Arson?" Tom asked.

Tom, one of his closest friends, was not in the dark about all that was going on.

"Absolutely," Jamie answered.

The fingers of both of Nora's hands wrapped around his biceps.

Dru came to his other side, and she grabbed his hand.

"AJ would burn down his house with both his son and his girlfriend inside?" Mika asked, and her voice was pitched far higher than normal.

His first thought was, if he was the beneficiary of life insurance on either of them, Jamie wouldn't put it past him.

But he said, "I don't know about that." He looked back to the TV to see Evan prattling mutely on about something. "The reporter might have been given wrong information."

Allegra plopped down beside her brother, with Valentina doing it on the other side, Allegra saying, "I'm so sorry, Jamie. Watching your childhood home burn like that has to stink."

Actually, he had no fucks to give. The ostentatious monstrosity of Oakbilly could burn right to the ground for all he cared.

It was just that his real dad and brothers would have no home to live in and as such, would have to rebuild if they decided to take over Oakbilly and live there.

"What's this about arson?" Valentina asked.

"I'll explain later," Nora said quickly.

Jamie sat back down, and since they were attached to him, both of his girls came down with him.

"Do you think that Charles and his group pulled out of the deal, and this was an act of desperation?" Nora asked quietly.

"I don't know what to think," Jamie muttered.

"What I think is, it's time for dessert," Mika decreed. "I'll go talk to Alyona. We'll serve it in here. Cozy and comfortable."

Jamie watched as Mika gave Tom's hand a squeeze and strode out.

"I'm gonna help Mom," Cadence said, shooting a sad look Jamie's way, then she ducked out.

"You okay, Dad?" Dru asked.

He turned to her. "I'm fine, darlin'. Just…stunned. But I had no ties to that place, and not many good memories."

She glanced beyond him to Nora before she came back to him and said, "Okay."

He squeezed her hand.

Then he looked to Nico and requested, "Can we talk in the hall for a second?"

All the women exchanged glances, but Nico got up quickly, saying, "Sure."

Jamie followed him to the hall, and when they were down it a ways, they stopped.

"We got interrupted. Are you good?" Jamie asked.

Nico blinked at him before he said, "I'm sorry, did we just watch your childhood home burning on the TV, they don't know where your dad and brother are, and you're worried about me?"

"I'm not close with my family," Jamie explained.

Nico started laughing softly. "No, man. You're just…*you*." He cuffed Jamie on the arm and went on, "I'm sick to my stomach my marriage is over. What comes next is gonna suck. But right now, I mean, Ma is pretty damned rad, so I understand how she earned you in this life, and I'm glad she did."

That felt really damned good.

Jamie nodded and clapped him on the back.

They returned to the hearth room.

Nora sought his gaze, and he did his best to communicate *It's going to be okay* with it.

He must have succeeded, because her face softened, her brown eyes warmed, and he returned to sit between her and Dru.

Mika and Cadence came in with trays of individual strawberry trifles, conversation sprang up, and although he weathered some concerned looks, and Nora nor Dru left his side, it was all good.

But Jamie couldn't keep his eyes from straying to the TV every so often to see if more news of the fire had come on.

This being more news about his father who had never been his father, or his dad. His brother, who fortunately was only half-blood to him, but he didn't want him dead. More news about a misguided woman who took a certain path in life and wanted others to pay for it.

No more news came on.

So he waited until everyone had left, outside Nico and Dru, before he went to the study to make his calls.

Jeff didn't pick up.

And neither did AJ.

The ranch house and all the outbuildings were burning to the ground. They might be busy.

No answer could mean anything.

And neither of them would think to call Jamie and tell him they were okay.

So he had to wait.

And to his surprise, the wait was excruciating.

———

It was after dinner.

Dru was gone.

Jamie and Nico were in the hearth room watching a baseball game, something which Nora had no interest in, so she said she was going to give herself a facial.

But just then, Nora came in.

Jamie looked to her.

He was flat out on one couch, Nico the same on the other, and she came to Jamie and sat by his hip.

Jamie didn't like the look on her face one bit.

"Elsa phoned." She drew in breath. "Darling, Jeff was in the fire. Paloma and AJ were in Dallas."

He felt his chest get tight. "He was *in* the fire? He died?"

Nico slipped out as Nora grabbed Jamie's hand and held tight.

He sat up.

"He died," she whispered. "And…Jamie…"

"What?" he asked tersely, not sure what he was feeling, he just knew it wasn't good.

"They haven't been able to inspect it officially, but Elsa says there are rumors flying that, preliminary evidence suggests he wasn't simply caught in the fire. He was caught while *setting* it."

Jesus.

Fucking.

Christ.

CHAPTER 19

GIVENCHY

Nora

"*H*ow's Jamie doing?" Chloe asked in my ear.

I was in my closet with Alyona, packing. Alyona was holding up a black dress.

I shook my head and turned back to Jamie's suits and my conversation with Chloe.

"I don't think he knows how he's doing," I confided.

"I can imagine," she murmured.

I pulled out a charcoal gray, bespoke, CKC New York suit and hung it on the valet rail.

I turned back to Alyona who was holding up my Givenchy, pleated-skirt, black silk dress.

I nodded.

She hooked it on a valet rail.

"Just so you know, Judge is going down to meet you guys, and Rix is going with him."

At this news, I stopped perusing Jamie's tray of precisely rolled ties to focus on the conversation.

"Chloe, that's a lovely gesture, but you know how Jamie feels about Judge leaving you and JT to go to the funeral."

"I know, Judge knows, but honestly, *ma belle amie*, do you think he's going to let his father go through this without him?"

Hmm.

"I've got Mom, Duncan, Heddy, Beth, and Alex all close to help out," she explained. "And Judge, who's his father's son, so he's overprotective, asked Gage to stay with me while he's gone. Gage was all over it. I can, of course, take care of a baby, two dogs and a cat by myself, but I won't have to. So Jamie doesn't have to worry."

"Is Judge going to tell him, or am I?" I asked, nodding my head to Alyona proffering my patent, black, slingback Louboutin pumps.

"Judge is packing. They have to leave soon to head down to Phoenix to catch their plane. He's going to call Jamie on the way."

"All right. I'm packing too, dearest. Dru will be here in less than an hour, then we're away to JFK."

"Okay, I'll let you go. Love you. Call if you need anything."

"I will. Love back to you."

We rang off and Alyona and I dug into selecting outfits. We were on to accessories when my phone rang again.

It was Charlene.

"Hello, Charlene," I answered.

"Hey there, Mz. Ellington. Wanted you to know that Arnold is on the way up with a packet that was dropped off."

"All right."

"And just to say, if you can get me a date with the guy who dropped it off, I wouldn't say no."

I smiled. "Always nice to have a handsome courier."

"This man was no courier. I think he gets his suits from the same place Mr. Oakley does."

Oh my.

Intriguing.

I wondered what the package was, considering neither Jamie nor I were expecting anything, and definitely neither of us were expecting anything to be dropped off by a man wearing a hand-tailored suit.

"Thank you for calling, Charlene."

"Never a problem."

I ended the call and looked to Alyona.

"I need to retrieve a package delivery," I told her.

"I can do it," she replied.

"No, I'll do it. If you could get started on folding?" I motioned to the suitcases in the corner of the closet with my head.

"Will do," she murmured, moving toward them.

I went to the door and was standing in it when Arnold got off the elevator.

He gave me the package with a tip of his cap, and I closed the door, holding a thick manila envelope that had my name on the front written in bold, black pen.

The metal clasp was sealed, as was the envelope.

I moved to the kitchen and furtively (my letter opener was in the study, which was too far away for the level of my curiosity, and Alyona would have a conniption if she saw me using one of her butter knives in this manner) slit open the envelope.

Inside, there was a notecard clipped to the thick pile of papers, and on it was another bold, black letter, this one simply an "R."

My brows furrowed at that, but I pulled it off, unclipped the papers, and drew in a sharp breath at what I saw.

The top was photocopies of bank statements.

And these statements belonged to Paloma.

Under those were more statements.

And those belonged to Chester Lynch.

Beyond that were LLC documents, and Articles of Incorporation, none of which I understood.

I didn't wish to, but I'd learned how Jamie felt about me keeping important things from him, so I sought him out, and found him with his laptop and some open files scattered across a coffee table in the hearth room.

Heiress was lounging on the velvet couch beside him.

He looked to me, his lovely blue eyes alert, but that hint of disso-nance behind them that had been there since he learned his brother had died was unhidden.

"Darling, we've had an unusual delivery."

I sat next to him on the couch and handed him the envelope with the papers on top.

First, after inspecting it, he lifted the notecard and flicked it to and fro.

"R?" he asked me.

"No idea," I told him.

He nodded, set that aside and started looking through the documents.

I sensed his surprise when he saw what they were, and then I sensed when he put it together.

"What is it?" I asked.

"The paper trail from Paloma to Chet, through a few shell compa-nies. Though it's clumsy and not at all buried." He turned from the papers to me. "She gave him money. Likely so he'd talk to the media and give them whatever bogus story he cooked up."

"How much did she give him?"

"From what I can tell, two hundred thousand."

Goodness.

That was a lot.

"Where is she getting that kind of money?" I asked.

Jamie turned back to the statements and shrugged. "Seems they're cash deposits."

"Does AJ have that kind of cash on hand?"

Jamie returned his attention to me. "He's got assets he hasn't tapped, but they'd be last ditch to anyone in his situation. Doesn't mean he hasn't sold them. Heirlooms. Jewelry. Art. Guns. He had the horses, which were worth a great deal of money, but all of their carcasses were found in that fire."

I winced.

In the three days since it had happened, it had become official.

It was arson, and all the evidence pointed to the arsonist being Jefferson Oakley.

It didn't take a genius to put together that Jeff had set fire to the entirety of the Oakbilly Gulch estate (save for one outbuilding that held tractor equipment, which he died before he could get to) in an effort to collect insurance. And as Jefferson Oakley was prone to do, he'd fucked it up, getting caught in one of the blazes he was setting.

The question that was beleaguering my beloved was if it was Jeff's idea, something that Jamie didn't think was possible, considering his brother wasn't the brightest bulb in the box. Or if AJ had not only told his second son to do it but did so knowing how gullible and dim he was, so also knowing there was a good possibility he'd get caught.

In other words, setting him up to take the fall, while AJ pocketed the proceeds and bought himself another chance to save his own hide.

Neither of us could wrap our heads around the idea that AJ did it thinking Jeff would perish, just that he could collect the insurance money, which was considerable, with his hands coming out clean, even if there was a chance that Jeff's wouldn't.

However, in all of this, the death of those horses, and how they must have spent their final moments, was the thing that could set Jamie into a fury. I knew because it had, on two occasions, and one of my old-fashioned glasses shattering against a wall was indicative of how deep his fury went.

This happened when Kateri had told him the horses had been insured as well, for quite a lot, and the stables were the first building Jeff set fire to.

Thus, it was clear the collection of that bounty was also on the radar for one, or both, of those Oakley men, and the hideous murder of those horses was done in pursuit of a payout.

Jamie took my mind from all this by continuing to talk.

"He could do private cash sales, which I couldn't track, nor could anybody, which means, even if he sold assets, the insurance companies would be none the wiser. We had Waterford. We had Limoges. We had an original Bierstadt and a Remington. My grandmother had an affinity for Royal Doulton and Cartier. I could go on. The payout of the insurance on the horses, the house, and the contents is enough to buy him years on that ranch, even if he erects a modest home in which to live there."

"If he sold, and didn't disclose, and the insurance paid on those items, that's fraud," I pointed out.

"If he talked my idiot brother into setting fire to his property so AJ could collect a payout, that's fraud too," Jamie returned.

I'd noticed of late that Jamie wasn't referring to AJ as his father or "Pop" anymore.

I thought this was good, especially considering he told me he shared important matters with Judge. It indicated to me that he might be moving closer to claiming his real father.

I just wished the final straw on that wasn't what it was: death and destruction.

Without warning, Jamie communicated what some of that disso-nance in his eyes was about.

"I feel responsible for this, Nora."

My body jerked in shock. "What, darling? My goodness, *why?*"

"I pushed him to it."

Oh no he didn't.

"You did *not* push AJ or Jeff into committing arson and equine homicide," I snapped. "I'll not hear you say that again, Jameson. For years, *you* did not actively seek to muzzle women who had been violated so you could protect the value of your shares, thus your tattered reputation shredded to oblivion when your foul behavior was outed. *You* did not make desperate and foolish deals that fell through. And *you* didn't light any matches. Of course, it can be said you know those men, but I can't imagine even if you had a functioning crystal ball, you'd believe they'd take it to that point."

I huffed out an annoyed breath.

And continued ranting.

"A real man would see he's bested and cut his losses so he could live another day. He had property. If what you say is true about his possessions, he could have easily put them to auction, making quite a bit of money, and found himself somewhere comfortable to live out the rest of his days. Or he could have done that and invested the capital in the one thing he had left, that ranch, and making it work for him. Simply because of his pride, he didn't do any of that. So what he did, if indeed he was the mastermind behind this latest plot, does not rest on your shoulders. It rests firmly on *his*."

Jamie said nothing, but he didn't have to, considering he cupped my cheek and rubbed his thumb tenderly over my cheekbone.

As such, I noticed some of the unrest in his gaze was gone, so I felt I'd done my job.

For now.

"I need to accessorize the outfits I'm packing," I announced. "And then we need to go. Dru will be here shortly."

Jamie removed his hand from my face and put the papers back in the envelope, saying, "Can you put these in the safe?"

"Of course." But he'd stilled, so I called, "Jamie?"

"R," he said, and looked to me. "Rhys Vaughan."

Well...

Heavens.

Rhys Vaughan—the sadly departed, immensely complicated, but it had been discovered after his death, intensely devoted—Corey Szabo's man on a mission.

And Vaughan's mission was to take care of any problem that anyone Corey loved had. He did this with dedication and meticulousness.

If he was behind this, an indication that he'd waded into the issues we were facing, that was a rather large bit of good news.

"I think we've been adopted, sweetheart," Jamie noted.

I took the envelope from him.

As I did, my smile was slow.

But Jamie's wasn't.

Thus, Rhys completed my job of clearing that dissonance.

Now we could get on with the next bout of unpleasantness.

And hopefully after that, my Jamie could have some peace.

THE ATMOSPHERE IN THE CAR WAS SO HEAVY, I WAS STRUGGLING TO breathe, but for the life of me, I couldn't think of how to alleviate it.

It was late the next morning, and we were on our way to the funeral.

Judge was driving, Jamie seated beside him (at my insistence, which Jamie was so against, it almost caused a row, but fortunately, Dru backed me, and Jamie couldn't fight the both of us) and Rix, Dru and I were ensconced in the backseats of the Cadillac Escalade Jamie had rented.

"Jesus, do I need to start cracking really bad, and really dirty, jokes?" Rix asked the general population of the car.

"We're going to my uncle's funeral, Rix," Judge reminded him.

"And Dad's going to have to see Granddad," Dru added.

"And Jeff was a putz and AJ's a dick, so what's the BFD?" Rix stated bluntly.

Judge opened his mouth, but Jamie got there first.

"He's right, kids."

And he was, because the heavy atmosphere wasn't coming from Jamie, me, or Rix, but from Judge and Dru.

They were worried about their dad.

"Dad," Dru said softly from the very backseat.

"I wasn't close with Jeff," Jamie shared something we all knew. "He was always a bully. He was ludicrously competitive, but bad at everything, which made it worse, because he was a shit loser. He made zero effort to keep in touch when I left. And he didn't respond to mine or Rosalind's efforts to do so. I haven't seen him in over ten years, and frankly, I didn't miss him. This means he not only didn't bother to come to Lindy's and my wedding, he also didn't show at Lindy's memorial, healthy indication that he was not a man who earned being missed. I'm here because he was still my brother, he was my mother's son, and I need this closure. But that's the only reason I'm here. This won't last long. Hopefully AJ will stay away from me. And then we can go back to the city and have a nice dinner."

"If that's where you're at, Dad, cool," Judge muttered.

"That's where I'm at, buddy," Jamie confirmed.

"Damn, now I don't get to tell any dirty jokes," Rix mock complained.

There was laughter and chuckles, and I was thankful Rix was there. Things were a good deal less tense the last fifteen minutes it took to get to the funeral home.

And Dru's gasp of delight when we saw Sully standing outside, I suspected, was how we all felt at this welcome surprise.

Sully walked to the Escalade so he was in position to help Dru alight when she followed Rix, something I took particular note of, even as Jamie was helping me out, because it was subtle, but it appeared he shouldered Rix out of the way to take the opportunity.

Noting the smirk on Rix's face as he watched this happen, I saw that Rix was having the same reaction to this happenstance as me.

Our crew was very close, and Dru was definitely a part of that.

But this seemed to be something different.

"Ready?" Jamie's voice came at me.

I looked up to him to note he hadn't seen what I saw, because he was looking toward the funeral home.

He might not be overly saddened at his brother's passing, but Jeff was still his brother, and AJ was probably already in that building, thus the next hour or so was not going to be enjoyable for my Jamie.

I curled my fingers around the crook of his arm and said, "Yes, darling. Let's go."

We walked toward the building but didn't make it when Jamie's steps stuttered to a halt.

So we all came to a halt.

His head was turned to the right, I looked that way, and I saw a lovely, tanned, robust woman of around my age walking toward us.

"Good Christ. Patty?" Jamie called.

My body tensed when I knew who she was, but the woman grinned largely as she called back, "In the flesh, brother boy."

Gently, Jamie extricated my hand from his arm, strode purposefully toward the sister he hadn't seen in years. She'd escaped the Oakley dysfunction by moving to New Zealand, and until this moment, as far as I knew, had never been back on American soil. And this included not going to her own mother's funeral (though, Jamie told me she did send a beautiful spray of flowers and a loving note to her mother, the reading of which Jamie included in his eulogy). That said, Jamie had gone to New Zealand to see her, though, considering the distance, not frequently.

The instant they were close enough to do so, they embraced.

We all edged toward them, so I heard her say to her brother, "Damn, it's so good to see you."

"You too, Patty. You too," Jamie muttered.

He broke their embrace and turned to us. "Judge, you won't remember her, because you were a baby when you last saw her, but this is your Aunt Patty."

She beamed at Judge, before she went to him, cupped his face in her hands and said, "Lord, son. You grew up good."

"Uh...thanks," Judge mumbled, his attention going between his dad and his aunt, uncertain which way to come down with the latter, in case, even if it gave no appearances of so being, this was another hit his father was taking.

Yes, Chloe was right.

Judge was indeed overprotective.

It was sweet.

"Congratulations on your boy, Judge," Patricia went on. "Jamie sent me photos. He's gorgeous."

Judge's, "Thanks again, Aunt Patty," was a little less hesitant this time.

Patricia turned to Dru and did the same. "Always so beautiful, just like your mother."

"Nice to see you again, Aunt Patty," Dru replied.

"This is Rix, Judge's best bud, and Sully, a good family friend," Jamie introduced. And after they all shook hands, he turned her to me. "And this is Nora, my future wife, when I get around to giving her a ring."

My entire body warmed, Patricia laughed, Judge and Dru grinned at each other, and Patricia moved in to embrace me.

"Lovely to meet you," she said in my ear, giving me a squeeze that was a mite overpowering, but I could take it.

"You as well," I replied.

We released each other, and she turned to the funeral home. "So, we got this shit to deal with."

"Yeah," Jamie agreed.

She looked to Jamie. "You ready to face the tyrant?"

"I've been in striking distance, Patty. The question is, are you?" Jamie asked.

"Brother boy, I've been psyching up for this for *decades*."

Jamie grinned at her, took my hand and curled it around his elbow, then ordered, "Judge, escort your aunt inside."

Judge offered his arm to Patricia, an offer she accepted, and in we went.

We'd timed it to be latecomers, and although there were a few people loitering in the vestibule, all of them turning our way with interest upon our arrival, Jamie didn't delay in leading us inside the chapel.

Standing at the back, two highly attractive women, one my age, one younger, both clearly related to each other, both who appeared to be waiting for our arrival, made their way right to us.

"Reid," Jamie greeted, giving the older woman a hug and me the knowledge of who she was.

Jeff's ex-wife.

So the younger woman was Greer, his daughter.

They both looked shaken, but neither appeared to be overly grieving or haunted. Perhaps because Jeff had left them, without affection or support, when he was done with his marriage and family.

More hugs, introductions and surprise that Patricia was there were exchanged before Greer announced, "We're up front."

"I don't think—" Jamie started.

"Damn straight we are," Patricia declared.

She then marched up the aisle to the front.

I had a feeling I was very much going to like Jamie's sister.

We all followed, and then I didn't know whether to gasp in shock or bark with laughter when Patricia made it to the first row, stopped, clicked her heels, and saluted AJ, who had Paloma seated beside him, before she greeted loudly, "Commandant Father."

There were titters among the mourners, and Jamie exhaled an amused sigh.

"On this day, we don't need your dramatics, Pat," AJ snapped, an interesting response to seeing his only daughter after decades.

"Of course, I forgot. This is a solemn occasion," Patricia replied, her tone belying her words.

Apparently, no love lost between Patricia and Jeff either.

AJ shifted in his seat to look at Jamie, and I pressed closer to his side.

"What are you even doing here?" he demanded.

"My brother died," Jamie drawled.

"Like you give a shit," AJ spat.

"We all don't consider family dispensable, AJ," Jamie retorted.

Was it only me, or did AJ flinch?

I took a moment to regard Paloma.

She was steadfastly faced forward, which was very unlike her. Paloma enjoyed oozing around the edges of a drama, and she was far from a wallflower.

Hmm.

Interesting.

Jamie took me out of my thoughts as he started directing our group to the empty front row opposite AJ and Paloma, which fortunately had ten seats, and that fit our entire crew. Jamie put Reid and Greer closest to the aisle, Patricia next to them, then him, me, followed by Dru, Judge, Rix and Sully.

It wasn't long before the service started, and it wasn't lost on me that the pastor who spoke the words had no idea who Jeff was, the light gray casket looked a bit (no other word for it)...*cheap*, there was a meager arrangement of flowers on top of it, and no other bouquets sent by friends and acquaintances scattered around.

Most awkwardly, when the pastor opened it up, no one came forward to say a few words about Jeff.

I had not met the man, nor had I heard a single word that was positive about him.

But I couldn't help but feel a sense of melancholy at this indication of a life so wasted.

I hoped, after it was over, we could get out and huddle in order to invite Patricia, Reid and Greer to enjoy the rest of the day with us. Or try to.

But Patricia had other ideas.

She got up and marched to her father, demanding, "I get it with me. You didn't have much use for women if they had a brain in their head or you couldn't sleep with them."

I pressed my lips together and watched AJ's face get red, Paloma's eyes narrow (ah, there was the Paloma I knew), but Patricia was far from done.

"But three of your grandchildren are standing right here, and you haven't said boo to them."

"They've all been disinherited," AJ retorted.

"Disinherited from what? Word I hear, you got a load of bupkis to lay on top of your other load of bupkis," Patricia shot back.

It was official.

I wouldn't pick the man's son's funeral as optimal timing for the messages she had to share.

But I liked her.

"I don't need this from you. I'm burying my son today," AJ snapped.

"Like you give a shit," Patricia was far from done. "The only one you cared about was Andy. Spoiled him so bad, he was useless in life, and died a useless death."

As an aside, AJ had another boy, his oldest. An inveterate playboy who died while on a yacht in Greece. He'd become inebriated, fell, hit his head then hit the sea. The only saving grace he'd had in his life was being unconscious while he drowned.

"One of the best days of my life was when you moved to a different continent," AJ returned.

"Thanks, Pop. Worked hard to make you proud," she sneered.

AJ turned to Paloma, and it wasn't the first time I noted what an odd pair they were, and this wasn't only that she was young enough to be his daughter.

She was tall and slender; he was round and squat. She was still a stunner; his personality wasn't the only unattractive thing about him.

She must be in hell.

"Let's go, baby," AJ muttered.

"That two hundred K…" Jamie started.

Both AJ and Paloma turned to Jamie, but I thought it was interesting only Paloma paled.

"Waste of your failing resources," Jamie finished.

"What are you talkin' about?" AJ demanded.

Jamie tipped his head to the side as this new development unfolded, before he suggested, "Ask your girlfriend."

AJ looked up at Paloma.

"Let's just go, my love," she mumbled.

AJ stared hard at Paloma as Paloma worked hard not to meet any of our eyes, including AJ's, and she practically dragged the old man down the aisle.

They didn't form a two-person reception line to receive condolences.

In fact, they were gone by the time we were out, and Reid, Greer, Jamie and Patricia received perfunctory condolences, though it was clear they all had the "mourners" respect, it was just that none of that was aimed at Jeff.

Most assuredly a sad waste of a life.

When we were alone, and only a few souls lingered in the parking lot, Reid turned to us and invited, "The ranch is a ways away, and if you're staying in Dallas, makes the return trip farther. But we'd love it if you'd come on over. I'll put some steaks on the grill and Greer makes a twice-baked potato that can't be beat."

"I'm in," Patricia said immediately.

Jamie's gaze went through our group, and getting nonverbal assents, he said, "We'll follow you there."

"Interested to know what that two hundred K comment was all about," Patricia stated.

"Me too," Reid added.

"We have a lot of catching up to do," Jamie said.

They sure did.

CHAPTER 20

WRANGLER

Nora

$\mathcal{I}$ sat in a rocking chair on Reid's front porch, a light breeze blowing at the silk of my skirt, looking out at a green lawn, a neat, attractive, flagstone path that led to another house in the distance (Greer's), and a lot of land on the horizon.

I did this as the sun set.

Never in my life, not even to Jamie (unless under torture, I sensed I wouldn't be good under torture) would I admit that I found beauty in the stark scrub, multitudinous cacti and dusty mountains of Arizona.

And the same could be said for this watercolor Texas sunset, with the rolling plain that stretched to the skyline having become the entire world before me, in the distance, cattle grazing lazily.

The door opened, and I looked that way, thinking it would be Jamie seeking some peace (much like why I was out on that porch) after he shared all he had to share with his family.

Including his paternity.

It wasn't.

It was Reid coming out.

When we arrived, she changed into a shirt that had embroidery across the shoulders and a pair of Wranglers.

Something else I would only admit under torture: There was a small part of me that wanted to own one of those embroidered shirts.

She came to sit in the rocking chair beside me.

"If you want time alone..." I trailed off on my offer.

"Grieved that sumabitch years ago," she replied and started rocking. She finished on a mumble, "Shitty way to go, though."

No denying, it had been a shitty way to go.

"How's Greer taking it?" I asked.

Reid blew out a long breath, before she answered, "I can say I'm glad you all came down, Patricia showed, and Jamie had a lot of big news to take her mind off things. She wasn't close to her dad, but he was the only one she had."

Poor Greer.

"Indeed," I murmured.

Civilities over, she launched in.

"I know Jamie thinks he's got things under control, and it isn't like he doesn't know this, but I'm gonna tell you. AJ seems like a snake, but he's a cat. Sneaky. Lethal. And he's got nine lives."

Before I could say anything, her hazel gaze pinpointed on me.

"And yes, I'd put money down AJ put Jeff up to that arson shit, because Jeff would do anything for his dad. I also think AJ was genuinely hurting today. Jeff was the only kid who hadn't turned his back on him. Now he's very alone, because that woman with him doesn't have her heart in it, and AJ isn't dumb enough about women to think she does. But I also think he's gutted Jeff bit it in that fire, and not because it might make things iffy about him collecting the insurance."

Oh dear.

"Might make things iffy?" I asked.

She shrugged. "If AJ left any trail that fiasco was his idea, sure. His insurance companies are set to lose a shedload on that payout. They're gonna be poking around to find anything that might let them off that hook. And the police are all over it. Jeff has been a pain in their ass for a long time, and AJ's attitude about his kid being able to do whatever he wants on their patch or any other hasn't been their favorite thing. Word I heard, they're turning over every flake of ash on that ranch. So AJ better have covered his ass."

Interesting.

"Another thing, Nora," Reid went on. "I know Morgan Rawlins. Known him for years. He's a good man. His sons are good guys. But my sense is, Jamie doesn't think Morgan knows about him, when I can tell you, he does."

My heart skipped a painful beat.

She kept talking.

"It isn't that he told me. It's that I already knew, or at least I suspected. I knew Morgan was foreman at Oakbilly, Jamie's the spitting image of him, and Jamie looks a whole lot more like Boone and Cassidy than anything close to Andy or Jeff. And we both know, even if it wasn't his doing, Jamie hasn't stayed out of the spotlight. Boone and Cass might have missed it, because they wouldn't be looking for it, but Morgan's also quick as a whip, so I can guarantee he didn't."

Oh dear again.

Reid wasn't done. "Since you're here, and he's got both his kids with him, I'd lean on Jamie to head out to Morgan's place. If you want, I'll act as go between so Morgan and Belle have a heads up."

"We're all leaving tomorrow."

"I'd suggest you stay an extra day."

"I'll speak to him."

"That's good."

"I'm very sorry for you and Greer, Reid," I said quietly.

She stared at me hard, then she said, "Leave it to Jamie to find a fancy, rich, city girl with a heart of gold."

I leaned toward her and whispered conspiratorially, "Don't tell anyone."

She grinned. "Woman, if you think you're pulling wool over anyone's eyes, I'm sorry to inform you, you aren't."

I shrugged.

She kept grinning.

And we rocked in the cool Texas breeze watching the sun set.

I WAS DYING TO GET JAMIE TO MYSELF IN ORDER TO TALK TO HIM ABOUT what Reid had told me.

I was also dying to get his take on Paloma and AJ's differing responses to Jamie's mention of those two hundred thousand dollars.

But I would be foiled in both of these, at least for a while, because Patricia had left Reid's early so she could change her hotel to ours, and at Jamie's request, I'd texted her to let her know we were arriving, so she could meet us at the bar.

I was also taking a backseat to Dru, who was leaning into her father and holding his hand as we walked into the lobby of our hotel in Dallas after returning from Reid's, because Dru was new to this information about Jamie's origins, not to mention, much of the larger story about AJ.

Dru needed to see to her dad.

And I needed to let her see to her dad.

Last, Jamie wanted more time with his sister, and what I had to say could wait so he could have what he wanted.

Therefore, I was walking arm and arm with Judge when we entered the hotel, Rix on my other side, when Rix muttered, "Well, fuck and shit."

I looked to him to see his gaze aimed across the lobby and his expression was stricken.

But before I could turn that way, Judge said urgently, *"Dad."*

My attention shot to where Judge was looking, and my stomach dropped to my feet.

Because...

Damn.

Reid was not wrong.

Jamie looked very like the tall, straight, broad-shouldered, handsome man who had just a hint of silver threading his dark hair, even if I knew he was in his 70s.

Jamie stopped dead, and Judge, Rix and I all hurried to his side.

There, we all stared at Morgan Rawlins.

But Morgan Rawlins only stared at Jamie.

A jolt scorched through my body when I heard, "See I don't have to make the introductions. Thought this would be fun. And hot damn, I was right."

We were so focused on Rawlins, we didn't see AJ hovering behind him until he stepped out of the taller man's shadow.

Judge moved, so Rix moved, and he did this to prevent Judge from doing what Judge was intent on doing.

Laying hands on his not-grandfather.

"Judge, please don't," Dru begged, hanging tight to her father.

"I got some kick left in me, boy, so let him loose," AJ said to Rix.

Truly?

God, this pathetic, little man was also delusional.

"Not worth it, Judge," Jamie said by way of a command.

Judge stopped pushing against Rix's hold but fixated on his not-grandfather.

I got close to Jamie's other side just as AJ turned his attention to him.

"Told you, boy, all your life." AJ's gaze shifted to me, he sneered, and then he concluded, "Women are nothin' but whores."

I heard Rix and Judge scuffling again, but I had to pay attention to catching hold of Jamie's forearm in both of my hands so he wouldn't act on that slur against his mother, which AJ had also used to slur me.

But Jamie didn't move, nor did he speak.

He just regarded his not-father.

"Got nuthin' to say about that saint you thought was your mama steppin' out on her man?" AJ jeered.

"You know," Patricia entered the conversation, coming around at our sides. "This is what women get that men don't. Maybe it's because you all try to make us feel irrelevant. Not that we take that on, just that we aren't driven, at the end of our lives, to do pathetic shit to convince ourselves we still are. We just put our feet up and bake bread or take cruises or whatever strikes our fancy and enjoy it. I've been home barely a day, and it literally exhausts me, Pop, watching you work so hard to stay relevant."

"Never knew when to stop runnin' your fuckin' mouth," AJ bit at her.

"And that was a real problem for you, since you're one of those who don't think women are relevant, so anything coming out of my mouth was just an annoyance to you," she retorted. "Probably hurt, too, when you paid attention and realized I wasn't scared of you, I didn't respect you, and I was embarrassed of you to boot."

"Keep runnin' your mouth, Pat," AJ ground out his threat.

"Don't mind if I do," Patricia drawled.

"Patty," Jamie grunted.

She looked to him, then seemed to become aware of the situation, so she looked to Morgan Rawlins.

And at this point, Morgan Rawlins made an approach.

So at this point, Dru pressed closer to her dad, I did the same, and Judge and Rix flanked us.

Like AJ wasn't there, Morgan passed him and stopped a few feet in front of Jamie.

"I knew before he told me," he said, his gravelly voice deep and attractive. "You should know that."

"I knew before I saw you, you should know that," Jamie replied.

"Didn't reach out because I didn't know if it would cause you problems," Morgan continued.

"I didn't reach out because of the same."

"My wife knows about you. She knows about Cordelia too."

Cordelia, as a reminder, was Jamie's mother's name.

"Your boys?" Jamie asked if Morgan's sons knew they had a half-brother.

The man lifted his hand and scratched the back of his neck before answering, "Well, see, that's a little tougher."

"I understand," Jamie said quietly, and Morgan narrowed his gaze on him.

"It isn't that I'm not proud of you," he stated.

"Oh, for fuck's sake," AJ groused.

"You still here, old man?" Patricia bit.

"Patty," Jamie whispered.

She fell silent.

Morgan was so focused on his son, it was like this byplay didn't happen.

"Moment I saw your picture in the paper, when you ran in that touchdown to win regionals in the last five seconds your freshman year, I knew," Morgan said. He shook his head sadly. "Back then, I shoulda—"

Jamie cut him off. "If you did, she would have suffered, and we both know it."

Morgan drew a visibly rough breath into his nose.

"Was she happy in the end?" he asked.

"She was free," Jamie answered.

My eyes started stinging when I saw the wet in Morgan's.

And I whimpered out loud when Morgan asked, his voice no longer gravelly, but croaky, "Can I hug you, son?"

It was Dru who whimpered when Jamie stepped out of our hold and into his father's.

Judge wrapped his arms around Dru.

Rix curved his arm around my shoulders.

And Jamie hugged his dad.

I WAS PACING THE SUITE, MY PHONE TO MY EAR.

"I knew we should have gone with you," Mika declared.

"It happened in the lobby, dearest. I don't think Jamie needed a larger audience when he went through that," I replied.

"I'm talking about supporting *you*," she retorted.

I *so* loved my dear friend.

"I can so totally believe AJ is not Jamie's sire," she remarked.

I'd had the time to fill her in on a great deal.

And it was, indeed, very believable, and not only because it was true.

"So, he's…what? Catching up with him now?" Mika inquired.

"I left him in the bar with Morgan, Judge and Dru," I confirmed.

"Jamie was down with you leaving?"

"I think Jamie sensed that Morgan doesn't need Jamie's entire posse breathing down his neck at this juncture. His grandkids, yes. His woman and sister, not as much."

"Posse?" she teased at my use of a word I didn't think I'd ever used my entire life.

"I'm in Texas. When in Rome…" I trailed off.

She laughed then said, "You know what I love most about this?"

I knew what I loved most about it.

The fact that Jamie, right now, was sitting down with his real father, drinking bourbon with him.

"What?" I asked.

"That AJ thought this was a big play, that he'd fuck with Jamie's head, and kick Jamie's real dad where it hurts, but they ended it hugging."

Yes, that was a good part too.

"I think we're going to be longer here in Texas," I noted.

"Or you'll go back," she said.

"Yes," I agreed.

"And how was Paloma at the funeral?"

I stopped pacing, sat in an armchair and crossed my legs. "I didn't have a chance to tell you. Before we left New York, Rhys Vaughan left us a package."

"Really?" she asked, not hiding she was intrigued.

Ah, yes.

The mysterious Rhys Vaughan perked up everyone's attention.

"Really," I replied. "And in it was information to show that Paloma, through some shell companies, paid Chester Lynch two hundred thousand dollars."

She asked the same question I did. "Where did she get that kind of money?"

"Would you like me to guess?" I offered.

"Please do."

"Jamie told me there was quite a bit of value at that ranch. So I think she got it by pawning AJ's valuables, likely things he wouldn't notice missing. Because Jamie went fishing by mentioning it at the funeral, and it was obvious AJ knew nothing about it, but Paloma's face grew deathly pale."

"Well, that's interesting," she remarked.

"It was a long ride back from Reid and Greer's, so I had time to think, and what I think is that you don't poke the bear that's mauling you. AJ has so much on his plate simply to keep his head above water, he isn't considering messing with Jamie, even if he threatened to do it. The man is all bluster. And I certainly don't think, if he could get his hands on nearly a quarter of a million dollars, he'd give it to the likes of Lynch."

"He sure showed up with a wallop in an effort to fuck with Jamie this evening," Mika pointed out.

"That didn't cost him any money."

"Right. That makes sense," she mumbled. "So that's all Paloma in a bid to fuck with you?"

"Perhaps."

"Therefore, what we have is maybe AJ accidentally killing his son in an insurance fraud scam that also ended with the tragic deaths of four magnificent horses. And Paloma manipulating Roland and Chester Lynch for the sole purpose of screwing with your happiness because you made her persona non grata at a couple of Prada stores."

"I also made sure she was struck off every list for every event that's of any consequence in New York City, which is her preferred hunting ground."

"Oh yeah, and there's that."

There was that, and that was at the heart of it.

I didn't regret it. She was trying to harm Tom for falling in love with Mika. If a lover moves on, you take it like a woman.

But it had certainly made things inconvenient.

I had no idea when Jamie would arrive in our room. I'd left them down there nearly an hour ago. But I had one more thing to bring up with Mika, so I needed to do it fast.

"Have you noticed anything…mm… *curious* between Dru and Sully?"

"You mean that they're totally in love with each other and for reasons unknown aren't acting on it?"

I sat blinking at my fabulous shoe.

"In love?" I forced out.

"Totally. Tom and I have discussed it, and we think Sully believes Dru needs to get some life under her belt before he goes there. They met when she was still quite young, and so was Sully. Or he doesn't want to go there at all just in case it doesn't work out and it makes things awkward for the rest of us. I like to think it's the first, even if that's foolish, and risky, because Dru might find someone else in the meantime."

I thought about Sully, and suggested, "It could be he's waiting so he can have time to deal with his own issues."

"What issues?"

"I don't know. But it always struck me as odd, in getting to know him, and how close he is with his father, his brother, and how quickly that family melded when Duncan and Genny got together. You'd think Chloe, Matt and Sasha were his blood, and he's known them since he was born, when he's known them what? Perhaps four or five years?"

"This is true," Mika mumbled.

"So why did he get a job far away from all that when he graduated? Gage didn't. He went right to work with Judge, doing something that doesn't even use his degree. And Sully told us today that the firm in New York that has been trying to recruit him for ages just upped their offer. And he's seriously considering taking it. Which leads me to believe he's escaping something, and that something isn't in our *posse*."

I paused to listen to her chuckle.

Then I finished, "Because half that posse is in New York. He's escaping something else, my dear. Did he have a bad break with a girlfriend?"

"Not that I know of."

"Hmm," I hummed.

"Should we make subtle queries to investigate?" she asked.

"Dearest, what a silly question. Of course we should," I drawled.

I listened to her laugh again.

We didn't talk much longer before we hung up, and I sat there, upending my phone on my knee, wondering if I should go down and check on Jamie, and I did this until the door opened.

I set my phone aside, took my feet and turned to Jamie.

He looked emotionally worn out.

So I used my feet to take me to Jamie.

He wrapped his arms around me, and I did the same to him.

"How did it go?" I whispered.

"It was a lot," he replied.

"I can imagine. Do you want to talk about it, or do you want some time away from it?"

He shook his head, guided us both to the couch, and brought us both down, pulling me into his arms again so I was twisted to him and resting my chest against his.

"He's headed home, and he's going to talk to his wife. They're going to figure out how to share about me with their boys. He asked me to give it some time just in case it didn't fly very well with them." When he saw my expression change, he went on hurriedly, "Not that he thinks they're going to pitch fits. But you have to agree, you reach your forties, and your dad tells you that you have an older half-brother, and he's me, they might need some time."

Yes, I had to agree to that.

"All right, darling," I murmured.

"Once that's done, we'll come back. So will Judge and Dru, though Dru might be difficult because she got the gig with Ashe. But that tour won't be running for a while, so hopefully they won't take that much time to get used to the idea of me."

"Hopefully."

"He was more worried about what was happening between AJ and me. It wasn't lost on him that AJ hit him up for the meet to do something spiteful and mean. He just refused to waste the opportunity presented him where he could meet me."

My God.

I loved that.

"I'm glad he didn't waste the opportunity," I said softly.

He gave me a squeeze. "Me too."

"This brings to mind that obviously, AJ knew who fathered you."

Jamie jutted up his chin. "Once I started to grow up, you have to admit, sweetheart, unless he was half-blind, it'd be hard to miss it."

Yes, seeing Morgan Rawlins live and in person, I had to admit that.

Jamie continued. "I'd seen pictures of my real father. Once I learned of him, I made certain of it. I simply thought AJ's pride blinded him to what was obvious."

"Why do you think he kept it a secret?" I asked.

"You don't play your ace until you know it's going to land precisely as you want it," Jamie answered. "Or hope you do. I've spent the last hour getting to know my dad, it felt good watching him with Judge and Dru. Judge has never had the opportunity to be close to his grandparents, not any of them, but now all of them are dead. And both Lindy's parents died before she did. Chet's parents were like Chet, so for Dru's sake, and frankly, for her safety, Lindy and I cut them out. It's wonderful they might have a chance to have a good man in their lives. But in the time I spent downstairs, I also had time to think, and AJ's always been hard on me. He's always been callous with me. So it isn't a surprise he knew I wasn't his, and even if I had no control over it, he found his ways to take that out on me."

I had nothing to say to that, no magic words to take that history away and give him, and his mother, something different.

Thus, the only thing I could do was stroke his jaw.

This I did.

His gaze grew sorrowful, and he whispered, "She would have loved me meeting him."

"Yes, she would."

"She would have been devastated about how Jeff died."

My poor, sweet Jamie.

"Yes, she would."

"She would have been ecstatic that Patty came home."

I smiled a shaky smile. "It would have been a rollercoaster day for Cordelia."

"Yes."

"As it was for you."

"Mm."

"Your sister is a firecracker," I noted.

The sorrow shifted from his eyes and humor lit them. "Always was."

"Any chance we can talk her into going back to New York with us?"

"She's taking this opportunity to visit some friends here she hasn't seen in a while. But when you were on Reid's porch, I asked her, and she said she had to take time off with short notice, so she can't. But she also said she'd be back."

"You don't talk much about her."

He lifted a shoulder. "Not much to say. She escaped dysfunction to live the simple life. She has a farm. Her husband is a farmer. She works in town at the post office. He had kids from a previous relationship, she never wanted her own, but she loves them. They grow wheat and barley. They all like each other and get along. And they vacation in Bali, Fiji and Thailand."

"So she has it made."

His arms got even tighter. "She's not the only one."

She absolutely wasn't.

I pushed up to kiss him softly.

Jamie angled his head to kiss me soundly.

When he broke it, there was yet another kind of light in his eyes.

"Let's go to bed," he murmured.

It was time to end a difficult day that had started all wrong, ended all right, and keep that last part going.

So that was what we did.

But I knew how much of a toll the day had taken on my Jamie.

Because, for the first time, he let me be on top.

CHAPTER 21

LIMOGES

Nora

$\mathcal{J}$ had never in my life had a sexual wrestling match with a man.

Or I hadn't, until right now.

By some miracle (unsurprisingly, I wasn't good at wrestling, but in my defense, Jamie was taller, bigger and stronger than I was), I got him on his back and managed to pin one of his wrists to the pillow by his head.

He shot me his beloved rogue's smile, which I took as a warning I wasn't going to have this position for very long.

Thus, I didn't dally.

I reached between us and wrapped my hand around his hard cock.

He hissed delightfully (oh *my*), stilled, and I took advantage, rubbing the head of his shaft through my wet before he caught. And then, at the same time, I slid down as he bucked up.

My head fell back at taking the fullness of him.

Jamie glided his free hand from my knee up my inner thigh and in, his thumb homing in on my clit.

I whimpered and rode, planting a hand in Jamie's chest for leverage, my eyes locked to his.

"You're so handsome," I whispered, my words breathy with effort and excitement.

"And you're fucking gorgeous," he growled.

He pulled his wrist from my hold, to lift it and fist his fingers in my hair at the back of my neck.

He held me there as we made love at the same time we fucked.

I started panting, Jamie put more pressure on his thumb, he started grunting, and then my orgasm hit me like it always hit me when given by Jamie.

I combusted, gasping and mewing and moaning through a transcendental climax.

In the midst of mine, I heard Jamie's, so after mine left me, I collapsed against his chest and burrowed my face in his neck.

He kept hold of my hair but slid the hand from between our bodies to wrap his arm around me and hold me close.

"I should have never let you have the top," he remarked, his deep voice thick and sexy.

I started laughing and pressed my face deeper into his skin, smelling his cologne, smelling Jamie, and closing my eyes as the bliss of understanding hit me.

A happily ever after wasn't always happy.

It was the "ever after" part that was.

In other words, you dealt with the fallout that life inevitably gave you, and then you went back to the joy of it.

Case in point...now, the Saturday after we went to Texas, Jamie and I were spending the day together in bed. Alyona had the entire weekend off. He was cooking for me later. But all weekend, we had no plans but to be together, eat together, nap together, sleep together and make love to each other.

I didn't need a superyacht.

I just needed my bed with Jamie in it.

As if to prove my point, his phone vibrated on the nightstand, evidence that life will leach into your happy.

But, just as long as you hold onto it, through all the ups, as well as the downs, you're good.

I lifted my head to look at him.

"I'm going to ignore it," he said.

With all that was swirling around us, we both knew he couldn't.

"Have a look," I replied. "I'll go clean up."

He nodded, and sadly, he didn't look happy about doing it. I touched my lips to his. When I was finished, he looked happy about that.

Then I slid him out, climbed off him and headed to the bathroom.

I saw to business, had my bra still on, and tried to decide if I should find my panties, or if they would be extraneous, all while I listened to the low murmur of his voice.

I returned to the bedroom (by the by, I decided not to bother with putting on my panties) just as he was setting his phone back to the nightstand.

I climbed into bed to the delightful invitation of Jamie's arms going wide, so I rested my chest on his, and he wrapped them around me.

"Who was it?" I asked.

"Nico," he answered.

I felt my brows go up.

Jamie didn't delay in giving me what I nonverbally requested. "He wanted to talk to me before he talked to you, because he knew you'd say yes, and he wanted to make sure it was okay with me before you said yes."

"Oh dear," I murmured, having an idea of what was coming.

"Yes, baby," he murmured in return. "He asked if he could move in here when they return from Vermont."

My heart squeezed.

"So, it's done," I stated.

"I could tell he didn't want to talk about it, but he's coming down every weekend, staying at their place, because they're sharing space during the week since there's no other choice. They're contractually obligated to teach those classes. But Felice has already found a room-mate to move in to help her with rent when she's back from Vermont, so Nico's out."

Felice didn't even let the grass die around their marital house.

I was glad I could more openly dislike that girl.

My mouth got tight, and Jamie didn't miss it.

"He says he's good with it. He's going to buy an apartment or find a co-op. He didn't want to rent in the first place. He thinks it's throwing away money, since he can't even claim it on his taxes. He just needs somewhere to be while he's looking."

"You two talked a lot in a short period of time," I remarked.

Jamie smiled. "We tend to lay it out there."

I would love him simply for being that man Nico could lay it out there to.

Fortunately, there was a lot more to love.

"Of course, you said yes he could stay here," I noted with mock severity.

That got him chuckling. "I did. Though, I wanted to run it by you the possibility of him staying at the brownstone. Work hasn't started, it probably won't for a while, and if it does, they can work around a living space for him. It'll set my mind at ease, having someone there. And he won't feel like he's third wheel to what we have going on here."

I melted deeper into him, "That's a lovely thought, Jamie. Feel free to suggest it, and I'll make sure he knows, if he wants to be home for a while, he's still welcome here."

"We have a plan," Jamie murmured.

I kissed his jaw, then his chin, before I parroted, "We have a plan."

He rolled us to our sides and tangled our legs together.

"Since we're taking a break from fucking," he started.

"A *short* break," I put in.

His blue eyes were dancing when he stated, "I'm not a machine, woman."

"You're my pleasure machine."

He burst out laughing.

"Well, you are," I declared.

He continued laughing and only stopped in order to press a hard kiss on my mouth.

"So, while I recalibrate," he started again, his lips still twitching.

"Yes?" I urged him to go on.

The residual amusement swept from his features, and he said quietly, "I'm pulling back from AJ."

I felt my eyes go wide.

"He might get the insurance and live another day," Jamie continued. "He might not. If he doesn't, the ranch will be mine, and I can make decisions then, and now I can do it while talking to Morgan about how he feels about it. But at this point, he's a lost old man, stripped of everything he had, everything he was. His two sons are dead, and he put them in the ground. His daughter can't stand to be in his presence. I was after vengeance, for Mom, for Judge, for me, and I got it. Continuing to go at him now is just cruel."

My morally upstanding Jamie.

"I think the same about Paloma," I admitted. "Seeing her with your father, it was just... pitiful."

"Yes," he agreed.

"And you have Morgan now."

He did.

Since Morgan was clearly hoping to make up for lost time, he called Jamie every day, even if it was simply to share the news they got rain down in Texas.

I loved that for Jamie.

No, I *adored* it.

As such, Morgan had told his sons. They took it as expected, being Morgan Rawlin's boys, shock but quick acceptance. They were all discussing when we'd go back at a time when Judge could take Chloe and JT, which wouldn't be long from now.

And they'd already accepted our invitation to come to the as-yet-unscheduled adoption celebration for Dru and Jamie.

The whole family.

AJ didn't need to factor in that.

Paloma didn't either.

"Whatever they can do to us now will be like a needle thrown at armor," Jamie said. "They can't hurt us. I couldn't live with myself if I kept up the drive to hurt them."

"Agreed."

Jamie tucked some of my hair behind my ear, a sweet look on his face.

Then he asked, "Want a snack?"

"Please," I answered.

"Stay here." He gave me a quick kiss before he knifed out of bed. "I'll be back."

He pulled on some joggers and left the room.

I watched him go, then stretched languidly on the bed, before I pulled the sheet over my lower half.

And I waited for my man to get back and feed me.

Definitely my version of happily ever after.

IT WAS THE NEXT DAY, SUNDAY MORNING.

We were in the kitchen, sitting on the stools at the bar by the window.

Jamie had made scrambled eggs, bacon, potato hash and toast (he was an excellent cook, even breakfast, then again, his mother taught him).

He was reading *The New York Times.*

I was fielding texts about the next Sunday lunch, to be held at Allegra and Darryn's, something she wanted to do soon, so we'd have a chance to check in on how Nico was doing.

Therefore, I was on my phone when the call came in.

Elsa.

"Elsa," I told Jamie (and the brows he'd raised at me) as I took the call. "Hello, dear."

"I'm going to send you something via email," she said. "I'd suggest you go to your computer to watch it. This definitely needs to be consumed on a larger screen."

"What is it?" I asked.

"Just…enjoy," she replied.

And with that, oddly, she rang off.

I turned to Jamie. "She's sending me something to watch, and she says I have to do it on a computer."

"Something bad?"

I shook my head. "No, considering she sounded like she was trying not to laugh the short time we were on the phone."

"I could always use laughter," Jamie noted.

I could too.

We took our coffee and left our plates when we went to the PC in the study.

I woke it up, pulled up email, found the one Elsa sent not minutes before, and clicked on the link.

It was a video from a gossipy news site.

And the still was of Ryan of G-Force sitting in what looked like a living room.

"Well, shit," Jamie said.

Shit indeed.

I hit play.

The video started in a newsroom, with the commentor saying, "It appears things are going to get complicated for the struggling AJ Oakley after several men came forward to report the cash sales of some of the Oakley estate's prized possessions. Reportedly, this happened only weeks, and in some cases, mere days before Oakley's son, Jefferson, allegedly set fire to the entire compound on the ranch known as Oakbilly Gulch."

The video switched to Ryan in his living room, gesturing to a number of vintage Limoges trinket boxes sitting on a velvet lined tray.

"I bought all of these from Paloma just two weeks ago," Ryan was saying. "Along with this." He jiggled his wrist for the camera, showing off a slim, gold Cartier watch. "She would only accept cash, *real* cash. Not Venmo or something like that. I didn't really think much of it at the time. I mean, cash *is* preferred, *always.* Now, I wonder if it was for other reasons."

The camera panned to Bryan, who was seated next to Ryan, and he was holding a pair of, to my trained eye, what looked to be three and a half carat diamonds studs pinched between his thumb and forefinger toward the camera.

He put his hand in his lap.

"I bought these from her, and yes, she demanded cash," Bryan announced. He grinned cheekily at the camera. "They're for my mom for Mother's Day." He leaned forward. "They're Tiffany's." After delivering that morsel, he winked.

The camera panned over Ryan to Wallace, who was seated on Ryan's other side.

"We all bought things from her," Wallace reported. "All for cash. She had a whole load of stuff to look through. It was like having a What Goes Around Comes Around store right in Ryan's living room. Except with tacky boxes."

Ryan could be heard gasping before he snapped, "They're *Limoges.*"

Wallace kept speaking over Ryan. "She asked us to tell all our friends about the things she had. She *said* they were from her private collection, and she's Paloma Friedrichsen, so we didn't question it. But now, with what happened down in Texas, we wonder."

The screen cut back to the newsroom commentator. "All told, these gentlemen say they purchased around one-hundred-and-ninety-thousand-dollars'-worth of pre-owned merchandise from Ms. Friedrichsen, and they're aware that friends and acquaintances made even more purchases. It's been noted by the police in Texas that a number of these items, which were listed on an inventory AJ Oakley provided to them, such as the diamonds in jewelry, wouldn't perish in a fire, even one that blazed as hot as the one in Oakbilly Gulch. Efforts are ongoing, but as yet, police report very few valuables have been recovered. It appears Mr. Oakley, and his girlfriend, ex-supermodel Paloma Friedrichsen, might have some uncomfortable explaining to do before they're able to collect what has to be a sizeable insurance payout after the disaster at Oakley's family ranch. We'll keep an eye on this story, and report as it progresses."

The video ended and I turned to Jamie.

He was looking down at me.

Fighting a gleeful smile (he and I did agree not to kick them now that they were down...*still*), I got up and walked (all right, it was more like ran-walked) back to my phone in the kitchen, whereupon I immediately called Teddy.

"Let me guess, you saw it," Teddy drawled as his greeting to my call.

"Did they really buy those things from Paloma?"

"They absolutely did. The deals were insane, darling. But they thought it was like a Paloma's Dying Breath Closeout sale, which, in and of itself was something to celebrate. Even so, they had no idea she was unloading AJ's belongings prior to what it seems this is about... that man attempting insurance fraud."

"I'm not certain AJ knows those things were missing," I shared.

There was a moment of silence before, "Well, that makes it even more delicious, don't you think?" Teddy asked. He didn't give me time to answer, probably because there was only one answer (that being "yes"). "They had other ideas up their sleeves to stop her shenanigans against you, but when Paloma sought them out, they were simply going to spread the word she was so desperate, she was having a clearinghouse sale of all her best pieces, something they did. Nothing makes a woman hide her head in shame more than being forced to divest herself of the items she *worked very hard for.*"

His inference wasn't even slightly veiled.

I so adored Teddy.

"Obviously," Teddy carried on, "when they saw the news about the fire, they put two and two together, and they contacted the police. That is, they did that before they contacted the media."

And I absolutely *adored* the G-Force.

I felt Jamie come in and watched him regain his stool.

I wasn't certain what his expression was relating, so I said to

Teddy, "I need to go. Tell them their last visit to the closet was just for fun. And you and I need to go shopping."

"You do know you don't need to take me shopping, and you don't need to give them anything else. We love you, Nora."

"We'll discuss it later, dear. Lunch this week?"

"Obviously. Ta-ta, darling."

"Goodbye, Teddy." I hung up and focused fully on Jamie. "Are you all right?"

"If AJ's smart, he'll press charges for theft."

I said nothing, and not because Jamie kept talking, because I didn't know what to say, and I still wasn't certain about his mood.

"At this juncture, I have no idea if he'll be smart. I don't know if he'd be able to live with everyone knowing his girlfriend was with him to steal from him, or if he'd better be able to live with an arrest for insurance fraud. I know that sounds ludicrous, but it's true, because that's the kind of man he is. And he's this regardless that he has to know fraud like that is a felony. At those amounts, he'd definitely be looking at massive fines and prison time. And he doesn't have the money to pay a lawyer, and anything she left for him went down with that fire."

"Jamie," I said gently. "He must throw Paloma under the bus. I can't believe I'm saying this, but he needs the insurance money."

"He needs the insurance money," Jamie murmured before picking up his phone.

I sat watching as he moved his thumb over the screen before putting the cell to his ear.

He caught my gaze briefly before he got up and moved toward the dining room, saying, "Yes, AJ, it's me. We need to talk."

Ugh.

My poor Jamie.

I turned back to our plates.

Jamie had cleaned his. What was left on mine was now cold, but regardless, I was no longer hungry.

Thus, I took them to the sink, rinsed them, swiped them with the handled sponge Alyona kept close, and put them in the dishwasher.

I set the skillets to soak and wiped down the counters so when Jamie was ready to make us lunch, he had a tidy kitchen.

He came back, glanced around and said, "I could have helped with that."

"It wasn't much." I went to him and put both hands on his chest, he rested his on my waist, and I leaned into him. "I didn't hear any shouting."

"He asked if I'd buy the ranch."

This was such a surprise, I sucked my cheeks into my teeth and bit them.

"Cute," Jamie muttered, his gaze on my mouth.

I let my cheeks go and urged him to continue by saying, "Darling."

"He did not know Paloma was stealing from him. He's going to be pressing charges."

My heart thumped with the shock of receiving confirmation of that news.

Jamie carried on, clearly reading my reaction. "He has no choice, sweetheart. It's either put her down or go down with her. And I believe him when he says he had no idea she was taking things. I asked him about Chet, and he didn't even know who that was."

Truly, the woman needed to learn how to lose a lover.

"Are the G-Force going to lose their money?" I queried.

Jamie sighed. "I can make them whole, but, probably. Those items weren't hers to sell. And unless she can prove that AJ gave them to her, as stolen property, they'll have to be returned."

I hoped the G-Force knew that before they called the police and the media.

"I don't know if the fire was his idea or Jeff's," Jamie went on, "because he didn't get into the fire. All I know at this point is, who I just talked to was a shattered man with all the fight kicked out of him. He's humiliated. Paloma humiliated him. The only thing he has is that land, and if it goes through, the insurance payout. He wants to sell the land to me for what he owes on the note, which is not what it's worth, especially now there's no house or outbuildings on it, so that won't be happening. But if he can get the payout, drill down the note, I'll purchase it from him at a price the market will bear, and, from what he says the payout will be, he'll have a nice sum to find someplace comfortable to live out the rest of his life."

"Did you tell him you'd buy the ranch for a fair price?"

"Yes."

"Was the call…antagonistic?"

Jamie suddenly appeared in mild pain. "He…" Jamie shook his head. "Fuck, Nora, he thanked me for calling."

Oh, *my Jamie.*

I slid a hand up to curl it around his neck. "It seems, in some cases, revenge isn't very sweet."

"This isn't that, darlin'," he declared. "He's not going to wheedle his way in because I'm the last one he's got, and I'm not even his. But I'm not going to let the man my mother loved once in her life, even if he conned her into that love, end up homeless or whatever is to become of him."

"You're a good man, Jamie."

"I'm my mother's son, Nora."

"Yes, like I said, you're a good man, Jamie."

His smile was small, but at least it was there.

"Paloma is in real trouble, isn't she?" I asked.

"AJ said he doesn't know all that she took, he does know it seems like it was hundreds of thousands of dollars' worth of property, so, yes. She's in a good deal of trouble."

I'd never experienced it before, but I was experiencing it then.

This being that fact that revenge sometimes actually felt awful.

Jamie slid his arms fully around me and suggested, "Let's not let this ruin our day."

"Okay then. Let's curl up in the hearth room and watch movies all day. We can make popcorn later. I think Alyona has one of those popcorn-popping gadgets, because she's made it for me before."

"Sounds good," Jamie agreed.

I got up on my toes to press my mouth to his.

He angled his head and deepened the kiss.

Jamie then let me go and went to the hearth room to fire up the TV.

I rinsed out our coffee mugs and put them in the dishwasher.

Then I joined him.

———

GETTING AHEAD A LITTLE BIT...

IN THE END, ALTHOUGH IT WAS IMPOSSIBLE TO TELL AFTER THE destruction of the fire, it was estimated that Paloma stole nearly a million dollars' worth of valuables from the Oakbilly Gulch estate.

She also took what was left of the proceeds of her sales of purloined merchandise and fled to the UAE. She did this within days of Jeff's funeral.

The UAE has no formal extradition treaty with the United States.

Nevertheless, deals between the countries could be made.

It was just that Paloma had been last seen entering the property of an obscenely well-off, as well as well-connected, not to mention quite elderly, sheik.

In other words, the police couldn't take her into custody for extradition talks to begin, because she disappeared in Dubai.

I had no idea what became of her, because she was never seen, or heard from, again.

———

AJ, ON THE OTHER HAND, RECEIVED THE INSURANCE PAYOUT.

There was no evidence that Jeff hadn't acted alone, and considering Jeff's reputation, it wasn't hard to believe that was true, and he came up with that lamebrained scheme to help out his father who was having a tough time.

We would never know.

AJ paid down the note, but sold to Reid and Greer, saying that would keep the Oakley ranch "in the family."

This wasn't a snub to Jamie. It was partially because Morgan said he had enough to handle, and Boone and Cass agreed, so Jamie had no use for that land.

I sensed Morgan's decision was also at least partially because he didn't want the memories of that place, bittersweet as they were, and he also didn't want his wife to face them, considering who the sweet part was.

AJ bought a modest property in Dallas, and mercifully, was forced to live in it for only six months, before he died of a heart attack while watching the Cowboys on TV.

Jamie told me that was the way he'd want to go.

And for the first time when it came to AJ Oakley, I was glad he got what he wanted.

———

Last, Jamie, Dru, and Judge had a Skype where they all decided to keep the Oakley name.

They did this because it was one of the names that defined Cordelia in her life, all of these names Jamie carried within his own, because she gave them to him.

Morgan, who was a very affable man, didn't feel slighted.

But that might be because Jamie legally added Rawlins before the Oakley, Dru would as well when she was adopted, and not only did Judge do it too…

He added it to JT's name.

EPILOGUE

HARRY WINSTON

Jamie

*I*t was Monday morning after his quiet weekend with Nora. Jamie was behind his desk in his office when Monica knocked then stuck her head in.

"I'm sorry, Jamie," she started when she got his attention. Along with the concerned expression on her face, giving him more indication he wasn't going to like what she had to say, she came in and closed the door, walking right to his desk before she shared, "There's a man downstairs who's demanding to talk to you. I asked security to escort him out, but he's being difficult, and loud, and he's claiming he's Dru's real father."

Jamie felt a muscle jump in his cheek.

Chet's latest meal ticket being in the wind (he was referring to Paloma, who AJ had reported during their phone call had "disappeared"), Jamie wasn't surprised Chet was now making a direct play.

He was annoyed, extremely annoyed, but he wasn't surprised.

Normally, Jamie would instruct Monica to have security deal with him and call the police if it became necessary.

But frankly, he was fed up with this shit.

Not to mention, with all that had happened recently, Jamie was also in the mood to be direct. And his version of direct was to deal with every annoyance that was dimming what was a bright future for him and everyone he loved.

And do it once and for all.

"Have him brought up, but ask security to accompany him," Jamie said to Monica. "Have them remain with you in your office while I deal with him in here. They can escort him out when I'm done."

Monica nodded and retreated.

As he waited for Chet to be brought up, Jamie considered texting Nora to let her know this was happening.

But he decided against it. He could give her the full story when it was all said and done. If he told her now, she'd fret until she knew it was over, and that was the last thing he wanted.

Two security guards escorted Chet in, and Jamie nodded to them that they could leave, which they did.

Chet stood opposite where Jamie sat at his desk, and he saw what Nora was talking about when she described his appearance.

The man looked rough, like he'd lived five years for every one of Jamie's. His face was lined and drawn, his once-broad shoulders were stooped, his once-thick hair now lank and fully gray, and it appeared he'd lost at least two inches of height, if not more.

When Chet seemed happy to stand there and glare at Jamie, Jamie started it.

"You'll pardon me if I don't offer you a seat."

"I wanna talk to my daughter," Chet spat.

Jamie raised his brows. "Sorry, do you have a daughter?"

Red crawled up Chet's neck. "Fuck you," he bit.

"Do you think that kind of talk is going to get you what you want?" Jamie asked calmly.

Chet's nostrils flared. "I got things I wanna explain to her."

"That's unfortunate, because I can assure you, whatever they are, she doesn't want to hear them."

"So, you stole them from me, both of 'em, and now you talk for her too?" Chet sneered.

"I see you've fallen on the strategy of revising history in order to be able to live with the man you are and what you've done," Jamie noted.

Chet threw a hand Jamie's way. "How was I supposed to compete with the likes a' you?"

"I don't know," Jamie drawled sarcastically. "Perhaps not stalking your ex, not beating her to make her become your ex, and giving that first shit about your daughter in the way a father should, rather than using her to extort money from me."

Chet moved his head like he was stretching the side of his neck before he proclaimed, "I wouldn't a' done that shit if I wasn't in a bind."

"You seemed to get in binds quite often. Including recently, taking money from Paloma Friedrichsen in order to cause more harm to Rosalind and Dru by sharing your revisionist history with anyone who might listen to it."

Chet didn't reply to that, but his eyes did flash with alarm at hearing all Jamie knew.

Instead, he jutted his chin stubbornly and stated, "I think it should be Drusilla's decision whether or not she wants to hear what I gotta say."

Jamie nodded. "You're correct. It should be. In fact, it is. She's an adult. She has resources. If she didn't wish to use those, she knows she can utilize mine. Therefore, if she wanted to find you, she would. That said, I suspect she doesn't want to see you, not only because she hasn't, nor has she asked me to find you, but also, considering that decision is now hers, she requested I adopt her officially. And although it's only a document to make what we already have official, it's important to the both of us, so we're in the process of doing that."

The pain and defeat in Chester Lynch's face at hearing this news was worth every bane Jamie had endured at this man's hands.

Not the ones his girls had endured, those Chet could never make up for.

But the ones Jamie had endured, absolutely.

AJ and Paloma's downfalls had left Jamie feeling morose and hollow. He was lucky, in the midst of all of that, Morgan Rawlins had become a part of his life in a way he was making perfectly clear he wanted a place in it, which shined a bright light through that darkness.

This victory, on the other hand, felt fucking phenomenal.

"She's the only kid I got," Chet stated.

"She actually isn't," Jamie returned.

Chet blinked in confusion. "What?"

"She isn't yours, Chet," Jamie said with studied patience. "She hasn't been yours since she was five."

"She's my blood," Chet ground out.

"You donated sperm," Jamie replied. "Congratulations. Other than that, you made her mother's life hell, as well as hers, every time you reared your head. That's what she's got from you. That's *all* she's got from you because that's all you gave her."

"I loved Rosie," Chet said softly, and if Jamie could credit it, there was regret in his eyes.

"That isn't close to true, considering how you treated her."

"We were young," Chet defended.

Fuck this asshole.

Jamie was done.

He stood, and he enjoyed watching Chet's eyes tip up as he did so.

Jamie's tone was cold and lethal when he declared, "I don't give that first fuck how young you were. That's no excuse. If you, a grown man, don't know that by now, there's no hope for you. You don't treat the ones you love with violence and intimidation."

"You don't know my life before Rosie came in it. She caught the brunt of me sorting shit out."

"I don't have that first fuck to give about your life either, Lynch," Jamie fired back. "That's an excuse too. And like all excuses, it's spineless and full of shit. And advice, if Dru does decide to seek you out, which is something that will be her choice *and* at her instigation, I'm not going to tell her about this conversation. She has to want to find you and it has to be her idea. But if that happens, don't land this bull- shit on her. She won't respond to it very well because she's highly intelligent and she'll read it for exactly what it is."

"It's all been so fuckin' easy for you," Chet scorned and threw his hand again toward Jamie. "Good-lookin', made a' money, probably took your first steps on a red fuckin' carpet."

"This is part of growing up, something it's clear you haven't done. But when you do, you realize, no matter what you think someone else has, they're living life just like you, and sometimes that life kicks them in the balls. The measure of a man is how he recovers from that."

"Yeah, and you recovered from Rosie real quick by nailin' that new, haughty piece of ass of yours," Chet shot back.

Jamie's voice was now low and deadly when he warned, "I'm keeping myself in check, Lynch. You'd do well not to remind me you put hands on my woman."

Chet visibly swallowed.

"Or, *another* of my women," Jamie corrected.

Chet said nothing.

"Are we done?" Jamie asked.

"I wouldn't a' hurt her," Chet said quietly. "I took that bitch's money, but I wasn't gonna say shit to hurt her."

"You're lying. I know you were talking to a news program."

Another visible swallow.

Oh yes.

Fuck this asshole.

Jamie continued. "Now, I can share with you that I will make it hurt if you try to approach Dru without her initiating it, but I'm assuming, since you're here, rather than bothering her, you already know that. However, if you've heard nothing I've said during this conversation, make certain to process that. She's lost her mother. She's lost the only blood who mattered to her.

She might be living her life, but she will never stop being devastated by that loss. If you cause her even a second more pain, by God, Lynch, I promise you'll regret it until your dying breath."

Chet stared at him but remained silent.

"Am I clear?" Jamie pressed.

"Clear," Chet grunted.

"Fantastic. Now get out," Jamie demanded.

He sat behind his desk and turned his attention to his laptop.

Chet hesitated only a second before he walked out on his own.

Ten minutes later, Monica stuck her head in and assured him Chet had left the building.

Only after the door closed on her, did he call Nora.

She demanded they cancel their dinner reservations for that evening so they could have a quiet night in, and Jamie translated that to: so she could look after him.

He demanded that they didn't, because that was the last time Chester Lynch was going to darken their lives.

His Nora always looked beautiful, even in a designer tracksuit with only mascara on her lashes.

But that night, she'd pulled out all the stops.

Therefore, when Jamie walked into the restaurant at her side, he was so proud, and so looking forward to good food and his woman's company, Chester Lynch wasn't even a memory.

In other words, Nora did what Nora was prone to do.

She found her way to look after him, no matter what.

"I'M RETHINKING THIS SUNDAY LUNCH SHIT," ARCHIE MUTTERED, sitting with Jamie and Nico in Allegra and Darryn's living room.

"Word," Nico agreed.

Both men took sips of their bottles of beer.

Jamie said nothing.

After being starved of a functional family while growing up and well into adulthood (until he met Lindy), he was always at one with any family time, no matter if the chaos that was currently ensuing at the dining room table was both confusing to follow, and even if it wasn't, he didn't have a lot of interest in it.

The results when they came, he was definitely interested in.

The road to get there, not at all.

This was because the women, with Darryn inputting regularly, were poring over some of the preliminary design schemes for the brownstone, at the same time they were discussing a variety of gowns for a variety of events, including Dru's adoption party. Not to mention, they were dissecting, with minute attention to every detail, plans for said party.

"You don't seem bored outta your skull," Archie observed to Jamie.

Jamie tipped his head toward the dining room table. "They're happy."

Archie looked that way.

Nico looked that way.

And both men with him settled in after they did, because when your loved ones were happy, that happened.

"Oh my God, Dru! Look at this dress!" Valentina shouted and shoved her phone in Dru's face.

"Oh my God!" Dru shouted back. "That's it!" She pulled Val's phone out of her hand and extended it to Nora. "What do you think?"

Nora glanced at the phone and decreed, "Perfection, dearest. Order it immediately."

Dru handed Val's phone back in order to dig out her own.

"They need a bed-length bolster pillow," Darryn declared.

"You and those bolster pillows," Allegra replied.

"Baby, they're the shit," Darryn said.

"Mom reads, and she says Jamie reads too. They need reading wedge pillows."

Darryn appeared revolted. "Those are ugly as fuck."

"They're useful. Not everything has to be about aesthetics," Allegra retorted.

"Since when?" Darryn asked.

"I'm *so* not coming to Sunday lunch when D and A start redesigning Momma Nora's place," Archie muttered.

"Word," Nico said.

As an aside, Nico had taken Jamie up on the offer to move into the brownstone when his courses ended in Vermont so he could keep an eye on it. Jamie was grateful because a home needed to be inhabited for more than safety. Nico was grateful because he didn't want to interfere with Nora and Jamie's new situation (even if it didn't feel new, it was), and it gave him a chance to take time to pick his own place and make it the right one.

The apartment phone buzzed, sharing someone was out front, and Darryn got up from the table to get it.

"Dearest, we need cake, so we'll have to make a cake tasting appointment, *tout de suite*," Nora said to Dru.

Now they were on about the adoption party.

"We don't have to have a big, elaborate cake, Nora," Dru replied.

Nora appeared stunned before she assumed her *Now, listen to me, I'm imparting wisdom on you* expression.

She then imparted wisdom.

"My beautiful girl, unlike most of the rest of the population, essentially, you've managed to be able to have *two* birthdays. As every woman knows, her birthday is *the most important day of the year*. More important than Christmas. More important even than her anniversary. It reigns supreme. You get *two*, darling. And if from this day forward you don't celebrate yourself to the absolute fullest on both, I'm disinheriting you. We're having an extravagant cake for your first one. No argument. I'll set up a tasting."

Jamie was careful to make note of his woman's views on birthdays as Nora started scribbling in her Mètier notebook that he'd long-since learned was the nerve center to all Nora's magic, and Dru turned to look at her dad. His girl's face was beaming with wonder mixed with happiness at the thought of having two birthdays.

Jamie had no idea he could love his daughter more, or Nora.

But in that moment, he knew he could, because he did.

Both of his girls.

Darryn's raised voice suddenly cut into the space. "I won't say it again, *back off*."

Everyone's attention turned to Darryn, but only Allegra got up and went to him.

She put her hand on his back as he listened on the phone, and he shook his head at her questioning look.

"You got some pretty big balls to pull this shit again," Darryn said into his phone.

At that, Jamie turned his attention to Nora. He tensed when he saw her face had paled.

"Is it Dad?" Allegra asked.

"Yup," Darryn answered.

Allegra held up her hand. "Let me talk to him."

"Nope," Darryn denied.

"Honey," she whispered.

Darryn's mouth grew tight, then he said into the phone, "Allegra wants to talk to you."

He handed over the phone, but he didn't move an inch out of his wife's space.

And Jamie was reminded just how much he liked Nora's son-in-law.

"Dad?" she said. She listened. She listened longer. Finally, she went on, "Okay. I'm hanging up the apartment phone. I'll call you if they say it's all right. I'll text if it's not, and then you have to promise to go."

Jamie blew out a sigh which corresponded with Nico mumbling, "Fucking shit," and Archie grousing, "Fuck me."

Allegra hung up the phone, turned to the room at large, but homed in on her mother.

"Dad's downstairs," she told them something they all knew.

"God! Did you tell him *again* we're having our family lunch and that's why he's here, messing up our family lunch?" Val accused her sister through a question.

"It shits me to say this," Nico put in. "But that was me."

"For fuck's sake, why? And when?" Val demanded of her brother.

"He called. He's been calling," Nico shared. "I've been ignoring him or answering and telling him to fuck off. It was stupid, I see that now, because a couple of days ago, in the middle of telling him to fuck off, I told him about lunch. But I did it to rub it in we're all good when he's not around."

"Actually, a boss play," Archie approved under his breath.

"He says he has something to tell us," Allegra announced. She turned uncertainly to Jamie. "I'm sorry, Jamie. He said it's something about AJ Oakley and some woman."

Fantastic.

Nico stood. "I'll go down and tell him to kiss off."

Val stood. "No, I will."

Nora stood. "No. Allegra will buzz him up, and we'll hear what he has to say."

Jamie got an acid taste in his mouth, but he said nothing.

"Mom," Valentina snapped.

"He's your father," Nora reminded her gently.

"You're too nice to him," Val returned.

"I love you, my darling girl, so it's with love when I say, maybe you're not nice enough," Nora replied, still going gently.

Val shut her mouth.

Allegra was on her phone.

Seconds later, the apartment phone buzzed again, and she hit the button to let her father in the building.

Jamie got up and moved to Nora.

"I'm all right," she told him the minute he was at her side.

"I know. Me being at your side is about me staking my claim."

She rolled her eyes and scoffed, "You hardly have to do that."

"Do we have to have a certain conversation again?" he asked.

Since he was talking about the one that referred to his cock, he saw her mouth quirk, her eyes flash with humor, and she shook her head.

Roland came in, and along with being happy he'd given Nora a moment of amusement before her ex showed, Jamie was glad he switched locations.

Because the man glanced at his children, but when he saw Nora, his gaze riveted on her, and his expression became ravaged.

"You were attacked?" he whispered.

He felt Nora stiffen, so Jamie moved into her and slid an arm around her waist.

"How did you—?" Nora began.

But Roland shook his head and cut her off. "It doesn't matter. I had no idea. I...I wanted you back. She told me she felt guilt for...for what transpired, and she wanted to help me do that, and she would, if I helped her get AJ out of financial trouble."

And the last puzzle piece slipped into place.

"I had no idea she...she'd..." he trailed off, his gaze moving to Jamie, then to Dru, and at that, Jamie knew Roland also had learned that Paloma had set Chet on them, including Chet assaulting Nora.

"This situation has been handled, Roland, so you needn't trouble yourself with it," Nora declared.

"I had no idea, darling," Roland whispered.

At the endearment, Jamie was unable to keep his silence, but he still spoke no words. Instead, he made a low noise of warning.

Roland's head jerked before he quickly, and surprisingly, said to Jamie, "Not my place, I'm sorry." He returned his attention to Nora. "I'm so sorry." He took a step back, looked at each of his children in turn, and again to Nora, he said, "That's all I wanted to say. In front of you. Our children. I'm sorry. Truly sorry. For all of it, Nora."

Without hesitation, Nora replied quietly, "Apology accepted."

Valentina was right, she was too nice to him, but that wasn't Jamie's call.

It was also part of why he loved her, that big heart she hid behind the uppity society dame, a heart that led her to him, time and again, over decades, and also led her to waiting for him to get his head out of his ass so they could have what they now shared. Thus, he also couldn't complain.

Roland looked to Allegra. "I love you."

She nodded, tears in her eyes.

He turned to Val. "And you."

His second daughter just stared at him.

Roland finally looked to Nico. "And you, son."

Nico said nothing, but held his father's gaze, his own contemplative and not shut down, like Val's had been.

"I'll leave you to your lunch," Roland murmured, then to Darryn, "Thank you for letting me in."

"Not my idea, man," Darryn replied, making it clear he wasn't over it.

Roland nodded, slid his gaze through his ex-wife and children again, and finally walked out.

The minute the door closed, Val launched in. "Allegra, if you told him about what happened to Mom—"

"I didn't tell him," Allegra asserted.

"I didn't either," Nico put in.

"Definitely not me," Archie said.

"Me either," Darryn added.

"It wasn't a secret. I reported it to the police," Nora reminded them.

"Dad hardly has police informants," Val replied.

"You're right. What I'm saying is, Mika knew, Tom, Cadence, the first or the last of those undoubtedly told Teddy, which means..." Nora didn't finish, but she didn't have to.

Teddy told the G-Force, and probably others, and the news made its way to Roland.

"That was a nice thing to do, Dad coming here and saying all of that. Wasn't it a nice thing to do?" Allegra, who desperately wanted to be her father's champion, if he'd give her any cause, asked.

"So he can act not like a dick one time and he gives a minimal shit about the woman who bore his children. Big whoop," Valentina, who desperately wanted to hold on to her hurt so she wouldn't get hurt again, returned.

Allegra pressed her lips together miserably.

"It was a cool thing to do," Nico proclaimed, and everyone looked at him, but he was looking at Jamie. "Right?" he asked, like Jamie could answer, which he couldn't. "Hat in hand, as it were, tail between his legs, putting his pride aside, making it about what it should be, an apology to Ma, it was a cool thing to do."

Since no one said anything, and Nico was still looking at Jamie, Jamie had to say, "You're right, Nico. It was a cool thing to do."

He felt Nora's arm wrap around his waist and she squeezed.

He squeezed in return.

"Do I need to break out the vodka, or are we down with deciding bolsters versus reading wedges?" Darryn asked, then he looked down at his wife. "And just to say, reading wedges are never gonna win, baby. I mean, do you know your mother?"

Allegra turned to Nora.

"They *are* rather unattractive, dear," Nora said.

"God, I married my mother, in hot-tall-brilliant-guy form," Allegra complained.

Darryn grinned wide and white.

Nora squeezed Jamie's waist again.

"Dad, do you want to see the dress I'm going to wear to the adoption party?" Dru asked.

"No, darlin', when I see you in it, I want you to stun me with your beauty yet again," Jamie answered.

Dru shot him another beam.

"I love this fuckin' guy," Val announced. She then stated, "We're all good, but you can still break out the vodka, D."

"Yankees are playin', man," Archie reminded Darryn.

"Fire it up, brother," Darryn replied as he headed to the kitchen for the vodka.

Archie reached for the remote.

Nora let him go, sat back down and reached for the design sheet of the primary bedroom.

Jamie headed back to the living room.

Darryn abandoned interior design for baseball, and the men sat around the TV, watching the Yankees, while the women remained at the dining room table, spending money.

Oh yes.

Jamie loved family time.

Any way he could get it.

Nora

"Someone turn the furnace down."

I shifted my attention from Jamie, looking resplendent in his dinner jacket, to Byron, who I was standing with.

"In...*deed*. We're all about to catch fire," Bryan, who was also standing with us, added.

Although I felt quite comfortable, I became alarmed. "Do I need to talk to management about adjusting the thermostat? Are you uncomfortable?"

"No, doll," Ryan joined the conversation. "They're talking about the lipstick on Jamie's collar, and the looks you two have been scorching across the room at each other since you got here."

Jamie was in a very good mood. Jamie had just officially adopted his beloved daughter. Jamie's son and daughter-in-law were there. Jamie's grandson was with his cousin Laird being babysat by Elsa's mother. Jamie's real father, his wife, and Jamie's half-brothers were there.

Jamie was in his element.

This being, surrounded by people he loved.

As such, prior to us coming out tonight, things had become rather...

Heated.

Delightfully so.

"It's not like she doesn't look at him *all the time* like she wants to devour him," Wallace put in.

"Or like she's remembering *having been* devoured by him," Ryan said.

"Or like she's preening, because he's staring at her like he wants to devour her," Wallace added.

"Or like he's remembering how he just devoured her," Ryan kept at it.

"I'm jealous, I want a man to look at me like he wants to devour me," Byron complained.

"Step behind me in that line," Bryan muttered.

But I was struck.

I turned my attention back to Jamie, only to find him watching me. When he saw my gaze on him, his danced down the length of me, back up to my face, whereupon he smirked in the most delightfully *scrumptious* way.

Yes, it was like he was remembering devouring me, and he didn't mind that I got lipstick on his collar when he did so.

Oh my.

"So, do tell," Ryan said, and as politeness dictated considering he was talking to me, I tore my attention from Jamie to give it to Ryan. "What's it like having it all?"

There was only one response to that.

Thus, I gave it to him.

"It is, of course, darling, *everything*."

Ryan smiled at me.

I smiled at Ryan, and all the boys.

I then moved my smile to Jamie, who was now talking to Tom, Dru had joined him, and father and daughter had their arms around each other.

Yes.

Having Jamie in my life…being able to claim Jamie as mine…

It was *everything*.

TikTok

THE WOMAN'S MINISCULE HEAD BOUNCED AROUND IN FRONT OF A photo of Nora Ellington, wearing a Carolina Herrera pinkish-nude, long strapless gown covered in crystal disk sequins and floating pearls. She was walking hand in hand into a restaurant that was closed for a private party with Jamie Oakley, who was wearing a perfectly tailored, traditional tuxedo.

"The Swans, Holloways, Pierces, Sharps and Oakleys never let things get boring, as you can see," the talking head in the TikTok video said. "Janora is officially oh-*ficial*. Because look at that ring."

A closeup of the Harry Winston Pink Legacy engagement ring that sported a nearly 19 carat pink diamond with colorless diamond shields at the sides rested on Nora's left ring finger.

"The handsome Jamie Oakley and the gorgeous Nora Ellington are going to tie the knot, and even though we didn't get a lot of pictures from Chloe Pierce Oakley and Judge Oakley's wedding day,"—the picture behind the head changed to one of the few photos of Chloe and Judge's wedding day that had been released to the press—"as you can see, what we did get was *fabulous*. I mean, who decides *mauve* as their wedding color? Chloe Oakley did, and she *worked it*. And now, of course, *everyone* is doing mauve weddings, such is the trendsetter that is Chloe. That said, Nora has more experience being *absolutely fabulous*, even more than Chloe. So I suspect we're in for a real treat when those two get hitched."

The picture changed to one of Dru Oakley, wearing a tea-length Oscar de la Renta dress with bos straps and sporting a crystal grid. She was standing very close to Sullivan Holloway, who was smiling down at her while she beamed up at him. Both were holding flutes of champagne.

"And something else that's official, public records show that Jamie Oakley has adopted his stepdaughter, Drusilla Lynch. The reason for this get-together of beautiful people. She's changed her name to Drusilla Rawlins Oakley, because rumor has it, AJ Oakley did not create the magnificence that is Jamie, or through Jamie, his son Judge."

The picture on the screen changed to a handsome older man standing with Jamie and two other men close to Jamie's age, along with Judge. All of them were wearing evening clothes (with three of the men wearing string ties instead of bow). All of them held old-fashioned glasses in their hands. All of them looked like they were laughing.

"But instead, this man, Morgan Rawlins, a Texas rancher, is the true sire to AJ's last boy. Now, this report isn't confirmed, but we all have eyes. So..."

The background pictures swirled through snaps of Imogen Swan and Duncan Holloway standing with Mika Stowe and Tom Pierce. This moving to Chloe Oakley laughing with Blake Sharp. Then Gage Holloway talking to Hale Wheeler and Elsa Cohen. Next was members of the G-Force striking poses with Valentina Castellini. On to a shot of Matt Pierce, Sasha Pierce, Gage, Sully and Dru all clinking glasses in a toast. This moved to a picture of Kateri True Arrow speaking with Elsa. After that Cadence Merriman giggling at something Nico Castellini said while he smiled at her. And last, Rix Hendrix and Alex Sharp listening to something Ned Sharp was saying.

"The gang was all there," the talking head said as the photos cycled. "Dressed to the nines, as usual, and giving no thought to how the little people live, as they shouldn't since they're just *that amazing*. Congratulations to Drusilla, Jamie and Judge for making their family official. And big congratulations to Jamie and Nora on their upcoming nuptials. All I can say is, it's about damned time. Now, be sure to hit follow for more news on the rich and beautiful. Elsa's out of the game, so someone has to share all of this, and that someone is me. There's always more where this came from, and I'm the one to give it to you. So hit that follow, folks, and see you on the flipside."

Swipe.

And done.

Jamie

. . .

THE HOUSE WAS ENORMOUS.

Tucked down a decline off Senator Highway, surrounded by trees, it was made of wood and stone, had five bedrooms, six baths, a chef's kitchen, front and back decks, his and hers closets in the primary bedroom—both walk-in— a study (for him), a large built-in vanity in the primary bathroom (for her), and a small guest house down a stone path fifty yards from the main house.

It sat on eleven acres.

Standing in the kitchen, looking out the window at Nora, Dru, Judge and Chloe (with JT in Dru's arms) all out on the deck, the sun shining on their hair, their attention aimed at the guest house—it wasn't until Jamie saw Nora turn her head and look at him through the window that he made his decision.

And what made his decision was his future wife, standing on the back deck of what was a mountain house, no matter how large it was, looking elegant, relaxed, immensely fuckable, and outrageously happy. She was wearing a sleeveless Prada, flower print, scarf collar dress and peach Gianvito Rossi flower, stiletto, slide sandals. Her gorgeous face was soft, he could feel the warmth emanating from her brown eyes all the way to where he was standing...

And she was smiling.

This would be their home when they were in Arizona, so yes, his decision was mostly about her.

But it was also about the other four humans out on that deck.

All he'd won. All he'd lost. All he'd earned. All he'd endured. All of it, every moment, every struggle, every heartache, every victory was about getting to this moment in his life with those five people firmly entrenched in it. Having the honor of watching them blossom, grow, live, love, including love him, and having the privilege of giving all of that back.

In other words, having a family.

Having *his* family.

The only thing in his life he ever truly wanted.

All of that, he read on Nora's face.

All of it was communicated in her smile.

Jamie smiled in return.

He then turned to the real estate agent and said, "Offer asking. I want possession in two weeks."

Her eyes grew large.

Jamie ignored that and walked into the Arizona mountain sun that shone down on the deck.

He did this because he had to gather his family.

They had a wedding rehearsal to get to.

The End

The River Rain Saga will continue...

ACKNOWLEDGMENTS

If you've been around for this River Rain ride, then you know that I work with my readers on the River Rain Team on Facebook to craft these stories. I try to take notes on who suggested what, so I can make sure to give credit where credit is due. So here goes, but I'll start by saying, if I misspell or just miss something, my sincere apologies! I love working with my River Rats on these books, so if I screw up, please know, it's entirely unintentional.

The name game:

Brianne Gavan gave Quincy Harrison, Nora's dad, his name. Katy Foltz offered up Valentina's name. Veronica Ines Garcia named Nico. Sara Matz suggested the name Charlene, while Asmaa Nada Qayyum gave us Arnold. Sheila Pieratt Curlin named Felice (and I hope you don't mind she turned into a pill, even I wasn't expecting that!). Jane Ulrich Pepin offered up Chester "Chet" (and man, was this name perfect for that freakin' guy, or what?). Danielle Pathmore Simmon gave us Marlo. Barbara Ponder suggested Winslet. And Ashlyn Dole named Ashe.

Now, Lee Cole El-Emari suggested Alphie, and somewhere in my fingers working the keyboard, I switched it to Archie, and since I liked that, I went with it. Sometimes, characters name themselves, and I think Archie was feeling a couple of letters changed in his name. Hope you don't mind, Lee.

Nora's mixologist skills:

Sara Lynne Levine made the hilarious suggestion that, on the yacht, Nora would want to muddle a mojito. And I hope you agree, she was right! Jane Kulbida said that Nora would mix up a French

Martini, her style, with Chambord, vodka and pineapple juice. She was right too. And Jamie agreed! Last, Susan Sneyers Parks gave us watermelon sangria (and see below for her recipe).

Heiress, the cat, was utterly perfect, and she was given to us by Lola Mac Harlow.

Jamie's (and Nico's) clothes:

Tina Stout introduced me to CKC New York. Michelle Thomas gave us Jamie's Bruno Cucinello polo and jeans outfit. Kate Tabor Yankey gave Nico his Tom Ford look. Denise Paul offered up a picture of Stanley Tucci in a velvet dinner jacket that I just *had* to give to Jamie (and he *so* worked it, just like Stanley). And Rita Book gave us Jamie's Christopher Key suit.

If you're interested in any visuals off all of this, be sure to check out the River Rain board on my Pinterest page. It'll all be there.

As ever, I need to give my shout outs to Liz Berry, Jillian Stein and MJ Rose of Blue Box Press for being so awesome at this publishing game, and just generally being so awesome. Not to mention, very patient since it took forever for me to submit this manuscript!

And I mustn't forget their fabulous team, Kim Guidroz, Stacey Tardif and Asha Hossain, who make the nitty-gritty of publication, the detail of proofing, and a gorgeous cover design all come to life!

Much love and gratitude, to all my sisters.

SUSAN SNEYERS PARKS'S (AND NORA'S) WATERMELON SANGRIA

2-3 cups of Watermelon, seeded & diced fine

1 cup of strawberries, hulled & diced fine (fruit can be food processed)

1 bottle of rosé

2 cups of orange juice

2 cups of Grand Marnier (or 1½ cups of brandy & ½ cup of triple sec)

1 orange, quartered & sliced

Place watermelon and strawberries in a pitcher and muddle a bit. Add the rest of the ingredients. Stir and refrigerate for at least 1 hour (longer is better).

Serve over ice, with a splash of bubbly water or seltzer.

BOOK CLUB/REFLECTION QUESTIONS

- Did you notice Nora decided the chapter headings? Did you enjoy them?

- What was your response to Judge's reaction to the birth of his son? Were you surprised, or did you think that was in character? And do you prefer JT or Jimmy?

- Felice, Nico's wife, is an interesting character. What were your feelings about her?

- In the end, both Jamie and Nora lose their desire for revenge. Did you agree with this decision, and as such, what became of Paloma and AJ, or did you wish they'd carried on with their retribution?

- Do you think we've heard the last from Chet?

DISCOVER MORE
KRISTEN ASHLEY

After the Climb: A River Rain Novel, Book 1

They were the Three Amigos: Duncan Holloway, Imogen Swan and Corey Szabo. Two young boys with difficult lives at home banding together with a cool girl who didn't mind mucking through the mud on their hikes.

They grew up to be Duncan Holloway, activist, CEO and face of the popular River Rain outdoor stores, Imogen Swan, award-winning actress and America's sweetheart, and Corey Szabo, ruthless tech billionaire.

Rich and very famous, they would learn the devastating knowledge of how the selfish acts of one would affect all their lives.

And the lives of those they loved.

Start the River Rain series with After the Climb, the story of Duncan and Imogen navigating their way back to each other, decades after a fierce betrayal.

And introduce yourself to their families, who will have their stories told when River Rain continues.

Chasing Serenity: A River Rain Novel, Book 2

From a very young age, Chloe Pierce was trained to look after the ones she loved.

And she was trained by the best.

But when the man who looked after her was no longer there, Chloe is cast adrift—just as the very foundation of her life crumbled to pieces.

Then she runs into tall, lanky, unpretentious Judge Oakley, her exact opposite. She shops. He hikes. She drinks pink ladies. He drinks beer. She's a city girl. He's a mountain guy.

Obviously, this means they have a blowout fight upon meeting. Their second encounter doesn't go a lot better.

Judge is loving the challenge. Chloe is everything he doesn't want in a woman, but he can't stop finding ways to spend time with her. He knows she's dealing with loss and change.

He just doesn't know how deep that goes. Or how ingrained it is for Chloe to care for those who have a place in her heart, how hard it will be to trust anyone to look after her...

And how much harder it is when it's his turn.

Taking the Leap: A River Rain Novel, Book 3

Alexandra Sharp has been crushing on her co-worker, John "Rix" Hendrix for years. He's her perfect man, she knows it.

She's just not his perfect woman, and she knows that too.

Then Rix gives Alex a hint that maybe there's a spark between them that, if she takes the leap, she might be able to fan into a flame This leads to a crash and burn, and that's all shy Alex needs to catch the hint never to take the risk again.

However, with undeniable timing, Rix's ex, who broke his heart, and Alex's family, who spent her lifetime breaking hers, rear their heads, gearing up to offer more drama. With the help of some match-making friends, Rix and Alex decide to face the onslaught together…

As a fake couple.

Making the Match, A River Rain Novel, Book 4

Decades ago, tennis superstar Tom Pierce and "It Girl" Mika Stowe met at a party.

Mika fell in love. Tom was already in love with his wife. As badly as Tom wanted Mika as a friend, Mika knew it would hurt too much to be attracted to this amazing man and never be able to have him.

They parted ways for what they thought would be forever, only to reconnect just once, when unspeakable tragedy darkens Mika's life.

Years later, the impossible happens.

A time comes when they're both unattached.

But now Tom has made a terrible mistake. A mistake so damaging to the ones he loves, he feels he'll never be redeemed.

Mika has never forgotten how far and how fast she fell when she met him, but Tom's transgression is holding her distant from reaching out.

There are matchmakers in their midst, however.

And when the plot has been unleashed to make that match, Tom and Mika are thrown into an international intrigue that pits them against a Goliath of the sports industry.

Now they face a massive battle at the same time they're navigating friendship, attraction, love, family, grief, redemption, two very different lives lived on two opposite sides of a continent and a box full of kittens.

Fighting the Pull: A River Rain Novel, Book 5

From *New York Times* bestselling author Kristen Ashley comes the new book in her River Rain Series, *Fighting the Pull.*

Hale Wheeler inherited billions from his father. He's decided to take those resources and change the world for the better. He's married to his mission, so he doesn't have time for love.

There's more lurking behind this decision. He hasn't faced the tragic loss of his father, or the bitterness of his parents' divorce. He doesn't intend to follow in his father's footsteps, breaking a woman's heart in a way it will never mend. So he vows he'll never marry.

But Hale is intrigued when he meets Elsa Cohen, the ambitious celebrity news journalist who has been reporting on his famous family. He warns her off, but she makes him a deal. She'll pull back in exchange for an exclusive interview.

Elsa Cohen is married to her career, but she wants love, marriage, children. She also wants the impossibly handsome, fiercely loyal, tenderhearted Hale Wheeler.

They go head-to-head, both denying why there are fireworks every time they meet. But once they understand their undeniable attraction, Elsa can't help but fall for the dynamic do-gooder.

As for Hale, he knows he needs to fight the pull of the beautiful, bold, loving Elsa Cohen, because breaking her would crush him.

Sharing the Miracle: A River Rain Novella, Book 5.5

Elsa Cohen has everything she ever wanted.

A challenging career. A bicoastal lifestyle.

And an amazing man—the kind, loving and handsome Hale Wheeler—who adores her and has asked her to be his wife.

She isn't ready for the surprise news she's received.

And she doesn't know how to tell Hale.

Once Hale discovers that his future has taken a drastic turn, a fear he's never experienced takes hold.

He just doesn't understand why.

Family and friends rally around the couple as they adjust to their new reality, and along the way, more surprises hit the River Rain crew as love is tested and life goes on.

Please note: This is a slice-of-life novella in the River Rain series. It was written to be read after *Fighting the Pull*.

Gossamer in the Darkness: A Fantasyland Novella

Their engagement was set when they were children. Loren Copeland, the rich and handsome Marquess of Remington, would marry Maxine Dawes, the stunning daughter of the Count of Derryman. It's a power match. The perfect alliance for each house.

However, the Count has been keeping secret a childhood injury that means Maxine can never marry. He's done this as he searches for a miracle so this marriage can take place. He needs the influence such an alliance would give him, and he'll stop at nothing to have it.

The time has come. There could be no more excuses. No more delays. The marriage has to happen, or the contract will be broken.

When all seems lost, the Count finds his miracle: There's a parallel universe where his daughter has a twin. He must find her, bring her to his world and force her to make the Marquess fall in love with her.

And this, he does.

Wild Wind: A Chaos Novella

When he was sixteen years old, Jagger Black laid eyes on the girl who was his. At a cemetery. During her mother's funeral.

For years, their lives cross, they feel the pull of their connection, but then they go their separate ways.

But when Jagger sees that girl chasing someone down the street, he doesn't think twice before he wades right in. And when he gets a full-on dose of the woman she's become, he knows he finally has to decide if he's all in or if it's time to cut her loose.

She's ready to be cut loose.

But Jagger is all in.

Dream Bites Cookbook: Cooking with the Commandos
Short Stories by Kristen Ashley
Recipes by Suzanne M. Johnson

From *New York Times* bestseller Kristen Ashley and *USA Today* bestseller Suzanne M. Johnson…

See what's cooking!

You're invited to Denver and into the kitchens of Hawk Delgado's commandos: Daniel "Mag" Magnusson, Boone Sadler, Axl Pantera and Augustus "Auggie" Hero as they share with you some of the goodness they whip up for their women.

Not only will you get to spend time with the commandos, the Dream Team makes an appearance with their men, and there are a number of special guest stars. It doesn't end there, you'll also find some bonus recipes from a surprise source who doesn't like to be left out.

So strap in for a trip to Denver, a few short stories, some reminiscing and a lot of great food.

(Half of the proceeds of this cookbook go to the Rock Chick Nation Charities)

Welcome to Dream Bites, Cooking with the Commandos!

Wild Fire: A Chaos Novella

"You know you can't keep a good brother down."

The Chaos Motorcycle Club has won its war. But not every brother rode into the sunset with his woman on the back of his bike.

Chaos returns with the story of Dutch Black, a man whose father was the moral compass of the Club, until he was murdered. And the man who raised Dutch protected the Club at all costs. That combination is the man Dutch is intent on becoming.

It's also the man that Dutch is going to go all out to give to his woman.

Quiet Man: A Dream Man Novella

Charlotte "Lottie" McAlister is in the zone. She's ready to take on the next chapter of her life, and since she doesn't have a man, she'll do what she's done all along. She'll take care of business on her own. Even if that business means starting a family.

The problem is, Lottie has a stalker. The really bad kind. The kind that means she needs a bodyguard.

Enter Mo Morrison.

Enormous. Scary.

Quiet.

Mo doesn't say much, and Lottie's used to getting attention. And she wants Mo's attention. Badly.

But Mo has a strict rule. If he's guarding your body, that's all he's doing with it.

However, the longer Mo has to keep Lottie safe, the faster he falls for the beautiful blonde who has it so together, she might even be able to tackle the demons he's got in his head that just won't die.

But in the end, Lottie and Mo don't only have to find some way to keep hands off until the threat is over, they have to negotiate the overprotective Hot Bunch, Lottie's crazy stepdad, Tex, Mo's crew of fratboy commandos, not to mention his nutty sisters.

All before Lottie finally gets her Dream Man.

And Mo can lay claim to his Dream Girl.

Rough Ride: A Chaos Novella

Rosalie Holloway put it all on the line for the Chaos Motorcycle Club.

Informing to Chaos on their rival club—her man's club, Bounty—Rosalie knows the stakes. And she pays them when her man, who she was hoping to scare straight, finds out she's betrayed him and he delivers her to his brothers to mete out their form of justice.

But really, Rosie has long been denying that, as she drifted away from her Bounty, she's been falling in love with Everett "Snapper" Kavanagh, a Chaos brother. Snap is the biker-boy-next door with the snowy blue eyes, quiet confidence and sweet disposition who was supposed to keep her safe…and fell down on that job.

For Snapper, it's always been Rosalie, from the first time he saw her at the Chaos Compound. He's just been waiting for a clear shot. But he didn't want to get it after his Rosie was left bleeding, beat down and broken by Bounty on a cement warehouse floor.

With Rosalie a casualty of an ongoing war, Snapper has to guide her to trust him, take a shot with him, build a them…

And fold his woman firmly in the family that is Chaos.

Rock Chick Reawakening: A Rock Chick Novella

From *New York Times* bestselling author, Kristen Ashley, comes the long-awaited story of Daisy and Marcus, *Rock Chick Reawakening*. A prequel to Kristen's *Rock Chick* series, *Rock Chick Reawakening* shares the tale of the devastating event that nearly broke Daisy, an event that set Marcus Sloane—one of Denver's most respected businessmen and one of the Denver underground's most feared crime bosses—into finally making his move to win the heart of the woman who stole his.

Rock Chick Rematch: A Rock Chick Novella

In high school, Malia Clark found the man of her dreams.

Darius Tucker.

But life hits them full in the face way before it ever should. Darius makes a drastic decision to keep his family safe and Malia leaves town with a secret.

When Malia returns, she seeks Darius to share all, but Darius finds out before she can tell him. At the same time, she finds out just how much Darius has changed in the years she's been away.

She just refuses to give up on him.

Until he forces her hand.

Secrets come between Malia and Darius, at the same time Malia has to worry about weird things going on at the law firm where she works, her kid wants a car and she's stuck in slow-cooker hell. Luckily, her ride or dies have her back.

And in the meantime, she might just learn she never should have lost hope in Darius Tucker.

Sign up for the Blue Box Press/1001 Dark Nights Newsletter
and be entered to win a Tiffany Lock necklace.

There's a contest every quarter!

Go to www.TheBlueBoxPress.com to subscribe!

As a bonus, all subscribers can download FIVE FREE
exclusive books!

DISCOVER 1001 DARK NIGHTS
COLLECTION ELEVEN

DRAGON KISS by Donna Grant
A Dragon Kings Novella

THE WILD CARD by Dylan Allen
A Rivers Wilde Novella

ROCK CHICK REMATCH by Kristen Ashley
A Rock Chick Novella

JUST ONE SUMMER by Carly Phillips
A Dirty Dare Series Novella

HAPPILY EVER MAYBE by Carrie Ann Ryan
A Montgomery Ink Legacy Novella

BLUE MOON by Skye Warren
A Cirque des Moroirs Novella

A VAMPIRE'S MATE by Rebecca Zanetti
A Dark Protectors/Rebels Novella

LOVE HAZARD by Rachel Van Dyken

BRODIE by Aurora Rose Reynolds
An Until Her Novella

THE BODYGUARD AND THE BOMBSHELL by Lexi Blake
A Masters and Mercenaries: New Recruits Novella

THE SUBSTITUTE by Kristen Proby
A Single in Seattle Novella

CRAVED BY YOU by J. Kenner
A Stark Security Novella

GRAVEYARD DOG by Darynda Jones
A Charley Davidson Novella

A CHRISTMAS AUCTION by Audrey Carlan
A Marriage Auction Novella

THE GHOST OF A CHANCE by Heather Graham
A Krewe of Hunters Novella

Also from Blue Box Press

LEGACY OF TEMPTATION by Larissa Ione
A Demonica Birthright Novel

VISIONS OF FLESH AND BLOOD by Jennifer L. Armentrout and
Ravyn Salvador
A Blood & Ash and Fire & Flesh Compendium

FORGETTING TO REMEMBER by M.J. Rose

TOUCH ME by J. Kenner

A Stark International Novella

BORN OF BLOOD AND ASH by Jennifer L. Armentrout
A Flesh and Fire Novel

MY ROYAL SHOWMANCE by Lexi Blake
A Park Avenue Promise Novel

SAPPHIRE DAWN by Christopher Rice writing as C. Travis Rice
A Sapphire Cove Novel

EMBRACING THE CHANGE by Kristen Ashley
A River Rain Novel

IN THE AIR TONIGHT by Marie Force

LEGACY OF CHAOS by Larissa Ione
A Demonica Birthright Novel

ON BEHALF OF BLUE BOX PRESS,

Liz Berry, M.J. Rose, and Jillian Stein would like to thank ~

Steve Berry
Doug Scofield
Benjamin Stein
Kim Guidroz
Tanaka Kangara
Stacey Tardif
Asha Hossain
Ann-Marie Nieves
Chris Graham
Jessica Saunders
Grace Wenk
Kate Boggs
Donna Perry
Richard Blake
and Simon Lipskar

Made in the USA
Las Vegas, NV
19 October 2024

10090155R00215